D0342847

MALIBU BLUFF

ALSO BY JANNA KING

The Seasonaires

MALIBU BLUFF

A Seasonaires Novel

JANNA KING

PEGASUS BOOKS
NEW YORK LONDON

MALIBU BLUFF

Pegasus Books, Ltd.
148 W 37th Street, 13th Floor
New York, NY 10018

First Pegasus Books edition May 2019

Interior design by Maria Fernandez

Library of Congress Cataloging-in-Publication Data is available.

ISBN: 978-1-64313-066-8

10 9 8 7 6 5 4 3 2 1

Printed in the United States of America
Distributed by W. W. Norton & Company
www.pegasusbooks.us

For my City of Angels

MALIBU BLUFF

PROLOGUE

Mia wrenched against the two hands that held her arms over her head. She tried to open her eyes, but the black bandana was pressed taut against her lids. *This is a joke. This is a joke.* She repeated the mantra to herself, though this was clearly not a joke.

The man mitts encircled her wrists like steel handcuffs. She kicked with every ounce of energy and fury she could find, but two other impossibly strong hands jammed her feet together. Rope wound fast around her ankles, binding them. She jerked her legs but couldn't bend her knees in this stretched and constrained horizontal position.

With all the struggling and squirming, her phone fell from her back pocket. She heard it smack on asphalt. A trunk creaked open.

"What the fuck are you doing?" she yelled, summoning all her anger instead of letting fear take over.

She was shoved inside a space that felt not much larger than her body, where she was maneuvered like a bag of groceries. The four hands released her, and the trunk hood slammed over her. Two pairs of heavy boots scuffled. One car door shut, then another.

"Let me out!"

The car came to life with the roar of a souped-up engine and growled over her screams. No one who could help her would hear her, because at midnight on the Tuesday after Labor Day, neighbors were ensconced in the heavenly slices of the Shangri-la that was Malibu. As the car lurched forward, she was propelled back—her head smacked on metal. Her heart raced, her breathing was heavy. The smell of gasoline mixed with the sex and sweat on her body and saltwater in her hair. She hadn't showered. With every bump, her body was jolted—hip against the rough treads of a spare tire, tire iron jammed into her neck.

She lost track of time in the darkness. Her energy and fight waned from punching and kicking, and lack of food. The air grew thinner, hotter, and staler, unlike the cool, fresh lightness of the eucalyptus trees that dotted Pacific Coast Highway and the hillsides—the ones that dropped oily bark and leaves she'd learned could start and spread fires.

The car straightened and accelerated. A distant siren became a deafening blare and the car veered, then stopped hard. Her body slammed back, her head clanking again on metal. The siren screamed by and the car continued on. It curved and snaked upward, keeping her back against the hard, rough spare. The winding road made her queasy.

This nausea was different from the violent wretching that had followed the discovery she'd made on July Fourth the summer before. She had walked into the backyard of Wear National's Nantucket estate. As a Lyndon Wyld clothing seasonaire, she shouldn't have been there, but she'd gone to check on her friends, Grant and Ruby. Grant had been on the right team, Ruby the wrong, both equally wasted. Mia had found Grant dead, then Ruby as good as dead, a silver revolver by her side.

Mia's current situation was a result of what she'd done next . . . or rather what she hadn't done.

Now, swallowed inside the trunk, she resigned herself to the fact that she deserved whatever she was getting. There was no point in guessing bleak specifics about the future, so instead, she thought of the shimmering Queen's Necklace view from the bluff and how the coast twinkled with Shangri-la lights. She steered her mind to the beach under the sun, a cool breeze in her hair. The ocean's silver blue stretched on forever. The image of the calm sea as she had waited for waves during her one time on a surfboard worked to slow her breaths until her heartbeat was like the staggered drips of the hose she'd used to wash the sand off her feet. Eventually the drips would stop.

And then it went black.

ONE

Six Months Earlier

Mia exhaled the air from her lungs and let herself sink. The tepid water weighed against her, keeping her afloat, so she blew out more air. Tiny bubbles rose from her mouth as she descended. She sat at the bottom of the pool, legs crossed in meditation pose, though she couldn't be paid enough to meditate. But as an escape, it was peaceful there, unlike the ocean, which had a mind of its own. The last time—the only time—she'd been in the sea, she had thrashed and kicked in an attempt to avoid drowning in the Atlantic. She'd coughed up salty mouthfuls until Ruby had grabbed her and swum to shore. Mia had been trying to save Ruby's life, but Ruby had ended up saving hers. Their karma points would never be equal.

A plunk in the water above. She looked up to see a red plastic swim school fish drop towards her in slow motion. Another plop. A blue fish sunk. Then a running shoe. With her bare feet, Mia pushed off the concrete, its sandpapery surface scratchy against the pads of her toes. She shot up like a bullet, bursting through the surface with a splash. She took a deep breath.

"What the—?" Water spit from her mouth. She turned her head to see her older brother Sean, distorted by the chlorine that burned her eyes. He stood poolside in his Boston College Eagles sweatshirt, track pants, and one running shoe, his white athletic sock damp on the wet edge.

"Are you crazy?" Mia's voice echoed off the walls, because the Y pool was empty. No one wanted to swim after dark during the remaining chill of early March in South Boston, even though the pool was indoors.

"I spent my free Sundays teaching you how to swim and I come here to find you at the bottom?" Sean's voice was shaky.

"I taught myself how to sink." Mia grinned as she treaded water, attempting to get a smile out of him. She failed, but Sean didn't smile much these days.

"I've been trying to reach you," he said.

"My phone's in a locker." Mia slicked back her hair with one hand.

Sean held out a white towel. "It's time to go."

Mia hesitated. She never used to want to go in the water. Now, she didn't want to get out.

—⁂—

Mia didn't have the chance to swim again that week. It was a balmy Sunday, and she couldn't take her eyes off her mother, whose makeup was heavier than usual. Kathryn had always been pretty, yet she didn't look like herself. Porcelain pale, her face was smooth—almost waxy—which emphasized the rose pink of her lipstick. Her meticulously separated lashes were long and dark, her brows chestnut brown arches that matched her hair, which hadn't been that silky in months. A shimmer of lavender eye shadow covered her lids. Mia wondered how her mom would feel if she knew she was on display. Mia had been on display, and it wasn't all it was cracked up to be.

"I would have done a kohl smudge instead of the harsh eye-liner," said a familiar voice, its sweet Southern lilt softening the r. Then the bite. "That look is dead." Mia turned, expecting to see the pageant smile and long, lustrous hair like spun gold. But Presley wasn't there.

Kathryn wore the dress that Mia had made for her the previous summer after Nantucket. Mia had sewn lace around the collar—not in a way that was Victorian and stuffy, but lovely and feminine, like her mom. The fabric's sky-blue hue was cheerful. Her mother was one of those cheerful people, even in the most trying times. Her cheer was authentic—not "fake it 'til you make it." Mia couldn't unearth that kind of unconditional cheer, no matter how hard she tried. She loved her mother for it.

That dress had clinched Mia's acceptance into MassArt, where she would start in the fall. It didn't hurt that Lyndon Wyld, the founder of one of the world's most successful clothing lines—her namesake—wrote Mia a recommendation letter. Mia was proud she'd had the balls to ask for one after everything that had happened. She had brandished a pair to apply for the coveted job as a Lyndon Wyld seasonaire, even though she hadn't been the required age of twenty-one. She'd never traveled anywhere in her life and hadn't known anything about being a brand ambassador. Social media was a glossy blanket of attention-grabbing influencers tagging clothes, shoes, makeup, and designer water in curated and filtered posts. Most were well paid, but only six made Lyndon's prestigious pack. The idea of creating a name for herself in the apparel world, plus $20,000 and eight weeks all expenses paid in one of the most beautiful places on earth, had bolstered her courage. Armed with one suitcase and a fake ID, she'd hopped the bus from South Boston to Hyannis and then the ferry from Hyannis to Nantucket.

It had turned out to be a fever dream of seaside brunches and country club fashion shows, vodka-crans in red Solo cups, house music, fast friends, hashtags, and a murder. Like any nightmare, the flashbacks of that night had come hard and fast after it had first happened, then faded in the weeks following. The walks on the beach, sea breeze misting her face, cool tide washing over her feet had diffused the macabre picture like the diluted blood in the pool water. She could finally see her friend Grant's wide, roguish grin instead of his floating dead body.

Six months had passed since what was supposed to have been the summer of a lifetime. After returning home in August, she'd deleted all her social media accounts despite her huge spike in popularity. The goal: to forget. So her heart had stopped when the blonde woman with the chic bob had entered the thrift shop in February. Slipping behind the rack of vintage overalls she'd been arranging, Mia had drowned again in ugly images. But she'd exhaled with relief when the woman had turned—her face soft, her eyes brown saucers, not sapphire sphinx; her earrings pearl studs, not diamond.

"Do you have any '80s Reebok high-tops?" asked the woman.

Lyndon would sooner fuck the devil than wear high-top sneakers or purchase anything in a thrift shop, for that matter. And the woman's accent? Pure South Boston, like Mia's. Lyndon's was crisp British.

Mia had been cherishing time with her mom before fall semester started. Sean had pinch-hit for Mia while she'd been away in Nantucket, but he'd become busy again with school and baseball. It was his senior year at Boston College. Major and minor league recruiters would appraise him like a prize show horse. Mia understood his ambition. Like her, he wanted more from life, in large part so they could give their mom more from life . . . which, to Mia, bordered on delusional.

Now Mia stared at her mother. She realized why Kathryn didn't look like herself. That wasn't her body. It was an empty shell, the contents stolen by cancer.

Mia didn't know she was capable of so many tears. She had cried over Grant's death, but the loss of her mother gutted the depths of her soul. Her heart hurt as if an ox stood on her chest. She wasn't one for church, and neither was her mom, but her brother wanted to be respectful. Kathryn hadn't written a will, because she'd possessed nothing to pass down to her kids. She'd never expressed her funeral wishes. It tore Mia's heart to see Sean weep—her older brother, who'd had his nose broken two different times after being hit in the face with a baseball. He'd powered through both games, bringing his team to victory. At the hospital, when Kathryn had taken her last breaths, Mia had held Sean, whose whole body had shaken with grief.

"We should tell Dad." Sean's voice was a hoarse whisper.

Mia swallowed with anger. "Why? He didn't care about her when she was alive."

"It's the right thing to do."

Sean always did the right thing. And he did it again when he called their father, because Mia had deleted the phone number. A few days later, an envelope arrived from Paramus, New Jersey. In it was a check with a sticky note that said: *For a proper coffin and funeral.* Mia didn't believe her mom would've wanted to end up in a box. But funerals were for the living. She remembered all the people who had come to Grant's memorial at the Nantucket Lyndon Wyld store. The #WearAMemory signage in the window with all his photos had made Mia feel sick. But the funeral was important to Sean.

Their dad never showed up. Mia wasn't surprised or disappointed.

The day after everyone else came to pay their respects, she and Sean roamed around the apartment. There was no hospital to drive to, meds to dispense, or sponge baths to give. They were restless, and the stale smell of long illness didn't help.

"Are we supposed to just go back to our regular life?" asked Sean.

"What's a regular life?" Mia touched the Lyndon Wyld cashmere blanket that her mom had been gifted by Lyndon and her sister Grace when Kathryn had visited Nantucket. It was the only cashmere Kathryn owned.

"I have a game, but I can't stand the thought of people feeling sorry for me," said Sean.

"I got over that a while ago. I let their pity and awkwardness wash over me." Mia wiggled her fingers down her head like a shower. "Go, Sean. Your team needs you and you love it. Mom would want you to do what you love."

After another twenty minutes of pacing, sitting on the couch, in the recliner, and looking out the window at the bright spring day, Sean grabbed his gear and left. The door click echoed more loudly than usual. Mia let herself cry again, then considered her own words: *Mom would want you to do what you love.* She entered her bedroom and sat at her sewing machine. She had been working on an ankle-length duster coat with jaunty epaulettes. She let the needle's rapid-fire pokes hypnotize her into some sense of momentary peace. The doorbell rang, causing her to jump.

"Shit!" She rose halfway, then sat back down and pressed the foot pedal, continuing to sew. *Maybe they'll go away*, she thought. But the doorbell rang again. She realized it was rude to pretend she wasn't home when someone may have been taking the time for a condolence call. She breathed deeply and stood, making her way to the front door. She peeked through the peephole and saw

6

a teen boy with curly red hair, whose freckled face was partially covered by a mass of white roses. Mia opened the door.

"Are you Mia Daniels?" The scrawny boy struggled to hold the biggest bouquet of roses Mia had ever seen.

"Yes, uh—" Mia held out her arms.

"I can bring them inside if you like. They're kind of heavy." The boy jostled the large beveled vase.

"No, it's okay. I've got them." Mia took the bouquet. It was as heavy as it looked. "Thank you." The delivery boy left and Mia pushed the door closed with her foot. Her arms trembled as she maneuvered the mass of flowers across the living room and placed the glass vase on the dining table with a clink. She counted the blooms, which had already started to replace the apartment's stale smell with a fresh, powdery fragrance. At twenty-four, she stopped counting, then reached through the thorn-shaved stems for the card. She lifted it out of its small envelope and read:

> I'm so sorry for your loss. You know I understand how you feel.
> Please let me give you another beautiful summer.
> Love, Lyndon

A surge of angry heat shot through Mia. *How dare Lyndon use my mother's death as a ploy to get me to come back? It was so like Lyndon to polish a turd to make it her own.* With that thought, Mia wanted to throw the flowers out but didn't have it in her to carry them to the apartment building's garbage. Plus, that would've looked wasteful. No one in her neighborhood received flowers like that.

Sean arrived home. "We won."

It was early enough that Mia knew he'd passed on going out with the team to celebrate. He eyed the roses. "Wow." Mia had tossed out the card.

Sitting on the couch, Mia shut the laptop that was propped on her thighs. "It's not so 'wow.' They're from Lyndon."

Sean's brow knit. "How'd Lyndon find out?"

"I texted Jade about Mom," replied Mia. "She must've told Maz, who must've told Lyndon."

"And the chain of gossip continues. I'm surprised they didn't post it." Sean affected a teen girl twang. "Hashtag: RIP."

"I wouldn't know since I shut down all my accounts. Jade wanted to come to the funeral, but she's at some new music festival Maz founded in Japan."

"You know how many shits I give?" Sean made a zero with his thumb and forefinger.

Mia eyed the roses. "I'm sure Lyndon had one of her assistants send them."

"Well, it wasn't her sister Grace, that's for sure," said Sean, chuckling dryly as he pulled off his sweatshirt on the way to the bathroom. Mia heard the shower turn on. She reopened her laptop. The screen showed the Lyndon Wyld Clothing website. She clicked on the *Be Wyld* tab to a page that showed a gorgeous, sparkling coastline view from bluffs above. The bold caption:

California Dreamin'! #BuWyld

"Bu Wyld?" she whispered to herself. Reading on, Mia learned that this summer, Lyndon Wyld's seasonaires would be going to Malibu. Mia wondered which six twentysomethings would win those spots and their $20,000 expense-free payday. *Good for them.* She closed her laptop and put it on the coffee table. Her arms spiked goose bumps, so she walked to the window and slid it down. She grabbed the only blanket in the room: that Lyndon Wyld blanket. She sat back down on the couch, wrapped the soft, fuzzy cashmere around her, and closed her eyes. Tomorrow, she had work at the thrift shop.

TWO

M anny, the landlord, stood in the door frame, his bull-dozer build filling it. For a scary-looking guy, Manny had puppy dog eyes that always made Mia feel safe and comfortable, especially when she was younger and dealing with the initial challenges of her mom's illness. He helped push Kathryn in the wheelchair while Mia lugged groceries. This past year, when things took a turn for the worst, Manny brought over an extra Thanksgiving turkey he cooked. He pretended it was to show off his skills with the new smoker on his balcony, because he had gotten used to Mia's pride.

Standing in that doorway, Manny could barely look at Mia and Sean. "I know you've both been through a lot," he said in a voice scratched raw by too many cigarettes. "But you're thirty days past due on rent."

Sean shifted on his sneakered feet. "We're really sorry, Manny."

"We'll get it to you." Mia's hand pressed against the wall. "We promise. Give us another couple weeks."

Sean glanced at her.

"That's about it." Manny lifted his empty hands from his pockets. "I'm sorry, but I've got a stack of applicants who want this place." He looked past Mia at the roses that had wilted, their petals molting to crispy, curling brown—some sprawled on the table. "Do you want me to throw those out for you?"

"No, thanks, I've got them," replied Sean.

The three stood in awkward silence, which Manny broke. "Well, I have a toilet to plunge. Please, guys, don't make me evict you."

"We won't," said Mia. Manny lumbered off down the hallway. Mia shut the door and turned.

Sean glanced back at her as he picked up the flowers. "We can't cover this apartment." He pulled the vase close to his chest. More crispy petals fell off their limp stems and onto the floor. "Maybe we shouldn't even try. We'll figure out a place for you. And if everything goes the way I want, then my new team will pay for my residence wherever I am next year."

"I say the Padres." Mia smiled. She thought about how her mom would try and spin Manny's unfortunate visit into a positive. Mia was bad at it.

Sean moved towards the door with the vase. "I like the cold. Hoping for the Twins. I'm not a sucker for beach towns like you."

"Ha, ha, very funny." Mia waited a few beats. She grimaced. "Lyndon has been leaving me voicemails. She wants me to be a seasonaire this summer."

"In Nantucket?"

"Malibu."

"Ooh, fancy."

"Yeah." Mia rolled her eyes.

"That's a patronizing eye roll," said Sean. "You're considering it."

Mia flipped him off as she opened the door for him. When Sean tried to return the bird, he almost dropped the vase. He pulled it securely back into his arms, then disappeared down the hall.

Mia hopped on the Red Line downtown to the Langham Hotel in the financial district. The buildings in her neighborhood were a blur of brick and concrete, then row houses with painted wood slats. Pigeons flew past the bus and into the trees, shrubbery, and tall sea grass that decorated a median. Mia thought of the sea grass border between the huge beachfront estates and the beach in Nantucket. Save for that trip, she never ventured out of Southie.

The bus entered a tunnel lined with two snakes of light over slick tile walls and came out the other side. Throngs of cars maneuvered around the heart of the city, with its businesspeople clicking along the sidewalk in power suits. More would soon spill from the stately buildings when the clock struck five. Mia admired people who worked banker's hours, though she could never see herself sitting in an office or cubicle. She knew that sounded bratty but hoped that her career would make each day different, like the varying patterns she created.

The bus pulled around a pink vintage taxi with the words *Experience The Langham, Boston* on the side. Mia disembarked the bus and entered the hotel, with its stone face, round red awnings, and dark glass roof. Clicking across the shiny triangle design of the lobby, massive halo chandeliers above, she asked a bellman where she could find the tearoom. She had never said "tearoom" in her life.

The bellman pointed. "It's in The Reserve." Mia followed his direction. When she stepped inside the restaurant, she was met with a cloud of perfume. She couldn't remember what she ate for breakfast, but she remembered the name of one scent she recognized: White Shoulders. Her grandmother wore White Shoulders but had never sipped tea at the Langham. In the kitchen of her apartment, she would make Mia "coffee-milk," which meant a smidge of coffee brewed in her percolator and the rest whole milk, plus three heaping teaspoons of sugar—all mixed in a big ceramic cup with a paisley design. Mia still loved paisley. The tea at the Langham was poured by uniformed servers into china teacups painted with English roses.

Mia felt out of place, but she was used to that. She wore a lavender dress she'd bought at the thrift shop with her employee discount but had swapped the plain ivory buttons with white enamel squares she hand-painted with tiny violet diamonds. She'd sewed on a Peter Pan collar that matched a thin raw silk belt, and the burgundy block heel ankle boots added necessary edge. Her ensemble was conspicuously absent of anything Lyndon Wyld.

She glanced around at the mostly middle-aged women who had the time to sip Earl Grey and chitchat while ignoring the tiny scones and tea sandwiches on the three-tiered platters between them. She wondered if they had ever worked a day in their lives when her own mom had worked two jobs for most of hers. Then she overheard a conversation between two of those middle-aged women about a trip to Puerto Rico to help reconstruct hurricane-ravaged homes. She chided herself for judging, especially because she felt judged. *Would they consider a summer in Malibu work?*

Mia spotted Lyndon across the room, seated at a prime window table, typing on her phone. As she walked closer, she could see her perfectly manicured nails tapping the screen. Mia thought about giving herself a manicure, but she loathed the idea of doing it without her mom. Friday nights had become Girls' Night for the two of them. Lyndon looked up and smiled. Her honey blonde bob was shorter and blunter, but just as glossy as Mia remembered.

"Mia, my darling." Lyndon rose to embrace Mia, though she didn't fully stand, forcing Mia to lean in for the customary air kiss on both cheeks. This power play wasn't lost on her. Lyndon sat back for an evaluation. "You look beautiful—tired, but I understand. I also understand that it's fucking irritating when people continue to offer their condolences, so I won't do it again. But just know you have mine."

She motioned to the chair across the table. The passing server stopped to replace the white linen napkin that had dropped to the floor. Lyndon's silence instructed him to leave them alone as she turned her focus back to Mia, who removed her small flower-appliquéd satchel and hung it on the side of the chair. Lyndon was still surveying. She sighed with a *tsk*. "You're a little slip of a thing—as if you weren't tiny already. How are you holding up?"

"I'm fine." Mia placed her white linen napkin on her lap.

Lyndon gave her new napkin a flick and positioned it. "I'm glad you decided to meet me, since I came in town just for you." She motioned over another server, who couldn't get his "Good afternoon" out before Lyndon ordered scones with Devonshire clotted cream, strawberry jam, and lemon curd. She looked at Mia. "I'm a snooty Brit, so I like black tea, but I think you'd like the English Flower here."

Mia looked at the menu to see that English Flower was a blend of chamomile, rose, elderflower, heather, lavender, and cornflower. "That's a lot of flowers for tea." The server nodded politely and ambled off with the order.

When the tea arrived, Mia waited for Lyndon to pour hers, which she did with an elegant dip of her delicate wrist encircled by a rose-gold-and-diamond Patek Philippe watch. Mia followed suit but added three heaping teaspoons of sugar. She stirred it in circular motions until she noticed Lyndon moving her teaspoon daintily back and forth, her clear sapphire eyes on Mia. Mia pulled her spoon out without another whirl and sipped the tea, which tasted like what she imagined a real English garden would taste like, with added sugar.

Lyndon didn't touch a scone. Mia was starving but too nervous to eat. She felt like she was about to give away something valuable. Lyndon's gracious, but practiced, smile revealed that she was relieved to see Mia. The sadness in her eyes was impossible to hide, the tiny crow's-feet more apparent, despite the skillfully injected Botox and fillers. Mia knew that sadness was not for her loss but for Lyndon's. In the entire conversation that ensued, Grace's name was never mentioned. Mia didn't know if it was because Lyndon was refraining or disdaining. After all, Grace had killed someone for the sake of the Lyndon Wyld brand name. The wrong person ended up dead: Grant. Grace's bullet had been meant for Otto Hahn, the scumbag who'd founded formerly reigning Wear National clothing. She'd confessed to the murder before summer's end and was now in prison.

"I don't know if you heard, but Maz bought out Wear National. He and I are getting ready to launch our co-branded streetwear," said Lyndon.

Mia shook her head, though she'd seen the MazzyLyn announcement on the Lyndon Wyld website. She had no idea what had become of Otto and wasn't going to ask. But she knew that singularly named Maz, one of the world's most prominent multimedia moguls, had been instrumental in taking him down.

Lyndon tapped her gold phone case with her spoon. "I'm not fond of the phone, yet I called you twice. Feel special."

Mia did not feel special. Mistrusting, cautious, curious, but not special.

"I want you to go to Malibu and give yourself a break, Mia. I tell all my new babies that being a seasonaire is work, but you and I both know that when you love what you do, it's not work at all. You'll relax and take in the City of Angels. But you'll also be crafting your collection."

She reached into the yellow tote that blended perfectly with her coral Lyndon Wyld bolero jacket, and pulled out a beige folder. Its color was bland, but the contents were not. Mia opened it to find a contract for the Mia Collection. Lyndon placed a black Mont Blanc pen next to Mia's teacup, then slid out the page behind the contract. It was a glossy ad that featured Mia on a beautiful silver gelding, wearing the green Lyndon Wyld dress she had altered and embellished with fringe to make her own. It had become the Mia dress. In the ad, Cole sat behind her, arms around her waist with the green pastures of the Nantucket hills surrounding them. Mia recalled the day of the photo shoot when she and Cole finally got together, ravaging each other and revealing more of themselves. But they had both kept secrets that came back to bite them in the ass like horseflies.

"I wish you had signed the contract last summer to see the Mia dress and your collection come to fruition. I was disappointed, as were fans of yours who waited for it. But we all deserve second chances." Lyndon pointed to the contract. "This chance offers even better rewards."

Mia's eyes landed on the numbers behind the dollar sign: 100,000.

"You'll get half your seasonaire's salary up front: twenty thousand like the others," said Lyndon. "The going rate for influencers has risen, but my babies work for me because they know they'll get the exposure that will move them to the next level. Then someone else can pay them more."

Mia knew there were now more people who called themselves "influencers" than there were monetizing gigs for them. It was becoming a saturated market.

"At the same time, you'll get twenty thousand as a deposit for your collection," added Lyndon.

Mia looked at the terms: $20,000 at five phases: to start; if Lyndon approves designs; if Lyndon approves samples; if the approved pieces go into production; and if the collection lands in stores. With the exception of the deposit—*all ifs* with a dependence on Lyndon's approval.

"I should have an attorney review this," said Mia.

Lyndon put the teacup down on its saucer, its hollow *plink* signaling it was empty. "Your money should go to better use than lining attorneys' pockets. You'll learn soon enough that they're fucking leeches. Lawyers will never have your best interest in mind unless you're paying them a percentage of your earnings, and right now, you have no earnings."

Mia shifted in her seat.

"I honestly *do* have your best interest in mind, Mia. I mean, what could be more healing than California sunshine during a summer that might otherwise be filled with grief? And as far as 'work' goes, distractions are helpful when the people we love aren't coming back."

Mia stared into her teacup, which was still full. She stirred, this time back and forth.

"My chosen mix of seasonaires will provide a good distraction for you and everyone else, given last year's tragedy," said Lyndon as she scrolled through her phone. "I've gone for aspirational in the past, but Maz thinks my choices, with the exception of his daughter, were, as he put it, '2-D catalog mannequins.'"

A small, wry smile crossed Mia's face. "I should probably be offended."

"Don't be. He's the one who pushed me to push *you* to come back. He heard about your mum, and since he recently lost his, feels a kinship. He thinks grief builds depth of character and depth of character is what the brand needs. Plus, Jade adores you, though this year Maz wants another offspring in the mix."

"Which offspring?" Mia had heard the rumors about one of Maz's two sons, both of whom had reputations. Maz liked it that way.

Lyndon tilted her head and clucked her tongue. "I have to leave some surprises, but here is my tease—" She placed the phone on Mia's contract and scrolled through four photos of eye-catching twentysomethings. "Chase Edelstein is our born-and-raised Angeleno with soul . . . Eve Dunn is bringing us social consciousness." She rolled her eyes. "Oliver Hay is our relatable Midwesterner, because we *must* have one of those, and Alex Ensol is multifaceted fabulousness." Mia marveled at Lyndon's ability to succinctly sum up humans as if they were clothing items like "high-waisted linen trousers with a cuffed hem," or "a Swiss Dot A-line skirt." What Mia had discovered through her work in the apparel industry was most garments had a damage: a loose thread, dropped stitch, or tiny hole.

She'd barely had a chance to identify each new seasonaire when Lyndon snapped up the phone and tapped Mia's face in the ad. "That leaves one spot."

Mia stared at herself in the pastoral setting. *That was an amazing day,* she thought.

"You can have your own bedroom." Lyndon's voice lifted with the coax.

Mia left the teaspoon in the cup and looked at her. "I don't need my own bedroom."

Grinning, Lyndon sat up and clapped her hands once. "That means you'll do it! Brilliant!" She retrieved her phone.

Mia wasn't smiling. Her heart pounded as she picked up the pen. "I want to do it like the rest of the seasonaires. If you haven't noticed, I'm not Presley."

"Well, now that I know you're in, I need to talk to you about Presley." Lyndon returned her phone to its facedown position next to her on the table, and smoothed the napkin in her lap.

Mia stopped, her pen in midair. "You didn't add a seventh seasonaire, right? I don't want to sound obnoxious, but I know that I had the most followers last summer. That means *I'm* the returning seasonaire."

"You did and she's not."

"Okay."

"She's handling my LA public relations."

Mia dropped the pen and sighed.

"She won't be living in the house," assured Lyndon. "And she has plenty to do besides lolligag at the beach, that's for certain."

Mia moaned with dread and looked up at the ceiling. "I don't know."

"Mia, Presley never did anything wrong, according to the law. And according to *me*. She would never have tried to push you into an oncoming car."

Mia looked at Lyndon. "So she didn't want me dead?"

"Oh, she absolutely wanted you dead." Lyndon laughed. "Figuratively. She couldn't stand that you replaced her at the top of the food chain. But honestly, she wouldn't really hurt a fly. That bitch is all bark and no bite."

"Does backstabbing count? Do you remember her posts? It's ironic that now she's in charge of PR."

Lyndon pulled lipstick and a compact from her satin makeup bag. "My darling, Presley's life almost ended because of your accusation. For a beat, people thought she killed Grant. We both know that wasn't right." She stared at herself in the compact mirror, then blinked away the gloom and applied the classic red shade. "But she made a silk purse out of a sow's ear by playing on the public's sympathies: 'Poor girl works her way up, then is taken down by jealousy.' It's a tale as old as time and she understood how to make it current, which is why I hired her as publicist."

Mia touched her forehead, perturbed. "I wasn't jealous." Presley was the one who had been envious of her social media popularity and her friendship with Ruby, as if they'd been in middle school.

Lyndon put her makeup bag away. "It doesn't matter. At the end of the day, you both came out on top, so let it go and move on. That should be the motto to your summer: *Move on*."

Mia doubted that a second seasonaire summer would count as moving on, but she needed the money or she and Sean would be homeless. And she had other reasons to go to California. After a long beat, she signed her name and sealed the deal.

"If I were you, I would keep the amount of your payday to yourself. You never know who'll come out of the woodwork when you rise, and you *are* rising," said Lyndon with a smile. She closed the drab beige folder over the contract and slid it back into her bright yellow tote. Teatime was over.

THREE

M ia walked down her street, arms wrapped around cardboard boxes she had snagged from the back of the bodega. She chose the ones that smelled like the Braeburn apples her mom had loved. Mia appreciated the blue sky that peeked between buildings as if they defied all the new construction that was taking over Southie. Nantucket, with its whitewashed perfection, had given her newfound love for her neighborhood's rough edges. She took solace in putting one foot in front of the other, though she was fried from trying to keep her mother alive during this last year. But when Lyndon gave her the first-class plane ticket to Los Angeles after their tea, Mia felt a spark of excitement she couldn't deny.

Then came the wave of dread at the thought of telling Sean. Two months had passed and it was time to deal with their mom's closet. She wasn't coming back no matter how hard Mia and Sean wished she would. Mia pulled out a pair of sailor-style pants with anchor-stamped buttons running parallel up the front. "I always loved these!" She folded them and put them in the box marked *Keep*. Feeling something in the right pocket of a ragged terry cloth robe, she lifted out a weed vape pen. "So *this* is where she hid it after I trekked to the dispensary to buy it for her."

"That's some surprising greediness!" Sean chuckled. "She taught us to share." They both broke into laughter.

"It did stop her vomiting." Maybe it would quell Mia's queasiness over the news she was about to impart. She held it out for Sean, who took the robe but not the pen.

"You know I don't do that shit during season." Sean put the robe in the *Giveaway* box.

Mia took a hit.

Sean's eyes narrowed at her. "And you never do it."

Mia exhaled. "In honor of Mom."

They put more items in boxes for a few silent minutes until a faint fuzziness covered Mia's head. "Speaking of seasons . . ." Going for nonchalance, she would toss out the information like the moth-eaten sweater she chucked into the *Giveaway* box. "I'm a seasonaire in Malibu this summer."

Sean lowered the skirt he was folding. "You're shitting me. You didn't really do it, did you?"

Mia put on a straw hat. "I can talk Lyndon into having you come, too." She heard her own voice rise in a singsong and grimaced.

"Travel three thousand miles away to live with a new set of douchebags posting selfies skipping down the beach drinking kombucha. Don't forget the flower crown filter!" Sean mimed a crown around his head. "Plus the possibility of an earthquake. No, thank you."

"Presley is head of PR in LA, so your description is about right. She'd love an earthquake. That's drama!" Mia dropped the hat in the *Keep* box.

"I'd rather eat a bag of toe jam, especially if she's around. What happened to 'I'm never leaving Boston again'?"

Mia ran the back of her hand across her forehead. "Um, Mom died and we can't afford to *stay* in Boston—or anywhere, for that matter. It's a good opportunity." She shook her head at the skirt.

Sean chucked it in the *Giveaway* box. "How much was the opportunity?"

"The seasonaire's fee, plus a contract for my entire collection. A little over a hundred grand." Off Sean's raised eyebrows— "Though not payable all at once."

"Of course not. That's business for Lyndon."

Mia plopped on the bed, dropping the shield of defensiveness because that never worked on Sean. "I have business in California, too."

Sean gave her a deadpan look. "That's where Ruby lives."

"Yes. Maybe," stammered Mia. "I don't know. I tried calling her a long time ago, but her number was disconnected."

Sean face-palmed. "Mia, c'mon. She was a mess."

"We're all messes." Mia took another hit. She had never told her brother or mother about walking into the Wear National backyard last July Fourth. She left the vape pen on the barren nightstand, closed the *Keep* box, and carried it to her bedroom.

—

At the tail end of May, Mia packed her own things, including her mom's wrap dress and straw hat, and some pieces she had been working on. Lyndon had texted her to leave her sewing equipment at home. In Nantucket, she'd bought Mia a new machine. Who knew what would be waiting for her in Malibu? Like the previous summer, Sean had to help her close the overstuffed suitcase. "At least you don't have to bring a fake ID this year," he said.

"Yeah, I'm a big girl." Mia recalled the thrill she felt knowing that she was cheating the system. Now she was *part* of the system, leading Lyndon's charge.

Sean slung his baseball gear bag over his shoulder and gave Mia a quick hug. "I feel guilty I can't drive you to the airport."

"No, you don't."

"You're right, I don't. But I'll miss you, turd." Sean put a hand on Mia's arm.

Mia returned the gesture. "I'll miss you, too, turd." She held her hand there. "This is for us—for our home."

"Keep telling yourself that, because without Mom, is this even our home anymore?" Sean left. Emptiness filled the apartment.

In the Lyft to the airport, Mia looked at her phone but couldn't bring herself to reconnect on social yet. Her finger hovered over the app store. She had deleted her accounts because they'd become a form of masochism: the memories—good and bad— and the trolls with their comments:

> Basic bitch
> Faux pixie-mom style
> #talentless

And the worst ones:

> Traitor
> #twofaced

Sean wasn't on social media. He said, "Anonymity gives people truck-nuts—noisy but impotent and they look fucking stupid."

It had been different with Presley's phone number. First, Mia had deleted the texts. Then, she'd deleted Presley from her contacts and blocked her. She couldn't find Presley if she'd wanted to, and that suited her fine. But now, pulling up to the domestic departures terminal at Logan Airport with a ticket to LAX, she was doing exactly that: heading for Presley. The thought made her want to turn around and stay in Boston, despite the increasingly sticky heat and throngs of sweaty, exasperated city people—most of whom would've given a kidney for a paid summer in a West Coast paradise. But before she could abort mission, her FaceTime buzzed: it was Lyndon. "Did you check your bags?"

"One bag, singular." Mia exited the car. The Lyft driver popped the trunk and set Mia's suitcase on the curb. "I'm about to do that now." She mouthed "thanks" to the driver and entered the terminal.

"I'll wait," said Lyndon. Mia hated when people were on their phones at the thrift shop or in line at the grocery store. It was rude. She put Lyndon on the counter as she checked her one suitcase and was directed to the gate. Security was the first gauntlet, and since it was the Thursday before Memorial Day weekend, the area was packed with travelers trying to get out of town early.

"Do you hate Logan as much as I hate Heathrow? The female security agents are such cunts." Lyndon's loud words made Mia look around. She caught the stink-eye of a female TSA agent and looked back at her phone.

"Can I call you right back?" Mia reached the front of the line. "I'm about to go through."

"Opt out of the body scan if you ever want children." Lyndon did not have children. Mia had always wondered if she wanted them or if she really considered her seasonaires to be her "babies." Mia clicked off and placed her smartphone in a plastic bin with her tote bag.

A hulking male TSA agent pushed bins and items through on the conveyor belt to be x-rayed. "Laptops out and in a separate bin!" Mia unzipped her laptop sleeve and put her laptop in a bin. Overwhelmed at the process, she glanced around at the lines of passengers. Most of them were removing their shoes, so she followed suit and placed her white sneakers in the bin. The female

TSA agent pointed her to the body scanner arch. People entered the vestibule and stood with their arms over their heads and their legs splayed wide as the machine scanned them.

"How do I opt out?" asked Mia. "Sorry, I don't know what I'm doing. I've never flown before."

The female TSA agent didn't say anything and, irritated, motioned Mia around. "Everything out of your pockets?" Mia nodded with a soft "yes." After the pat-down, she fumbled to gather her belongings and slipped on her shoes, leaving them untied. Feeling disheveled, she checked the fly on her long, tailored shorts to make sure it wasn't down, then hauled herself to the rows of chairs at the gate. She found one and sat. A text came in from Lyndon:

> Are you through?

Mia replied:

> Yes.

Lyndon followed up:

> Were the women cunts?

Mia pinged back:

> 😔

Lyndon ended with:

> Told you. Bon voyage!

Mia realized that Lyndon wanted to ensure her investment got on that plane.

The flight was full, according to the terse male voice over the speaker, which demanded that passengers volunteer to check their carry-ons so there would be more room in the overhead compartments. No one volunteered. Fifteen minutes later, the voice added that the airline would pay passengers to switch to a later flight in order to reduce the plane's weight. An older couple stepped up to the gate agent at the counter to sell their places. Mia wondered how their thin bodies would make a difference in keeping a technologically advanced aircraft aloft. Her heart started to beat faster.

The flight was delayed, first by an hour, then by three. The wait didn't bother her. She sketched and caught up on fashion and beauty blogs. She breathed for the first time in months. After three and a half hours, Mia was starting to hope the flight would be canceled altogether. No such luck. Passengers were called for boarding. Mia was in the first group, while others crammed together, waiting impatiently for zones two, three, and four. As she walked through the gauntlet, passengers in the other groups threw her bitter stares, as if she had personally relegated them to coach.

Mia maneuvered into the aisle seat next to a forty-something woman who stared straight ahead and clutched the front of her armrests. "Hi," said Mia. The woman mouthed "hello," her neck pink from forcing her breath in and out.

Following the voice-over instructions, Mia slid her Lyndon Wyld monogrammed tote under the seat in front of her and buckled up. A flight attendant wearing a tight smile to go with her uniform strolled down the aisle carrying a tray of glass flutes filled with bubbly. She nodded to Mia's seatmate and the shrouded window next to her. "You'll have to put up your window shade for takeoff and landing."

"Oh," said the woman, who appeared frozen.

"Do you want me to—?" Mia unbuckled and awkwardly reached across the woman to slide up the shade. The flight attendant gave Mia a "thank you" look, then pushed the tray of beverages closer. "Prosecco?" Mia's seatmate unglued a hand from the armrest long enough to take a flute and down the bubbly. Mia re-buckled and took a flute. "Thank you." She sipped. Looking back, she could see through the split in the curtain between first class and coach, where passengers were squeezed in tight rows of three. No one had prosecco.

Mia's seatmate re-gripped the armrest with her fingers still around the stem of the empty flute. "I hate flying, but I won this trip to California in my job's holiday lottery."

Mia smiled politely. "Congratulations."

"I haven't seen my sister in five years, but with the free ticket, I didn't have an excuse anymore." The woman winced. "I'm looking forward to landing."

Mia didn't know if she could say the same. She closed her eyes as the plane took off and discovered that she liked the sensation of defying gravity. Once the plane leveled off, Mia pulled her sketch pad from her tote and started to work on a romper design. Mia's seatmate barely moved until the plane dropped and lurched, and she grabbed Mia's wrist. The pilot assured everyone that the turbulence was normal and temporary, so the woman let go. But she grabbed back on with each bump, making it hard for Mia to work.

The woman started crying and repeating, "I'm so sorry" on a loop, unable to detach herself from Mia.

Mia patted her arm again. "It's okay."

The woman's voice trembled. "I have this superstition that if I imagine the worst thing that could happen, that thing won't happen. But my mind is stuck on the worst thing."

Mia understood but felt like the worst things had already happened. She patted the woman's arm. "We're in good hands," she said, though she had no idea if that was actually true.

FOUR

Coming into Los Angeles, the plane tipped so that Mia could catch a glimpse of the landscape through the sliver of window visible past her seatmate. Sludgy-brown haze covered the city, as if to shroud its rumored beauty like an antique veil over what could be a blushing bride or the Bride of Frankenstein. All she knew was that she had arrived.

The passengers applauded when the pilot landed with minimal jostling. Mia's seatmate released Mia to clap, a relieved grin widening on her tearstained face. Mia's arm remained moist from the woman's sweaty fingers as they deplaned after exchanging final pleasantries.

Mia walked through the plane's exit tunnel and stopped for a beat to lift her tote onto her shoulder. She started to pull out her phone, then dropped it back in. She wove around the mass of travelers, most of whom had their eyes on their phones as they pulled luggage or pushed children. Following the signs to baggage claim, she headed down an escalator and along a tunnel plastered with LA-friendly ads. It ended at a wall of welcomers. Happy couples hugged. Tired kids cried. Selfies were snapped. She watched her seatmate embrace an older woman, touched by the joy of their long-awaited reunion. As they moved off to baggage claim, Mia's eyes landed on an iPad turned horizontally with the last name *Daniels* written in cursive. The man holding it was in a brown blazer with a Lyndon Wyld embroidered logo patch on the breast pocket. His hair was a thin halo of graying wisps.

Mia pointed to the iPad sign. "That's fancy. I'm Mia Daniels. Are you waiting for me?"

The man offered a friendly smile. "Sure am. Welcome to Los Angeles, Mia Daniels. I'm Marcus, your driver for the summer."

"I have a driver?"

Marcus ushered her to baggage claim. "You and the five other seasonaires."

Mia saw her suitcase come around on the baggage carousel. Though she reached, Marcus got to it first.

"Oh, thank you." Mia awkwardly pulled in the arm aiming towards the suitcase. As Marcus rolled it, Mia followed, not knowing what to do with her hands. The glass double doors opened and they exited.

Mia didn't realize how cold the AC was in the terminal until she stepped out into the Southern California air, which was warm and thicker than she imagined. A cacophony of car honks greeted her. Drivers were juking their vehicles around each other on their way into the loading lanes. Airport traffic cops blew whistles, and shuttle buses narrowly missed fenders. She and Marcus made their way into a multilevel parking structure.

A beep emitted from a spotless white Tesla Model X with beige and green Lyndon Wyld logos—small, but noticeable on either side of the hood. After placing the suitcase in the back, Marcus pressed his remote and the passenger doors lifted like wings. Mia slid into the second of three rows and Marcus into the driver's seat. The car's motor was silent as he maneuvered around the honkers to reach another domestic airline terminal. He parked in the nearby parking structure and turned to Mia. "I have to retrieve one of your colleagues. I'll be right back." He pointed to the center console. "There are waters for you—cold and tepid, sparkling and flat."

Mia was now alone in the car that felt like a small spaceship. She took a deep breath and lifted her phone from her tote, then stared at it for a few minutes. She pressed it on. After it came to life, a text buzzed in from a 470 area code noted as Atlanta, Georgia:

Welcome to the City of Flowers n Sunshine, sunshine! 🌷 ☀

She didn't need to know Presley's new phone number. That text was obviously from her. Mia didn't text back but instead let Lyndon know that she'd safely arrived. Lyndon's text response:

Greet everyone for me. I'll see you at the store opening.

In Nantucket, Lyndon and Grace had greeted all the seasonaires. Mia wondered why this was now her responsibility. But she didn't question Lyndon. Instead, she reinstalled the social apps and, with a hard swallow, reactivated her accounts. She wished she could see her Instagram Story with Grant—the last photo she'd ever taken with him, but it had disappeared with all the others that vanished after twenty-four hours. She found her last post on the Fourth of July at The Rabbit Hole. The party was in full swing around the seasonaires, moments before shit went down.

A comment came in. Mia's brow furrowed as she read it.

It's never over. 😊

"Fuck." Mia couldn't delete it fast enough to forget it. Unable to stop herself, she searched for Ruby Taylor but didn't find her on social. Ruby's posts and stories, which had featured her in tiny Wear National bikinis, loose minidresses, and thin tanks, accompanied by her stack of bracelets and blissed-out smile, were gone. Wear National didn't exist, but Mia hoped that Ruby still did.

"Ooh, a Tesla," said a cheerful female voice, muffled by the closed car window. The back passenger door lifted and a girl jumped in, her wild mane of thick, curly auburn hair bouncing. She glanced around. "It's very cush, but the whole zero emissions thing is bullshit. It's about where you plug in. The grid has to be greener. But the grid's pretty good in California, so I don't feel like too much of a sham riding in it."

"Thank goodness," mumbled Marcus as he started the car.

"*Yet.* I don't feel like too much of a sham *yet.*" The girl's heart-shaped face was covered with freckles that she didn't camouflage with foundation. She looked straight into Mia's eyes. "You're Mia. You were a seasonaire last summer. How long did it take you to feel like a sham, because I'll bet the whole pretense feels 'sham-ish' after a while?"

Mia rubbed the back of her neck, confused by Eve's perspective, given that Eve had applied to be a seasonaire. "Don't we all feel like occasional shams?"

"Good answer! You are down-to-earth, Mia! I'm Eve." Eve stuck her hand out. Mia shook it. "And you shake! Girls never shake."

Mia chuckled. "You're right. They don't. They either hug or air-kiss, even when they don't know each other, which is wildly disingenuous."

"In other words: a sham. See?" Eve slapped her bare legs in the short, flouncy floral skirt. "You are *not* one. I can tell."

"Where are you from, Eve?" asked Mia.

"Portland. You're from Boston. I saw that on your social." Eve's enthusiastic ramble didn't give Mia a chance to answer. "I was there once when my parents went to a conference at Emerson. They're both English professors at Reed. I was about eight and loved it, even though it was during the Big Dig—all that construction! The nav in our rental nearly combusted, and so did my dad's head."

"Try living in LA full-time," said Marcus, who joined the dissonant symphony of honks as the Tesla crawled out of the airport fray. "Everyone is a rideshare driver, most of whom just moved here and can't find their way out of a paper bag. I've been here for twenty years and now you can't get anywhere in less than an hour." He honked again and pressed the Ludicrous Mode button on the car's control screen. The Tesla rocketed off, the g-force propelling the girls back.

Eve chortled. "That's some big dick energy right there."

Mia reached forward and touched the right side of the driver's seat. "We're not in any hurry."

Eve tapped Marcus's headrest. "Yeah. Mia and I are getting to know each other."

Marcus gripped the steering wheel tighter. "I have to drop you off at the house, then pick up another one of you, so I *am* in a hurry."

Mia sat back and exchanged a look with Eve, who shrugged. They whizzed along Century Boulevard with its dull stucco buildings, billboards for ambulance chasers and fat freezing procedures, and striking lack of greenery.

Eve took in the sights. "So far I'm not impressed."

"It's Westchester—" Marcus said flatly. "Not the nice part." The Tesla flew onto the 405 Freeway going north and was immediately stuck in bumper-to-bumper traffic, despite its place in the carpool lane. A man in a coupe gained on them from the side to get into the lane. Mia did a double take at the car's passenger. "Oh my God!" Eve looked. The passenger was a blow-up sex doll. The girls' peals of laughter stoked Marcus's road rage, so when the sex doll driver cut him off, Marcus laid on the horn.

"That looked like a passenger Otto Hahn would have—from what I've read about him." Eve was still chuckling.

Mia's smile stiffened.

"Is this what it was like landing on Nantucket?" asked Eve, still chuckling.

"Not remotely."

"I didn't think so. Well, I hope the rest of the summer is different, too. I mean, one of your friends was murdered," said Eve, her green eyes wide.

Mia couldn't keep the corners of her mouth lifted. "You sure know how to kill a conversation."

"I'm actually starting one. I suck at small talk. What was his name again—your friend?"

Mia caught Marcus staring at her in the rearview mirror. "Grant," she answered. Mia's mind flashed to Grant's bright white smile as he stood by the Lyndon Wyld G-Wagen convertible on the dock. His perfectly chiseled, golden-tan body had made her wonder if she would fit the image of the brand.

"He was hot," said Eve with a *tsk*. "What a tragedy."

"He was a good guy." Mia's voice caught for a beat. She was surprised at how quickly her emotions overtook her when talking about Grant. "Kind of like a puppy who couldn't control himself."

"Aren't most men like that?" Eve eyed Marcus. "No offense, Marcus." Marcus refrained from response. Eve sighed. "That's why we give them a pass far too often. Do you agree, Mia?" She held her phone out to Marcus. "Can you plug this in?" Marcus connected the USB and The Mamas and The Papas' "California Dreaming" started to play from the speakers.

Amused, Mia released a dry snort. "That's a little on the nose."

"I made a playlist. I wanted to include Tupac's 'California Love,' but given that I'm a white girl from Portland, it seemed wrong."

"It's a great song," said Mia.

"Cultural appropriation."

The four-part '60s harmony filled the car, making it easier for Eve and Mia to have a conversation that Marcus couldn't hear. Eve leaned in close. "Did you hook up with Grant?"

"No." Mia brushed invisible lint off her shorts. "We were just really good friends. He slept his way around Nantucket. I was glad he had enough respect for me to pass me over."

"I would've fucked him for sure." Eve grinned. "Some might say that's disrespectful to the dead, but from what you're telling me, I think he would've appreciated the compliment."

Mia bristled for a beat, but then smiled at the thought. "He probably would have."

Eve leaned away to survey Mia. "Did you hook up with *anyone* last summer?"

Mia struggled with her desire for privacy and her hope to make friends this summer. Being a seasonaire, she knew privacy was impossible, so she decided to answer. "I had a thing, but it was short-lived."

"As summer *things* should be."

"Yeah, I suppose it was fine for a minute, but it got complicated." Mia didn't talk about Cole with anyone. After finding out he was DEA, she felt stupid—her relationship could've cost her much more than her heart. But she had betrayed him, too.

Eve shook her head, her curly hair growing more untamed. "Oh, shit. Nope, nope, nope. No complications." She made a cross with her forefingers.

Mia crossed her own forefingers. Since Cole, she had avoided relationships. The occasional hookup was fine with her—she just wanted to feel good.

Eve fixed her loose, violet cap-sleeve top, which revealed the softness of her arms and the fullness of her breasts peeking out from a powder-blue cotton bralette. She possessed an earthy sensuality. "Studies show that one night of sex can boost your mood the next day. Pleasure, not intimacy, enhances mental health, so I say get your drama-free freak on!"

Marcus tapped the steering wheel. "What's your major, Eve?" *Apparently the music isn't loud enough,* thought Mia.

Eve crossed her arms. "Rhetoric and media studies."

"What are you going to do with *that* degree?" asked Marcus with a snicker.

"Talk to me in ten years when we're controlled by AI and need humanities majors. Everyone will want to know how humans'll survive, and we'll be able to tell them. That's part of why I wanted to do this seasonaires gig."

"As extra credit?" asked Mia.

"Don't get me wrong. I'm grateful to be a seasonaire with twenty thousand bucks in my pocket by summer's end. College is fucking expensive, and my parents don't get paid what they're worth as educators. But I really took the job as an experiment on the growing pretension behind social media. It plays to our innate narcissistic tendencies, and I wanted to immerse myself in it—kind of like self-taught summer school."

In the rearview mirror, Mia could see another silent snicker from Marcus. She looked at Eve. "That's an interesting experiment if we don't become part of the problem in the process."

"Never gonna happen." Eve twirled a curl around her finger. "That's Munchausen syndrome."

They passed a billboard that looked like a plug for a science fiction movie because it displayed a microscope shot of spiny cells . . . until Mia read the words *Gonorrhea Alert!* "The clap is back in a big way, especially here in the Golden State," said Marcus in an extra loud voice. "Antibiotic-resistant clap."

Mia and Eve shared a disgusted grimace. The Eagles' "Hotel California" came on the stereo. "Can you turn it up, please, Marcus?" asked Mia. Marcus met her request. Tension spiked in Mia, which could have been due to Marcus's creepy interjections or the fact that he was getting right up on the asses of the cars. She glanced around at the suffocating hug of the freeway meridian on one side and cars on the other. Every single driver was either tapping, swiping, or talking on a phone. No one tried to hide it. Mia wondered what they could be texting or posting from this uninteresting clusterfuck that made Boston's Big Dig streets seem like empty country roads.

Eve sang along with the songs: "West Coast" by Lana Del Rey, "Californication" by Red Hot Chili Peppers, "Hollywood" by Madonna. She swayed and waved her hand out the open window—her nails were short and polish-free. Mia watched the 10 Freeway turn into Highway 1; Pacific Coast Highway presented the Santa Monica coastline like the jewel of the city.

Eve gasped. "Now *that's* more like it!"

And there they were: "Palm trees," said Mia with a smile. The tall, ridged brown trunks topped with sprays of leafy green fronds bordered PCH as they passed the Santa Monica Pier. Its Ferris wheel, with its red and yellow gondolas, was wrapped in the red track of the roller coaster. Mia had never ridden a roller coaster, but this one looked invitingly tame.

The Tesla floated along the endless stretch of beachside highway, watched over by hills and cliffs—thrones to the homes perched on them. The houses varied in style, in addition to a couple of mobile home parks that didn't look like any Mia had seen before. The double-wides were like upscale-cozy beach hideaways. All the homes had one asset in common: a bird's-eye view.

The car approached the iconic wood sign with its yin-yang of blue and green, and the white letters that announced:

MALIBU

21 MILES OF SCENIC BEAUTY

Eve smacked Marcus's seat. "Stop! We need to take a pic!" Before Marcus could pull over, Eve unbuckled and yanked her phone from the USB. The car rustled onto the shoulder's gravel and the two girls got out. Eve grabbed Mia's hand and pulled her over to the sign. She fervently motioned for Marcus to get out. "Photog!" She tossed her phone to him, and it narrowly missed the asphalt. As he aimed it at the two girls, Eve jumped with her arms up. Beaming, Mia gestured to the sign as if it had been a game show prize. Marcus snapped the photo and tossed the phone back to Eve.

Mia was calmed by the sea air, which smelled different from Nantucket's. Malibu's air was lighter, tinged with the cool sweetness of eucalyptus trees.

Eve posted. "Just know that if you're in one of my posts, it's going up as is, despite this giant zit." She pointed to a sizable pimple on her chin that went uncovered by concealer. Mia's phone buzzed with the tag notification as they got in the car:

New summer. New friends. #seasonaires #BuWyld
#nofilter

Marcus pulled the Tesla back onto the highway and was overtaken by a thunderous pack of motorcycles that seemed to come out of nowhere. The dark shadow of leather and chrome surrounded them in a deafening roar.

"Holy shit," said Mia. She and Eve laughed, but Mia's heart raced as the pack growled off like a serpent.

FIVE

Marcus drove a few more miles before turning down a road off PCH. It looked like they were going to soar straight over the bluffs into the sea. They were stopped by a modern architectural masterpiece of wood, glass, and concrete. The estate's angular lines were juxtaposed against the rounded, uneven edges of the cliff beneath it, as if to make the statement that it was more important than the earth it sat on.

Marcus parked the car in the horseshoe driveway. "Your castle awaits."

Eve yelped with glee. "This is insane! And it's *extra* because of the drought-tolerant landscaping. I might've had to leave if I saw sod!" Mia glanced around—the home was surrounded by green and purple succulents, agave plants, and aloes. Bright yellow African daisies and red daylilies were sunny pops of color.

The car doors lifted, and the girls got out. Marcus was already at the back, pulling out their suitcases. "Thank you," said Mia as she gazed at the twin sky-high palm trees—the only palm trees among the property's fruit trees and one stately oak.

Eve abandoned her luggage by the car. Marcus stared at it. "Does she think I'm a bellhop?"

Eve skipped up to the front door. "We have *so* arrived!" Mia couldn't remember the last time she'd skipped.

Marcus watched, shaking his head. "She is definitely going in my script."

"You're writing a script?" asked Mia.

"You gotta create your own content in this town. That's the only way to get anything done."

"Oh." Standing near him, Mia couldn't shake her uneasiness. "You can just leave my suitcase here. I'm going to take a look around."

Marcus pulled his iPad from the front seat, perched it on the car's hood, and typed. He got back into the car with it. "I have to go pick up another one—at the Expo terminal. Kid wouldn't get on a plane from Denver, so he came by bus and Metro Rail." He rolled his eyes as the Tesla whirred off.

Instead of heading towards the house, Mia walked to the bluff's edge and took some deep breaths. The sound of the crashing waves filled her ears. She couldn't believe how close and *loud* they were. She wondered if that sound would grow to be peaceful, because right then, it was overwhelming.

"Well, well, well, look what the help dragged in," drawled that familiar Southern Peach lilt.

Mia turned around. Before she knew it, Presley was air-kissing her on both cheeks. Her cornsilk hair was as shiny as ever, but shorter and styled straighter and sleeker. Her look was more British queen and less beauty queen in a cropped white Lyndon Wyld raw linen jacket, crisp white blouse, and daffodil-hued

A-line skirt that covered a conservative amount of her pageant-perfect shape. The cleavage she revealed was respectable but flattering—a far cry from the low necklines and high slits of the previous summer.

"How's life, sugar?" She touched the amethyst solitaire in the center of her delicate necklace. It was similar to the sapphire necklace that Grace used to wear, though much of Presley's look mirrored Lyndon's.

"Life has been . . . life," replied Mia, who mustered a wry smile and swallowed her sadness.

"I was sorry to hear about your mama." Presley released an overdramatic sigh. "If one of our mamas had to go, I wish it would've been mine."

"You have a special way of offering condolences," said Mia. She couldn't help the comfort she felt getting exactly what she expected from Presley. *The devil you know*—that adage calmed her nerves in an odd way.

Presley brushed a strand of hair off Mia's face. "You and I were tight, Mia. I loved you like a sister—the sister I always wanted, not the one I have of course, because Gemma is hopeless trailer trash." She chuckled.

Mia touched the strand that Presley had brushed.

"But you didn't believe my loyalty, and your active mistrust made me doubt yours forever," said Presley.

Mia looked at the mossy-green ground cover. "It was a fucked-up situation, to put it mildly."

"Fucked-up situations reveal people's true colors, and yours clashed with mine like that shirt with those . . . what are they? Pants or shorts?" Presley flicked a hand towards Mia's outfit.

"This is a pattern pair I'm going to present to Lyndon with my new collection." Mia smoothed her Lyndon Wyld pinstripe pants that she had shortened to just below the knee. They sat below a ruffle-sleeve top with mini polka dots. She looked back up, into

Presley's eyes, and mustered confidence. "It'll hit retail in the spring."

Presley clapped her hands together. "I loathe the shants but love your new proverbial peacock feathers! I think you should include some plumes in your designs!"

"You asked how my life was. I'm telling you." Mia's tone was slightly defensive.

"That you are, sugar." Presley grinned. "That you *are*."

"I'm trying to move on."

"Move on from that Millennial Pink." Presley pinched the blush-hued fabric of Mia's top. "It's over, like the past. We're still working towards the same goal, you and me: Bring Lyndon Wyld to the next level. Who else really counts here?"

"*Five*—five other people count here," said Mia, turning towards the house. Manning a camera was a good-looking guy in a distressed heather-gray M-Kat T-shirt under a Lyndon Wyld navy button-down paired with rigid black denim. He filmed a tall brunette with legs for days who strutted out of the house and down the limestone walkway in six-inch stilettos like it was New York Fashion Week.

Presley nodded to the cameraman. "Do you recognize him?" There was something familiar—his Cheshire Cat grin and cocksure presence. "That Maz's son."

"*The* son?" asked Mia.

"No. That one's too old and too far off the rails for Lyndon. This is the younger one: Brandon."

Mia crossed her arms, staring at Brandon. "Didn't he go off the rails, too? Beat the living crap out of some guy in a club?" She tried to stay away from the tabloids, but Maz's family exploits were hard to miss.

Presley side-eyed Mia. "Rumor. You and I both understand the stink of rumor. And Lyndon didn't really have a choice, with the co-brand and all. Maz is the new money."

"Have you heard from Jade?" asked Mia.

Presley crossed her arms. "Nope. Baby sister has moved from fashion to the entertainment side of their daddy's world."

Mia hoped that Jade was making a name for herself separate from being Maz's daughter—a moniker that bothered Jade enough to self-sabotage. After Jade had broken the rules and left Nantucket for her dad's annual July Fourth Blue Bash in the Hamptons, Lyndon had kicked her off the island.

"That's Alex." Presley's eyes were on the tall, leggy stunner who struck a pose—chin tilted down, shoulders back, arm closest to the camera on an angular hip, and ankles crossed like a pro. The marigold bell-sleeve minidress and cascading choker necklace complemented Alex's slender model's body.

Mia didn't remember Alex from the photos Lyndon had shown her. "Well, Alex could carry off a garbage bag," she said with a smile.

Presley grimaced. "Working the sexy way too hard. Lyndon picked all the seasonaires herself, without my input." Mia could tell that she was chapped. Alex's long, shiny chestnut ponytail was the same length as Presley's hair before the new cut. Presley had paraded her mane around like she was Rapunzel. She turned to Mia. "Enough about you and them. Before we move on, where are your manners? Aren't you going to ask me how *I've* been doing?" She flipped her own hair back—her bob barely grazed her shoulders.

"How have you been doing?"

"If you hadn't've asked, I was going to tell you anyway. My short stint in jail, thanks to you, made me stronger."

Prickling heat rose through Mia's body and she started to sweat. She'd known this would come up, but she'd applied some magical thinking: If she avoided the subject, it wouldn't rear its ugly head. She was wrong.

"But I'm not going anywhere . . . except my Hotel Brentwood suite. The penthouse is positively smashing!" Presley's tone was sharp with bitterness, but the British term sounded awkward coming out of her mouth. "It all worked out, but I do have to say it's a tad hard to get hired at a law firm, even as a lowly clerk, with that on my resume. My degree from a great school didn't help much."

Mia shoved her hands in her pockets. "I dropped the charges. If you were innocent, I can't imagine that legal professionals would hold anything against you."

"They don't admit to that. It's like having a new boyfriend who's all about realness. You tell him your tits are one hundred percent, then he sees your boob job scars. He'll say he wants to fuck you, but he won't."

Mia stared blankly at Presley.

"Oh! That reminds me—" Presley held up her phone. "Remember Jill from the Nantucket store?" As Presley scrolled on her phone, Mia thought back on Jill and Cole's friendship, and her needless jealousy over it. Jill had also accused her of shoplifting. It was easy to access the humiliation she'd felt as the other seasonaires had stared at her. Presley had taken the fall and put Jill in her place. Putting people in their places was one of Presley's special skills.

"She had her face redone so she wouldn't need to filter." Presley showed Mia Jill's Instagram feed. She had been an attractive woman in her late twenties. Passed over as a seasonaire, she'd ended up working at the store instead. In the new posts, Jill's lips looked fuller and her jawline more defined. "But now the pout is out!" Presley made duck lips and clicked off her phone. "Next year, I might get a little somethin'-somethin' right up here." She pointed to the smooth skin between her brows. "My 'what the fuck' line is digging in." She motioned to Mia's face. "You might want to think about it yourself, honey. Tough times can age a girl faster than a plum left out on the counter in July."

Mia pushed a stone with the tip of her sneaker. The last of the sunlight glinted off the LW buckle on Presley's ballet flats. Mia had never seen Presley in a heel lower than kitten. "I'm sorry about the jail stint."

"Oh, well. My mugshot trended." Presley bumped up one shoulder, then pouted. "But you didn't call. You didn't write."

"You weren't there long enough for a letter. Besides, no one writes letters anymore."

"You see? We're sisters with our twinning dark senses of humor." Presley caressed Mia's arm. "But don't cross me again." She squeezed for a beat and released.

"Presley, I'm not here to compete with you. I would never have signed on for this job again if you were living in this house."

Presley put a hand to her chest, mock offended. "I was a model roomie!"

Mia obliged with a closed-mouth smile. "You had your moments."

"We both have a passion for this business. This brand is my life now, and I'm going to get it the exposure it deserves." Presley lifted her chin.

"I have no doubt. You are all about exposure."

Presley glanced at Alex, whose dress was lifted just enough to tease Brandon's camera with the back of a thigh. "Hm." She sniffed with judgment, then locked eyes with Mia. "Just know that I can make you look really, really good or really, really horrible."

"Hasn't that always been the case?" Mia squinted into the sun as it lowered over the water, creating an ombré of purple, red, and orange.

"Shall we hug it out?" Presley didn't give Mia a chance to answer before tugging her in for a hug and whispering, "I haven't made you look really, really horrible . . . yet." She pulled away and grinned as if she was kidding.

"Maybe there's a way that we can be cordial and adult. Is that possible?" asked Mia.

Presley snickered, motioning to the house. "Who under thirty calls themselves an adult? No one here, that's for sure." Eve had joined Alex and was swigging from a bottle of Dom, which burst with bubbles, while Alex sipped Perrier from a straw. The two "flossed" for Brandon's camera, shifting their hips the opposite way of their arms.

"And see that Muppet right there? Chase?" Presley pointed to the round plexiglass swing hanging from the far end of the long porch. It spun to the front to reveal Chase—barefoot, his legs crossed underneath him. He was shirtless in knee-length surf shorts, his golden tan offset against shoulder-length, sun-bleached, sea-salt-matted waves. He smoked a joint. "All I know is that he still lives at home with his mama in Santa Monica. He could practically walk there." Presley grimaced with disdain.

Mia pointed to herself. "*I* live at home."

"It's fine for a girl. Wrong for a man. How *is* your brother, by the way?" asked Presley, fiddling with a button on her blouse.

"Working hard."

"I'll bet he could've come, had you asked Lyndon. And he would've enjoyed himself. I mean, look how relaxed Chase looks."

They watched Chase twirl in the swing. "You mean, high," said Mia.

"Snooze, ya lose." Presley nodded towards the house. "We should go inside. You have some welcoming to do. Did you practice your speech?"

"I didn't practice it, because I don't have one." Mia patted her empty shants pockets.

Presley placed a hand on Mia's shoulder. "Wing it from the heart. That's what I do. At least that's what I've got everyone thinking."

"No one's thinking that." Mia gazed out at the Pacific Ocean.

Presley pointed at the sweeping coastline to the east. "That's the Queen's Necklace—not to be confused with a 'pearl necklace,' which is a common sugar daddy gift out here." She skimmed the curving line of her collar. "When it gets dark, the lights from the homes twinkle like pearls."

Mia lifted one corner of her mouth. "Thank you for clarifying. I look forward to seeing it in all its glory—the *Queen's* Necklace, that is."

"This whole place is a goddamn Shangri-la," said Presley, beaming. "Fuck Nantucket."

The water's shimmer was magical. Mia couldn't wait to take the wood steps from the house down to the beach and walk along the shore. "Fuck Nantucket," she said as she took a photo and posted.

Presley gasped. "What? No filter or caption? You're not even in the pic!"

"That would've ruined it," replied Mia.

Presley *tsk*ed. "First mistake."

"It won't be my last, I'm sure." Mia slipped her phone in her back pocket and walked towards the house.

SIX

Presley strode past Mia to the house's walkway. As she crossed the parked white Volvo XC60 SUV hybrid, she pulled her key from her white crocodile shoulder bag to lock the doors with a *beep*. Brandon turned the camera from Alex and Eve to Presley and Mia. Presley flipped him off.

Brandon placed his camera on a woven wood table. "Don't chew the scenery. It's not yours to eat anymore."

"It's stale anyway." Presley dropped her hand by her side.

"That's why *I'm* here." Brandon angled to film Mia. She stepped to the left so she was partially hidden by Presley, who was a good head taller, but Brandon found Mia with his lens. "You can't hide, little girl." He finished getting what he wanted, then lifted his face above the camera, catching Mia with his grin, which was wide and bright against his smooth, dark skin. Mia remembered Cole's smile when he greeted her at their Nantucket estate. It was humble, his green eyes sweet. There was nothing humble about the way Brandon carried himself, but then again, Cole had not been what he'd seemed. The spark in Brandon's magnetic amber eyes told Mia he was exactly as he seemed, which attracted and repelled her, given what Presley was calling "rumor."

"You're pointing that thing in the wrong direction," said Alex in a velvet voice, long fingers touching Brandon's shoulder.

"Everybody's already fighting for airtime," said Brandon.

Eve reclined in a teak chaise, toking on the joint. "Airtime is for people who have something compelling to say."

Presley let out a riotous laugh. "Oh, honey, please!"

Chase retrieved the joint from Eve and held it out for Presley. "Hey."

"Is for horses. No, thank you," replied Presley.

Chase offered up to Alex. "You sure?"

Alex put hand to heart. "My body is a temple."

Chase lifted his chin towards Mia. She hesitated a beat then took the joint, inhaling and holding. "Thanks." Smoke wafted from her mouth with the exhale.

"Any time." Chase grinned at the small cough Mia let escape.

Presley's eyebrows were frozen in a knit as she stared at Mia. "This is—"

"Mia." Mia wasn't going to let Presley step on her. She returned the joint to Chase. "You're Chase."

"I am." Joint in mouth, Chase grabbed the skateboard propped against the house. He dropped it on the driveway with a clack and rode it around, passing a line of Lyndon Wyld mono-grammed electric bikes. The adjacent two-car garages were open. One held an electric Smart car with beige and green trim. The other was a glorified surf shed, with surfboards of every size and shape stacked against one another like colorful, wax-covered dominoes.

Mia turned to Alex and smiled. "You're Alex, right?"

Alex beamed. "In the flesh, pretty."

Mia shifted to Eve. "We've met." Eve offered a peace sign. Mia turned to Brandon, who reviewed footage on the camera. "And you must be Brandon."

"I must be." Brandon looked up and put out his hand for a shake. Mia made sure her grip was strong and firm. "You don't mess around," said Brandon with a chortle.

"Nope." Mia released. She tilted her head, surveying him. After she made sure she had confirmed his assessment, she appraised the surroundings. "Well, this place is ugly," she said, her voice thick with sarcasm. Her face lit up when she saw the two long ponds that bordered the walkway. "Oh, wow!" Swimming in the clear water were six beautiful fluorescent-orange-and-pink koi fish the size of Chase's skateboard—three in each pond. "These are incredible!" She glanced at Presley. "Just your color."

"Bubblegum is no longer my shade." Presley wiggled her French-tipped manicured fingers. "It was fun while it lasted—and I still love the pink of a strawberry daiquiri— but we all need a little transformation."

"Every day," said Alex, smoothing the dress.

The Tesla pulled back up in the driveway. It rolled to a stop a couple of inches from Chase, who, unfazed, flipped his skateboard up and caught it. Marcus got out of the car and opened the back to remove an aluminum roller suitcase.

"That's Oliver," whispered Presley to Mia.

Stepping out of the car, Oliver removed his straw fedora and ran a hand through his sandy brown hair. "Look at this place!" In light blue chinos, a polo shirt, and boat shoes without socks, Oliver wore an ear-to-ear grin like a kid at the Magic Kingdom for the first time. When the car doors descended and locked, he tapped the flat silver door handle three times, then strode towards the group. "I've never been anywhere like this!"

"Hi, Oliver. I'm Mia." Mia offered a friendly wave.

"Nice to meet you." Oliver repositioned his hat and pushed his black-rimmed glasses up on the bridge of his nose. "I'm super happy to be here, like *beyond* super happy." Nobody could doubt that from his smile—it was infectious.

"How long was the bus ride from Denver?" asked Mia.

"About twenty-five hours."

"Hell on wheels," said Presley under her breath.

"No one rides the bus to LA," said Brandon as he filmed Oliver. "Why would you do that when Lyndon offered to fly you here?"

Mia glared at Brandon and Presley. "Not everyone likes flying. It was *my* first time and I can see why a bus might be a good alternative."

Eve bent down to admire the fish. "It's more eco-friendly."

"I took the Metro Rail, too. It was very cool," said Oliver with unbridled enthusiasm. He pulled the dark blue nylon backpack off his shoulders and unzipped it. He reached inside. "I have welcome gifts."

Presley nudged Mia and whispered, "That would've been a nice idea on *your* part."

Oliver presented each seasonaire a wood key fob with the Lyndon Wyld logo carved in the center.

Mia touched the craftsy masterpiece in her palm. "Thanks, Oliver. These are amazing!"

Oliver was empty-handed when he got to Presley. "I'm so sorry. I only have six."

"I'm good." Presley smirked. "Those must've been from Lyndon's old antique accessories collection. Did you find them on eBay?"

"No. I made them the night before I left." Oliver hoisted his backpack over his shoulders.

"*All* of them?" Alex touched the intricate wood detail. "This has as much detail as a Givenchy Oscars dress!"

50

"Dude, you *whittle?*" Chase twirled his fob around his forefinger.

"Yep." Oliver's smile was humble. "Dorky, right? Like this question, but I'm gonna ask it anyway."

"Of course you are." Presley rested a shoulder against one of the concrete columns.

"Think we'll see celebrities?" asked Oliver.

Marcus stepped onto the far end of the porch. "You will definitely see celebrities, but keep your wits about you. Don't photobomb or accost them for selfies. You might end up disappointed by their reactions."

"There are some stars I love who would break my heart if I found out they were jerks," said Oliver.

"I've driven around plenty of actors who have nice reputations but are total assclowns in real life. It always chapped me, because I worked my tail off for decades just to land bit parts in B movies. I have talent, and I've never been an assclown."

"That kind of behavior doesn't fly anymore because everything ends up on social," said Mia. "Haters are quick to hate, so let's try and be kind."

"Ever so wholesome." Presley yawned.

Alex brushed a high cheekbone. "I'm prepared to be read. Bring on the rant vloggers. I'm not going to keep quiet about it either. It's sick that there are people who find pervasive nastiness entertaining."

"You feed the beast," said Marcus, sitting in the swing.

Eve lifted her phone. "We have a *forum*. It's our job to bring social media back to what it was meant for, and that's to have a positive voice." She sat tall. "But I am Teflon and I don't have a problem clapping back. You'll see."

"I've found it's better to just not respond," said Mia.

"You've been off social for a year, Mia," replied Eve. "It's on the upswing in certain ways. After the school shootings, kids are speaking out. I'm proud of them. But there are others who just want to shit on people because *they* feel like shit. That creates a whole future of shit."

"Articulate," mumbled Marcus.

Brandon lowered his camera. "That's enough from the peanut gallery, Marcus." He and Mia exchanged a look.

A matte black Bentley with tinted windows rolled into the driveway. Presley clapped her hands. "Inside, everyone. Taka is here for *omakase*."

"Oma-what?" asked Mia.

"Sushi. Chef's choice," answered Brandon.

"Taka's the best sushi chef in the world. He's going through the kitchen entrance. No one is allowed to look him in the eye, so get your hineys in the front." Presley shooed the seasonaires in the house. Marcus pushed past them.

Mia pulled Presley aside. "Is there a reason why we need a driver?"

"Ask Brandon. I'm pretty sure that Marcus came from Maz." Presley nodded towards Brandon, who filmed Oliver's awe at the skylight through the foyer's reclaimed wood beams.

Mia caught Brandon's arm. She spoke in a low tone. "Did Lyndon or your dad hire Marcus?"

Brandon shrugged. "One and the same."

Marcus fingered a wire sculpture of a child fishing. "How much do you think this cost?" he said to no one in particular.

"I mean, is he living here?" Mia walked with Brandon and Presley into the living room, which opened out from the foyer. Their conversation remained private because the ocean-facing floor-to-ceiling glass doors were slid fully apart, welcoming the sound of the rumbling ocean below. The crashing waves seemed close enough to rise up and swallow the house.

"No, Marcus isn't living here," said Presley. "But it's a complete pain to drive in LA. I should know, I've been hauling my own sweet ass around for two weeks."

Brandon shrugged. "I'm not in LA that often, so I like driving. Put on some tunes. Take in the sights."

"I don't mind driving either," said Mia. "We drove ourselves around Nantucket just fine." She looked at Brandon. "Sometimes our photographer drove, but it looks like you're handling that job." Mia turned her eyes to his Hasselblad DSLR camera.

Presley flicked her wrist. "He's dubbed himself producer with that camera his daddy bought him. Cost more than y'all are making."

Mia brushed at a sleeve, knowing this was untrue. Presley didn't appear to be privy to the financial terms of Mia's design deal, or she wasn't letting on.

Brandon squinted at Presley. "I bought this baby myself. And everyone here is going to thank me for it later."

Mia looked at him. "You're a seasonaire like the rest of us, even though your father did some hiring on our behalf." She ignored the scowl that had taken over Brandon's cocky smile. "To that point, I think Marcus's talents would be better utilized somewhere else."

Presley shifted a hip. "Strut those peacock feathers, girl."

Mia shot her a look.

"What talents?" asked Brandon.

They glanced at Marcus, who roamed around the house like it was his own.

"He told me he's a screenwriter," replied Mia.

Presley snorted. "I've been here a month and you can't throw a rock without hitting a screenwriter. They're at every coffee place in the city. Most of them are Facebook stalking their exes and making their half-caff-one-Splenda-no-foam lattes last eight hours while the rest of us actually *work* for a living."

Marcus tickled the keys on the baby grand piano nearby. "Is that what you call what you do? *Work?*"

"Suck a prairie dog's whang," said Presley in her sweetest Georgia peach voice.

"Can I quote you on that? Or can *you* quote you on that, since you're supposed to be the publicist?"

Mia remained serious, watching Marcus take a giant bite out of a green apple he'd plucked from a white porcelain platter atop the sleek white credenza. She'd had her fill of unsavory middle-aged men after dealing with Otto Hahn the summer before. In addition to his sketchy business practices, Otto had preyed on his nubile Wear National seasonaires and employees, including Ruby. Chewing, Marcus walked off towards the curved wood bar, where Chase mixed gin and tonics for Eve and Oliver while Alex stuck to Perrier with a straw.

Mia looked at Brandon and Presley. "Marcus can't work here if he's going to write a movie about us. He says that's what he's doing."

"I know he's an old friend of your dad's, Brandon, and Mia might be paranoid because of the weed she just smoked, but no fucking way," said Presley.

Brandon rubbed his eyes. "Man, I told my dad not to push Lyndon into hiring him. But my dad is loyal. Marcus did him a solid back in the day by signing away the rights to a movie he pitched him. My dad paid him, but he spent all his money on hookers and blow, or some shit like that, and now he's left doing menial jobs for the likes of us."

They watched Marcus, who was now behind the bar with Chase, pouring himself a glass of expensive scotch.

"I've got this," said Brandon.

"I love to see a dirty old man cry, but I need to check on Taka." Presley sashayed through the living room. "He likes to serve the fish while it's still moving." She disappeared into the kitchen.

Brandon and Mia made their way to Marcus, who had polished off one drink and was pouring another. Eve, Alex, Chase, and Oliver brought their beverages to the taupe micro-suede couches. Eve and

Oliver started a game of tic-tac-toe on an oversized plexiglass game board. Brandon tapped his knuckles on the bar, causing Marcus to look up from pouring more scotch. "What are you doing, Marcus?"

"Having a well-deserved cocktail, my man. I'm not driving anyone anywhere again tonight, so cheers." Marcus lifted his generous pour towards Brandon and took a swig.

"That's right. You're not driving anyone anywhere, and you're taking an Uber home. So, feel free to drink up before you leave, because you won't be seeing this bar or this house again."

"What do you mean?" Perplexed, Marcus put his drink on the bar.

"You're fired," said Brandon. "You signed an NDA and now you're writing a screenplay about this? Not that it will ever sell—"

"It's *fiction*. I don't need an NDA to write fiction."

Mia stepped in. "Maybe you should explain that to Maz, because I don't think that's part of your job description. I mean, your *former* job description."

Marcus swallowed the rest of his drink, slammed the glass on the bar, and stomped towards the foyer, glaring at Mia before exiting. "Little fish in a big pond." The heavy wood door slammed shut, the sound echoing between the smooth plaster walls and high ceilings. All eyes were on Mia and Brandon.

Presley stepped out from the kitchen. "Who's hungry?" she said cheerfully.

Chase patted his lean belly. "I could eat. I could always eat." He pulled on the T-shirt that was tucked into the back of his surf shorts and walked with Eve, Alex, and Oliver to the dining room, which was separated from the living room by a two-sided concrete fireplace. Its glass rocks flickered with blue flames.

Mia looked at Brandon. "Marcus is pissed."

From Brandon's fiery look at the closed front door, so was he. He turned to Mia. "I'm definitely not here to do your dirty work."

He left Mia standing in the living room, alone.

SEVEN

The Marcus situation hadn't given Mia a chance to appreciate the house. Her excitement about seeing it beat out her eagerness to eat "still-moving fish" and, more importantly, give a welcome speech. She decided to take herself on the ten-cent tour. The ten-million-dollar tour was more like it as she scanned the expansive, open-air living room with its sleek yet beachy-chic furniture upholstered in serene earth tones. She stared out at the ocean-facing deck with its firepit area, lounges, and an infinity pool that met the horizon.

She snuck down the floating birch stairs that seemed to be suspended in midair. At the bottom floor, she found a media room with a gigantic flat screen, vintage pinball and video game machines, a pool table, and air hockey. Another bar sat next to a connoisseur's wine cellar. The adjacent gym was fully loaded. Double glass doors opened to a succulent garden and concrete steps that led up to the deck and pool. She walked back upstairs and headed to the third floor, her light buzz adding a dreamlike quality to the house.

"What are you doing?"

Mia whirled around to see Presley standing at the bottom of the stairs, with her hands on her hips.

"I had to pee." Mia put her hands on her hips as if to defy the need to explain herself—despite her explanation. She had been placed in de facto charge by Lyndon and, even though she didn't know if she was up to the task, she couldn't let Presley bulldoze her.

"Well, I hope you washed your hands, since you're probably going to eat with them. Doubt you're a pro with the chopsticks."

"Hey, I know my way around chopsticks." Mia descended the stairs and strode past Presley. She entered the dining room and peeked into the kitchen, still itching to see the rest of the house. Taka, wearing a white collarless chef's jacket, apron, and hat, had taken over the expansive culinary paradise. The shiny, high-end appliances seamlessly blended into the red lacquer cabinets. It was the cleanest kitchen Mia had ever seen. But when she saw Taka chop the head off a whole fish with his gleaming, sharp knife, she took it as her cue to leave, even though he was too focused to notice her or make eye contact. She let the kitchen door swing shut and sat down at the dining room table.

The same red from the cabinets accented the chairs around the long wood table that looked like it had been carved off the side of a maple tree. The knots were shellacked smooth. Brandon pulled the chair at the head of the table out for Mia.

"Thanks," Mia said, a bit taken aback.

Brandon leaned into her ear as she scooted in. "You're the MC for this circus." He gave her a patronizing closed-mouth smile and took the seat to the side of her.

Mia cleared her throat. "I'm not one for the head of the table, so I'm going to move over once the meal starts. But I wanted to welcome you here to Malibu on behalf of Lyndon. She's proud to have you all as seasonaires representing the brand."

Presley snapped a photo of the group in the beautiful setting with the backdrop of the obsidian Malibu night behind them through the glass doors.

"I'd tell you to get my best side, but you have a choice." Alex offered both profiles, which were equally enviable.

Soon everyone else's phones, which were face-down on the table, were buzzing and dinging with tags. They all checked to see themselves on the Lyndon Wyld feed.

New crew in the 'Bu. #BuWyld #seasonaires #dreamsummer

Presley pointed at them as she exited into the kitchen. "Repost!" More notification buzzes and dings came in.

"When are we going to meet Lyndon?" asked Eve. "I have so much to talk to her about."

Mia folded her hands and smiled. "Not tonight. I'm her welcome wagon for now. I think she wanted us all to get to know each other on a level playing field." She shifted in her seat, painfully aware that her position at the table contradicted her words.

Brandon picked up one of the two hand-painted ceramic sake carafes. "The best way to do that is sake. Never pour for yourself."

Oliver pointed to the carafe in front of Eve, slightly out of his reach. "I'll pour yours, Eve. Pass me the carafe."

"It's called a *tokkuri*," said Brandon. "Put two hands on it when you pour it into the *ochoko*." He motioned to the small rounded ceramic cups. Oliver followed Brandon's instructions and readied to pour for Eve. Brandon held a hand up. "Wait! We pour for Mia first because she has seniority. She can hold her ochoko with one hand, but the rest of us have to hold ours with two." The resentment in his voice was thick. Mia shifted again in her seat, then sat up straighter, taking one hand off the small round cup.

"Thank you," said Mia. Brandon poured, avoiding her gaze.

"How do you know all this?" asked Oliver after pours were complete.

"My dad does a lot of business in Tokyo."

Chase lifted his ochoko towards Brandon. "Your dad's a baller. I've been listening to his music and all the stuff he produces since I was a kid."

Brandon's smile froze. "We're here. *We're* ballers." He lifted his ochoko. "*Kanpai!*"

Everyone lifted their ochokos. Eve wrapped her arm around Alex's as everyone drank, Alex taking a tiny obligatory sip. Mia realized she'd forgotten to suggest they all look each other in the eye to avoid seven years of bad luck. Last summer, Grace had made known Lyndon's superstition. Despite adherence, Grace's luck ran dry.

"Is the pouring ritual tradition or superstition? I'm never sure of the difference," said Mia as she moved from the head of the table into the chair between Brandon and Oliver. She poured her own sake. "I'm not a big believer in superstitions, like I step on cracks on purpose." She had discovered that *her* luck was no better or worse than anyone else's in the long run. They would all end up in the same place. She privately drank an ochoko of sake for her mother. The weed and sake started washing away her uneasiness. "Anyone else silly enough to be superstitious?"

Brandon pulled out a smooth black silk rope necklace from under his T-shirt. "My mom gave me this when I was going through a tough time." He revealed the necklace's round silver engraved medallion. "It's a Tibetan mandala."

Chase stood and leaned across the table to get a closer look. "Those are the Eight Auspicious Symbols."

Brandon pointed to Chase and nodded with a grin. "She gave my dad one, too, so I'm going to call it tradition and not superstition—though I'm pretty sure it's kept me alive. I never take it off."

Alex peered at it. "I'd never take it off either. Your mother, Tatiana Chen, has ruled the runway and graced the cover of every major magazine. She's used her power to lift up the disenfranchised *and* she's a fierce protector. She is a *goddess*."

Eve put her elbows on the table, chin in her hand. "Brandon, I can't live in this house without saying something to you about your 'tough time.'"

"Shoot."

"Violence begets violence."

Brandon's jaw tightened for a beat before he smiled at Eve. "Agreed." He turned to Oliver, who examined the medallion.

"You don't take it off in the shower?" asked Oliver. "Because the medallion I got in scouts turned my chest green when it got wet." He touched his own chest. "I wanted hair so badly, I settled for green stain."

Alex poured more sake for Oliver. "*You* are lucky, Oli! I spend a fortune to get silky-smooth and it hurts like hell. Girls, you feel me?"

"I'm for full bush." Eve lifted her arms to show off small auburn tufts of hair peeking from under her cap sleeves. She lowered her arms and drank her sake. "Why do women have to shave and wax and alter our appearance in order to be loved? It's such a double standard."

"In some cases, I beg to differ," said Alex. "But you should do whatever you want with your body, as long as *you* love it."

"You have to admit there's a disparity," replied Eve. "Older men—balding, wrinkled, and paunchy—end up with younger trophies, while older single women end up with cats."

"Hey, I grew a mullet one year because this girl I was crushing on told me she liked them," said Oliver, pulling on the back of his hair. "But then I found out when she group-texted my entire freshman class that she was trying to prove I'd do anything for her."

Alex placed a hand on Oliver's arm. "Fuck that bitch! You're a romantic. She'll end up buried in cats."

Girls are cunts. Mia recalled Presley's motto—even if it was said with a ladylike twang that implied jest. Lyndon said the same thing about the female airport security agents. Mia understood how mean women could be to each other and how it would be hard to trust during this summer. She didn't trust herself. But that was part of the reason she was in Malibu, sitting at the table with new strangers: She couldn't live the rest of her life mistrusting herself.

Presley brought out the first long platter of sushi. "Just a reminder: I'm not your server. The sous chef got sick."

"Hopefully not from the sushi," said Mia.

"Sh! Don't let Taka hear you. He will have a goddamn conniption!"

Presley placed the platter down. Mia exhaled, because nothing was moving. Phones snapped photos of the pink raw slices laid over small beds of white rice. Brandon rolled his eyes and refrained from taking a photo. Instead, he skillfully lifted a piece onto his plate with his chopsticks, topped it with a dab of green wasabi, and popped it into his mouth.

Seeing Mia's hesitation, Presley gave her arm a tap. "Well, go on, Mia. Dig in." Mia tried to maneuver the chopsticks, but the piece kept dropping on her plate. She eyed around her, put down the chopsticks, picked the piece up with her fingers, and slid it in her mouth.

"That's how you do it!" Chase grinned and ate a piece with his fingers.

Mia covered her mouth with her hand. She wished she could spit out the slimy morsel but was afraid to upset the "best sushi chef in the world." She swallowed and plastered on her best smile. "Mm! Good!" Mia believed she sold it, because Presley appeared irked as she exited into the kitchen.

She came back a few minutes later with more platters. Each was more artful than the next, with delicate scallion curls, cucumber flowers, and tiny sprinklings of orange roe. Chopsticks clicked and fingers picked as the seasonaires tucked in. Mia did her best. Thrown together as colleagues and housemates, they ate in awkward silence, despite the sake lubrication. Mia didn't know how to make the situation more comfortable, being uncomfortable herself, especially since Presley was keeping such a close watch. Every time Presley brought out another platter, it was placed down on the table with a tad more force.

"Thank you," repeated Mia. Her attempt at civility was met with contempt.

Chase tapped Oliver with a chopstick. "Hey, Oliver, are you up for an ice-breaking challenge?"

"Sure, why not?" Oliver's voice quivered.

Mia's smile was just as twitchy—she had one job at that table and someone was doing it for her. This wasn't lost on Brandon, who eyed her.

Chase pulled Alex's lipstick-stained straw from the Perrier bottle and handed it to Oliver. He pointed to the small mound of wasabi on Oliver's plate. Oliver, seeing everyone staring at him with expectation or dismay, grinned nervously. "I've got this." Since there were no utensils besides chopsticks, he took a pocket knife from his pants pocket and sawed off a short piece of the straw.

"A scout always carries a pocket knife," said Alex with a chuckle.

Oliver laughed. "Never know when you might get the urge to whittle or snort wasabi."

"Oliver, you don't have to—" said Mia. Brandon put a hand on her arm and lifted his camera to film.

"Get all your phones ready." Chase aimed his at Oliver, who took a small toot. His eyes grew wide and watery. He leapt up from his chair and hopped around. Grabbing his napkin, he gagged and coughed into it. Hysterics among the seasonaires ensued, though Mia's eyes were wide.

Presley rushed in. "What'd I miss?" She saw Oliver's gurgly convulsing and flapped at all the photo snapping and filming. "No! Do not post that!" She released a groan that sounded short of combustion. "This was not the plan!" She stormed back into the kitchen. More seasonaires' laughter ensued.

"I guess *Jackass* was not her favorite movie growing up," Oliver croaked. When he sat down, Chase patted him on the back.

"You crushed that, dude."

Oliver tossed back sake, which quelled his hacking. "Sorry."

Eve dropped her chopsticks. "It *is* actually disgusting."

"Snorting wasabi? Yes," said Mia, trying to stifle a chortle at the absurdity.

"No, the *straw*." Eve glared at Alex. "Plastic straws are the worst environmental offense. You know, the city of Santa Barbara passed an ordinance that punishes restaurant employees for giving out straws. After the second offense, there's up to six months of jail time or a one-thousand-dollar fine."

"Why don't we play a different game, because I like the ice breaker idea," said Mia, though she would stay away from Truth or Dare. In Nantucket, a dare had almost drowned Jade.

Brandon side-eyed Mia. "Games?"

"Game nights are big in my dorm," said Oliver. "I'm pretty good at Charades."

Brandon shook his head. "Not playing Charades."

Eve waved a chopstick. "How about Two Truths and a Lie?"

Alex sat tall. "Lies are secrets. And I don't believe in secrets."

"'Nothing weighs on us so heavily as a secret,'" said Chase. "Jean de La Fontaine."

Mia fidgeted in her seat. Oliver finished off his sake. He reached for a Sapporo from one of the silver ice-filled buckets in the center of the table. Opening it, he filled his beer glass and chugged.

Brandon nodded from behind his camera. "Okay, I'm digging it, because this house is going to be open to the world. That's what'll make Lyndon Wyld and MazzyLyn the hottest brands on the planet."

Oliver put down his empty beer glass and threw up all over the table.

"Whoa!" Brandon got it all on film.

"Brandon, stop!" yelled Mia. She ran into the kitchen.

Presley was leaning on the counter, tapping on her phone. "What in Loretta's pants is happening out there, Mia? This is not the way Lyndon would want to start the summer."

"I know, I know." Mia struggled for a beat to find the refrigerator, which was camouflaged into the cabinetry. She found it and grabbed a water. Turning, she saw Taka frozen in anger, listening to the noises of vomiting.

"Sorry, that was disgusting," they could hear Oliver say in a hoarse rasp.

Mia winced at Taka. "Too much sake?" To add insult to injury, she had made eye contact.

Taka, seething with rage, wiped his knife off with his apron. He slid it into his black roll bag with his other gleaming-sharp tools and stomped out the kitchen door—the second slam of the night. Arms crossed, Presley glowered at Mia.

EIGHT

Although Mia was concerned about Taka taking off in a furious huff, she was happy that Presley had followed him out. She had endured enough pestering and needling for one day, and there were so many more weeks to come. After the climactic shitshow at dinner, everyone was too drunk on sake and tired from traveling to process any new information from Mia about the summer's upcoming activities. She was relieved about that, too.

Oliver was already asleep upstairs in one of the bedrooms when two boxes of swag were delivered. Chase carried them into the living room. Mia watched the others' energy reboot as they attacked the contents.

Brandon filmed. "Like hyenas with fresh gazelle."

"Please tell me you don't hunt," said Eve as she rifled through a box filled with sleepwear.

"I've hunted, but I don't hunt now, no."

Mia lifted out a handwritten note from Lyndon and read out loud:

Sweet dreams. I'll see you in your posts.

The second box was filled with swimwear. "For our first beach day tomorrow," said Mia. Alex read the note:

Be a picture of SoCal sunniness.

"Already done." Chase held up a pair of long trunks with a curvy orange and yellow pattern.

Mia's phone buzzed with a private text from Lyndon:

Call me no matter what time.

Mia walked up the stairs, having snagged a pair of mono-grammed pajamas and a high-waisted striped bikini—the kind worn by classic pinup queens and current pop culture princesses. Bedrooms had been staked out. There wasn't a dud in the joint.

Brandon stood in the hallway and motioned with his thumb to the door behind him. "Did you get a load of this yet?"

Mia shook her head. Brandon opened the door to a room that might as well have been a giant toy store for Mia. She gasped. Inside was a long worktable facing the ocean. Bolts of fabric hung on two walls. The colors and patterns were Mia's favor-ites—Lyndon knew her so well. Baskets of buttons, zippers, and hooks sat next to wicker bins holding their more frivolous counterparts: fringe, poufs, studs, feathers, and trims of all kinds. In the center of the workspace proudly sat a brand-new computerized sewing machine. Mia generally shunned bells and whistles, but a dream sewing machine to her was like a dream car to her brother. Sean always thought that was weird and funny. Sean wanted a Bugatti Chiron Sport. Mia got a Janome Memory Craft 14000.

"You're looking at it like you want to fuck it," said Brandon.

"I actually want to marry it. This is real love." Mia ran her hand over the sewing machine she could never have afforded before. Now she had the money, and it was free. She considered the irony: *Wasn't that how it worked?* Celebrities never had to pay for anything—not that she was a celebrity.

Brandon appraised the extravagant workspace. "If I were Lyndon, I would've never done this to you." He shook his head. "Not cool."

Mia furrowed her brow as she ran her fingers over a spool of satin ribbon. "You're acting like it's a punishment." The smell of fresh denim and muslin was a reward she would covet every day here in Malibu.

"Well, it's not going to ingratiate you with the other seasonaires." Brandon flipped some Lyndon Wyld patches. "I could tell you were stressed out about that at dinner. You couldn't handle the head of the table. That's too bad."

"You and Presley didn't make it easy."

"Are we supposed to? She has a job. I have a job. *You* have a job. You knew what you were signing up for."

Mia squeezed a pink fuzzy pouf. She understood she was going to have to work extra hard to make sure that the others didn't feel she was superior to them. In a stomach-turning way, she felt that she didn't deserve to be a seasonaire for the second year. Some of her social media notoriety came from the wrong kind of attention.

"You're taking one of the single rooms, right?" asked Brandon. "I'll admit, I've never shared a room in my life." As far as Mia knew from having lived with Jade, Maz's heirs didn't share rooms or sleep in beds that might have a bothersome pea under the pillow-top mattress. Brandon pointed to the couch. "Although you could prove your worth by sleeping on that pull-out right there." His voice lowered to a whisper. "*I'm* going to sleep in my studio."

"What studio?" asked Mia.

"The studio I asked Lyndon for."

"We are not the king and queen of this castle," said Mia, lifting a straw fedora off a shelf topped with accessories. It looked like a hat J.P. would've designed. She smiled, remembering her seasonaire-friend from the previous summer and how hard he'd hustled to get Lyndon, Maz, or both to take his haberdashery concept seriously.

"Wow, what's this?" Eve stood in the doorway, surveying Mia's workspace. She wore a mask of judgment and bitterness. "I don't sew. I can guess no one else sews here either—besides our fearless leader." Her focus landed on Mia.

"That's a pretty hardcore stereotype," said Brandon. "I can work a machine." He pointed to the sewing table.

"Come in." Mia gestured to Eve, who refused to step through the threshold, as if the space was filled with plastic straws. "Brandon and I were just talking about who's taking what room, and I was telling him I'm sharing a bedroom with you."

Eve tilted her head. "Don't do me any favors. Alex is happy to be my roommate if you're not into it."

"Well, will there still be a bed for me?" asked Mia, genuinely hopeful.

"They're measly fulls. Knock yourself out." Eve walked off, her footsteps slow and plodding. She called back. "But I'm never sloppy seconds."

When the bedroom door across the hall shut, Brandon looked at Mia and smiled. "Smart choice. Benevolent rulers live among the people."

Mia put the hat back on the shelf. "No one is *ruling*. I know you think you do. Maybe it's your upbringing. I thought the same thing about Jade when I met her, and then she proved me wrong. Are you going to prove me wrong?"

Brandon crossed his arms. "I have nothing to prove. It doesn't matter if I bunk with anyone else because everyone already thinks I'm an asshole. They pretend they don't, but it works out great for me." He placed his hands on his chest.

"Personally, I think it would feel lonely in a room by myself. This house is so huge."

"Are you offering to sleep with me instead of bunking with Social Justice Warrior?" Brandon motioned to where Eve had been standing.

"No, I think you're an asshole, too. But I read an article that said it's unhealthy to sleep in your workspace. I couldn't help it at home in South Boston. We don't have as much space as this—" Mia whirled her arm in the air. "Or in the homes *you're* used to. Now I can increase my productivity by separating work and play. The article said that, too." She plucked a pencil from a white mesh cylinder on the desk, next to the seasonaires' activity schedule printed out in calendar form.

"Work is play and play is work here. You know that," said Brandon.

Alex stepped up to the open door with two roller suitcases and pointed across the hall. "I'm bunking with you and Eve. Lyndon told me I could have my choice of roommates, and I choose *you*."

"I'm honored," replied Mia with a grin.

"But if either of you snores, I'm with Chase and Oliver."

"I talk in my sleep," said Chase, crossing behind.

"Ooh, that's another story." Alex winked. "I might reserve the right to change my mind."

"I'll be in in a bit," said Mia. "I'm a little wired from this first day, so I'm going to do some work."

Alex held up a Lyndon Wyld baby doll nightie. "I'm saving you this little number. It will look insane on you."

"I'm partial to sleeping in pj's." Mia put down the pencil and lifted the pajamas she'd slung over the desk chair.

"I'm partial to sleeping buck-naked, but we'll all adapt." Alex wiggled the nightie at Mia, then disappeared down the hall.

Brandon lifted a brow. "You're not going to feel lonely, that's for sure."

"*You* might."

Brandon smirked and left. Mia shut the door and shook her head. She checked the time on the neon wall clock. It was the middle of the night for Lyndon in New York. Mia looked at the text message requesting a call. She dialed.

"Mia," said Lyndon.

"Thank you for my workspace. It's fantastic." Mia gazed at a large framed print of the first glimpse of the Mia dress. Vincent, last summer's photographer, had caught her soaking wet after nearly drowning at Brant Point. Mia had lied about her sopping condition, telling the other seasonaires that she'd finally decided to try a swim in the Atlantic. After the photo had posted on Instagram, Mia's social blew up, and Lyndon took notice of the dress and Mia's talents. But the dress had never been made because Mia hadn't signed the original contract. Now she was getting another chance.

"I'm glad you like the accommodations," said Lyndon. "But you're there one night and you've already fired the driver *and* pissed off the guest chef?"

"What can I say? I'm good at my job." Mia offered a nervous chuckle.

"Marcus wasn't just the driver. He was the caretaker. Maybe I'll have Presley handle those tasks, like she did dinner."

Mia's eyes went wide. "Her head would explode."

"Always an attention-getter."

"We can drive and take care of the house ourselves. Maybe this summer, you don't spoil your seasonaires so much."

"Says the girl who loves her workspace."

"I do. But like I told you, I'm sharing a bedroom. That way I'm hoping we can avoid one-upping each other here."

"My darling, one-upsmanship is the whole point."

"Honestly, then I don't know what I'm doing. Why didn't you just make Brandon your point person? He seems to think he is."

"Don't you dare get intimidated," snapped Lyndon.

"I'm not intimidated. I just don't understand why you would choose him to be a seasonaire, given his—"

"Reputation? We all have reputations. And those of us who don't, will. His family's public image—whether good or bad— has made them exceedingly wealthy. Obviously, they're doing something right."

"Is wealth a measure of what's right?"

"Get off your high horse, Mia. You have skin in the game."

Mia looked around at her workspace.

"Sleep tight, my darling," said Lyndon. "I'll see you soon." She clicked off.

Mia hadn't been lying to Alex when she'd said she was wired. After pacing for a few beats, she sat down at her desk. She slid over one of the drawing pads from a stack, picked up the pencil, and tapped it on the white paper, making tiny dots. She looked out at the moon for inspiration. It was full.

Mia started awake to a bloodcurdling scream. She sat straight up in the chair at her desk where she'd fallen asleep sketching new sleepwear, since she wasn't crazy about the choices, in particular the nightie Alex had chosen for her. Squinting in the morning light shining through the huge windows, she rubbed her eyes and rushed out towards the scream—it was like the scream she had wanted to let out when she'd found Grant dead in the pool. She raced down the stairs and held her breath as she ran towards the sound of weeping. Outside the front door, she found Eve and Chase standing over the left-side koi pond.

Mia stopped in her tracks. "What's wrong?" The two seemed unharmed. Chase wore a wetsuit pulled halfway down. His hair was damp. Eve was in a short cotton robe, crying.

She pointed to the pond. "The fish!"

Mia slowly approached and looked in the direction of Eve's trembling forefinger. The three koi, still beautifully fluorescent, floated on their sides. Their round eyes stared straight up. Mia exhaled and took another deep breath, turning to the pond on the opposite side of the walkway. The other three koi were dead, too. "Oh, no," she whispered.

Chase's expression was somber. "I went surfing at dawn. But I left through the back doors. I didn't see them."

"I was just going to take a walk around the grounds and—" Eve broke down again.

Mia tried to tell herself that they were just fish, but they were more than that. She decided to do her job and take care of Eve, who couldn't stop crying. "Let's go inside. I'll make you some tea." She put her arm around Eve's waist and escorted her into the house. Chase removed his wetsuit and hung it over a chaise, then followed the girls in.

They entered the kitchen to find Oliver organizing translucent plastic containers of salads, fruit, and cookies into a woven-wood picnic basket. Cold cuts, veggies, condiments, and loaves of bread sat on the island in an assembly line for the dozens of sandwiches he'd made. Wearing earbuds, he looked up from packing and smiled at the sight of the others.

"Sammies for the beach," he said, brimming with too much energy for the morning, his speech rapid-fire. "I'm sorry if I don't know what everyone likes yet. To be safe, I went the whole nine yards: turkey, PBJ, grilled veggie . . ." When he saw Eve's tearstained face, he pulled out his earbuds and stopped the music. "What happened?"

"The koi fish died," whimpered Eve.

Oliver's bright expression dimmed. "That's sad." He busied himself, spreading mayo on more bread.

"It could've been because of the water," said Eve with a sniffle. "Californians are good about recycling, but it's not helping—another broken infrastructure. Who knows what kind of bacteria is growing in that pond?"

Chase plucked green grapes off a bunch on the counter. "The fish didn't die from that water. A house like this has a water filtration system that would make my pee clean enough to drink. But they're gone. Maybe it's just a reminder to live in the moment. That's why Dadaism poetry was my favorite course. Presentism, man." He ate a grape.

Mia looked up from the stove, where she put on a kettle of water. "You studied Dadaism?"

"You *studied*?" asked Brandon, who entered in track pants and nothing else.

"English-lit major at Pepperdine. Just graduated." Chase tossed up a grape and caught it in his mouth, then left the kitchen.

Mia scanned the pile of sandwiches—more than they could ever eat—and looked at Oliver, who was neatly stacking them into containers. "Did you make all these yourself?"

"I did." Oliver held up a PBJ. "Who's allergic to peanut butter? I have an EpiPen just in case. *I'm* allergic to bees."

Mia remembered Grant's swollen face after he had been stung at the trunk show. He was sweet—she was sure that that's why the bees had loved him. She promised herself she would never judge a book by its cover again, even if it had a smoking body and an attitude. Brandon leaned against the counter and scrolled on his phone.

"I'm allergic to bullshit and that screaming was some bullshit so early in the morning," he said. "Unless someone was gettin' some." Mia tried to concentrate on his face and was met with his annoyed expression. "Was someone gettin' some already?"

Mia scowled at him. "All the koi, they're . . . gone," she said in a low voice, hoping not to stoke Eve's feelings further. No such luck—more tears.

Brandon *tsk*ed. "Oh, man, that's too bad." Mia was surprised he had enough respect to take his bluster down a notch.

Chase returned with a bottle of tequila and margarita mix. He intercepted the mug of tea Mia had made for Eve and put it on the counter. Sliding over a brushed stainless blender, he closed his eyes. "I can make a bombdiggity margarita with my eyes closed and no jigger. I'm missing a testicle from a surfing accident, and in middle school Timmy Jenkins asked to see my horns."

Brandon squinted, nonplussed. "What?"

"That's my Two Truths and a Lie." Chase blended margaritas as he attempted to lighten the mood.

Oliver tilted his head at Chase. "I'm guessing the last one is a lie, because why would someone ask to see your horns?"

Chase opened his eyes and poured the lime green slush into juice glasses he removed from the cupboard. He handed the first to Eve. "His name wasn't Timmy Jenkins. That's the lie."

Eve sipped. "This *is* bombdiggity. Definitely better than tea."

Oliver scratched his head, pressing. "Wait, Chase, *why* would someone ask to see your horns?"

"I'm Jewish. That's what some people believe about us," answered Chase. He handed Oliver and Mia margaritas.

Mia held the cold glass. "I didn't think that kind of awful thing happened in LA."

"Unfortunately, that happens everywhere," said Brandon, exiting.

Mia looked at the door swing close and sipped, crunching the crushed ice. She put her hand on Eve's shoulder. "You okay?"

Eve drank and nodded. "Better."

Mia brought her cocktail upstairs to grab her phone from her workspace and saw a slew of texts from Presley:

> I'm here.
> Get your asses to the beach!
> Do not make me wait.
> You better have been snatched.

Given all that had happened, Mia should've been dismayed by Presley's choice of words. But she wasn't. She polished off her breakfast margarita, put on her bikini, a gauzy cover-up, and sandals, and headed out.

NINE

M ia, Eve, Chase, Oliver, and Brandon, armed with his camera, walked down the rustic wood staircase built into the bluff. Oliver carried the picnic basket with both hands, because it was so full—three bottles of wine and a large Perrier stuck out of one flap. "This is a movie set beach day!"

They stepped onto the sand. Unlike the beaches that Mia had seen from PCH while she was driven to Malibu, this stretch was without a lifeguard station or the mass of summer tourists and beachgoers. There were only two other souls. One was a crispy tanned man building a rock mandala with an intensity that said "Notice me." The other was Presley, who didn't give a shit. She sat in a high-back beach chair on an oversized Lyndon Wyld blanket under a green and beige umbrella. Barefoot, in a sundress, she rose and snapped phone photos of the descending group. Crispy

Tanned Rock Sculptor appeared disappointed that the photos wouldn't be of his geological masterpiece.

Presley lowered her phone. "Took you long enough. How was your first night? Everyone survive?"

"Everyone except the koi," said Eve, wearing sunglasses over her swollen, bloodshot eyes. She walked off towards the low tide.

"What's with her?" Presley sat back down.

Chase shrugged. "Circle of life."

Presley lifted her Jackie O sunnies to give Mia a perplexed look. Brandon filmed Chase and Oliver. "What's the craziest thing you've ever done on the beach?" he asked.

As the three guys headed for the water, Oliver answered, "My dad buried me up to my neck in sand and left to go eat lunch."

Presley watched them. "I can't stand all this realness. Why won't Lyndon let us use a *professional* photographer?"

Mia joined her on the blanket. "For the same reason all the seasonaires should share rooms."

Presley glared at her. "You gave up your single?"

"I never wanted one in the first place."

"You're a moron." Presley's attention went to the photos she had taken on her phone. "These are shit."

Mia peered around at them. "I think those look great. Plus, you have all the video Brandon's shooting, though the whole producer thing is mildly annoying."

"Speaking of annoying—" Presley looked down the shore a few yards. "Nature Girl looks forlorn, like she got her period in white pants." Eve plodded along as she filmed herself with her phone. Presley checked Eve's Snapchat. "I have some sad news, guys," said Eve on the screen. "Our beautiful koi fish have passed away."

"She was the first to see them," said Mia.

"I couldn't keep a goldfish alive. It happens." Presley clicked off Eve. She filtered and enhanced the photos of the seasonaires and posted to the Lyndon Wyld feed.

"It was more than one. All six of them are dead." Mia picked up a small broken shell.

Presley shrugged. "Maybe Marcus forgot to feed them. But he made it easier on you, because now *you* won't have to."

"Presley, that's terrible!" Mia slapped her thighs, which were growing pink from the sun. She reached into her woven beach bag, pulled out sunscreen, and smoothed it on. "But what if he did it on purpose because he was pissed?"

"Brandon will lose his shit if you mention that to him. It's one thing to say that guy was creepy, but his daddy would have your hide for implying he'd hire someone *that* creepy."

"Unless that creep is related to him," replied Mia, eyeing Brandon, who snapped a photo of her from the shore.

"Don't piss on me and call it rain, sugar. You think that boy is hot."

Mia huffed and put on her sunglasses.

Presley applied sunscreen to her lissome legs. "And God only knows why you would tell Lyndon you'll do housework. You need to concentrate on more important things than fish and toilets, like whether to wear your hair up or down to the Malibu store tomorrow, or which spin class you're going to take to show off the new Lyndon Wyld athleisure."

"There were *six* fish," pressed Mia. "There are six of us. What about Taka. Would he—?"

"He doesn't need to kill *koi fish*. Oh, Mia, don't start."

Mia kept her eyes on the water to avoid seeing Presley roll hers. "Maybe it was what they looked like. They reminded me of—" She looked at Presley. "What if it *was* on purpose?"

"Honey, you tend to be paranoid. That's what landed me in jail."

"Not everyone loves us."

"You're influencers. I'm still an influencer. We're going to have haters." Presley re-positioned her sunglasses, donned her wide-brimmed straw hat, and snapped a selfie.

"Well, this comment came in the minute I landed," said Mia as she showed Presley her phone:

It's never over. ⚫

Presley waved it off. "That emoji is tired. The least they could've done is send you a stupidly amusing GIF of an angry cat or a tantruming baby." She filtered and posted to her own Instagram, captioning:

A publicist's work is never done. #LyndonWyld #lifesabeach

Mia decided to address the pink elephant in the sand. "Have you heard from Ruby?"

Presley, vexed, put down her phone. "Why would I hear from her? Just because I was nice to her doesn't mean we're BFFs."

"You weren't that nice to her, but don't you care?"

"Not one teeny, tiny bit. I did catch a *Jezebel* piece on the fall of Otto Hahn and Wear National. Lyndon requested that I scrapbook the failings of our competitors. It gave a little backstory on his former seasonaires and mentioned that Ruby's daddy is out of prison, but her mama's an inmate at the California Institution for Women. Makes my trailer trash family look positively royal."

Mia stared at the shore. "The California Institution for Women?"

Presley jabbed Mia's arm. "Don't you go playing 'Where's Waldo?' We left, she left. Door closed."

Eve approached, putting a period on the conversation. She stood in front of the two girls at the blanket's edge. "I had a heart-to-heart with myself—"

Presley lowered her sunnies and waved her phone. "I saw. You might want to try a little mascara or the fairy filter."

"A heart-to-heart means honesty, so no." Eve wiped a tear. "But I need to let the fish go." She motioned outward.

"You're not the only one," said Presley in a low voice with a side-eye at Mia.

Chase jogged up to them with Oliver behind him. "Hey, who wants to body surf with me? Oliver passed."

"This body isn't built for surfing," said Oliver, motioning to his thin build.

Chase motioned to the girls. "Eve? Mia?"

Mia kept seeing flashes of those six fish, belly up. She smiled politely and shook her head. "Here are *my* Two Truths and a Lie. I just learned to swim this year. I can hit a fastball at 110 miles an hour, and I *love* sushi."

"You made that too easy, because I saw your face during dinner." Chase chuckled. "And if you can hit a fastball, I'm sure you picked up swimming pretty early on."

"I can catch a wave like a legend," said a familiar, throaty voice. They turned to see a gorgeous, sinewy twentysomething male with short chestnut-brown hair striding down the steps from the house, shirtless in color-block swim trunks. Brandon filmed.

Presley smirked. "Well, Alex knows how to make an entrance."

Mia grinned as Alex approached looking just as striking in swim trunks as in a dress.

Presley applauded. "The contouring yesterday was a little heavy-handed." She ran a finger up her cheekbone as Alex reached the blanket.

"The fuck it was," said Alex, inhaling the sea air. "The gym in the house is one hundred percent! What a way to start off an incredible day!"

Eve's melancholy returned. "You obviously didn't see the koi."

Sensing the bad news, the corners of Alex's mouth dipped. "I went out the back door."

80

"Six floaters," said Chase.

"Those beautiful creatures?" replied Alex, upset.

"I didn't really think about this before, but is it weird there were six fish and there are six of us?" asked Oliver as he twisted his watchband.

"Get a grip, people!" snapped Presley. "You ate fish last night and you'll eat it again." She flicked her hand at Alex. "For fuck's sake, the stilettos you were strutting in yesterday used to graze on grass!"

Eve glared at Presley. "Where's your empathy?" She plucked the strap of her green and blue striped one-piece. "I picked this bathing suit because green is the heart chakra. This world has become void of compassion. We can't keep looking away! And blue is the throat chakra, because this summer, I want to *speak*. I'm tired of going to protests and being one of thousands. This is my chance to stand out."

Brandon lowered his camera. "I'm going to have to edit that chakra shit."

"Why? Your mom believes in chakras, right? She gave you that medallion," said Eve.

Brandon's necklace hung on his chest, bordered by an open short-sleeve button-down. "My mom spends time with the Dalai Lama. I think you learned that crap because you knew you were coming to California."

Mia whipped off her glasses. "Give her a break," she said. "I want to know more about this. In swimwear, you're more exposed than usual. Why shouldn't you use it as an opportunity to express your identity through color?" She smiled at Eve.

Eve put her hands on her hips. "Exactly."

Chase nodded. "Buddhist teachings can be applied to a lot of life. For the past year, I've been practicing *brahmacharya*."

"Brahma-what?" asked Mia.

"*Brahmacharya*—the renunciation of sex."

Eve admired Chase's lean, tanned surfer body, and pouted. "Aw, really?"

"I thought you said you're Jewish," said Oliver.

"Jew-Bu," replied Chase.

Brandon motioned to Chase. "California."

"I'm drawn to elements of Buddhism," said Chase. "That one has worked to save my energy for more rewarding activities, like being out on the water or up on a powdery mountain."

Two surfers ambled along the shore: a curly mop-headed ginger and a beanpole with a green faux-hawk. They passed a joint back and forth. A panting bulldog wearing a yellow smiley face collar trotted behind them.

Curly Mop-Headed Ginger called towards Chase. "Whaddup, broheem?" He jumped over a sandcastle, both feet smashing it when he didn't make it over. Faux-hawk Beanpole stepped up behind him and held the joint out to Chase, who took it.

"Just enjoying the day with my new friends." Chase toked.

Curly Mop-Headed Ginger grinned at the group. "We're his old friends. I'm Wyatt." He and Eve locked eyes. Eve returned the smile, twirling an auburn ringlet.

"Nils." Faux-hawk Beanpole poked his own rib cage—the right side bore a tattoo of a macabre-looking eyeball-man riding a wave. He turned to Brandon and put out his bony hand. "Yo, I love your dad's stuff."

Brandon hesitated for a beat, then shook Nils's hand. "My dad thanks you."

"You've been up against the wall, brother. I've been cited for a few minor transgressions—peeing in public and whatnot." Nils nodded in appreciation. "Nothing like yours."

Brandon shoved a hand in his shorts pocket. "I'm not your brother, so quit while you're ahead with the 'compliments.' You shouldn't say shit unless you know what you're talking about."

"I read the news."

"No, you don't," said Chase with a snort.

"I'm just saying that you've come out the other side. You keep livin' the life." Nils attempted to give Brandon the rock, but Brandon just stared at his lifted fist.

Presley waved her hat at Chase. "Tell your friend to put it away." Nils lowered his hand, shaking it out.

Mia felt embarrassed for him, but she also felt ashamed of herself because she had made the same assumptions about Brandon, and her assumptions weren't based on facts. Brandon squinted out at the ocean. "Let's move on to the business at hand," she said, hoping to deflect the attention from Brandon, who seemed to love and loathe it at the same time. She looked past him to see the bulldog relieving himself in the sand. "But it looks like someone is doing *his* business first."

Everyone turned to see the squat, wrinkly pooch kick sand over his fresh, steaming pile. "Hey, hey, hey!" yelled Crispy Tanned Rock Sculptor. He pointed to a wood sign that read:

WARNING DOG OWNERS:

LAW REQUIRES YOU TO PICK UP AFTER YOUR DOG

AND SO DOES COMMON DECENCY

"Chill, brah. Boomer is a good burier." Wyatt motioned to the dog, who had plopped down in the sand a smart distance away from his own excrement.

"This beach is also private, not public. Slackers like you seem to get confused," said Crispy Tanned Rock Sculptor.

"I'm not the one spending the day playing with rocks."

"You're trespassing."

"We're hanging with our buddy." Nils put his hand on Chase's arm. "He's staying at that sick house up there." He pointed at the seasonaires' house perched above them on the bluff.

Crispy Tanned Rock Sculptor refused to look in that direction, instead pointing at Wyatt and Nils. "Pick up your dog crap or it'll end up in *your* ass."

"*That's* harsh," said Wyatt.

Mia opened the picnic basket and pulled out a sandwich. She walked to Crispy Tanned Rock Sculptor and removed it from the baggie. "Are you allergic to peanuts?"

"No."

Mia handed the sandwich to him. She reached down to pet Boomer, who snored through his pushed-in snout, then scooped up the sandy poop with the baggie and tossed it in a nearby garbage can. As she walked past Chase to the towel, she whispered, "You owe me." She turned to Wyatt and Nils and raised her voice to a curt, professional tone. "We're having a business meeting, so if you'll excuse us."

"That's cool. We just wanted to say 'hey,'" said Nils. Chase punched him in his long, twiglike arm, which was a signal to leave, but the two friends didn't go far, moving to survey the rock mandala—really to annoy Crispy Tanned Rock Sculptor. Presley strode over to them and handed them some cash, then returned as they made their way up the beach.

She whispered to Mia. "I gave them fifty bucks to flush the koi."

"They're too big to flush!"

"It's not like I gave them a key. They'll figure it out."

Brandon handed Presley his camera. "Presley, take a photo for the channel's banner. You know how to work a regular camera, right?"

"Yes, but again—drives home the need for a professional photographer."

"What channel?" asked Mia.

Without an answer, Brandon pulled her in as the others gathered around them. Their arms touched and electric heat rose through Mia. She attributed it to the sun, because she refused to think she was attracted to Brandon in any way. Presley snapped a slew of photos. At that angle, the beach and the bluffs created the quintessential Malibu shot.

Oliver poured rosé and passed around the rest of lunch. He knocked on the top of the picnic basket three times. "Keep the lid closed or the beach chickens'll swipe our food." He waved off a seagull. Mia flinched as it flew off, since she was not fond of *any* birds—"beach chickens" in particular. One had haunted her dreams when she was young, even though she hadn't spent much time at the beach near her home in Boston. There had never seemed to *be* any time. But as the bird disappeared into the one puff of white cloud in the sky, Mia was struck by *this* beach that seemed to stretch on forever in both directions, with its ocean's remarkable shimmer. The breeze felt good on her face. She inhaled and released, ready to do her job. "Let's talk about the schedule," she said. "Tomorrow, we're going to the Lyndon Wyld store at the Malibu Country Mart—"

Presley waved a hand, a thin gold bracelet glinting in the sun. "Blah-blah. Come on, Mia, if you're going to get down to business, set the rules."

Mia shot her a look, then turned back to the others, trying to maintain her composure while feeling like she had just had her hand smacked by an old-time schoolteacher. "Right, okay. The most important rule is to post on social. Tag the brand, tag each other." She was repeating Grace's words from last summer.

"The algorithm changes every day, so do your research and keep up with those changes," said Presley. Mia's jaw tightened.

Brandon gestured. "Why do we want to try and guess the algorithm, right? We need to be miles ahead of any algorithm. Stay relevant, or this brand will become as extinct as 8-track tapes."

"What's an 8-track tape?" asked Oliver, who wiped an errant splotch of mustard off his shirt with a cloth napkin.

"How do you suggest we stay relevant, Brandon?" asked Mia, taking a healthy swig of her wine. She watched the translucent pink liquid swish around her stemless glass, ignoring Crispy Tanned Rock Sculptor when he walked by.

He pointed at them. "No glass on the beach."

Mia took another sip.

Brandon clapped once. "First of all, the hashtags *lit*, *cray*, *af*, *onfleek*, and *shook* have expired. That fucking fire emoji? Dead. And stop with the shit that doesn't say anything about you: acai bowls, planks, pedicures. The only time that's *remotely* riveting is if those fucking baby piranha bite off your damn toe. Each one of you needs to be the *GOAT. GOAT, GOAT, GOAT.* Or better yet, claim your own damn acronym."

"GOAT," repeated Mia. It had been a long while since she'd had any interest in hashtags or acronyms.

"Greatest Of All Time," said Alex with confidence. "But if I share my day, what am I supposed to give my followers? The finger?"

Presley lowered her sunglasses to peer at Instagram on Alex's phone. "Impressive number, but you can do better."

Brandon patted his camera. "They don't just want to *see* everything, they want to *watch* everything, and not only in ten- to sixty-second increments. Video makes up the lion's share of internet traffic."

"I have a self-care vlog—mostly ASMR videos," said Eve in her most soothing voice. "That's one of the reasons I ended up here. They're pretty popular."

Presley sniffed. "Scratching a plastic water bottle and cooing for twenty minutes? I don't think so."

Eve looked away, offended. "I would *never* use plastic."

"Our followers will want to be in it here with *us*, not just you or me." Brandon motioned outward, then to himself. "It's about community. They want to *be* us, so we're going to film everything we do."

Oliver straightened his glasses. "Everything?"

"Almost everything." Brandon tilted his head at Oliver. "We don't need over-sharers. For example, no one needs to see the giant wax ball you pulled out of your ear."

"It *was* pretty awesome," said Oliver with a chuckle. He picked at the crust of his sandwich, glancing at Alex. "I'm sorry to sound like an idiot and I hope this isn't a rude question, Alex, but what's your preferred pronoun?"

"I'm a gay man who finds beauty in my femme side. I call myself 'he/him,' but I'm not into labels unless they're on amazing clothes," replied Alex.

Mia smiled at him. "We should all be proud of our individuality. That's why we're here, and that's why we post." Her smile waned when she turned her focus to Brandon. "But I don't want to be filmed all the time. I mean, don't you like it when you see people on the street and there's *some* sense of wonderment about who they are?"

"I like to make up the story and then I want to know if I'm right," answered Brandon.

Presley gave Mia's sunburned thigh a light slap. "Guess where y'all are putting these videos?"

Brandon rose on one knee. "Our own digital channel: Wyld World. There are cameras around the house."

Mia threw her head back in disbelief. "What?"

"Don't worry. I'll show you where they are," said Brandon with a cocky snort. "They're not in your bedroom or the john, but our fans are going to want an authentic connection."

Mia glared at Presley. "I'm not understanding. Why didn't I know about this?"

Presley popped a grape in her mouth. "Let's not have mommy and daddy fighting in front of the kids."

"The more you see someone online, the more you trust them," said Brandon. "So when a celebrity or influencer posts something, you're more liable to trust them than if that info came from a quote-unquote stranger. Like with doctors—we assume they know what they're doing even though it's called a *practice*. We're style experts, so the more fans see us, the more they're going to trust that they *need* Lyndon Wyld and MazzyLyn to survive."

"Survival of the Wyldest—with a *y*," said Presley with a grin.

Alex reclined flat to soak up the rays. "Like I said last night, I have nothing to hide."

"Neither do I." Eve sat taller.

"Me, neither." Oliver twisted his watch around his wrist one more time.

Chase shrugged. "I was going to do promos for a new surf brand, but that fell through. As the poet Virgil said, 'Fate will find a way.'"

"Mia?" Presley gave Mia's arm a light pinch.

Brandon put his forearms on his knee and leaned towards Mia. "We're here to sell ourselves, and this is the way. *We're* the brand."

Mia stood. "I'm going up—too much sun." She brushed the sand off her butt.

"You're done?" Presley chucked a grape in Mia's empty wineglass.

Mia strode back up the beach to the house.

TEN

Mia entered and fell onto the couch that looked plush and inviting but was actually uncomfortable. Flopping her legs—pink and hot—over the side, she felt the sand on her heels rub against the smooth fabric. She'd forgotten to wash off her feet with the hose on the deck, but she didn't care, consumed as she was by the information that she was going to be a reality show for the next twelve weeks. She dialed Lyndon's number on her phone and got voice mail: "You've reached Lyndon Wyld. Please leave a message at the tone and your call will be returned. Cheers." Mia recognized Grace's voice and wondered why Lyndon didn't change that outgoing message. Feeling like she was a kid tattling on Brandon, she hung up.

"No one went into anaphylactic shock from my sandwiches, so I'm happy," she heard Oliver say. She looked at the open glass sliders to see the rest of the seasonaires spray the sand off their feet. Presley dipped hers in the pool and entered.

"Mia, you're still here!" Presley's voice rose with faux cheer as she sat on the couch's arm.

Oliver disappeared into the kitchen with the picnic basket while the others took their places on the living room couches.

Brandon started towards the hall. "I'm going into my studio to edit. I'll be out of pocket for the next four hours."

"Why will it take that long?" asked Mia.

Brandon stopped. "Because we need a story arc. If this is as boring as *Moby Dick*, people are going to turn it off."

Chase sprawled in the armchair. "Why does everyone dis *Moby Dick*? It's a sweet story of friendship."

Mia looked at Brandon. "Editing doesn't sound 'authentic' to me."

Oliver reentered and sat on the ottoman near Mia's sandy feet. He clapped his hands together. "You said we're going to the Malibu Country Mart. When do we get to see Rodeo Drive?"

Presley tapped her phone on Oliver's thigh. "I realize you're from middle America, Oli, but have you lived under a rock? Rodeo Drive is for tourists."

"*I'm* a tourist," said Oliver without the least bit of embarrassment.

Mia put her elbows on her knees so her head was near Oliver's. "I'm a tourist, too."

"What she means is, Beverly Hills doesn't represent LA's retail culture anymore," said Brandon. "It's all happening on Melrose, La Brea, and Fairfax."

"That's where Lyndon is launching MazzyLyn, the co-branded streetwear line. I don't question her need to branch out." Presley smoothed her sundress.

Chase pumped his arms in the air. "More dope swag! My buddies are gonna freak."

Oliver beamed. "I can't believe we're getting twenty grand to live this life!"

Alex sang the chorus of ABBA's "Money, Money, Money." Eve sprawled across him and sang along as Brandon filmed them. Mia edged back into the corner of her couch, alone and uncomfortable with the knowledge that she was making more than the others. She had to remind herself of the extra work she would be doing.

"Brandon is donating his wages to charity," said Presley. She must've sensed Mia's discomfort. She knew how to poke people where they were weakest, like tapping a fragile vase until it cracked.

The room became silent. Eve started laughing hysterically.

"What?" Brandon leaned against a wall.

"That hits me in my giggledick—you donating your wages to charity." Eve could barely get the words out between peals. "Our wages are like a weekend's allowance for you." After composing herself, she added, "I think you can do better than that."

"I can and I do. I deejayed a sixtieth birthday party for some rich bougie jackhole—a producer whose last movie tanked because he didn't know how to talk to an audience that didn't carry AARP cards. I donated five figures from that, too."

"Talking about it makes *you* bougie," said Eve.

Brandon rested his camera on a plexiglass side table. "Oh, I get it. I know shit disturbers like you. You celebrate Opposite Day every day, picking the cause that's contrary."

Eve stopped laughing. "That's so demeaning."

"You'll overlook a positive contribution because it will never be enough in your opinion."

Eve stood. "It should never be enough! That's how change happens."

"You're probably one of those millennials—"

"*You're* a millennial!"

"Not one of *your* millennials, the kind who wants to move to Canada but doesn't realize that Canada doesn't want us."

Eve stormed past Brandon and up the stairs.

Presley offered a woeful sigh. "Aw, you just crushed her dreams."

"I'll show you the ticket to our dreams." Brandon motioned down the hallway. The group followed him along a wall lined with giant black-and-white framed photos of rock legends like Jimi Hendrix, Jim Morrison, and the Rolling Stones. He led them into a study that had been transformed into an elaborate production studio. Film equipment filled the space: lights, tripods, DSLR cameras, and gadgets. Laptops and monitors were perched on a long glass desk. The windows were covered with blackout shades.

Chase roamed in awe. "This is some wicked gear."

Oliver touched the camera set up on a tripod.

"You break it, you buy it," said Brandon.

Mia motioned around. "So *this* is the studio you asked for." Everything with Brandon was for show, including this display.

"It's where the magic happens," said Brandon. "We'll sprinkle in live confessionals with the episodes." He motioned to the video camera on the tripod in front of the Lyndon Wyld logo backdrop.

"Confessionals?" Mia ran her hand through her hair in exasperation.

Presley sat in one of the high director's chairs. "I'm going to monitor your success—or failure. The first four hours after you air are crucial. If there's a lot of traffic, you'll go right to the top of the search."

"That won't be a problem," said Brandon.

"This sounds like a million other reality TV series, which everyone knows are scripted," said Mia.

Oliver frowned. "They are?"

Mia walked to the backdrop and pointed to the Lyndon Wyld logos that covered it. "We're here to represent a *real* brand."

"You're right, Mia." Brandon turned on the camera and pointed it at her. "We have to be different. Here's how we're going to blow shit up." He pointed at Chase. "Chase, you had the right idea with the wasabi challenge, though that was—"

"Dumber than a box of hair," said Presley.

Brandon pointed to the laptops. "There'll be challenges presented by our viewers. We're going to be scripted in a *real* way, because we'll let the *fans* write the script. They'll tell us what they want to happen, and we'll put that in motion."

Mia saw herself on a monitor and moved out of the frame. She groaned.

"They don't control the outcome. Just like life, no one does," said Brandon.

Alex crossed his arms. "What if they don't like our choices? Because I don't live by anyone else's choices."

"Believe me, they'll let us know. That starts a conversation."

Mia scoffed. "This is ridiculous."

"It *is* a little Orwellian," said Chase.

Presley looked at the footage in Brandon's camera. "Lyndon loves the idea."

Mia's head was spinning. "Is anything off-limits?"

"Dead bodies," answered Brandon. Mia looked down at her bare feet and shook her head.

Oliver cringed. "Too soon?"

"No. It's not too soon," said Brandon. "That's happened online. We're also not going to tase dead rats or, in our case, dead koi for the camera."

"How considerate," said Eve, who was now standing in the doorway, a sour look on her face.

Brandon put his hand on a monitor. "That's about it for what's off-limits. There *will* be surprises."

"Goodie," said Mia, her expression as flat as Eve's.

Chase picked up a signed Dodgers baseball. "I think the player of our universal video game is going to press the Reset button anyway, because our parents fucked up and we're not fixing it."

Eve stepped into the studio. "Some of us are trying to fix it."

Chase tossed the ball in the air and caught it. "It's broken beyond repair. That's why I'm in this bitchin' house for a summer of fun." He put the ball back on the desk.

Brandon moved to Mia. "If you're worried about your privacy, why'd you even sign up for this gig again?" Mia didn't answer. He shooed the group towards the door. "Okay, everyone out. I'll show you the finished edit when I'm done." He stopped Mia. "There's no camera in your workspace. That would be giving away trade secrets."

"At least some things are sacred," said Mia, exiting. As the group made their way down the hall, she pulled Presley aside. "This is not cool at all. I'm going to talk to Lyndon about it."

"You'll be shouting into the wind. This is happening." Presley continued down the hall. "I won't be at the store opening. I have a strategy call."

Mia heard the front door slam. She stopped and stared at the classic rock icons on the wall. They hadn't had to deal with their lives on camera every minute. There were stories and rumors. There was mystery. Her mother had loved classic rock, so Mia grew up listening to it, especially the Stones. Mia stared at Brian Jones, with his long bangs almost covering his eyes as he played guitar. He had been found dead in a swimming pool.

That night on their way out to dinner, Eve tried to maneuver down the walkway with her eyes shut in order to avoid seeing the dead koi. Alex put his face close to hers. "Open. They've gone to fishy heaven." As a memorial, Eve suggested they eat at a vegan restaurant on PCH.

Afterwards, the group settled in the living room. Brandon turned on the widescreen TV set into the wall and pressed the remote. Their digital channel came up with a Wyld World banner across the top that displayed the group shot at the beach. He clicked on *Episode 1: We're Coming For You.* Since Presley had promoted the channel on the brand's social, it already had a significant number of subscribers. The episode featured Oliver and Chase roughhousing and Eve strolling down the beach.

Snuggled on the couch watching, Alex squeezed Eve. "Work it!"

Eve batted her mascara-free eyelashes. "Thick thighs and pretty eyes." She didn't have what the "masses" would call a "perfect" body, but she exuded a self-assurance that Mia envied.

"You look great, Eve," said Mia, pulling her legs to her chest on the ottoman. She could easily access the pang of insecurity she had felt when she'd walked into the Nantucket house filled with beautiful people. She felt that pang now. She was on-screen for a total of four seconds: waving as she made her way down the wood steps to the sand. She couldn't help thinking that Brandon had edited her out on purpose because of her resistance.

On the screen, Alex held out an upside-down Lyndon Wyld baseball cap full of shells. The close-up displayed his striking features and flawless complexion, even without the makeup he so expertly knew how to apply.

Chase's surfer friends, Wyatt and Nils, managed to photobomb some footage.

"Those jokers need to get their own channel," said Brandon. His agitation was quelled because Boomer the bulldog was a hit, according to the comments that came in. The episode's viewer count grew and so did the channel's subscribers after Brandon's footage of himself sitting by the Crispy Tanned Rock Sculptor's abandoned mandala. His shirt was open, his demeanor sexy-cool as he demanded that everyone keep tuning in to find out more about the MazzyLyn streetwear launch: "Check this giveaway: front of the line entry to the store," he said as he pointed at the viewers.

The seasonaires cheered when the big bold words #BuWyld closed out the episode. In celebration, they drank tequila and swam. Alex refrained from tequila, Mia from the pool—she wasn't ready yet, despite cajoling from the others and a couple of hits off Chase's joint. The mood became as breezy as the late night air.

Mia headed upstairs to her workspace. Brandon caught her wrist. "The episode: no problem, right?"

Mia pulled away. "No problem." She didn't want to admit that the episode was harmless and did its job of showcasing the line's swimwear. Brandon, who had pulled it together in one afternoon, was just so *smug*.

Mia sat at her desk, staring at her sketches. Unable to concentrate, she looked around for a hidden camera but didn't see one. A couple of unproductive hours crept by, and she finally abandoned her pencil and paper. She found Eve and Alex sleeping soundly in their beds. They didn't seem worried about having their lives broadcast for the rest of the summer—they welcomed the opportunity. Maybe their ease would rub off on her while she slept . . . *if* she could sleep, because every time she closed her eyes, she saw the six dead koi fish.

ELEVEN

After breakfast on the deck, the seasonaires loaded into the Tesla for their trip to the Lyndon Wyld store. Chase drove while Brandon briefed them on the success of their first episode. Mia caught periodic words: *analytics*, *core metrics*, *engagement*, and *deprecation policy*. Mostly she was thinking about seeing Lyndon at the store and if it was worth telling her she was unhappy about the channel.

"PCH is bumper-to-bumper on weekends, especially when the weather's nice," said Chase as the car slogged through traffic.

Eve glanced around them. "The drivers don't look nearly as agro as they did at the airport or on the freeway."

Oliver smiled at the flawless ocean view from the car. "That's because everyone wants a piece of this!"

The Tesla wound its way into the Malibu Country Mart parking lot and the seasonaires got out. The sun filtered through the colorful paper lanterns that hung above one of the pathways leading to the upscale shops, galleries, and eateries.

"I've been to the country, and it's nothing like this," said Oliver as he gawked at the lush grounds dotted with contemporary sculptures and well-heeled patrons. The seasonaires walked through to the Malibu Lumber Yard, where the new store joined other high-end, trendsetting boutiques in an architectural cluster of wood and glass structures. A dad wearing a straw porkpie hat played Ping-Pong with his young son on the deck of the James Perse store. Their three-legged pitbull-mix sat near a water bowl. Mia noticed that rescue mutts seemed to be the dogs of Malibu.

"This was an actual lumberyard," said Chase while Oliver bought everyone cupcakes. Brandon shot footage. Alex, short hair spiked, rocking blue Lyndon Wyld men's trousers and a floral women's blouse, fed his frosting to Eve, who wore a cream-colored romper and espadrilles. Mia went for simplicity: a cap-sleeve dress and flats.

The Lyndon Wyld store was airy, with floor-to-ceiling sliders that opened onto the shared deck. The racks and shelves were filled with pieces that were more sophisticated-boho than their preppier counterparts in Nantucket, though Oliver represented that classic look. He threw it off kilter with a nylon Lyndon Wyld fanny pack.

"Different styles for different coasts," Mia said to Brandon as they perused.

"It's all online anyway. Brick-and-mortar stores are becoming obsolete. You mostly shop online, right?"

"No. I tend to make clothes instead of buy them. My seasonaire's fee from last summer went to this fall's college tuition and my mother's hospital bills."

Brandon tamed his swagger. "I'm sorry about your mom. My mom is everything to me. I don't know what I would do if I lost her. She's seen me through a lot of shit. I keep giving her more, but she's always there for me."

"You're lucky."

As they walked through the store, they were met with a crowd of great-looking people dressed in relaxed summer ensembles that seemed like they took hours to put together. Mia landed on a descriptor: *planned casual.* All the smiles turned towards the seasonaires with a constant chorus of enthusiastic greetings.

Brandon nudged Mia and chuckled. "You look like a deer caught in the headlights."

"I expected people to be—I don't know—snobbier."

"It's been called the rudest city in the US, but I think in LA, everyone's a friend you haven't met yet," replied Chase, paraphrasing Yeats with a grin.

"You're born and raised here. You have to say that," said Eve as she plucked a mimosa from a table topped with them. The scent of freshly squeezed orange juice met with the lemon verbena soy candles placed around the store.

Chase took a drink. "Malibu isn't all rich celebrities and industry VIPs. Back in the fifties and sixties, surfers and hippies staked ground here because it was a mellow, fun place to live. A lot of those residents never left. They're a super chill, tight-knit bunch."

Alex gasped and straightened the shoulders of his blouse, eyes on the entrance. "There she is!"

Lyndon—a pale peach, silk caftan grazing her jeweled sandals as she wafted in—was anything but "earthy." Her blonde hair was freshly highlighted and twisted in a low chignon, her makeup a summery shimmer.

The crowd quieted to a hush. Guests snapped photos, as did photographers and camerapeople who stood with journalists.

Lyndon opened her arms and smiled gracefully. "I want to welcome everybody to my beautiful Malibu boutique. This year, I was so thrilled to finally open a store in my favorite city on earth."

Applause all around.

"I'm not kidding. I know California is about as far across the pond as you can get, but there is just *something* about this coast that makes me gain perspective. It even makes me want a dog, because everyone here seems to have one." She motioned to the dad with the rescue pit. Guests tittered as they sipped their bubbly libations. "I don't know if you're aware, but all of today's profits will go to the Children's Hospital Los Angeles. I don't have any children of my own, so I consider my seasonaires my children. Every summer I have new ones, but I get to keep my girlish figure." She shifted, hand on her hip. More crowd titters.

Eve gave Mia a disapproving glance and whispered, "Ooh, I don't like that."

Lyndon motioned to the seasonaires across the store from her. "They will be making a visit to the hospital to spend time with those brave kids and their families, many of whom are without health care. I have assured all funds will go to cover those young patients' care. I'm going to have Mia, who has returned to lead my seasonaires' charge *and* design her own collection, say a few words." She gestured to Mia. This was also her savvy way of giving guests the chance to scan all the merchandise as they turned their focus.

Mia tried to steady the shake in her voice. "I'm really excited to be here on the beautiful West Coast." She was nervous, but she wanted to find pride in the fact that Lyndon had chosen her to speak for the brand that day—and for the summer. "I've never been west of Boston . . . or far from Boston period. I'm honored that Lyndon has again given me the opportunity to make my dream come true." She exchanged a nod with Lyndon. "Ever since I was a little girl, I've wanted to be a fashion designer. My goal is to continue to learn about the industry through this experience."

Mia was relieved that Presley was nowhere in sight. She refrained from talking about the harder lessons she'd learned about competition and backstabbing, because she looked around the room and saw the faces of people her age and younger. "I've been off social media for a year and have to say that I've been a little nervous to start up again. I know you understand how brutal it can be. Being out there makes you a target, so just know that if you've ever suffered at the words of some jerk who's hidden behind a handle, you're not alone. But it's also a way for us to connect and for you to get to know the rest of my new friends here in Malibu." She smiled and motioned to the other seasonaires, relaxing when she saw their smiles returned.

Brandon was the only exception. He handed the camera to Chase, then stepped up next to Mia. "We're also pumped to announce the opening of the flagship MazzyLyn store on Fairfax!" The crowd applauded. "Here's a sneak peek." He revealed his white and gold MazzyLyn high-tops underneath the cuffed hem of his pin-striped linen pants.

"How do we find out where and when?" asked one reporter, taking notes.

"You haven't watched our new channel, Wyld World?"

"Not yet."

Brandon pointed at him. "Get on it!"

Everyone laughed. Mia shared a glance with Lyndon. Both maintained cheerful smiles.

"I have a question," called out a reporter in the corner.

"Yes, it's spelled with a *y*," replied Brandon, chuckling.

"My question isn't for you." The reporter's focus shifted from Brandon, who appeared irked. "It's for Lyndon. Grant Byrd, the seasonaire who died last summer, has a younger sister in his hometown battling leukemia." Mia didn't remember Grant saying anything about a sister who was ill, but he hadn't said much about his family. She had discovered that he'd felt unloved by his father and tried to cover that unhappiness with fraternity boy bravado. "Is that why you're donating to Children's Hospital?" asked the reporter.

Lyndon fidgeted with her watch. "It's part of the reason, yes."

Oliver turned his watch around his wrist twice. The reporter ignored the store's awkward silence and kept his focus on Lyndon.

"After the murder of one of your seasonaires by your sister last summer, why didn't you shut down your program?"

"Shit," muttered Brandon.

Mia now understood why Presley wasn't there. Lyndon and Presley might have seen this PR glitch coming, and "the strategy call" Presley had mentioned was to keep her unfettered mouth from making it worse. They both knew diplomacy wasn't one of Presley's strengths.

Lyndon clasped her hands together to stop them from trembling. "We all have tragedies that we must move past, and—"

Mia blurted, "I was there last summer—" She immediately regretted her interjection, not wanting anyone to infer that she was at the Wear National house that fatal night. "—in Nantucket. Like Lyndon said, a tragedy happened, and to call it upsetting is an understatement. But justice is being served. I felt confident enough about that to return as a seasonaire. Lyndon is a strong woman and an even stronger entrepreneur to forge on after someone so close turned on her. I'm inspired by her." She looked at Lyndon, who held back tears.

The reporter was still focused on Lyndon. "How do you see the trajectory of your brand as a whole after the controversy?"

"Kick-ass," said Brandon, loud and clear. "The owner of a popular chicken joint was involved in a murder-suicide, yet people keep eating his chicken. A hot athleisure brand's salesgirl stabbed another salesgirl but those yoga pants are still on many of the women here . . . though now you have another choice, because Lyndon Wyld is crushing it in the athleisure department." He pointed to the store's section featuring chic leggings, joggers, tanks, and hoodies. The athleisure-attired shoppers clapped lightly.

"Yes, thank you, Mia . . . and Brandon," said Lyndon, composing herself. "Now, please, everyone, enjoy and remember, today is for Children's Hospital Los Angeles." She walked off, striding through the store and out the doors onto the deck. Mia and the seasonaires followed her.

When Lyndon saw them, she put on her brightest smile. "You're all smashing—the lot of you!" She gestured to Alex. "That top looks far better on you than it does on me!" Alex touched the floral silk and beamed. Lyndon air-kissed Mia on both cheeks. "Thank you," she whispered. She pulled away and scanned the seasonaires, who stood straighter in her presence. Brandon filmed the "kiss the ring" moment.

"Brandon, my darling, turn off the camera."

Brandon obliged, but it was clear from his expression that he didn't appreciate being chided like a child.

"I'm thrilled for you to be here and start your summer, which I'm positive will be the bee's knees." Lyndon grew more subdued. She tucked a lock of hair that had escaped from her chignon behind her ear. "I know you're all aware of what happened in Nantucket, and if you weren't, you are now, thanks to that reporter's inappropriate sidetrack. I appreciate that you're putting what you've heard aside in order to embark on this adventure." She gave Mia's hand a squeeze. "Mia has suffered the brunt, especially after the passing of her mother. She is the epitome of resilience and bravery, coming back for a second summer, but she was the reigning seasonaire with the most followers, and that's how we do it here at Lyndon Wyld. You'll all have the chance in the future, so I want you to communicate with your fans in the most relatable way possible."

"I have that handled," said Brandon, lifting his camera.

She brushed Brandon's sleeve. "I know you do. I've never been a micromanager. I let the experts rule their wheelhouse."

Mia considered this. Lyndon had allowed Grace a good length of the reins. She really couldn't understand how someone as put together as Lyndon let her horse run so far out of control.

Lyndon put up a finger. Her pale peach nail polish matched her silk caftan. "My mandate is that you do not talk to the media about our 'personal' business without going through Presley first. You've all met her."

Alex shoved a hand in a trouser pocket. "Yes, we have."

Lyndon lifted her handbag onto her wrist. "Before I leave you, do you have any questions for me?"

"I hope you'll give all of us the same attention," said Eve, eyeing Brandon.

"Not really a question," said Brandon.

"You hired influencers who are already popular, which puts the rest of us at a disadvantage," said Eve, whose focus shifted to Mia.

Lyndon lifted Eve's chin. "Everyone needs to work their way up. That's why work is called *work*." She turned to Mia. "Come with me for a moment."

"Sure."

Lyndon waved at the others. "I will see you all soon. Be safe. Tah!"

With a quick brow furrow at Eve, Mia accompanied Lyndon to the parking lot on the other side of the shopping center. Lyndon positioned the handle of her embroidered mini-satchel purse on her wrist. "We've got live ones this year."

They approached Mr Chow, where patrons on the patio were ensconced behind a wall of tall green ficus. In the lot, the flashiest cars—a red Lamborghini, yellow Ferrari, and a silver Porsche Carrera GT—were parked up front. At the curb, not yet ready for the valet, sat the white Volvo SUV with Presley in the driver's seat, tinted window rolled down.

"Presley, will you let Mia and I chat for a moment in private?" said Lyndon. "I'll meet you inside." Mia fiddled with an earring as her stomach knotted.

Presley got out of the car. "You don't have to ask me twice." She sashayed into the restaurant.

Lyndon sat in the driver's seat. Mia entered and closed the passenger door. The car was running to enable the air conditioner. Goose bumps covered Mia's arms. Lyndon put her hands on the bottom of the steering wheel. "Since the word of the day seems to be *transparency*, we need to get an issue out in the open."

"Okay." Mia smoothed her dress. The knot in her stomach tightened.

"I know you were close with Cole, who was involved in the drug investigation that surrounded Otto Hahn. I'm not sure if he had anything to do with Grace's arrest, but I could bet my bottom dollar that *he* did. If you're in contact with him, you need to let me know right now, because I will not tolerate secrets. Trust is tantamount to our relationship."

"Honestly, Lyndon, I haven't talked to Cole since last summer."

The corners of Lyndon's mouth lifted, and she caressed Mia's arm. "We're a real team now, you and I."

Mia nodded. Silence and frigid air filled the car. Mia's hands were numb.

Lyndon's tone lightened but was still firm. "Don't let the little prince step on you. I've known Brandon since he was a tot, and he was formidable even then. I expect you to hold your own."

"I will."

"Would you like to join Presley and I for lunch? I go back to New York first thing tomorrow morning."

"No, thank you. I should be with the others."

"That's my girl," said Lyndon. She patted Mia's arm, which Mia took as a cue to exit the car.

"Safe travels," said Mia. She walked across to the other parking lot, worried that "trust" was an issue. When she met the rest of the seasonaires at the Tesla, she knew she had to let it go.

"Lyndon is as fabulous as my dreams of her," said Alex as Mia slid into the car next to him. "The way she handled that reporter was *eleganza* but fierce! And you, Mia, are following in her kitten heel footsteps!"

Eve sat tall, her jaw tight. "She basically ignored me. I think it's because my idea of a girlish figure is different than hers." She fiddled with the waistband of her jumper.

Oliver tapped the door handle three times. "She seemed nice to me, given the circumstances."

"Yeah, that kind of sucked for her," said Chase, driving.

Brandon checked the Wyld World channel on the car's touch-screen. Looking through the comments, he stopped on one:

Challenge: seasonaires versus bikers at Stingray's,

"Who wants beers?" he asked.

"I'll take *that* challenge," replied Chase and glanced back. "You?"

"Yes!" shouted the others as Brandon punched off the screen and Chase whirred them off. Mia was in definite need of a beer.

TWELVE

D riving to the Malibu Country Mart, Mia had been too distracted by the upcoming store opening event to notice the packs of bikers that roared by in both directions. But now back on PCH, she was aware of the growling tailpipes, studded saddlebags, heavy black boots, and helmets of all styles and colors. Some women rode solo—hair in long ponytails or braids. Some sat on the back, arms loosely wrapped around drivers of all ages and sizes.

"Malibu's always been a biker destination," said Chase, lifting a peace sign to one, who returned the gesture.

"Looks fun," said Mia, who found these packs less ominous than the one that had overtaken her and Eve when Marcus had driven them from the airport. At this moment, still stressed out from the store event, she would've loved the blast of fresh air on a bike.

The Tesla pulled up to Stingray's, with its stringray tail sign poking out from top of the simple one-story bar and grill. A crowded line of motorcycles and conversing bikers obscured the patio. The parking lot was full, so Chase drove the car past it and found a spot a few yards away when a cherry vintage VW van pulled out, surfboards strapped to the top.

The group spilled out of the Tesla and walked along the highway to the restaurant, passing throngs of patrons eating and drinking on the patio. Mia was fascinated by the diverse blend of surfers, tourists, and bikers. Now, seasonaires would be added to the mix. As they entered, framed photos of stingrays, dolphins, and other West Coast sea creatures welcomed them. Souvenir tees hung from the wood pillars, and the fans above spun around, circulating the air, which was thick with the smell of leather, smoked cigarettes, perfume, and the sizzling grill behind the open kitchen.

"I'll order," said Chase.

"I'll come with you." Mia started towards the counter with Chase while Alex, Eve, and Oliver looked around. Through the window, the three saw an empty table on the patio.

"We'll meet you outside," said Alex. His floral blouse, lush lashes, and glossy lips caused a few heads to turn. He basked in the attention.

Brandon had moved off to talk to a couple of bikers by the door. Mia watched him as they laughed with the familiarity of friends. After several minutes, Mia could hear him say, "Catch you at the store" as he walked towards her. He motioned to the bikers. "My dad and I used to do the Love Ride with those guys."

"What's the Love Ride?"

"A charity trek for underserved kids and vets."

"Do you have your own bike?"

"Bikes—plural. But after I dropped my Triumph, my mom didn't want me riding anymore."

"She sounds overprotective." Mia eyed the black rope of his necklace.

Brandon patted the spot where his T-shirt sat over the medallion. "She is—almost more than my dad."

Chase picked up a tray of fish tacos, hamburgers, fries, and a grilled salmon salad for Alex. Brandon grabbed the five bottles of beer and a LaCroix, and the three made their way out to the table. Mia took the empty wood seat next to Oliver, whose eyes were wide as he peered around at a few of the tougher-looking men. Mia chugged her beer thirstily. The heat, mixed with her addled nerves, was getting to her, so the beer was more refreshing than she'd expected. She took a hungry bite of a burger.

Eve dipped a French fry in ranch dressing. "I think Lyndon needs to work on the body positivity angle, especially since she's selling athleisure." She ate the fry.

Brandon flicked the condensation off a beer bottle. "That reporter was a tool."

Eve ate another fry. "It's his job as a journalist to ask the tough questions."

"At a fashion event?" said Alex, stabbing a forkful of lettuce. "I don't think so."

Mia was distracted by someone inside, past the stickers on the windows: a whip-thin girl with long blonde hair and a violet streak sitting in a booth, her body decorated with ink. Mia's heart stopped until the girl turned around and they caught eyes—she wasn't Ruby. Mia exhaled and took another bite of burger, which caught in her throat with her disappointment. She finished her beer. "I'm still parched." She looked at the others. "Anyone else?"

"Who knew you were the type of girl who could shotgun a beer?" said Chase, impressed. He chomped on a taco, food falling from his mouth. Alex handed him a napkin.

Once Mia was back inside, she waited for some patrons to order at the counter. Tapping her foot, she glanced around at the crowd. In the corner under a Flag of California on the wall was a table with three bikers. A girl—porcelain pale and just north of scrawny—leaned her left hip on the shoulder of the muscular biker in a white tee and black leather vest who was sitting facing away from Mia. With light pink hair piled messily on her head, the girl wore a loose tank top that dipped low in back to reveal a tattoo between her angular shoulder blades: a sunflower, like the one on Mia's ankle, but bigger and in color instead of black and white. The hair color was different, but when the girl shifted her head to kiss the muscular biker, Mia saw the silver septum ring. *This was Ruby.*

An older biker, with a thick tuft of silver hair and matching beard, kept his eyes on the couple—his blue deep-set eyes like Ruby's but piercing and bordered by deep crow's-feet. The younger, with a brown ponytail and gauges in his ears, had similar eyes and Ruby's identical nose. He removed a pack of Marlboro Blacks from inside his leather jacket as the three men rose and headed out. They passed Mia, missing her, thanks to the patrons between them. She looked away until they exited the restaurant and were out of sight.

Mia's heart beat faster, and she couldn't stop her legs from carrying her over to Ruby, though the rest of her wanted to turn around. The restaurant was crowded enough that Ruby might never see her if she left. Ruby picked at the dark blue polish on her fingernails, lost in thought as the din of conversations grew louder. Mia inched her way closer and touched Ruby's shoulder.

Ruby whirled around, more frightened than startled. "Fuck!" When she saw Mia, her eyes immediately filled with tears.

"Hi," said Mia, the word coming out as air.

Ruby lifted her shoulders back and sniffed once, extinguishing her emotion. Her body was more rigid, her face more angular than Mia remembered. "What are you doing here, Mia? You're not exactly a biker bitch."

"I'm working in Malibu this summer." Mia hesitated. "I'm a seasonaire."

"I meant *here* at Stingray's." Ruby's eyes darted around for a beat, then landed back on Mia.

"How are you?" asked Mia, fidgeting with her thin blue enamel bangle bracelet.

"Amazed that you would go back to work for Lyndon Wyld," replied Ruby.

"I'm a little amazed myself," said Mia with an awkward chortle, then grew somber. "I'm sorry we lost touch." She tried to find softness in Ruby's face.

"It's fine." Ruby's voice lowered to a concerned hush. "Listen, do *not* try to contact me again. I'm willing to bet I'm part of the reason you took this job."

"It was a chance to see you, yes."

"You saw me, now go do what you were hired to do this summer."

"Just tell me if you're okay." Mia didn't see any fresh track marks on Ruby's arms or cuts on her wrists, which were unsheathed by the stacks of bracelets she used to wear. The matching bangle Mia had given her was gone.

"I'm good," said Ruby, crossing her arms. "I've given up fashion for a career in hair. People seem to like my way with color." Her high, swirled bun reminded Mia of her mom's favorite type of roses: Angelica.

"You changed it. It's pretty," said Mia.

"You haven't changed." Ruby's eyes finally softened. "Still pretty, too. How's your mom?"

"She passed away."

"I'm sorry. That's why I'm staying as close to mine as I can." This jab prompted Mia to look away. Out the window, she saw two beefy bikers lumber over to Alex, Oliver, Eve, and Chase at the table—they didn't look friendly.

"Go hang with your new friends, Mia," said Ruby, a bitter bite to her tone. She shook her head and strode off to the ladies' room.

"Shit." With a sharp exhale, Mia turned and wove her way through the restaurant and back outside. At the table, the two bikers hovered over the group.

"Get the fuck up. You're at our table," said the beefier of the two. Mia couldn't process what was happening, her mind still on Ruby. At this point, she felt like her work in California was done. Or more to the point, she *wished* it was done, but she was shackled to the job.

Oliver smiled politely at the bikers. "I'm sorry. We didn't see it was reserved." His genuine smile remained as he twisted his watch around twice.

"Are you being a smart-ass?" The smaller-giant biker pounded his fist on the table. The fourth beer—untouched by Brandon, who was nowhere to be found—toppled and spilled on his jeans. He glared at Oliver like the accident was Oliver's fault.

"No, actually I'm not that smart." Oliver's expression remained innocent. "I don't do well on tests. I'm happy to share some of my Adderall with you. I have it right here in my fanny pack." He reached for his nylon fanny pack to pull it around to the front.

"I can't believe you're wearing a fanny pack," said Chase, chuckling. He didn't seem to be taking the situation seriously as he polished off another taco.

Alex leaned away from Oliver in mock offense. "It's a fashion don't."

The bikers turned their glare to Alex. "*You're* a fashion don't," said Beefy Biker.

"Look who's talking." Alex brushed at the sleeve of his blouse, clearly judging the Beefy Biker's attire.

At this point, Mia had no tolerance for the bullshit that was transpiring, so she stepped closer to the table to cut it off at the pass. "Fanny packs are back in. They actually never went out, kind of like *knife holsters.*" She side-eyed the knife holster on the smaller-giant biker's belt.

Oliver maintained his charming grin as he motioned to the bikers. "I'm kind of a sucker for the nineties, which have made a resurgence. I mean, Backstreet Boys' 'I Want It That Way' was my jam as a toddler—or so say my folks—because I would only eat my food if it was in sections. Nothing could touch." He pointed to his plate: a taco was neatly in one corner, fries lined up in another. "I want it *that* way."

Eve raised her eyebrows at him. "What are you talking about?"

"Yeah, Oliver, what are you talking about?" asked Mia, glancing around. No one seemed to care about these threatening men. *Where was Brandon?*

"I'm saying—" Oliver broke into the song "I Want It That Way" with so much enthusiasm that everyone on the patio stopped to listen. The two bikers were stunned. Mia stared, mouth agape, at Oliver, whose voice was terrible but whose enthusiasm made up for it. When he reached the chorus, Alex harmonized, pulling Oliver up onto the table where they finished the song with finesse. Applause and cheers erupted all around. When the adulation died down, the bikers fortified their stance.

"We're going to kick your ass!" growled Knife Biker.

"Oh, shit," mumbled Oliver, mid-bow.

Mia put her hand on Knife Biker's sleeve. "You don't have to do that." His stare burned into her.

Beefy Biker yelled towards a curvy middle-aged woman relaxing against the high backrest of a fully loaded Harley touring bike. "Mama! Hit my favorite song!"

The woman turned on the bike's stereo, and NSYNC's "Bye Bye Bye" started to blast from the top-rate speakers. Mia's eyes went wide. Not only did the two bikers start singing, they performed

the choreography from the boy band's famous puppet video—
bopping up and down, bouncing their heads, and jutting their
fists out. Knife Biker motioned for Oliver and Alex to join them.
"You're right. I have no sense of style," he said to Alex between
stanzas. The two hip-bumped. In no time, the whole patio was
grooving.

For a moment, Mia forgot about Ruby. She forgot about the
reporter at the Lyndon Wyld store. Her grief over her mom was
farther from the surface. She sang and danced. As she jutted her
fist out in time with the beat, she caught Brandon standing on a
table in the corner, filming. She laughed and shook her head. He
peeked around the camera and laughed as well.

Mia stopped laughing when she saw Ruby and the three men
slip through the jubilant crowd. Without looking back at her,
Ruby was gone.

THIRTEEN

When the seasonaires returned to the house from Stingray's, Brandon blew past them. He unlocked the front door. "This episode is going to kill!"

"I still can't believe you got that all on camera," said Oliver.

"It was amazing! I mean, *I* was amazing!" Alex strutted up the walkway with Eve next to him.

Mia followed Brandon in. "It was *scary*. I should be pissed, but I'm not."

"Because it was fuckin' funny," replied Brandon.

"Don't you have to get consent from those bikers? What about the restaurant?"

"Everyone is going to be stoked. It's eyeballs! Who doesn't want eyeballs?"

Mia wondered if Brandon had caught her talking to Ruby. Those weren't the kind of eyeballs Mia wanted. He disappeared down the hall to his studio.

"I'm going to change and go for a run," said Alex, who strode upstairs. Oliver followed when he got a phone call he "needed to take."

The faint smell of weed tickled Mia's nostrils. She looked around, curious and a little nervous. "Did Lyndon hire a new caretaker?" She followed the scent, with Chase and Eve behind her.

Mia could hear snoring as she walked into the rec room. Boomer the bulldog was sacked out on the carpet. Wyatt and Nils were shirtless, in full manspread on the couch, wearing virtual reality headsets with headphones. A bong sat on the coffee table in front of their bare feet, with an array of snacks from the open cupboards behind the bar.

Mia turned to Chase. "Did you give them your key?"

"They got rid of the fish—proper burial at sea and all. So I thought it'd be cool if they hung out."

"A burial at sea? That's so sweet," said Eve, eyeing Wyatt, who had no idea anyone besides Nils was in the room.

Mia picked up an empty beer from the floor. "Maybe they shouldn't be in the house when we're not here."

"Do you want them to leave?"

Oblivious, the two surfers batted at invisible aliens, balls, asteroids, or whatever they were watching.

"Lyndon is paying *us* to be here, not them," said Mia. "I don't think she'd appreciate it."

"Does he practice *brahmacharya*, too?" asked Eve, still ogling Chase's tanned, ginger-mopped buddy.

Chase broke into laughter. "Wyatt? No."

Eve turned to Mia, looking serious. "Mia, I think Lyndon would promote inclusion—or at least she *should*."

Chase kicked the sole of Wyatt's foot. Wyatt jumped, pulling off the headset. "What the fuck, dude?"

"Yeah, what the fuck?" answered Chase.

Wyatt flopped his arms. Chase mimicked. Nils continued playing, remaining clueless. Wyatt yanked off his goggles. "We're not wanted here."

Chase rubbed his forehead. "Dude, that's not what I said." He glanced at Mia.

Eve shifted a hip and waved at Wyatt. He lifted his chin towards her with a grin. Mia sighed and looked up at the ceiling's wood beams. All the action had riled Boomer, who whined by the glass doors to the outside. "It's just . . . if you could be here when we're here, I think that'd be better," said Mia.

Wyatt ate a chip off the table. "Yeah, no worries."

Boomer squatted by the door and did his business. Mia shook her head, the weed smell now met with the steamer's stench. "And if you're going to be here, you can't let your dog do that."

Nils pointed at Boomer. "Aw, look how sorry he is!" Boomer *did* look sorry.

Mia ascended the stairs as Eve scooched next to Wyatt. Chase grabbed the bong and moved to the vintage Pac-Man machine. "You don't want to kick us out," Nils called up to her. Even in his stoney voice, this sounded like a threat. But everything sounded like a threat to Mia.

Wyatt and Nils slept in the rec room that night and the next and the next. They left with Chase in the early mornings to surf but returned for snacks, alcohol, and video games. The weed they brought themselves, and it overpowered the home's scented candles, which Mia lit.

The following evening, Brandon followed her down to the rec room to retrieve two bottles of Baileys from the cellar. Eve and Wyatt were making out on the couch while Nils and Chase played at adjacent pinball machines. Boomer snored by the glass doors.

He tapped the couch's arm with the Baileys bottle to get Eve's attention. "Come on, we have work."

Chase jammed the buttons on both sides of his machine. Bells clanged and dinged, lights flashing as the ball hit the bumpers and popped out of holes. "I don't know if I'd call a slumber party work."

Nils slammed his hips into his machine, shaking it. "A slumber party? That's so fuckin' cheesy."

Brandon marched up next to him. "I didn't hear anybody ask you. But I did see Mia ask you to leave, and you rudely ignored her." He glanced towards the upper corner of the room. Mia looked in that direction and saw a small camera. Brandon unplugged Nils's pinball machine.

Nils slapped both sides of his faux-hawk. "Are you joking, man?"

"Go home," said Brandon. Mia knew he was posturing for a potential future episode. The idea of the cameras still made her skin prickle with angry heat, but she was glad that Brandon was the one riding the two freeloaders, because she had felt like the buzzkill of the group.

Eve stroked Wyatt's ginger mop. "We'll have a slumber party right here."

Mia wasn't about to show Eve Presley's text message:

Promote sleepwear. I don't care if you have to fuck in it.

Eve might take it literally, and *she* didn't seem to mind the cameras.

Brandon motioned. "Let's go."

Eve kissed Wyatt for a last time while Chase took a final hit off the vape pen that sat on the air hockey table. The four seasonaires went upstairs and put their Lyndon Wyld sleepwear on, along with the others. Mia had emailed Lyndon her sketches, and received the pithy response: *Pass.*

Chase caught her in the hallway. "I know those guys seem like chodes—"

"Squatters, more like it."

"They've done a lot for me. I joke about the one testicle thing, but I'm lucky that's all I lost. I had a surfing accident when I was fifteen. Wyatt pulled me out."

Mia flashed on Ruby pulling her to shore.

"I was in a wheelchair for a year. Didn't think I'd walk again, and they stuck by me," continued Chase. "They pushed me around—made me laugh, and that wasn't an easy thing to do."

"Oh, wow. I'm really glad you're okay," said Mia. From his daring athleticism, she would've never guessed that Chase had been through such an ordeal. She took his arm and they headed downstairs to the living room.

Hearing jazz piano, they entered to find Brandon playing the baby grand. Mia shouldn't have been surprised at his expertise, given his dad's infinite talents, but the easiness with which he moved his hands over the keys contrasted with the cocky edge he'd just displayed. He caught her eye and she crossed her arms over her pajamas, feeling decidedly unsexy, while Brandon wore Lyndon Wyld lounge pants and a white tank. When he finished the tune, the other seasonaires applauded. He humbly nodded.

"That was fire!" said Alex with a whoop. As Mia sat next to him, he whispered, "You should've worn the nightie."

The applause continued. "Alright, alright, don't make fools of yourselves, because you already did that at Stingray's." Brandon's bravado had returned. "You'll see in a few minutes."

They all settled into the couches and chairs. Mia was relieved when she watched the channel's second episode: *Wyld Karaoke*. It featured Lyndon at the store in her best light—Brandon had edited out the reporter's tough questions. The impromptu karaoke battle at Stingray's opened with Mia trying to come to the rescue of Alex, Oliver, Eve, and Chase. She watched the stress in her face until the songfest began. Watching Oliver warble the Backstreet Boys' song, the group broke into hysterics.

Brandon gave Oliver's shoulder a good-natured pat. "Lil pitchy." Oliver laughed.

Alex beamed at the spectacular tabletop performance. Everyone cheered. The episode ended on the seasonaires and the bikers hugging it out.

"So ridiculous," Mia said about the spectacle on-screen. But secretly she was also referring to her paranoia. She didn't want to be caught with Ruby—and she hadn't been.

"Check it out." Brandon pointed to their exponentially growing subscriber number. More cheers. "Presley's stupid fucking slumber party idea is going to be a quick Instagram Live broadcast. I have an idea how to make it interesting." He motioned everyone outside.

They grabbed blankets and moved to the deck, where Brandon set up his camera on a tripod, keeping it running. Oliver brought out a tray of hot chocolate as they sat around the firepit with its flickering lava rock. Alex poured Baileys into the others' mugs. He wore drawstring sleep shorts—slung low—and a pink satin sleep mask that he used as a headband. Mia thought this would make Presley crazy because *she* slept with a pink satin sleep mask and no one this year would know it, since she was behind the scenes.

"We're going to take follower requests for scary stories," said Brandon.

Oliver lifted a flashlight under his chin and talked straight to the Lyndon Wyld Instagram on Brandon's phone. His face was a macabre shade of white-yellow, and he adopted a deep voice that was scarier than Mia thought he could muster. "Ask us anything and get ready for the fright of your life! At this slumber party, someone might never wake up!" He cackled and handed the phone to Mia.

She attempted a ghoulish face. "I go *crazy* for 'Headless Mary'— the one about the girl with the velvet choker. If you untied it, her head fell off."

Alex took the phone and looked into the camera, deadpan. "I think wearing a velvet choker in the first place is where Mary made her fatal mistake." He squinted and read. "Someone has a question for you, Mia: 'What did you do last summer?'"

All eyes turned to Mia. She froze. Seeing dread wash over her face, Brandon grabbed the phone and talked into the camera. "Last summer at this time, I was spinning at a club in Vegas. Afterwards, we were walking on The Strip at about four A.M. A car drove by and some dude leaned out the window and asked me if I was Maz's boy. He was grinning and laughing. I assumed he was just some ass-kissing fanboy. Then the bullet hit me right here." He pulled down his blue hoodie and showed the scar on the top of his shoulder. Mia's brow knit. *What is he doing?* She exchanged a look with Eve, who rolled her eyes. Brandon was swinging the testosterone extra hard. "I jumped on the side of that car. They didn't know I was even there. I climbed around front like it was motherfucking *Mission Impossible* and when I reached the window—surprise! I jammed him right in the neck with a pen. Blood spurted!" He fanned his fingers around his neck. "I jumped off the car and rolled to the side, then went out for a drink." He mimed a mic drop, then clicked off the live Instagram.

"Wow, you are really some tough guy," said Mia, her voice tinged with sarcasm.

"Yea, that's some badass shit," said Eve, equally patronizing.

Brandon chuckled. "Hey, don't mess with me!"

"Oh, I won't." Mia mimicked his tough voice.

Brandon lunged for her, scooping her up. She tried to maintain her irritation despite the comfort she felt with his strong arms around her. "What are you doing? I'm going to kill you!" The words came out of her mouth before she could stop them. She hoped they were cloaked by the seasonaires' laughter and the crashing waves. Brandon dumped her into the pool. Everyone else jumped in. There was splashing and handstands. Eve, Chase, and Alex turned the moonlight swim into a skinny-dip while Brandon filmed.

Mia floated to the pool's edge that spilled over the bluff. In the dark water and looking out at the blue-black ocean, she felt like she was immersed in the sea. She noticed the absence of chlorine smell and burn in her eyes. Instead the air was filled with eucalyptus and sage. Her view was interrupted by the bright white and bronze MazzyLyn trainers, water running up and over them. Mia looked up to see Brandon, without his camera.

"Your new shoes are getting wet," she said.

"I have more."

"I'm sure you do."

Mia looked past him, out at the beach night. "You're blocking my view."

"It won't be the last time."

Oliver yelled towards Brandon. "Are there cameras in the pool?"

"Nah," answered Brandon.

Oliver jumped in and removed his pajama pants. He tossed them at Alex. "Because you're a shower and I'm a grower."

Brandon shook his head. "No one wants to see that." He turned to look at Mia. "I'm not going to air anything that'll make you look bad. But you gotta give me *something*."

Irked by his sense of control, Mia avoided his stare. "You'd better be telling me the truth, because I already don't like you."

Brandon bent down, keeping his focus on her. "Good, because I like you. That *is* the truth."

She did like him, so *she* was the one who was lying. She turned her gaze to the dark emptiness in front of her.

"I paid those bikers," said Brandon.

A lump caught in Mia's throat. She looked at him. "Which bikers?"

Brandon squinted with curiosity. "The singing and dancing ones, that's why they did it. You have to stop stressing. I've got this. Let me do my job."

"We have the same job."

Brandon walked off. Alex swam over to Mia. "No one can *make* you look bad. Believe me, I know, because people have tried." The moonlight made his green eyes emerald—they were steadfast.

Instead of a confessional that night, Eve did an ASMR video in Brandon's studio. She brushed her fingers lightly over the camera lens and cooed into it, "Are you calm? Is your mind at ease? I want to sleep with youuuuu."

In the bedroom, Mia and Alex sat on Mia's bed against her pillows and watched Eve on the laptop.

Mia chuckled. "I can't believe you can control people through a screen. That's so creepy."

Alex was mesmerized by Eve's unintelligible whispering. "It's relaxing."

"Not for Brandon. The lens-touching must be chapping him so hard."

Eve went on doing the bizarre soft lens brushing for a solid two minutes and whispered, "I want you to sleep well and have beautiful dreams." Then she held a MazzyLyn shoe box and tapped on it—first fast then slow, then fast again.

"Well, that should make him *less* chapped," said Alex.

Eve's shoebox-tapping continued for fifteen minutes more.

"I guess my scalp is the teeniest bit tingly, but mostly I'm just annoyed." Mia turned to Alex, who had fallen asleep. She closed her laptop and rested her head against Alex's. She picked up her phone from the nightstand and looked at the Instagram Live that would remain up for twenty-four hours. There was the question, floating up on the screen from someone named *TankSlapper18*:

What did you do last summer, Mia? 🐛

She had the sinking feeling that *TankSlapper18* didn't need an answer.

FOURTEEN

A news notice buzzed in on Mia's phone: a fire had broken out in Brentwood along the 405 Freeway. Chase sat behind the wheel of the Tesla as all the seasonaires buckled in. "We're going to take Sunset to Children's Hospital. The traffic heading east isn't bad this time midmorning. And if the road is open, no one will want to be near that fire, though coming back'll be a bitch."

Brandon clicked his belt in the front passenger seat. "LA is like a jigsaw of separate cities. Whenever I'm here from New York I want to examine every piece."

"I've never been east of La Cienega," said Chase.

Brandon shook his head. "Why would you admit that?"

Chase drove them out of the driveway and onto PCH. "Westsiders don't go east or to the valley unless they have to. My mom was born and raised here. She told me that when her parents used to fight, her dad would go for a drive to cool off. Can you believe that? No one in this city would get in their car now and go for a drive *to cool off.*"

They could see the smoke as they made their way up to Sunset and drove towards Brentwood. Ash dusted the car's windshield like the lightest sprinkling of snow. Mia noticed that no one appeared to care about the fire that was only miles away. Drivers went about all their business while driving—texting, talking, and even FaceTiming.

Oliver snapped the flames that flickered in the hills around the freeway. "Wow."

Mia stared out the window. "I've never been this close to a wildfire before."

"This happens every year at least somewhere here in the Golden State," said Chase with more somberness than usual.

Eve did a Snapchat Story with the fire in the background. She put on the flower crown filter. "Fires used to be Mother Nature's way of regenerating. In California, the oily bark and leaves dropped by eucalyptus trees can start or spread them, but the trees themselves are resilient, like *we* are . . ."

Mia recalled the first time she'd fully breathed in the cool sweetness of eucalyptus as she and Eve had stood by the Malibu sign. Now all she smelled was smoke, because Eve had her window down in order to take better video.

"I thought you didn't filter," said Mia about the flower crown.

"I'm not filtering out flaws." Eve motioned around her face. "I'm just adding color to my Story." She put on the deer filter. "Now there's so much more to these fires . . . and hurricanes . . . and tornadoes. Global warming is real, people."

"When are they going to come out with a muzzle filter, because you need to give it a rest with the tree hugger shit," said Brandon.

Eve huffed and put down her phone.

As they drove towards Hollywood, the landscape changed. On the Sunset Strip, they passed rock-and-roll staples like the Whisky a Go Go and the Rainbow Bar and Grill. Ten-foot-tall guitars commemorating musicians were perched along the boulevard. People chatted and ate on the patios of cafés along Sunset Plaza, oblivious to the fires directly west. "It's midmorning on a Monday. What do all these people do for a living?" asked Mia.

Alex adjusted his gold-rimmed aviator sunglasses. "They don't."

At a stoplight, Oliver pointed to a real estate billboard that advertised a $25 million home. "The address is on there!"

"Anyone can find anyone anytime, anywhere," said Brandon.

"But I heard those maps people sell on the corner take you to fake homes. You think you're looking at Brad Pitt's house and it's just some regular rich person."

Chase told a story about the one time his mom went east of La Cienega. It was to see Red Hot Chili Peppers at some club when everyone used to hitchhike. She went with a group of her high school friends, but one never made it home. "They found her dead in a Bel Air ditch. Her killer was never caught."

Eve shivered. "Cold cases are so creepy."

"There's a bus tour that takes you around to famous death and murder sights," said Chase.

"Let's not do that," replied Mia.

Chase almost hit an electric scooter rider who swerved into the street.

"Hey!" Brandon yelled at the rider. He turned to Chase. "I'd rather drive a gas guzzler, because no one can hear electric cars, especially those e-scooter idiots." Chase veered around a sawed-off tour bus that had all but stopped in the middle of Sunset to point out The Comedy Store. He tapped the horn. "I hate honking."

Mia saw herself in the faces of the tourists—the wonder, excitement, and disappointment at the sites of such a famous city. Some pointed to the small Lyndon Wyld logo on the side of the Tesla. Brandon lowered all the windows so the seasonaires could wave. Photos were snapped. He lobbed MazzyLyn caps to them. "Sun protection! Come by the store next week! Watch us on Wyld World!" The tourists cheered, and Chase sped ahead.

"Poor bastards," said Brandon. "Honestly, who gives a fuck where some comic shot up his last balloon of heroin or where a pop star got a knob job in a bathroom?"

"Maybe it's that celebrities are messed up like the rest of us," replied Mia.

"Maybe." Oliver tapped on the door handle three times.

Brandon pointed to Carneys, an old yellow train car on the side of Sunset Boulevard. "I want a *dog*."

"I could eat," said Chase. He pulled into the lot, past the train crossing sign that touted hot dogs and hamburgers, and parked. The seasonaires got out and walked around to the restaurant's metal steps. A man in stained, ripped army pants and no shirt with dirty bare feet was lying on the ground nearby, eyes closed, motionless. Pedestrians walked up and down the sidewalk. Patrons entered and exited the restaurant. Not one gave him a glance. The desensitization made Mia's stomach turn. There were homeless in South Boston, but in Los Angeles, the juxtaposition of sprawling mansions along the stretch of Sunset through Beverly Hills, the Bentleys and Porsches parked along Sunset Plaza, and this man was unnerving. She stopped at the bottom of the restaurant's stairs.

"Come on. I'm inching towards hangry," said Brandon.

Mia stared at the motionless man. "I wonder if he's okay."

A guy on a scooter whizzed around him and said, "He's fine. Get used to it."

"It's called 'The City of *Angels*,' asshole." Mia glanced at the other seasonaires. "If he hasn't moved when we come back out, I'm going to call nine-one-one."

They entered the train car. While the others ate hot dogs, Mia barely touched hers. She could see the man from the window. He hadn't moved. Eve prattled on about how "homelessness is a chicken or the egg problem. Do we deal with chronic substance abuse and mental illness before creating housing, or do we create housing before dealing with chronic substance abuse and mental illness?"

Oliver put down his food and gazed out at the man.

"Who's 'we'? Are you doing either of those things?" asked Brandon.

"Education and awareness are the first step," answered Eve.

Brandon scoffed and sipped his soda.

When the meal was done and the others headed back to the car, Mia stepped up to the man.

Alex stopped and watched her, concerned. "What are you doing, Mia?"

Mia spoke softly. "Sir, are you okay?" The man didn't move.

Mia approached a police officer who was standing against his squad car at the curb nearby. He had just sent off a perturbed driver with a ticket and the warning, "Put your phone away." The warning would probably be ignored, despite the expense of the ticket and the traffic school time.

"Hi, um, excuse me, officer," said Mia.

The cop finished writing up a report. "Yup?"

Mia pointed to the homeless man. "I'm worried about that man. He hasn't moved since we were inside the restaurant. Is there any way you can check on him?"

The cop looked as perturbed as the ticketed driver he'd sent off, but he obliged. He stepped up to the man and leaned over him. "Are you alive, sir?"

No answer or movement.

"This is the police."

The man opened his eyes. "I'm resting." Now *he* was the perturbed one.

The cop turned to Mia and shrugged. Mia walked back to the car. Brandon had been filming her. She pointed at the camera. "Put that away!"

He chuckled and lowered it. "Education and awareness, right, Eve?"

"Exactly."

Mia slid into the Tesla next to Alex, who put his arm around her. "You interrupted his nap. I would not be having any of that!" He was teasing, his eyes soft and empathetic. Oliver reached over the backseat and gave Mia's shoulder a squeeze.

Chase pulled out of the parking lot. "You did a mitzvah, Mia. A good deed. That's cool." He and Mia exchanged a smile. They drove deeper into Hollywood. A man with a tattooed face rode a unicycle across Fairfax Boulevard. The buildings became less flashy.

"Fairfax—is that where the MazzyLyn store is?" asked Oliver.

"Down a couple miles," answered Brandon. "We'll be back."

Chase slapped the steering wheel. "Another trip east of La Cienega."

In the next few blocks, the windows of retail stores were boarded up. Brandon nodded to the barrage of *For Lease* signs. "Everything's changing around here. Pretty soon, nobody except my dad will be able to set up shop, prices are so high." Mia thought about the gentrification of South Boston and how her hometown was starting to feel less like home.

They pulled into the main entrance of the circular driveway at Children's Hospital Los Angeles. A valet took the car and they entered the sliding doors, moving through security and past the families waiting to see their sick kids. Their expressions revealed either hope or despair, but mostly a combination of both. The opposing smells of antiseptic and stale mustiness was all too familiar to Mia.

Presley waited for them on the fourth floor, holding a canvas tote filled with Lyndon Wyld tees. She gathered the seasonaires. "This is a nice human interest story for the mainstream media, but I warned Lyndon that it's not very sexy, and sexy is what brings

eyes to our channel and social. Try to ramp it up where you can."
She smoothed her vivid green sheath dress. As they dispersed, she
handed Mia a small package of tissues and whispered, "Do not
look into their eyes."

"Are you afraid you'll turn to stone, because that's already happened," said Mia, only half-joking.

The seasonaires split up. Brandon followed Mia and Presley.
Mia felt his eyes on her as if he could feel her discomfort. She
entered a room where a girl, about thirteen, sat in bed, an oxygen
tube in her nose and feeding tube in her arm. She was tiny and
pale, with saucer brown eyes and a charming smile. A long scarf
covered in red roses was tied around her bald head. The knot on
the side sent the fringe falling on the girl's frail shoulders. The
walls were covered with cards and drawings.

Presley motioned Mia towards the girl like she was ushering
a baby duck off into a pond. "Mia, this is Katie. She's a fan of
yours."

"Hi, Katie. I'm honored." Mia sat in the chair next to the bed
and scooted in.

"I want to be a fashion designer like you," said Katie. Her voice
was weak and breathy.

This was the first time Mia had officially been called a "fashion
designer." She almost turned around, as if Katie had been speaking
to someone else.

Mia admired the drawings on the wall, all of which were
signed by Katie. "If you drew these, then I would say you're well
on your way."

Katie nodded and sat up, shoulders straighter.

Mia overheard Presley question the nurse, and her heart
stopped. "What kind of cancer does she have?"

Katie found the strength in her voice. "I had a Wilms' tumor
that spread to my lungs, so I'm kind of a hot mess." Her mouth
curled into a small, wry smile.

Mia forced a smile at her, though she wanted to burst into tears. "You look beautiful to me."

Katie's translucent cheeks blushed with the faintest pink. "Right now, there's no cure yet, but thanks to Lyndon Wyld, my family has been able to get me really good doctors."

Mia glanced at Presley, wondering if she'd put those words in Katie's mouth, because Brandon was filming the whole encounter. She focused on Katie. "Science is amazing. I'm sure there will be a cure before you know it." She didn't know what else to say. There had been no cure for her mom. She reached towards the fringe on Katie's scarf. "I love your scarf. Roses are my favorite flower."

Presley gave Mia a Lyndon Wyld tee to hand to Katie as if Katie's disease were infectious. Mia placed the tee on Katie's lap. Katie touched it. "I wanted the Mia dress."

"I'm sorry, it's taking a while to come out," said Mia.

"That's okay. I don't wear dresses very often. I'm more of a T-shirt fanatic."

Mia kept her hand on the tee. "How about if I make this one special—just for you?"

"That would be awesome."

"Roses?"

Katie nodded with a grin. Mia couldn't believe this young girl's vibrant spirit. The two took a selfie and Katie posted, tagging Mia. When Mia pressed the *Follow* tab on her phone, Katie's eyes sparkled.

"I'll be back with the Katie tee." Mia hugged her, careful of all the tubes and wires, and Katie's tiny, frail body. She flashed on feeling her mother's bony frame when her arms were wrapped around it. Holding back her tears, Mia turned and left the room after one last wave.

She joined the other seasonaires in the playroom where young patients congregated. Alex braided a girl's hair, while Oliver did card tricks for two boys. Brandon picked up a guitar that was near a cluster of instruments and asked for requests. A boy in a wheelchair asked for one of Maz's earlier hits—from when Maz used to perform before he moved on to producing and "world domination," as the boy put it. Without the customary rancor at hearing his dad's triumphs, Brandon played the unplugged version. Mia softened again towards him but chalked it up to her raw emotions after sitting with Katie, and being with these kids who were the kind of heroes she felt she could never be.

The group left. Presley bolted so quickly that Mia thought she saw sparks fly from her kitten heel ankle boots. But while the seasonaires waited for the car, they looked at each other with expressions of shared emotion, gratification, and gratitude.

As they headed back west, Oliver pointed out the Hollywood sign in the hills above. As a reward for their "day of mitzvahs," Chase drove them to Hollywood Boulevard and said, "This is the only time we will be on this street, because it's definitely not the reason to come to Los Angeles." Hordes of tourists meandered, heads down, fingers pointing at Walk of Fame stars. A dirty costumed Spiderman and ripped Elmo solicited photo ops from unassuming families and freaked-out kids.

Oliver tapped on the window three times. "This is kinda depressing."

More tour buses caused traffic jams by stopping in front of Grauman's Chinese Theatre and the Hollywood Wax Museum. Rideshare cars dumped out passengers in front of Ripley's Believe It or Not! without pulling over to the curb.

"I have two words: *Happy Hour*," said Mia.

They turned back down to Sunset and stopped at Chateau Marmont for cocktails. Paparazzi clustered by the bushes in front of the famed hotel, waiting for the celebrities who would emerge from their hideaways. They counted on selling the photos to tabloids that would pay thousands of dollars.

"Junior!" one yelled out as Brandon headed inside. Brandon flipped him off. The clusters of cameras clicked.

"That's friendly of you," said Mia.

"I'm giving them what they wanted." Brandon entered the hotel followed by the other seasonaires.

They sat on the restaurant patio, surrounded by tall, green hedges bursting with red trumpet flowers that matched the woven chairs' red vertical stripes. The umbrellas provided shade and added protection from any lookieloos in the rooms above. Over cocktails, they chatted about the brave kids they had met that day. Mia thought about Katie, and hoped that she would be around when the T-shirt was finished.

Eve sipped the fizzy sunset of an Aperol spritz. "Do you think that Lyndon is making this donation to Children's Hospital for Grant's benefit or for hers?"

"Does it matter?" said Brandon. "It's a win-win." He refrained from drinking, giving Chase a break from driving. He steered them back past the fires that were still burning, though less ferociously. Helicopters flew above, dropping water to tamp them.

The Tesla pulled into the driveway when dusk was casting a silver shine over the Malibu sea. The fire seemed a world away. When the group went down to the rec room, they discovered that Wyatt and Nils were also gone.

Alex put his arm around Chase. "Where are your boys?"

Eve flicked Alex's ass. "Hey, Wyatt is mine."

Chase nodded to Brandon and Mia. "You hurt their feelings."

Brandon rubbed his thumb and forefinger together: "World's smallest violin." He clicked on the TV, which was even bigger than the one in the living room. "Let's watch the sleepover episode. I got some stuff after everyone ended up in the pool."

"Some of us weren't wearing any sleepwear at that point," said Alex with a laugh.

Brandon grabbed the remote. "That's the point."

The seasonaires sprawled on the couches and recliners. They laughed along with themselves as Brandon threw Mia into the pool. Mia could see herself mouth, "I'm gonna kill you," but the words were obscured by M-Kat Records music that Brandon had added. Comments came in:

> You're a goddess, Eve.
> Alex! I'll be your bottom, your top, your everything.
> Oliver, so adorbz.

And then:

> Who's next?

"'Who's next' what?" asked Oliver.

"They probably mean seasonaires," answered Mia, covering her immediate jitters. "Like 'Who will be next summer's seasonaires?'"

"Fuck those guys. We just got here!" said Chase. He took a hit off a vape pen and passed it to Eve.

Brandon shut the laptop and the widescreen TV went black. He pointed to it. "That comment is gold. Like I said, they want to *be us*."

Mia wasn't so sure, especially when she opened her own laptop that night. She had scanned a few designs to email to Lyndon and saw an email from an unfamiliar sender. As she opened it, she reminded herself not to click on any links or attachments for fear of a virus. But the contents felt worse than a virus:

> Fathers & daughters. One is always paying.
> Now it's your turn.

The hair on the back of her neck stood on end.

FIFTEEN

A buzz underneath her rib cage woke her with a start. She had rolled onto her phone in bed during the night. After getting the weird email, she'd sought the comfort of her bedroom and her sleeping roommates. She'd waffled over texting her brother Sean until it had gotten so late that she'd fallen asleep with her phone on her chest—she must've rolled over onto it.

She pulled it from under her and looked. A text from Presley:

Hospital trip was a snoozefest. 😴

Mia tucked her phone under her pillow. Presley's opinion didn't matter right now. Mia was looking forward to working on the Katie tee and forgetting about the weird email. She closed her eyes as Eve and Alex stirred awake, pretending she was sleeping until they left the room. "This goddess needs coffee!" said Eve as the door shut behind them.

Mia thought about the conversation she'd had with Lyndon during their tea in Boston—about how people will come out of the woodwork when someone rises in the world. But she had heeded Lyndon's advice and hadn't shared her payday with anyone . . . except Sean. Mia had texted him a couple of times since she'd arrived eleven days earlier, but he hadn't responded. She chalked it up to the fact that he sucked at texting. His texts usually amounted to one word if he pinged back at all. She tried again:

Have you disowned me?

That morning, her serene walk on the beach was interrupted by thoughts of the email, so she dialed Sean. He picked up, sounding like he was in a hurry. "I just saw your text," he said. "No. I didn't disown you."

"Good, because you're all I have." Mia hesitated a beat. "Have you talked to Dad?"

"Not since he gave us money for the funeral."

That was all Mia needed to hear.

"What's up?" asked Sean.

"Nothing. Everyone is talking about their family here, so ours has been on my mind." The truth was no one had shared much about their families. Brandon's family was famous, so everyone was familiar by all public accounts. But the seasonaires were still basically strangers.

Sean's voice softened. "I'm your family, Mia. I know you're still pissed that I talked to Dad, but it was necessary. Now it's just you and me."

"You're right. So why don't you return my texts?"

"Some other coaches have been scouting late. I've been busy doing my best show horse impression."

"They'll see you're a prize."

"That's what I'm hoping. Are you 'hashtag: living the dream'?"

"I am," said Mia, looking out at the whitecaps. "It's gorgeous here—perfect, really."

"Yeah, I'm sure," Sean snorted. "Okay, I gotta go brush my mane. Make sure it's nice and shiny."

"You do that. Break a leg."

"I'm an athlete, not an actor. I hate that saying." He clicked off.

Mia waited a long beat, then scrolled through her contacts to *Him*. She started to dial, then pressed the FaceTime icon because she wanted to see his expression when she asked him about the email. She'd be able to better ferret out the truth. She jumped slightly at the trill of the ring. After three rings, a man's face filled the screen.

"Mia?" he said. His eyes were almond-shaped like hers. "Is everything okay?" He looked the same as he did fifteen years earlier, the day he left—with a few more lines around those almond-shaped eyes and across his forehead. His hair was still full, cropped close, though now graying at the temples.

"I don't know if everything is okay. Is it?" asked Mia. Her heart was racing.

"When you get a call from your daughter who you haven't heard from in years, that's a little worrisome. The last time I got one from your brother, it was because your mom died."

Mia had to stifle the smidgeon of happiness that she felt over his concern or she wouldn't have the nerve to ask him the question she needed to ask at that moment. "Do you feel like I owe you something?"

"What?" Mia's father's salt-and-pepper eyebrows knit in confusion. "Why would you owe me anything?"

"Maybe for paying for Mom's funeral."

Her dad's eyes softened with sadness. "You didn't ask me to do that. I did it because I wanted to."

"I feel like I owe you."

"You don't owe me anything, Mia. I'm doing really well."

"Sean told me." Mia brushed back her hair, which was blowing in the wind.

Her dad grinned. "You're at the beach, so it looks like you're doing pretty well yourself. Your half-sister—"

Mia swiftly exhaled. "She's not my half—"

Her dad put up his hand—not in protest but surrender. "Okay."

"I've never met her," said Mia.

"The invitation has always stood. But what I was saying was that Kayla told me you're Instafamous? Is that the right word?"

Mia's face flushed with embarrassment. "I'm a fashion designer. I'm working on my own collection." Mia was pissed at herself for correcting him. *Why do I need his approval?*

"I'm proud of you."

That was why.

"Dad, you don't know me. How could you be proud of me?"

"I tried, Mia, but, honestly, your mom didn't make it easy. When we were together, I wasn't doing well financially, and that was stressful." He took a deep breath. "She was disappointed, and I felt like crap for disappointing her. It was a vicious cycle. When I decided to leave for the sake of both our sanities, she was really angry. But she would've been angrier if I had stayed."

Mia's face furrowed in anger. "You don't get to say anything about Mom when she's not around to defend herself."

"I'm sorry. I just wanted to explain my side, since you're giving me the chance."

"This wasn't why I called."

"Whatever the reason is, I'm glad you did." He was smiling. This wasn't the smile of a man who would send an aggressive email to his daughter. It was still the man who wouldn't send an email to his daughter at all.

"I'm going to go, Dad. Be well."

"You, too."

Mia clicked off and put the phone down. When she returned to the house, she was drawn again to her laptop. She looked at the email again and her anxiety quickly spiked, so she deleted it. It was probably just a sick joke. It just wasn't her dad's sick joke.

She entered the kitchen to find Eve and Alex sitting around the island while Oliver made stacks and stacks of pancakes. Eve read on her iPad while Alex poured agave from a clear bottle into his nonfat latte.

Mia grabbed one of the empty red mugs on the counter. "Morning."

Oliver made her a latte—he was becoming the house's barista, topping coffee drinks with foamy hearts, dolphins, and suns. "Thank you." She looked at breakfast. "Wow, that's a lot of pancakes." Hearing clacking and shushing outside the open window, she looked to see Chase doing a handstand flip on his skateboard in the driveway while Wyatt rode past. Nils was in the middle, sitting with his board on his lap, rolling a joint.

Eve drizzled syrup on her pancakes. "I was just saying that I think it's awesome Lyndon implements fair trade practices. What do you think of them?"

"I think it's too early in the day for that kind of discussion," answered Mia, perturbed as she took a sip of the coffee, its heat burning her tongue.

Eve pointed to her iPad. "Why? I'm doing a little reading on the company I'm working for."

Mia eyed the camera above Eve by the hanging pot rack—a perfect angle. "You're doing it in a very convenient location."

Alex moved to lean against the counter. He tilted his head at Eve to ensure he was in frame.

Eve put her hands flat on the island. "I know that Lyndon hires foreign-born workers on visas. I mean, it's common in the fashion industry. A significant portion of manufacturing workers in the US are undocumented. How many of those workers fear being deported, detained, and separated from their children? Lyndon is an immigrant. And because she became so successful in this country, she owes it to every other immigrant to speak out, don't you think?"

Mia burned her tongue again on her coffee. She couldn't handle this conversation after coming up empty-handed about the unnerving email. "I do think this is all important, but I also think you took this job to promote your own agenda and are using our platform for your political benefit."

Eve's eyes went wide in outrage. "*My* political benefit? Do you believe what's gone on in our country is okay?"

Mia blinked hard, bristling at this pointed question. "No, it's *not* okay. But this isn't the time or the place."

Eve stood from the tall stool. "It's *always* the time and place. I was hired to be *me* and *I* don't always talk about fashion and makeup. In fact, I don't even understand makeup."

"I agree that we all should speak our true selves," said Alex. "But I can also help you understand makeup. It's a form of expression, too." At 11:00 A.M., he looked dewy fresh in light foundation and mascara, a Lyndon Wyld baseball hat on backwards, with his jeans and basic white tee.

Frustrated, Eve rubbed her bare face. "We're all here to express ourselves. Just because I know the camera is watching me doesn't mean I'm going to filter what I say or do."

Brandon entered, scrolling on his phone. "I've noticed that you have a lot of new followers, Eve."

Eve lifted her chin. "I do. What difference does it make?"

"About two hundred and fifty thousand more from when you got here."

Oliver handed Brandon a plate piled with pancakes. He grinned at Eve. "Nice job!"

Eve looked at Mia. "You told us to work our social and that's what I'm doing." Her focus shifted to Brandon. "You *told* us you didn't want us talking about stupid shit like acai bowls and pedicures."

"*Exclusively*," said Mia.

Oliver poured more batter into the pan. "So *some* stupid shit is okay? Because I've been posting a lot of stupid shit and *I* don't have two hundred and fifty thousand new followers."

"I was going to talk to you about that," said Brandon, holding up his phone to reveal one of Oliver's recent posts: a selfie in a tide pool, poking the mushy center of a sea anemone. The caption read:

> Is this what it feels like? #40yearoldvirgin #lifegoals
> #humblebrag #BuWyld

Eve put a hand on her hip. "You're here for your own benefit, too, Mia, and I don't disrespect you for it. Everyone knows you want a do-over because last summer was a shitshow."

Mia looked into her mug, tapping its ceramic side.

Eve pointed at her. "I don't see why that's any better or worse than what I'm doing." She pointed at herself. "Do I like the attention? Yeah, I do!"

Alex removed his cap and ran a hand through his hair. "Who here doesn't?"

"But if I can open a couple people's eyes because they overhear me talk about the way the business is run as a reflection of our country, then I'm doing my job—not just as a seasonaire but as a human being."

"Lyndon is a savvy business owner who, as you pointed out, practices fair trade," said Mia. "You can be confident about her sense of ethics." She put her mug on the counter. *How much did she really know about Lyndon's ethics?*

Standing at the island, Brandon cut into the pancakes. "Lyndon is in business with my dad. My mom would have his ass if he practiced anything other than fair trade. She's the reason he does it." He took a bite.

Alex beamed with reverence. "Of course she is."

"But you're right, Eve. I have no right to censor you," said Mia.

Brandon chewed and nodded to Eve. "Instead of biting the hand that feeds you and the face you're using to express your views, why don't we talk to her and see if we can come up with something that'll show we're about a bigger picture."

Eve brightened. "Let's bring people together."

"Hashtag: woke," said Oliver.

Brandon dropped his fork and covered his ears. "That's dead, too."

Oliver shrunk and flipped a pancake.

Alex stood. "I know exactly what's going to bring people together: The LA Pride Parade in West Hollywood."

That evening, they watched the hospital episode. Presley was right. Views were paltry, and subscribers were dropping off. None of the comments that came in were about the young patients. One stood out:

Presley's dress 🔥

Eve sniffed. "She's not even a seasonaire and she's still getting attention."

"She probably wrote that herself," said Mia, though the handle wasn't *hounddogdayz*.

Viewer challenges were interspersed in the comments:

Brandon records the acoustic track of his dad's song.

Brandon shook his head. "Hell will freeze over before I do that."

The episode included an edited version of the kitchen discourse. From the dissatisfied look on Eve's face, she wasn't happy with the amount of her contribution. Then another challenge came in:

Alex dresses everyone for Pride.

Alex beamed, reclining on the living room's chaise. "I will most definitely do that!"

"I'm sure Lyndon will be on board, but let's confirm," said Mia.

She scheduled a group Skype the following morning. Lyndon was in the penthouse office of her Manhattan headquarters, and Presley was lounging at her hotel's rooftop pool, which she called *her* office.

"I'm thrilled we're going to be a presence at Pride!" Lyndon clapped her hands together. Her excitement was genuine. Mia grinned at Alex.

"We're all going to look amazing!" Alex motioned to his Lyndon Wyld sarong, cotton tee, and platform sandals.

Mia touched the hem of Alex's sarong. "I'll do some tailoring."

"You shouldn't have to tailor anything," said Presley. "Lyndon's pieces are flattering on a variety of body types."

Eve pursed her lips. "As long as you're not a size ten," she said dryly.

"Or have broad male shoulders," added Alex. "The floral blouse you liked on me will never fit—let's say—Brandon." He motioned to Brandon, who made his entrance in a royal blue knee-length Lyndon Wyld pleated skirt and black blazer with an M-Kat tank underneath.

Presley's eyes went wide. Lyndon looked shocked at first, but a delighted grin quickly spread across her face. Alex looked at them. His tone was serious and confident. "Other brands have tried to go gender neutral and failed, but they skewed on the side of traditional male clothes. Boyfriend jeans—"

"Which make me look like a sack of flour," said Mia. "But I *do* like a wide-leg trouser." She stood and revealed her ecru linen wide-leg men's cotton trousers. She had them cinched at the waist with a brown leather Lyndon Wyld belt.

"So do I," said Lyndon, looking tickled.

Alex continued, "I've seen 'male' items for your women—basic tees and tanks, sweatshirts, bomber jackets. And don't get me started on Grunge plaid—mostly shown tied around the waist. That's just plain indifferent, no offense."

"None taken," said Lyndon, still smiling.

"Really?" Presley's brow was furrowed.

"My dad wore a kilt at family reunions," said Oliver. "I saw things I never wanted to see, because you're supposed to go commando with those."

Brandon manspread on the couch. "Don't worry. I'm covered."

Presley *tsk*ed. "Aw. An upskirt with you would break the internet."

Brandon revealed his black MazzyLyn briefs. "That'll break it, too."

Alex sat next to him but remained intent. "Gender *fluid* clothing is sexy. It's chic. It's modern. It's relevant."

"Pink and pastels look great on *people*—not all women, not all men," said Mia, touching Oliver's sky-blue chinos and a pale pink polo. "Black, gray, and dark blue—same thing. Why does color need to point to gender?"

"This trend isn't new," said Chase, wearing a green kimono over surf shorts. "It's just lost. Think about the late sixties and early seventies when it was rock-and-roll. Think about David Bowie, Patti Smith, Freddie Mercury."

Mia read from her laptop. "There are studies. People were presented with a list of twenty-five traits and attributes, then asked which ones applied to men, women, or both equally. Most traits overlapped. Gender is just one aspect of who we are."

"I couldn't agree more," said Lyndon, her eyes sparkling.

Eve stood, hands on her hips, wearing a jumper that hugged her curves. "The same should be said for size. I think that the styles can be more forgiving. Honestly, they're not inclusive."

On-screen, Presley fixed her bikini top. "There are the popular kids and the losers. We go after the popular kids. Is that elitist? Absolutely, but everyone wants what they can't have."

Eve motioned to all the seasonaires. "From this conversation, I'd say that our collective goal is to promote inclusivity."

"Oh, for Pete's sake, not everyone has a goal!" Presley's voice raised in irritation. "Look at Chase."

Chase sat cross-legged on the ottoman. "You're right. I don't really know what I'm going to do with my life, but why do I have to figure it out? I'm lucky enough to get ski in the winter and surf in the summer." He gestured out the window—the beach view was magnificent. "We're all going to end up like Sisyphus—pushing a boulder up a hill just to have it roll back down. I'm putting that off as long as possible."

Presley sighed with ennui. "You live with Mommy and her platinum card. You've never had to push a boulder in your life."

"I appreciate that we're talking about goals, but one person's goals matter the most here, and those are mine," said Lyndon. "Eve, part of the reason I chose you is that, among your many admirable causes, you volunteered at a women's shelter. You speak for women." Eve's hunched shoulders released. Lyndon continued, "Now, I'm *paying* you to promote my brand and speak for me. If you can squeeze your views in with that mandate, be my guest. But if you ever pull that shit again on camera—putting my business up for amateur scrutiny—I will not only fire you, I will sue your bodacious bottom. Your parents on their honorable professorial wages will never recover."

Eve's shoulders hunched again. "I don't understand. Everyone here has an agenda, including Mia. I mean, isn't that why you hired *her*?"

Brandon answered. "She's a talented fashion designer." Mia's brows lifted in surprise. Brandon kept his focus on Eve. "This is a clothing brand and she gets to show her stellar work to the world because the world will be *buying* it. So, '*honestly*,' it's about capitalism."

Alex stood. "My goal is business oriented, too, because a modeling career is the ultimate for me. I don't want to do strictly male shows or female shows. I want to walk all runways." He strutted across the room and back. Lyndon applauded.

Oliver watched in awe. "I just want to be able to walk across the room in those shoes."

On-screen, Presley waved a dismissive hand. "Those turns are too sharp."

Alex looked at Presley. "I'm doing high fashion, not beauty pageants."

"Both commendable and deplorable in their own rights," said Lyndon with a smirk. "Now less chatting and more working." She clicked off.

"Mia, we have *our* work cut out for us," said Alex. "But we will crush it!"

Mia grinned and vogued, breaking any tension in the room. Everyone laughed, except Presley.

"You have ten days. You'd better pull this off." Presley exited Skype, and the TV screen went black.

SIXTEEN

Mia spent all her time in her workspace—nipping, tucking, hemming, and letting out pieces for the seasonaires. She made alterations to the back of a purple Lyndon Wyld column dress. Alex supervised this collection with a precise eye—so precise, it was exhausting Mia. "Don't get me wrong—I love camp, but we need couture," he said, leaning over her.

"It's a parade, not a runway show."

Alex straightened the pieces on their hangers. "To me, it's the same thing."

Mia put down the purple fabric and rubbed her eyes. "My eyeballs are going to fall out, Alex. I need to get some sleep or I'm not going to be able to walk a parade or a runway show."

"Then tape those eyeballs in!"

Mia leaned back in her chair. "Why are you riding me so hard?"

"Because we need to shine."

"We'll shine!" replied Mia, annoyed. She jerked her hair into a low, messy bun.

Alex put his hands flat on the worktable. "Do you know what it's like to be judged for your entire life? I don't just mean now, while we're posting and vlogging. I mean your *entire life*."

"No," said Mia softly. Her life had been hard growing up, but her struggles were different. Until she started posting and vlogging, she hadn't really given a shit what people thought because she'd assumed they weren't thinking about her at all.

Alex looked at himself in the mirrored wall. "I never let judgment change who I am. It makes me want to be *more* of who I am."

Mia reached for a wicker bin full of faux feathers and pulled out a handful that looked like a peacock's, remembering Presley's off-handed suggestion on the first day in Malibu. She pointed to the bodice of the purple dress and smiled.

On the day of the parade, they all got ready in Mia's workspace. Their excitement was stoked by a free flow of Chase's "eyes closed" margaritas. Presley was there to ensure everyone wore at least one Lyndon Wyld piece. She watched Alex, sipping a virgin margarita, apply makeup on each seasonaire. As he dusted light glitter on Chase's chest and brow bones, he said, "Your skin is flawless. What's your secret?"

"I don't wash my face," replied Chase.

Alex squinted in disbelief. "Shut the fuck up."

Chase shrugged. The guys were more cooperative than Eve, who only allowed Alex to give her a blush glow and some clear gloss.

"Lip liner would make them look more voluptuous," said Presley, who took the opportunity to re-apply her own lipstick in the mirrored wall. "You're all about voluptuousness, Eve."

"I don't need blowjob lips."

"I'm sure that surfer who's been squatting downstairs would beg to differ." Presley put her lipstick back in her Lyndon Wyld satchel and stepped up to Mia. She leaned in and whispered, "What a motley crew you've got here."

"They're growing on me," said Mia. "And I think I'm growing on them."

"Like mold on attic clothes." Presley eyed Mia's ensemble: the trousers with suspenders over a white ribbed tank top.

Mia grinned at the group—the clothes fit to perfection. "We all look fabulous, if I do say so myself."

"Bam!" Alex slicked his hair back and expertly affixed a lustrous booty-length ponytail. He looked stunning in the purple column dress. "Let's go strut." They all strode out of the room past Presley. Mia was last.

They loaded into the Tesla, which was wrapped in Lyndon Wyld logos—not green and beige but rainbow for the occasion. As Brandon got in the front passenger's seat with his camera, he looked at Presley. "You sure you don't want to come? There's a seat for you in the back."

Presley sashayed to the Volvo. "I drive or ride shotgun. And I've done my last parade. I was queen of the International Cherry Blossom Festival in Macon. Can't top that." She got in her car and lowered the window. "I've already made sure that every major media outlet is at your finish line. I promised them that Brandon is going commando." She smirked and drove off. Brandon let out a perturbed grunt and bumped his fist on the Tesla's window sill.

With Chase at the wheel, the seasonaires made their way to West Hollywood. Countless street closures and traffic jams frustrated Chase at every turn. "'The strongest of all warriors are these two—time and patience.' I'd rather read *War and Peace* again than sit in this clusterfuck."

"Spoken like a true Angeleno, except that you're the only one in this city who's read that book," said Brandon with a chuckle.

They took their place in the parade line with other cars and bright, fantastic floats just ten minutes before the start. When Mia heard the roar of motorcycles over the floats' dance music, her heart jumped. She turned, relieved to see a pack of women cheering on bikes.

Santa Monica Boulevard was packed with people dressed to the nines and undressed to almost nothing. There were older couples, and families with children who held mini Pride flags in their strollers. Dogs were adorned with rainbow collars. There were fishnet shirts and high school football jerseys, camo joggers and leather pants, sequins and sailor hats, tutus, flower crowns, paper leis, feather boas, and lots of Mardi Gras beads. Banners and balloons burst from stores, bars, and restaurants that were filled to the rafters with revelers.

Eve, Chase, and Oliver accepted free hugs from a head-to-toe rainbow-painted man.

Mia grinned as the group started walking. "This is the best parade I've ever been to!" She wiped the sweat from her brow but didn't mind the steamy sun and crush of revelers one bit.

"How does it compare to Boston's St. Patrick's Day Parade?" asked Alex, who never seemed to perspire and always smelled like vanilla musk.

"It doesn't," replied Mia. "This is way more fun, and so far, not as many drunk, belligerent, middle-aged guys starting fights."

"Oh, there will be fights."

The dueling signs were the first indication:

LOVE ALWAYS WINS
BEING GAY ISN'T A CHOICE
TRANS RIGHTS ARE HUMAN RIGHTS

Versus:

Turn Or Burn
Homosexuality Is A Sin
God Did Not Make You Gay

Mia's upset over the offensively intolerant signs was tamped by by the sight of a fire truck blasting Lady Gaga tracks for the bare-chested male dancers in fireman overalls. When the parade began, Chase continued driving while Brandon, wearing a plaid pleated skirt and MazzyLyn high-tops, sat on the roof with his camera.

Oliver, in a white tank, sheer Lyndon Wyld blouse, and white "shants"—as Presley would call them—was joined on either side by two beautiful, tall goddesses in silver flapper minidresses. They linked arms with him and strutted down the street, taking in all the cat calls and cheers.

Eve sashayed in a long men's blazer, unbuttoned to reveal a a lace bra, accessorized with fishnets, and platform boots.

A young man, his body wrapped in black belts, wearing leather bunny ears and combat boots, draped the Pride flag he waved around Mia's shoulders. Mia grinned. He dropped away with his flag to kiss a friend.

Alex ran up to a handsome man in his thirties wearing jeans, fitted tee, and a baseball cap that said *We Are All Equal.* They wrapped their arms around each other in a joyful embrace, then kissed. They parted. Alex turned to the seasonaires and gestured to the man.

"This is my husband, Luis."

"Hi, Luis," said Mia with a smile. The other seasonaires waved.

"I feel like I know all of you," said Luis. "Alex has told me so much, but I've also seen your channel. It's very cool." He offered a peace sign to Brandon, who filmed while perched on the Tesla behind them. Brandon returned the gesture.

"How do you like sharing Alex with five other people?" asked Oliver.

"It's not the first time." Luis kissed Alex.

Alex wrapped his arms around him. "I'm all yours, baby."

Eve ran a finger across the peacock feathers on Alex's dress. "I'm jealous, because *I* want Alex."

"Everyone wants Alex," said Luis with a chuckle.

"Ain't that the truth." Alex threw his head back with a throaty laugh, long ponytail swinging.

"I have to go back to the SoCal LGBTQ Center booth," said Luis. "I love what Lyndon Wyld is doing." He pointed at Mia. "I want those trousers."

"That can be arranged," said Mia.

Luis kissed Alex again. "I miss you." He walked off.

Alex gazed after Luis, who disappeared into the crowd on the sidewalk. "He snuck down here from Austin for Pride to see me, and decided to volunteer. He's the best person I know."

"Three months is a long time apart," said Mia.

"My boss at the construction company where we both work wasn't as understanding. But Luis supports my dreams. I support his. And we're all supporting this!" Alex motioned to the festivities.

They were interrupted by a heavy-set woman who yelled into a megaphone, "If you shut out the voice of God, you're an abomination! Repent! Seek the Lord and call upon Him or you will spend eternity in the Lake of Fire!"

"That sounds hot," purred Eve. Alex laughed.

Mia bristled at the wall of protestors, though parade revelers were undaunted. The rainbow-painted man gave Megaphone Woman an unsolicited free hug. She shoved him away. The man didn't shrink, instead blowing a kiss. "I love you. Don't hate us," he said.

"If I hated you, I wouldn't be here warning you." Megaphone Woman's voice was dire. "This is a warning from someone who cares about you."

"You have a very skewed definition of 'caring,'" replied Mia, brow knit.

"You don't have to be a murderer to go to hell, ladies and gentlemen," shouted a lanky, bald man in a *Homosexuality is an Abomination!* T-shirt. Next to him was a girl in a unicorn costume holding a sign that read *Never Misses a Gay Event* with an arrow pointing to the man.

"Time is running out! Judgment Day is approaching!" roared Megaphone Lady.

"Let me put it in my calendar," said Eve, who lifted her phone and pretended to type.

"You're out here to celebrate Pride, isn't that true?" asked Lanky Bald Man. "God is a foe to those who are proud of their sin. Turn away from that wickedness! People have this idea that God loves everybody, but that's a lie! You have lived your life as a criminal, breaking His law." He motioned to Oliver's sheer blouse. "Do you realize that?"

Oliver reached up and "pulled" a quarter from the man's ear. "Here's a quarter. Call someone who'll listen." The man swatted away the coin.

"Did your dad not love you enough?" Eve asked the man. He ignored her, but Mia noticed Oliver turn his watch around his wrist two times.

Two women walked by with their arms around each other. "God said lesbians are sinners!" Megaphone Lady yelled at them in her loudest voice.

"Did you actually *read* the Bible, ma'am?" asked Chase from the open window of the Tesla.

The crowd around the protestors started to chant: "Go home! Go home! Go home!" Mia was the first to join in. The rest of the seasonaires became part of that collective voice as Brandon filmed, chanting at the protestors as well. Two cops nearby in Day-Glo yellow vests stood with their arms crossed, watching while impassively chatting.

The protestors were not impassive. They were scornful and disgusted.

Mia glared at them. "I'd really like to check a bitch right now."

As the seasonaires and the rest of the Pride supporters continued their fervent chants of "Go home," Mia felt like she was shouting into a sign-carrying, megaphone-shouting void that would never return their views.

Alex caressed her arm and nodded towards the protestors. "*They* don't belong here."

The seasonaires all moved on. Mia's eyes filled with tears. "I don't understand. What difference does it make who you love as long as you love?"

Alex held her hand. "Think about it this way: you're brought up by parents who close you away from life. They tell you that this type of person is the devil—anyone who is different than you. You're not allowed to see a broader spectrum of life, and you're punished if you even entertain the idea of something other than the lessons you're taught. That's how terrorists are raised."

Eve glanced back at the strident protestors. "Some of them are ignorant, yes, but most are just plain horrible," she said with a scowl.

"How do you break the chain?" asked Mia.

"My dad beat me when I was little," said Oliver, causing Mia, Alex, and Eve to turn to him. "You either succumb to the fate of becoming who they are, or you decide to go the opposite direction. I would do anything to avoid being my dad."

"I'm sorry that happened to you," said Mia, thinking about her own father, who abandoned but never hit. She thought about the email. *Who sent it?* She brushed away a lock of hair, trying to brush away the image.

She took Oliver's hand and the four strode, linked, to the end of the parade. Presley had summoned an impressive cadre of media. Journalists, reporters, and camera operators gathered around the Tesla, ready for a sound bite. Brandon stepped up to Mia and whispered, "As Eve says, be inclusive. That means mention MazzyLyn, too."

"Really, Brandon?" snapped Mia, annoyed at his constant need to promote.

Alex leaned in to Mia. "Watch what you say, girl. One slip of the lip and you will be eaten alive."

"I'm not saying anything." Mia brushed confetti off Alex's shoulder. "This is *your* runway."

A reporter called out to the group. "The Lyndon Wyld camp looks incredible this year!"

"Natch." Alex did a slow, elegant full turn so the cameraman could capture every flourish.

"What's on trend right now?" asked the reporter.

"Anything and everything," answered Alex.

Mia noticed Brandon drop his head in disapproval.

Alex stayed focused on the reporter. "Whether it's a dress or a skirt or a pair of men's sports shorts, you should wear it. What you put on doesn't define your gender or your sexuality. It defines your *individuality*." He motioned to Eve, who beamed.

"But it helps if it's Lyndon Wyld or MazzyLyn," said Brandon, doing his own charismatic version of Alex's turn from atop the Tesla's roof. The crowd of revelers cheered. Mia furrowed her brow, pissed that Brandon was stealing Alex's spotlight.

"What are you wearing under that amazing kilt, Brandon?" asked another reporter. As Brandon's face furrowed, Mia couldn't restrain a chuckle.

On the way home, Mia and Alex leaned on each other in the back of the Tesla.

"That was so cool," said Chase, driving. "I've never been before. Traffic was totally worth it."

Alex leaned his head back. "Being here means everything to me—at Pride . . . in Los Angeles . . . as a *seasonaire*. I had no doubt it would help me make a name for myself in the fashion industry and live my best life with my love."

"You whipped my ass getting here, but you totally inspire me," said Mia.

"Right back at ya," replied Alex.

Brandon looked up from his phone with a grin. "You're inspiring a lot of other people, Alex, because *you*, my friend, are trending."

Alex put an arm around Mia and whispered, "Peacock feathers." He ran his hands through the feathers on the purple dress and looked at Mia with admiration. The two nuzzled close. He snapped a selfie and captioned, tagging all the seasonaires:

PRIDE forever. #LoveWyld

Mia reposted, then let the steady stretch of PCH and Alex's breathing lull her to sleep.

That night Mia watched Alex film his confessional. He talked about how his parents always told him he could do anything, then capped it off by encouraging viewers to think for themselves. "Say this every, single day: 'Your opinion of me is none of my business.'"

Mia smiled but knew some opinions that *were* her business. She cared about the harm she had done.

"You want to get yours in the can?" Brandon asked her.

"No, thanks." Mia wasn't ready for her confessional.

SEVENTEEN

M ia was learning to navigate her den mother role with more joie de vivre, as Vincent, their photographer in Nantucket, would have put it. She enjoyed days on the beach, evenings grilling on the deck, and even a sushi dinner at Nobu—she stuck with the tempura. Presley set up a private tour of the Getty Villa, where the seasonaires spent less time viewing the art and sculptures and more time taking photos of each other around the Roman architecture and verdant gardens. The Malibu store was consistently busy, with clothes displayed in a more gender-fluid fashion. Lyndon was pleased, and Mia was working on new designs.

She felt closer to the rest of the seasonaires after Pride. Maybe it was the weeks that had passed since their arrival, and the familiarity of living in the same house. Maybe it was the sense of connection she felt coming together for the same cause. Maybe it was a combination of both, but she felt herself relaxing into

Malibu in the way she imagined Malibu was supposed to relax people. It didn't hurt that the weird texts, emails, and social comments had stopped.

The day of the #BuWyld Beach Bash, Mia spent the afternoon embroidering delicate roses on a sample of the Katie tee. She was sure that Katie would love it and that they would sell fast in stores and online. She emailed Lyndon that she wanted to keep the Children's Hospital LA campaign alive by donating the proceeds from the tees. They would cost more than the line's other tees to make, given that they had to be stitched by hand instead of machine, but the price tag could be higher for the same reason. Lyndon signed off on the idea, giving Mia more confidence about the business aspect of the summer. She was making career headway instead of just posting and preening for the camera. As the sun set outside her workspace, Mia could see that the beach was decorated like a scene straight out of '60s Woodstock.

Brandon knocked on the open door. "If I can take a break, so can you." He was dressed in distressed jeans and a loose-fitting light blue linen shirt, open to reveal his rope medallion and two prayer bead necklaces—no shoes and a toe ring.

"I need to change," said Mia. "I'm not 'groovy' enough for this party right now." She motioned to her white tee and relaxed cotton joggers.

She walked across the hall to her bedroom and put on the wrap dress she had made her mother. She took a daisy from the vase on the dresser, broke the stem, and slipped the yellow flower behind her right ear. As she headed out of the room, she realized that she hadn't closed the door completely. Butterflies flitted in her stomach. But when she walked into the hall, Brandon was standing several respectful feet away, leaning against the wall, staring at his crossed feet.

Mia motioned to him. "Let's go." Brandon pushed himself off the wall and followed her.

They made their way down the steps to the beach, where the '60s flower children scene was more current up close because of the deejay with his laptops and mixers, power generators, and the party's co-sponsors with their signage and swag.

The seasonaires and guests drank elderberry wine from a Malibu winery that prided itself on the fact it was *not* from the usual Northern California wine country. Two blonde girls with beach-wavy extensions—the winery's brand ambassadors—manned the table. They reminded guests that "millennials are drinking more wine than any generation" as a push to sign up for the "Counter (Wine) Culture Club." Membership meant a new bottle of the sweet nectar every month. On a wide woven beach mat, two goats with rainbow ribbon wrapped around their horns walked on the backs of partygoers.

Mia chuckled at the sight. "There are no dogs allowed on this beach, but I guess goats are okay?"

"You can't have a party in LA without party goats," said Brandon.

A colorful spread of hummus, pita, olives, and grapes was arranged on a long wood table sprinkled with daisies and wildflowers.

"This makes me imagine a time when peace and love were actually a thing," said Eve as she fed red grapes to Wyatt. The two were entwined on a jumbo corduroy beanbag chair underneath a tie-dye overhang wound with vines. Nils and Chase passed a joint, smoked from a hookah, and drank straight from a wine bottle. Boomer, with his pushed-in bulldog snout, snored on a small heart-shaped pillow nearby.

A voluptuous girl, braless in a tank top, bounced by towards a friend. Nils winced. "With those saggy puppies, that is *not* a good look."

Eve removed her own shirt. "Free the nipple!" Wyatt cupped a full, round breast.

Mia glared at Nils, who, with Wyatt, had all but moved into the house. She wanted to like them for Chase's sake, but she didn't. "You know that natural boobs are bags of fat, right?" she said to Nils. "And there's this concept called gravity, so if you take away the bondage device"—she motioned to her chest, strapped in a bra beneath her dress—"gravity pulls them towards earth. Your dick flops around and it's pulled earthward. It's not at a salute all the time."

Nils grabbed his crotch. "Speak for yourself."

Brandon looked at him, deadpan. "She doesn't have a dick."

Mia knelt to pet Boomer so her face was next to Chase's. "Honestly, your friend really doubled down in the douche department." She walked off with Brandon through rows of electric candles that created shimmering, winding paths around patchwork blankets. They approached Alex and Oliver, who sat in a big circle with a group of guests, all dressed boho-chic for the occasion. At the tip of the circle was a thin guy with patrician features shrouded in a bushy beard and mustache. He strummed an old, scratched acoustic guitar covered with worn and torn stickers: a peace sign, a rune symbol of some sort, and the M-Kat Records logo.

Mia stared in disbelief. "Is that—?"

"Seamus Galloway," said Brandon, his voice thick with disapproval. "My dad's into this whole unplugged revival. It puts me to fucking sleep." He strode off. Mia stood alone, listening to Seamus's music, which was, at best, mundane.

Presley slipped behind her. "That hair took two hours and more product than you own." Watching Seamus, her arms were crossed in a paisley shift dress, accessorized by Lucite earrings and a modified bouffant. Mia noted Seamus's stringy, shoulder-length hair as he finished the song to applause and whistles. When it quieted, Presley, in her flirtiest Georgia peach twang, called out, "Those bracelets are positively divine."

In his charming Scottish accent, Seamus revealed that they were handmade by the jeweler wife of one of his "good mates," who was also one of the world's biggest action stars. "Soon 'nough, you'll all be able to wear 'em, too." Excited murmurs bubbled through the crowd.

Presley leaned into Mia. "Those bracelets are Lyndon's next frontier: a line of jewelry with celebrity artisans." She eye-fucked Seamus. "I *would* like to put those beads somewhere. But I should keep it professional, even though he sang me his newest song yesterday at the office . . . with a giant boner."

"I'm glad you're taking your job as publicist seriously," said Mia, knowing that *should*s didn't apply to Presley, whose patchouli perfume was a departure from her signature jasmine–orange blossom scent. They watched Oliver pull a quarter from a pixie girl's ear while Seamus took a selfie break. "I had a date with a guy who did a magic trick for me once," said Mia. "I bailed after ten minutes. The same would hold true for a serenade. That's beyond cheesy."

Presley frowned at Mia. "Where's your sense of romance, sugar?"

"Says the woman who wants to do bad things with those beads." Mia lifted an eyebrow at Seamus's bracelets.

She and Presley moved in closer to Oliver and Alex, who wore Lyndon Wyld flare jeans and a purple silk blouse knotted at his chiseled waist. Presley sat with her bare legs tucked beneath her and gave Alex's thigh a squeeze. "Honey, your ass looks *delicious* in that denim! I spotted it from the steps."

"That's the goal," replied Alex, playing with one of his oversized silver hoop earrings.

Mia sat and smiled at him. "You do look gorgeous."

Alex kissed Mia on the cheek. "You're sweet." He shifted to Presley. "You, not so much."

Presley grinned and shrugged. "Overrated."

Oliver scanned the scene. "The last time I went to a party, a girl from my dorm was in that outfit—" He pointed to the girl taking a selfie with Seamus. She wore a tiny tube top and even tinier shorts. "It was fifteen degree weather and she passed out on the porch. No one found her 'til morning."

"She froze to death?" asked Alex, mouth agape.

Oliver nodded with a grimace. "I don't want to think about it."

"Then don't," said Pixie Girl, who held out a baggie filled with pastel pink and blue pills embossed with smiley faces. Oliver hesitated. He twisted his watch around his wrist twice, then plucked out one pill. They toasted with their wine and swallowed. The girl offered the baggie up to Mia, who passed, lifting her wine towards the girl. "I'm good."

Presley nudged her. "Live a little, Mia. I'd partake if I didn't have to oversee this *amazing* soiree I planned."

"It's pretty amazing," replied Mia with a smile. No expense had been spared, including the fake bonfire prop because fires weren't permitted on Malibu's beaches.

Female screams filled the air as Seamus started another acoustic tune. Then he played another. They all sounded the same to Mia, like the repetition of the waves she watched. She caught sight of a man walking along the shore. He was a shadow in the darkness, but the moonlight caught the silver streaks in his thick hair, and bounced off of sunglasses that had no place at night. A chill ran up Mia's spine. *Otto Hahn.* Repelled, she tried to focus on Seamus's innocuous melodies, but she was compelled to check the shore again. Otto—or the shadow—was gone. She finished her wine and took another cup from one of the blonde girls who walked by with a tray.

"Don't forget to—"

"Sign up online. I got it." Mia pasted on a closed-mouth smile. She downed the second glass—sweetness bathing her mouth, warmth filling her body in the cool night. She snuggled into her buzz, reminding herself to feel grateful that she wasn't in Southie, where she had spent many muggy summers feeling stifled. And this *wasn't* Nantucket.

Presley's holler cut through Mia's buzz. "Rumor has it that Brandon, aka Monarch, is guest spinnin', y'all!" The fans around Seamus dispersed quicker than Whole Foods hipsters after the last avocado had been grabbed.

Presley showed Mia her phone. The last comment on the Wyld World channel was the challenge:

Private Seamus concert for Mia.

Presley leaned in to Mia's ear and whispered, "I texted him to play this song for you." She winked, then turned to Alex and held out her hand. "C'mon, Alex, time to make another round with that ass."

Alex, Oliver, and Presley walked off, leaving Mia sitting alone with Seamus. She sighed and rolled her eyes up at the moon. It was full.

"Can't be that bad," said Seamus with a wry smile.

Mia looked at him, pulling her knees into her chest. "I like your music."

"I call bullshit."

"Okay, I wouldn't have known a song of yours before tonight."

Seamus released a guffaw. "An honest girl! Come sit closer, truth-teller. Don't embarrass me by making me sing to you from so far away."

"I wouldn't want to do that." As Mia moved next to him, she noticed that his eyes were the most golden-green shade of hazel, like a cat's. He started to strum his guitar. Mia cringed on the inside. "You don't have to play for just me," she said.

"I've played for less, many times."

Seamus played a new original song for her that "he hadn't played for anyone else before." Even though she thought the lyrics about love, trust, and "soul resurrection" were cloying, she didn't have the heart to get up and walk away. She let his silky-airy voice wash over her like the tide smoothing jagged rocks over time. When he finished, he stared at her, not so much expectantly but hopefully, like a little boy wanting praise from his mama.

"That was nice," said Mia.

His face crinkled in a grimace. "*'Nice.'*"

Mia patted his leg twice, the rip in his jeans forcing her skin on his. She pulled her hand towards her lap, but he held it and leaned in to kiss her. She allowed it for a beat—their mouths meeting—then broke away, sitting back and straight.

"I'm sorry," said Seamus, though his eyes said he was butt-hurt.

"I'm not gonna do this." Mia motioned between them.

House music began to blast through the sound wall of waves. Partiers across the beach were dancing—a pulsing mass of bodies. Brandon was in his element, spinning.

Seamus abandoned his guitar, brushing his hands off. "I'm being overshadowed."

"Don't feel badly. I don't listen to his music either," replied Mia, getting up and walking towards the group. "Thanks for the serenade." Seamus chuckled and nodded. There were clearly no hard feelings.

Mia approached the rest of the guests in their gyrating and jumping frenzy. She grinned at the sight of Oliver and Pixie Girl making out. Suddenly, female shrieks cut through the music. Everyone turned to see three squealing girls running up from the tide. After having spotted who she'd thought was Otto, Mia was relieved to hear their shrieks turn to giggles. Around their feet were hundreds of silvery-white oblong fish jumping and flopping on the wet sand and in the foamy tide when it came in. Presley and the other seasonaires joined Mia to watch.

"The grunion are running," explained Chase. "The lady grunions dig their tails in the sand to lay their eggs, then the dude grunions wrap around them to deposit their loads."

Alex put his hands over his face. "That's disgusting."

164

"Agreed," said Presley, turning to stride up the beach.

Eve beamed. "It's life-affirming!"

"I don't do orgies," Presley called back, continuing away through the crowd of guests squealing, jumping, laughing, and snapping photos.

"You have to appreciate their tenacity," said Mia, who watched the wet, sandy moshpit of fish. She scanned the shoreline and surrounding rocks to see if Otto or his ghost was spying on the mating ritual. It would be just the type of thing that would entertain him in his creepy way. Neither was there.

EIGHTEEN

The party broke up around 2:30 in the morning—about an hour after the caterers had left and all the swag was gone. Chase and his two buddies were so high that they had sacked out in the sand with Boomer still curled on the heart pillow. Mia, Alex, Oliver, and Eve were back at the house, sprawled in the living room. They were all too bushed to go upstairs, while Brandon had enough energy to close himself in his studio to edit.

Alex offered Mia, who was sandwiched between him and Eve on the couch, a cheeky smirk. "I'm surprised you're back here with us."

In the nearby armchair, Eve sucked on a lollipop. "Yeah. I thought you'd be with that hot Scottish piece of haggis."

Oliver was lying on the floor but jumped up, still wasted. "A haggis comes whole, not in pieces, and it's not 'hot'—it's gross. Sheep guts."

"You know what I meant," said Eve, poking the back of Mia's bent knee with her toe. "Yet you passed up a chance to hook up with him."

"Yup." Mia closed her eyes, annoyed by this line of inquiry. She could still feel Seamus's lips on hers, his tongue darting in her mouth like a lizard's. The kiss was more soulless than his serenade song, which she highly doubted he wrote himself. She hoped no one had seen the kiss, so she wasn't going to bring it up.

Oliver pretended to juggle. "Who wants eggs?"

Eve crinkled her nose. "That sounds revolting right now."

Alex stuck his tongue out. "Yeah, kinda does."

"I'll prove you both wrong." Oliver whipped into the kitchen like a cartoon character scramming out of frame—elbows out, smoke coming off his heels.

"Wyatt and I got each other off under the blankets," said Eve. "I'm not ready to fuck him. He's a little relentless."

"That's a nice word for him," said Mia with a sniff.

With the double-paned sliders closed, the living room was oddly silent. The ocean was so dark outside, it was as if it had disappeared and the house was suspended in space.

Mia sighed. "I'm so tired."

Alex echoed her sigh. "But in a good way."

It dawned on Mia that she had let herself have a good time, despite the ridiculous rock star who was a shockingly bad kisser. The corners of her mouth curled up. "Yeah, in a good way."

The three started drifting off to sleep against each other as the smell of grilled peppers and onions filled the air from Oliver's cooking. Mia rested her head against Alex's smooth chest, while Eve's soft thighs rested across Mia's.

A roar of motors broke through the silence. The thunder of tires on gravel got closer by the second until it overwhelmed their ears. They opened their eyes.

Eve's brow furrowed. "What's that?"

"It's baby kittens," said Alex with an exaggerated eyeroll.

Mia's heart beat faster as she recognized the sound. Adrenaline pumped any remaining party buzz from her body.

The motors cut and the silence returned. Mia was afraid the others could hear her loud, hard heartbeat. After seconds that seemed like hours, there was a rap on the front door. Alex rose, lightly kicking his platform sandals to the side.

"It's late. You don't have to answer it," said Mia.

Alex looked at her with concern. "Right. Maybe there was a motorcycle accident, or someone got a flat." He checked the peephole and spoke through the door. "Can I help you?"

"I hope so," said a gruff male voice.

"Don't answer it," said Mia.

Eve elbowed Mia. "Are you saying that because they're bikers? Isn't that making a snap judgment about people on the basis of how they look? Did you not learn anything from our karaoke lunch?"

Alex opened the door before Mia could answer. There stood the three men who were with Ruby at Stingray's. The older man with the shock of thick silver hair and beard crossed the threshold, his barrel chest forcing Alex to step back. "We've got a problem."

Eve sat forward, her tone dramatic. "Is everything okay?"

"No." His voice was deep and gravelly, as if he'd swallowed razor blades. "Rocko, Caleb, and I weren't invited to your little shindig down there at the beach." He pointed to the biker with the ponytail and ear gages first, then to the well-built, tattoo-sleeved biker who had kissed Ruby.

"Do we know you?" asked Alex.

Rocko glared at Mia. "Do you?"

Mia realized that no one else recognized these three out of all the bikers at Stingray's, nor had they seen the older man on the beach earlier. That shadow figure's shock of silver hair didn't belong to Otto. In the foyer's light, it was white and belonged to Teddy, who was taller and broader than Otto.

"The party was private, but we weren't trying to offend anyone," said Mia in her most diplomatic tone.

"We don't get offended." Teddy chuckled. "We get even."

"We don't want to go to parties *like* yours," said Rocko. "We want to get paid to party like *you*."

Eve motioned to them. "You can apply to be a seasonaire for next summer. You've got a very authentic look."

Alex nodded in agreement. "The brand could use more edge." He crossed his arms as he scrutinized the three men.

Rocko squinted at Alex. "Look at you! Judging me like that."

Alex grew serious. "Oh, I don't judge."

"I do." Rocko guffawed and pointed at Teddy. "Dad, you're too fucking old to be a seasonaire."

Eve waved a dismissive hand at Teddy. "Don't listen to him. That's ageism."

Teddy batted Rocko in the back of the head. "Yeah, that's fucking ageism!" Eve grimaced at the gesture.

Rocko smoothed his ponytail and sniffed the savory air. "Smells dee-licious in here."

Oliver poked out from the kitchen, frying pan filled with eggs and vegetables. "Huevos rancheros—fights off a hangover every time." He was surprised by the sight of the bikers. "Oh, hey."

"I'll take some of those," said Rocko. He crossed Mia, a wave of cigarettes and leather wafting past as he grabbed the pan from Oliver.

Oliver kept his empty hands in the same position. "Careful—"

Rocko ate the eggs with his fingers.

"—Hot," said Oliver.

Caleb glanced around and saw the video camera in the upper corner of the wall. It faced the living room. He reached up with an arm sheathed in tattoos and smashed it with his silver skull ring as Brandon padded in from the hallway that led to his studio. He glared at Caleb and the broken video camera. "What the fuck is happening?"

Teddy spread his thick fingers out by his face. "We don't like being watched." He opened his eyes wide so that he looked like the king cobra that Mia's neighbor had accidentally let loose.

Brandon stepped towards the three men. "If you don't like being watched, why are you here?" He motioned to Mia, Alex, Eve, and Oliver. "We're all about being watched."

"Yeah, we've been watching—for a while now," said Caleb.

"Then we're doing our job," said Brandon. "What do you want?"

"We want your money, and yours and yours and yours and *yours*." Teddy pointed to each seasonaire, landing last on Mia. She stood, her arms stiff against her body.

Oliver started laughing. He slapped his thigh three times. All eyes turned to him as he elbowed Brandon. "This is one of those surprises you talked about. Nice!"

Brandon furrowed his brow, then stared at Mia, who shifted on her feet. She breathed deeply, hoping for more oxygen. She tried to will away the sweat that started to bead around her hairline. The other seasonaires joined Oliver's laughter—now in on what they assumed was a joke.

Oliver put his knuckles to his mouth. "I'm acting scared."

Alex leaned back against the wall, crossing his long legs in the snug denim bell-bottoms. "I don't do scared."

Teddy crossed his thickset arms, scanning all the seasonaires. "I *want* your money."

"I have about twenty-four dollars. I'll go upstairs and get my purse," said Mia.

Eve chuckled. "I never carry cash."

Brandon face-palmed. "This is fucking stupid," he muttered under his breath about the theatrics.

Teddy snorted. "Twenty-four dollars? How about twenty-four *grand*?"

"That's a drop in the bucket for you posers. We know what you make from your website," said Caleb.

Rocko chewed the eggs. "We're taking ten percent of your total earnings, like an agent's fee. Isn't that what agents make?"

"That's not really the math," mumbled Alex.

"An agent's fee for what?" Eve laughed louder. "That hits me in my giggledick!"

Teddy pointed to the wall clock. "I'm being a generous guy and giving you a week."

"Is that a week from now or tomorrow, because now is really tomorrow—" rambled Oliver, still high from the ecstasy.

Teddy rolled his head in exasperation. "Next Saturday night. We'll be back for it."

"And we'll have it for you," said Oliver with a wink at Caleb.

Caleb grimaced. "Eat me."

Alex gazed at Caleb and recrossed his legs. "I would ask you to do the same, but you're not my type. And I'm taken."

All the seasonaires, except Mia and Brandon, continued to laugh. Teddy slammed his fist on the table with the key bowl, its contents jangling. "This is no joke! And if you tell anyone that we made this visit, someone's going to end up swimming with the fishes."

Mia flashed on the six dead koi and the email:

Fathers & daughters. One is always paying.
Now it's your turn.

From the family likeness, this was Ruby's dad. A trickle of sweat slid between Mia's shoulder blades.

Brandon scratched his head, amused with Teddy. "I think you can do better than that bad Tony Soprano cliché."

Oliver pointed at Teddy. "Or say it with a mobster's accent."

"Since you don't seem to see the gravity of the situation, we may have to fire a warning shot," said Teddy.

Mia locked eyes with him. "We'll make it happen. What I say goes here, so you have my word."

Alex applauded. "Mia! Puts a little extra on it!"

Brandon scoffed and shooed out the three bikers. "Okay, enough. Get out of here. I'll edit the shit out of this later."

Caleb got in his face. "Don't go running to your daddy, because we've handled bigger men than him."

"Yeah, yeah. Whatever." Brandon opened the front door for them.

"I turned my back on the biggest club in the country. My days are numbered," said Teddy. "But I take care of my own." He gave one last look at Mia, threw open the door, and marched out. After the three men were gone, the room was silent until the motorcycles out front roared again to life. The rumble quieted as they retreated from the house.

Oliver, Alex, and Eve broke again into peals. Oliver knocked on the credenza three times. "Man, I've watched enough prank robberies online, and none of them could hold a candle to those guys. They really sold it."

Brandon checked the video camera, which was now broken. "No. They *broke* it." He turned to the others. "Whose idea was this? Because it wasn't mine."

"Mine," Mia blurted. "Revenge for Stingray's."

"Well, you failed. We've got nothing."

"My eggs were a success," said Oliver, picking up the empty pan from the coffee table.

Alex caressed Mia's arm before he and Eve moved up the stairs. "You tried."

Mia was alone with Brandon. He shook his head. "You can figure out what to tell Lyndon about this." He pointed to the camera and exited down the hallway.

Mia knew what she would tell Lyndon: nothing.

NINETEEN

Mia holed up in her workspace until the others turned in and fell asleep. She couldn't face them, knowing that the shit may have hit the fan. For hours, she wracked her brain about who would be safe to tell. She needed a reality check, but her gut told her that the visit wasn't some joke or idle threat. If the situation was real, then no one was safe to tell, even Sean—*especially* Sean. He would push her to contact the police—or worse, contact them himself—and the possible fallout was too much for Mia to consider. Last summer, Mia had kept a secret to save her own ass. This summer, she would keep one to save everyone else's.

She logged into her bank account. She had used the seasonaire's deposit to pay three months of rent. That left her just enough to pay the bikers. She opened her sketchpad and picked up a pen, feeling a surge of pressure to finish her designs, knowing that her balance would soon be close to $0. Her next fee installment wouldn't happen until Lyndon's approval. She fell asleep on the 2-D assortment of long-sleeve tops with lace and bead inlays.

A symphony of notification buzzes woke her a few hours later. She'd been tagged in a post from *hounddogdayz* that had been reposted countless times: She and Seamus were kissing. Mia had confronted Presley the previous summer about the identity of *hounddogdayz*, but that hunch was never confirmed. Then she saw the comments:

> Homewrecker
> @miamamasgrl backstabs again. \
> Southie Slut

She poked the app off and left her workspace to find her bedroom empty. After getting dressed, she threw her hair in a ponytail. She would sneak out before anyone could catch her. On a Saturday, after the first big party of the season, the only activity would be nursing hangovers. Her temples throbbed from too much sweet wine, but the aspirin was in the kitchen, where she assumed the others were congregating. Alex wouldn't be hurting like the rest, but he was most likely in the gym for his morning workout. She padded downstairs in her sneakers. Oliver was cleaning the house in the energetic way that he did everything. Thankfully, he was focused on getting a scratch out of the living room's wood floors with a mop, so she quietly grabbed the key to the Smart car from the bowl by the door.

"Dammit," she whispered to herself when she stepped outside. The rest of the seasonaires were out front, drinking Bloody Marys while watching Chase, Wyatt, and Nils skateboard.

Brandon stopped filming when he saw Mia. "You managed to do one thing right last night. Seamus has a girlfriend."

"I didn't know he had a girlfriend, because I'd never heard of him."

Brandon showed her an Instagram Story of a balayaged and Brazilian-straightened brunette with eyelash extensions like spider legs. Snuggling a teacup poodle, she went ballistic for the camera. "Bitch better keep her hands off my man!" Spider Eyes turned on the water works. "I'm hurt!" Then turned them off to yell, "But I'm still standing! You think you're better than me, you low-rent, trash-wearing piece of—"

Mia pressed the X on Brandon's phone to stop the rant and strode off towards the open garage. Eve sat on a double chaise with Alex, braiding a woven bracelet. "It was his responsibility to be transparent, not yours, Mia. Why are women responsible for contraception and morals?"

Alex lifted his sunglasses to peek at Mia. "Maybe they have an open relationship."

Brandon looked at Mia. "Well, his album sold a million more copies because everyone hates his chick. You may have pissed her off, but you made my dad happy."

"Glad I could help." In all sincerity, Mia didn't give a shit. She needed to get to that car.

Chase skated next to Mia. "Oli told me last night was rad! Those bikers! I'm surprised dudes didn't have prop guns." He bent low on his board, arms out in the shape of a rifle.

"Where you going?" Brandon called out to Mia while he resumed filming Chase.

"To apologize."

Eve's eyes were wide, appalled. "To the girlfriend?"

"Yes. Presley'll know where she is, since she planned the whole thing."

Mia got in the Smart car. Her anxiety made the car's tiny size feel claustrophobic. She rolled down the window as she steered out of the driveway. Nils hung onto the bumper until the last minute when Mia jetted onto PCH.

She had discovered that a branch of her bank was located across from the Malibu Country Mart. She tried to keep her hands from shaking as she filled out a withdrawal slip for $20,000. When she reached the window, the bank teller—a portly man in his fifties—scrutinized it. "You'll need to fill out a large cash withdrawal form so that we can report it to regulators."

"Why? It's *my* money."

"They want to make sure it's not for illegal use."

Mia looked at him, deadpan. "I'm buying a black market baby." Off the teller's look—"It's for a car."

The teller filled out the new form and Mia signed it, keeping her hand steady. She requested hundreds. The teller disappeared through a door, and after a few minutes, he returned with the cash. Mia was surprised at the small size of the bound bundles. The teller placed them in an envelope, which he handed to her.

"Name it after me." The teller pointed to his badge, which read *Max*.

"The car or the baby?" Mia managed a smile, slipped the envelope into her crossbody bag, and hurried to the car. Motorcycles roared by her on PCH in both directions as she headed to Stingray's. She didn't know if she'd recognize Teddy, Rocko, or Caleb in leathers and helmets, and she had no idea what kind of bikes they rode. Her hope was that they would be hanging out like on the Saturday when she first saw them.

As she approached the restaurant, she squeezed the car into a tight spot along the highway, then walked to the full patio and made her way through the crowd. She peered in the window and saw Teddy and Rocko sitting at their table in the back. She didn't know if she was relieved that Ruby wasn't there or if she felt Ruby would be able to help her in some way. But before she could think about it further, she found herself back in her car, hyperventilating.

A few minutes later, she saw Teddy and Rocko get on their motorcycles and ride off—southeast on PCH. "Shit." She peeled out of the space and across the highway to make a U-turn, narrowly missing a Mustang convertible, whose driver blared the horn. She kept on Teddy and Rocko's tails. Teddy's bike was matte black like the darkest storm cloud. Rocko's was also black, but shiny with tall handlebars. Both men wore black half helmets, Teddy in sunglasses, Rocko in goggles.

Mia pressed the acceleration pedal to the floor and was surprised at the little car's peppiness. But it was silent, like the Tesla, so the two men didn't notice her, even when she got close. She honked, but they still didn't stop. No one in Los Angeles seemed to notice honking—it was like white noise. As they got into the turn lane to head up Kanan Dume Road, Mia was desperate to get their attention. She did the only thing she could think of: She clipped the back tire of Rocko's bike. Since the Smart car was so small, it knocked Rocko off balance but didn't take him down. He caught the bike, then turned and yelled, "Are you crazy?" *Yes, I am*, Mia thought, especially when Teddy and Rocko recognized her. Teddy, face furrowed in anger, motioned her to follow them.

They led her up the windy road and curved onto Latigo Canyon, turning into a parking lot where Backbone Trail was marked for hikers. They all cut their motors. Teddy and Rocko dismounted their bikes and hung their helmets and goggles on the handlebars. Trembling, Mia got out of the car and walked with them into the mouth of the trail. They were surrounded by coastal sage and scrub, but for Mia's taste, not nearly enough people.

A couple with a terrier mix made their way onto a path ahead. Teddy leaned against a eucalyptus tree while Rocko lit a cigarette, despite the *Fire Danger* signs throughout Malibu. Mia's breathing was quick, her legs weak and shaky.

"I'll add that scratch on my fender to your tab," said Rocko with a gruff exhale of smoke.

"I'm sorry. I was trying to get your attention." A pebble that had slipped into Mia's espadrille stabbed at her insole.

Teddy crossed his arms. "I didn't get yours with my email, so we decided to relay our message in person at your fancy digs."

"How did you find me?"

"We know people," said Rocko.

Teddy shot him a look, then shifted his focus back to Mia. "Geotag. See? I'm not a dinosaur like everyone thinks."

Mia took the envelope from her purse and handed it to him. "Here."

"You're preempting our upcoming visit," he said. "I'm offended you don't want us around."

Mia nodded to the envelope. "I know you asked for twenty-four, but twenty was all I had."

"There will be penalties."

Mia rubbed the back of her neck. "Are you serious?"

"As a heart attack, which I had after my only daughter tried to overdose." Teddy opened his denim shirt, revealing a pink, raised vertical scar in the center of his chest. "You remember when Ruby tried to overdose, don't you?"

"Yes." Mia's eyes filled with tears and her lips trembled. "I'm so sorry about everything that happened, but the new seasonaires weren't involved."

"They're involved now. They took a job for a company built on blood money. Your cunt boss had the balls to send them here—to *my* backyard—after what her sister did to my baby girl!"

"But *I* knew Ruby, and the others didn't, so I feel responsible—"

Rocko poked a finger square between Mia's brow. "You called yourself a friend, but you were no friend to her!"

"You want to be responsible, fine." Teddy shoved the envelope inside his leather vest. "Because you're right—none of this would be happening if you had stayed away from her last summer."

Mia was so breathless and dizzy, it was all she could do to stay on her feet. "I'm sorry" was all she could get out.

Rocko pushed his face towards hers. "Your sorries don't mean shit!" Mia leaned back, eyes wide. Rocko punched the air.

Teddy's mouth screwed in anger. "She told us you let her leave that poser bar, The Rabbit Hole. If you had stayed with her, she wouldn't have gone back to the house."

Mia felt the knot turn to fire in her belly. "*You* let her live with that scumbag Otto Hahn. That's why she was at the house in the first place. You knew about the times she tried to take her own life before she even reached Otto or Nantucket."

Teddy looked like he would eat her if it hadn't been for the tourist family walking past in their LA, Malibu, and Hollywood souvenir T-shirts. The father furrowed his brow at Rocko, who dragged on his cigarette. "You shouldn't smoke here," he said.

"You shouldn't wear those shorts anywhere." Rocko flicked ash towards the sunburned father's plaid Bermuda shorts. The tourist hurried his wife and three kids onto the hiking trail. Mia watched them disappear, wishing they had found something odd about a small, simply dressed brunette standing alone with two scary-looking bikers.

Teddy stared at Mia and gave his beard a stroke. "You were right to take this on yourself, because you're the one who owes her. But something good came out of it all—Caleb made an honest woman out of her. They got hitched—cost me a pretty penny." Teddy stamped a heavy boot on the ground, then looked up at the sky. "So Rocko's bike plus Ruby's wedding equals how much?" He turned to Rocko.

Rocko furrowed his brow. "I was never good at word problems."

Teddy slapped him on the back of the head. "Another twenty." He turned to Mia. "I'll take four off your next payment and give you two weeks."

Mia brushed at her brow. "I don't have it."

"Ask your boss," said Rocko. "She's got bread coming out of her tight British ass."

Teddy loomed over Mia. "I will prove to you how serious I am, so don't even *think* of shafting me again." He nodded to Mia's ankle tattoo—the sunflower that now adorned Ruby's back. "Interesting ink. Stay away from my girl."

Rocko tossed his cigarette butt at Mia's feet. The two men marched off as the pile of dry brown leaves started to smoke. Mia ground out the butt, then picked it up. She held it in her fist and waited for the roar of the motorcycles to start and disappear. She slowly walked to the trashcan by the trailhead and threw it in. This wouldn't be the first or the last fire she would try to put out.

<hr />

That night, the seasonaires watched the episode Brandon titled *Beach Blanket Bikers*. It was a hit, especially when the bikers showed up at the house, ending with the smash of the skull ring into the camera. The screen went black.

"I thought it might be redundant after biker karaoke, but I'll admit, this was gold," said Brandon as he saw the viewer count double, then triple, as did subscribers. He glanced at Mia, who laughed like the rest of the seasonaires again over the "prank."

"I know what I'm doing," said Mia, mustering swagger, because she had absolutely no idea what she was doing. The gin and tonics that Chase had mixed were barely helping after her day.

Eve chuckled. "Too bad they really broke the camera. That extortion thing was hilarious."

"It was a little over the top. My dumb mistake, so let's never mention it again." Mia gave one more guffaw before she finished her drink and escaped upstairs to her workspace. Shutting the door, she collapsed into her chair and put her head between her knees. "Fuck me," she whispered to herself.

TWENTY

I n the week that followed, Mia spent every spare moment toiling away on the designs. She went to sleep working on them and she woke up to work on them, breaking for mandatory appearances and photo ops: a beach club brunch and trunk show, sand sledding on the dunes, kayaking, and another trip to the boutique. She needed to finish the designs quickly, but they had to be good or Lyndon wouldn't approve them. Mia stopped to log into her bank account and stared at it, hoping that somehow more money would magically appear.

Brandon knocked on the door and peeked in. Mia slammed the laptop shut. He lifted an eyebrow. "Porn on a Sunday? Blasphemous!" He chuckled.

"Despite my conflicted feelings about faith, I'm not watching porn."

"Good, because it's exploitative. What we do is exploitative enough."

"And it's scripted, though there are no sexy librarians or hot pizza delivery guys."

"No badass bikers either," said Brandon.

Mia cocked her head. "How much mileage are you going to get out of that? It was a lame prank. I get it." She went back to her sketches.

"I haven't decided yet, especially since they didn't come back last night, like they so ominously threatened to do." Brandon chuckled. "And it pumped up our numbers. I texted Lyndon about your genius. She was happy and not surprised. I think you're her favorite."

Mia erased the hem on a polka dot tunic. "Moving on."

Brandon touched her sleeve and motioned her out. "We're meeting to talk about our next challenge." Mia followed him. "You okay?" he asked. "You didn't come down for breakfast."

"Is breakfast mandatory?"

"Eve will tell you: pin-thin is out." Brandon eyed Mia's loose white jeans. Mia's appetite had disappeared since the bikers' visit.

"I forget to eat when I'm working."

"I hear ya. How are your designs coming?"

"They're coming."

Brandon squinted at her. "That's what I say when I don't know how my shit's panning out."

They joined the other seasonaires in the living room. Mia looked outside the open glass doors. She hadn't fully taken in the day, which was overcast and gray. "June gloom," said Chase from his cross-legged position on the couch next to Eve, who ate a bagel sandwich.

Presley sashayed in from the kitchen, holding her phone and an espresso, Oliver in tow. "The fans have a challenge for you, barista boy. Hopefully, you'll get as much attention as Lil Miss Groupie, who's still raking it in from her beach blanket boff session with Seamus." Mia scowled at her.

Brandon pressed the remote—the flat screen came alive with cuts between Oliver cleaning the house and Chase performing skateboard tricks, Oliver making pancakes with Alex sprinting down the beach. The cursor blinked at the challenge in the comments section:

Oliver, prove ur not a pussy.

Alex pulled Oliver in for a hug. "What jerks!"

Oliver laughed it off. "It's okay. I'm a little bit of a pussy."

"You couldn't even get a blowie on ecstasy at the beach party," said Presley. "But the house is pretty damn clean." She ran her finger along the piano's keys, which plinked with dissonance. "Marcus didn't look like he could wash his own ass, let alone the kitchen counter."

"Ew." Eve dropped her bagel on her plate in disgust.

Presley sipped from her tiny cup. "Your after-party with the big, tough motorcycle daddies was cute, but this challenge will give you *all* a chance to prove you have real balls while promoting our athleisure. Forget spin class—you're going to do a show at the Airflip Acrobatics Academy in Venice."

Oliver flexed his plum-size biceps. "Yes! Muscle Beach!" He did a double take. "Wait—acrobatics? I signed up for high school robotics so I could get out of gym class."

Presley waved a hand. "Hence the challenge." Mia had never heard Presley use the word *hence*. It was straight out of Lyndon's mouth.

Alex ruffled Oliver's hair. "You have to face what scares you."

Eve twirled her wrists in the air. "Does this mean we're doing trapeze?"

"It means you're going to do anything that will show off leggings, sports bras, and low-slung terry sweatpants." Presley pointed at them.

"Balance beam instead of runway is a natural for me. I was born in six-inch Louboutins," said Alex, lifting high up on his toes.

Oliver winced. "Balance beam?"

"You all signed release forms." Presley handed Oliver her empty espresso cup.

Mia followed her outside. She turned as she strode to the Volvo. "I'm looking forward to seeing you hang."

"That's obvious from the photo you posted at the beach party. You had to set me up for drama, didn't you?"

Presley shrugged. "That's why Lyndon pays me the big bucks."

"Wasn't there enough last summer?"

"There's never enough." Presley got into the car and drove off.

⁂

Venice Beach in the summer was a circus, so the Airflip Acrobatics Academy's red-and-white canopy fit the atmosphere. The seasonaires arrived an hour early because Brandon wanted footage of what Presley called "the freak show"—the boardwalk. The weather was still gray, but its dullness made all the color around them pop.

They passed the row of shops selling *I'm With Stupid* T-shirts, rainbow snow cones, and tarot card readings. Outside a cannabis dispensary, a shirtless man with wild, curly hair grinned at them. "Weed if you need," he said, his lids heavy. They browsed the wares of vendors selling candles, crystals, and wood trinkets.

Presley put her hand on Oliver's shoulder. "If this seasonaire thing doesn't work out, you can sell your twig art."

A girl with long braids and countless piercings gave Eve a henna tattoo of a phoenix. Mia flashed on Ruby's new sunflower tattoo—a permanent personal connection. Presley crinkled her nose at the $50 price tag and Eve's painted forearm. "For that price, a blowout would last longer and look better."

Brandon shot a bubble gun at Presley. "When did someone steal your sense of fun?"

Presley batted away the slick clear spheres, popping them. "Ask Mia." She strode ahead of the group. The others looked at Mia, who stopped at the outdoor gym where tanned, oiled men in tight sports shorts lifted heavy dumbbells and women with equally ripped muscles in jog bras did pull-ups. Oliver joined her. "Muscle Beach!" After some gawking, the group moved on.

Weekenders on their beach cruisers and recumbent cycles beeped and honked at Presley, who couldn't have cared less that she was in the middle of the bike path. Drunk coeds flailed on rollerblades. Mia walked with the others on the proper path.

Chase met Wyatt and Nils at the skate park and expertly navigated the smooth gray cement bowls and pools.

"This isn't play time!" yelled Presley. "You're an ambassador for a fashion brand, not a skate brand." In response to a skater girl's stink-eye, she shot, "You're not a brand ambassador for either, I assume."

"You assumed right," said Skater Girl with a sneer. She carried her board to the top of the pool and jumped off. She was as skilled a skater as any of the boys.

As Brandon filmed Chase, he threw a side-eye at Presley. "You're forgetting we're a streetwear brand, too."

"MazzyLyn is a distraction," replied Presley. She tapped her shiny new Patek Philippe watch—a smaller version of Lyndon's. "We paid for trapeze time, so let's go."

Oliver turned his own watch around his wrist twice as he gawked at the skaters twisting, soaring, and tumbling. "They're getting a lot of air." His voice trembled.

Alex grinned. "So will we!"

Eve took Oliver's hand and pulled him towards the Acrobatics Academy's canopy. "It's going to be amazing!" The others followed.

The academy was open on all sides so that passersby could take in the action. Lyndon Wyld #FlyWyld signage stood out front. Inside, two bars hung from red steel beams—a lake's leap across from one another. Rings and vibrant silks also hung over the net that ran the concrete floor's length.

Oliver pushed his glasses up on his nose. "That net's thinner than I thought."

"You won't need the net," said a clear male voice with a thick Italian accent. The group turned to Francesco. His name was embroidered on the pocket of his Airflip Acrobatics Academy shirt—the Lycra snug against his broad chest and shoulders. "You're going to stay in the air."

Presley flicked a wrist. "Well, that's not very exciting." Mia gave her a look as the seasonaires signed another release form—this one for Francesco.

Presley had talked Wyatt and Nils into rolling the racks in from her Volvo and their beat-up van, both parked nearby. "Groupies are put to work." She stole Francesco's attention with her eyelashes, pageant figure, and questions about "Rome, The City of Love" while the seasonaires changed into their designated athleisure ensembles. Mia donned black yoga pants with lace-ups down her calves and a matching tank with a crisscross back. Only Brandon remained in his regular clothes as he manned the camera.

Mia crossed her arms, eyebrow raised at him. "This is some bullshit."

"We don't have an episode if I don't shoot it. And I don't wear anything called 'athleisure.' I'll talk about it, but I won't wear it."

As M-Kat artists' music played over the speakers—loud enough to be heard on the boardwalk—a crowd gathered inside. Francesco tore himself away from Presley to give the group instructions.

Alex was first up and didn't need much direction. He turned the balance beam into a catwalk—his shoulders back, body beautiful in liquid-black leggings and a white mesh long-sleeve top. He dismounted with extraordinary grace. The crowd cheered.

Bare-chested, in Lyndon Wyld sports shorts, Chase shimmied up one rope and leapt his body over to the other. He lowered himself down, then pushed off with his bare feet and soared through the air like a lemur. Brandon laughed, filming the gathering crowd's enthusiastic response.

Francesco crooked his forefinger to motion over Mia. "Bella."

"I'm pretty happy with my feet on the ground," said Mia as Francesco lowered one of the trapeze bars so that Mia could reach it on a stool instead of climbing the tall ladder.

"We'll start here."

Brandon booed and hissed. Mia shot him a look.

Francesco instructed her to rest her pelvis on the bar. At five feet off the ground, he was able to spot her, holding her legs. "I'm going to swing you back and let go to give you some momentum."

"Okay." Mia squeezed her eyes shut for a beat when he let go. He told her to tighten her core and lower herself off the bar so that she was hanging. As she swung, she felt weightless. The more she swung, the lighter gravity pulled her. Listening to Francesco's steady instructions, she made hip circles—right and left. She tightened her core again and was able to pull herself back up onto her pelvic bones, then lower back down to swing some more. She managed a fairly poised release and landing—to a smattering of applause. She smiled, feeling a twinge of pride.

Presley walked behind Eve. "Why don't you show Mia how it's done, Eve? Fuck that toddler stool."

"Yeah, fuck it," said Eve. She kissed Mia on the cheek and winked at Oliver. "If I can do it, *you* can do it, Oli." She pranced over to the canopy-high metal ladder, her loose scoop-back tee swaying. Francesco stood at the bottom, hands on her waist as she started climbing. When she got three-quarters of the way to the top, Mia noticed that a rung was loose. Eve smiled for Brandon's camera and the cheering crowd as she reached up.

"Stop!" Mia screamed and raced over to the ladder with her arms out. But Eve had already grabbed the rung. It slipped diagonally downward and knocked her feet off balance from the rung below. The crowd gasped as she slid down. The net was between the trapeze bars but not under the climber's side of the ladder, so there was nothing to break a fall on the concrete floor. Eve managed to grab a rung with one hand. Her body jerked below, yanking her arm, and she screamed in pain. Francesco quickly climbed the rest of the way and grabbed her around the waist, carrying her down while swearing in Italian.

The show was over. Eve wept as she sat in a folding chair. Her arm hung limp.

An ambulance siren blared over the din of Venice traffic, but the sound that rose above for Mia was the roar of motorcycles that flashed by. As the paramedics examined Eve with Chase and Oliver by her side, she cried out. Oliver winced. The crowd snapped photos and took video while Presley, Mia, and Alex watched on, closer to the canopy. Brandon approached. He reviewed the footage on his camera and nodded his chin toward Mia. "You were quick to play superhero."

Presley gave Mia's rear a pat. "I told her to work the tights."

Francesco marched up to Mia, barrel chest first. "You distracted her! If she'd been focused on the ladder instead of your shouting, she would have avoided that fall!" He strode off under the canopy.

Alex zipped his sweatshirt, smoothed his hair, and looked at Mia. "Francesco's right. Eve wasn't focused, and neither were you during your performance."

"I wouldn't call it a performance. I mean, we're not professionals," replied Mia. She wiped her forehead, wrestling with her guilt.

"Yes, we are. Maybe not professional acrobats, but we're here to give it our best. You know that, Mia."

Mia stepped in towards him. "If you think I'm doing such a shitty job, Alex, then why don't you go back to Austin?"

"Whoa, whoa, whoa!" said Brandon, separating Mia and Alex. "Tensions are high right now."

Presley lifted her phone to video the impending kerfuffle. "Ooh, I'd like to see *this* go down."

Brandon was right—Mia was wound tightly. If Eve's accident was the biker's "warning shot," Mia didn't want anyone else getting hurt.

"Alex is bringing a lot of fans to the brand, but there's strength in numbers," said Brandon. "Let's keep it together."

Alex glowered at Mia, shifted on his heels, and strode to the others at the ambulance.

Presley watched him and turned to Mia. "Judges probably would've given his dismount a ten—and not a strand out of place." She touched her own hair, which was slicked back in a low ponytail.

Mia shook her head and stormed away from Presley and Brandon. She stood on the academy's perimeter and surveyed the equipment, the canopy, and its openings. Anyone could've snuck in while they were changing before the exhibition. Wyatt and Nils had left, and there were no spectators at that time to witness ladder tampering. Plus, Francesco was the only instructor. He had been engrossed in Presley's flirting. Mia didn't see Teddy, Rocko, Caleb—or any bikers in the crowd. But she had gotten caught up in the acrobatics and her own safety. *Maybe it was just an accident*, she thought.

Brandon touched her arm. "Haven't you had enough?"

"I think I left my purse inside."

"Mia! I have your purse!" called Oliver, who was next to Eve at the ambulance with Alex and Chase. Mia's purse was slung across his chest. Chase was filming for Brandon.

Brandon kept his hand on Mia's arm. "I know what's happening," he said in a low voice.

"You do?" Mia searched Brandon's face. His eyes were soft and deep, as if he was looking through her.

"Yes. Let's talk about it in private," he said.

"How are we supposed to do that?"

"I've learned from life with my family that anyone can find privacy if they want it badly enough."

While he ushered her toward the others, Mia scanned around one last time.

Presley was annoyed that the paramedics wouldn't turn on the siren as the ambulance drove off. "Boring exit." She got in the Volvo and left.

The rest of the seasonaires met up with Eve at Venice Community Hospital. They waited five hours in the emergency waiting room among the chaotic collateral damage of summer heat stroke, alcohol poisoning, car accidents, and e-scooter falls. A woman almost gave birth right in front of them. When Eve's name was called, Mia turned to her. "Can I keep you company?" Eve nodded, her face twisted in pain.

In the examination room, Eve took her place on the table, and they waited another forty-five minutes for the doctor. Mia paced around the room, past the CPR poster and plastic models of skeletal sections.

"Mia, chill."

"Are you going to leave?" asked Mia. She tried to tamp the hope she heard rise in her voice. She didn't want anyone to get hurt, but she realized that if seasonaires started making a mass exodus, suspicion might arise.

Eve winced. "Hell, no. Never say die."

Mia stopped pacing. "I feel guilty for distracting you."

"Guilt is a useless, passive emotion. It's like when a tragedy happens and people say, 'My thoughts and prayers.' What good does that do? Plus, this wasn't a tragedy. It was an accident."

Mia thumbed through a blood drive pamphlet as her mind raced around the word *accident*.

Eve held up her phone. "The bright side is I gained ten thousand followers." She patted the examination table. Mia sat. "I can tell you're committed, Mia. We might not be here for the same reasons, but we're both committed." A handsome, young doctor entered, and Eve straightened up. Mia stood from the examination table and let Eve receive the attention. According to the X-rays that were then taken, Eve had a dislocated shoulder.

At last, back at the house, they drank their dinner *and* dessert— White Russians mixed by Chase. "Calcium for strong bones," he joked as he poured the cream.

An enormous box of expensive bath products from Lyndon arrived for Eve with a note that promised an at-home facial and massage by LA's premier aesthetician and massage therapist the following day. The others would get their choice of spa treatments as well.

"Happy ending, yo," said Wyatt, entering through the open deck doors.

"Not for you," said Brandon.

Wyatt saw Eve's arm in its sling. "Well, she's not gonna be able to give me one for a while."

"I'm ambidextrous," said Eve with a laugh. "But you might never find out with that attitude."

Chase descended to the rec room with his buddies. Boomer panted behind them.

Everyone else retired to their rooms. Mia, Eve, and Alex sat on Eve's bed. Eve winced in pain, holding her arm. "Fuck." She opened the vial of Percocet prescribed for her. She shook one out, then held the open vial towards Alex and Mia, who put their palms up to decline. "More for me, until Wyatt and Nils get to them."

Alex lifted his mug of tea to Eve in a toast. "To making a sling stylish."

"'Out of the mouth of *babe*.'" Eve returned the gesture with her good arm and swallowed the pill with a swig of the sweet, creamy cocktail. She eyed the box of fragrant soaps, body oils, and bath bombs. "I almost had to kill myself to get back in Lyndon's good graces."

"Don't say that," said Mia softly.

Alex moved in next to Eve. "Yeah! Bite your tongue!"

Mia reached out for Alex's leg. "Hey, I didn't mean what I said today."

"Of course you didn't, because this summer would turn into a hot mess without me." Alex gave Mia's hand a squeeze.

The jokes about happy ending massages turned into talk about their first sexual experiences, which moved to a deeper conversation about relationships. Mia tried to participate but was consumed with worry. *She needed to get that money.*

Eve plucked her earbuds off her nightstand so she could fall asleep to one of her favorite political podcasts. As Alex started for his bed, she grabbed his arm. With an alcohol-meets-Percocet whine, she said, "Don't leave. Cuddle."

Alex pointed to the earbuds. "You lose one of those every night. If it ends up somewhere I don't want it, I'm going to be pissed."

The two snuggled up, and when they grew tired of chatting, fell asleep. Mia was jealous of their friendship because she wasn't sure—with the way the summer was going—that she could make any true friends. She was the problem before she even arrived, and now her problem was becoming everyone else's.

TWENTY-ONE

E ve was sore and cranky when she woke up, both earbuds in her ears. Despite her mood, she was committed to doing a confessional, singing Lyndon's praises in getting her excellent medical attention. She would use it as an opportunity to rant about the sorry state of health care. "If I didn't have a generous employer, I would've been stuck at a sub-par hospital with insufficient care since my parents' coverage is lacking."

Brandon leaned in to Mia, who watched the monitor with him. "This beats that ASMR bullshit."

Eve's impassioned speech gave Mia an idea. She closed herself in her workspace and FaceTimed Lyndon, who opened the conversation. "Mia, I was hoping you would keep everyone out of the hospital this year."

"I'm trying. Acrobatics were Presley's idea."

"It *was* good social media fodder, but I'm certainly glad that Eve is okay."

"We got a lot of attention, that's for sure." Mia waited a beat. "I saw her hospital bill, and it reminded me of the pile my mom left behind." Mia hesitated again. "Is there any way you could advance me my fee for the designs so I can start to pay them? I'll scan more sketches right now and email them to you."

"Haste makes waste. I don't want you to rush them. The ones you sent were just decent," said Lyndon, touching her pearl-and-diamond necklace.

Mia sighed, her heart sinking.

Lyndon sighed in return. "However, I'll wire transfer you the money, because I understand your burden. You should have it in a day or two."

Mia brightened. "Thank you! I really appreciate it." Mia's request was only half a lie. Her mom's bills *had* piled up, but they weren't the more pressing burden.

Lyndon lifted her forefinger. "But consider it a loan. If I don't like what you show me, that fee reverts back."

Mia nodded, her pulse rushing.

"Enjoy spa day." Lyndon clicked off.

A massage therapist, facialist, and manicurist arrived to pamper the group. Alex encouraged Oliver to get a manicure. "You bite your nails to the quick." The manicurist encouraged a paraffin wax treatment for Oliver's dry, rough hands.

"That's because you spend all night scrubbing the kitchen," Chase said to Oliver. "You were going to town on the oven at two in the morning when I came in to get a snack."

"I didn't see you."

"That's because you were jamming with your earbuds in." Chase busted an Oliver move.

"I was working off a little steam from yesterday. I was worried about Eve."

"Dude, you didn't seem worried. You seemed happier than a pig in shit."

Oliver shifted on his feet. "I wasn't. I was worried."

"It's okay. *I'm* okay," said Eve, who squeezed Oliver's hand, then quickly let go. "Ooh, you do need a manicure."

Mia couldn't enjoy hers. Her only spa experience was in Nantucket with her mom, who'd suffered a scary allergic reaction to the tea tree oil used in the healing massages Lyndon and Grace had gifted them. *That* had ended in a trip to the hospital. The stress over the impending transaction with the bikers caused her to fidget so much during her pedicure that the manicurist clipped a cuticle too short. Mia hobbled upstairs in the foam toe separators, claiming she had work to do.

Alex rested his head against a couch pillow while his charcoal face mask dried. "All work and no play makes Mia a dull girl."

"Or a rich girl," said Brandon, who disappeared down the hall to edit after a neck massage.

In her workspace, Mia contemplated emailing Teddy for a meeting, but instead spent the next half hour—as Presley had said—"playing 'Where's Waldo?'" She discovered that the California Institution for Women was in Corona. Then she did an internet search of every salon in that city and called all of them, asking for Ruby Taylor. The Golden Strand salon was the winner.

"She has an opening at one the day after tomorrow," said the receptionist. Mia made an appointment under the name "Justine Timmons."

That night after dinner, Brandon showed the group the Airflip Acrobatics Academy episode. Fan adoration came in fast after Alex's balance beam turn and well wishes during the Eve debacle. Mia was hailed as a "baller," heroine," and "fierce as fuck," but the adulation only made her feel worse. The viewers were disappointed that Oliver never took his turn. One comment of many:

Oliver is still a pussy.

"Can't teach an old cat new tricks." He knocked on a side table three times. Mia noticed that this was one of his habits. He seemed to have a few.

On-screen, the camera had caught Brandon and Mia in close conversation by the canopy. A viewer challenge popped up:

Brandon and Mia date. Make Seamus Galloway jealous.

Brandon and Mia laughed, but on Mia's way back up to her bedroom, Brandon stopped her. "I'll take that challenge."

Mia smirked and shook her head. "Number one: Seamus Galloway hasn't so much as sent me a text since the party. Number two: You and I have zero chemistry."

"I beg to differ. That's why I wrote the comment."

Mia noted that the comment was from *WyldFan97*. "That's you?"

"It's a breakfast date, so don't freak out. We'll have privacy to talk."

The following morning, Mia checked her account. Lyndon's money had transferred. She was relieved the "date" would be over in time for her to scoot to the bank for a withdrawal.

After a slew of teasing from the rest of the seasonaires, Brandon and Mia left the house. Brandon drove—he was steering them far from Malibu. Mia stared out the Tesla's window as they took exit 6B off the 60 Freeway east towards Monterey Park.

Mia shifted in her seat. "Where are we going?"

"To eat congee—best breakfast in the city."

The landscape had changed to pale stucco and off-white brick one-story buildings. Weeping Chinese banyan trees lined the street. On Garfield Avenue, they passed one of the neighborhood's many churches. The kiosk read: *It's okay. Your lifeguard can walk on water.* Mia twisted her head to see the other side, which read: *Wear sinscreen. You don't want son-burn.*

"Do you believe everything you see or read?" said Brandon.

"No."

"Neither do I."

Mia wasn't sure if he was talking about the church's punny rhetoric or something else.

They arrived at a strip mall and parked. Brandon gestured her towards an unassuming restaurant with blue awning and red letters: *Delicious Food Corner.* He opened the door for her. The line was long, so customers busied themselves on their phones and iPads or watched one of the several hanging TVs while they waited. No one in this small traditional Hong Kong café almost an hour away from Malibu gave the couple a second look. Brandon ordered in flawless Chinese and was given a Post-it Note scrawled with a number. He and Mia scooted across from each other in a tiny booth.

"You can't get in here on a Saturday," said Brandon.

Their tabletop was soon covered with platters of steamed buns and rolls accompanied by various sauces. Brandon walked to a nearby table, where a preteen boy was eating with his dad, who was watching TV. Mia couldn't hear the conversation, but she saw Brandon hand the boy his camera and some cash. The dad nodded and went back to his TV-watching. The boy started filming Brandon and Mia.

Mia's brow furrowed. "I thought you said we'd have privacy."

"Gotta get something for the fans." Brandon sat back down. Mia wasn't happy about the production, but she relaxed when Brandon started explaining all the dishes. He pointed out the *youtiao*—unsweetened Chinese crullers wrapped in sticky rice noodles. "My grandmother's favorite."

Mia smiled with surprise as she tried the Spam and egg on toast. Brandon passed her a golden pineapple bun. "Push the butter in there." He pressed the melting yellow pat between the warm sliced rounds.

"I never liked porridge, but this is incredible," Mia said of the congee. She savored all the flavors and textures. Brandon bought her a frozen red bean drink and a chrysanthemum tea for himself. Mia sipped the double layer concoction topped with condensed milk and red beans. "That's sweet." She swapped with Brandon.

"Everyone's throwing shade at Oli, but *you* need to take bigger risks, too," said Brandon.

He has no freakin' idea, thought Mia, but instead of revealing more, she pointed to the sandwich and said, "I'm eating Spam!" She took a bite.

"I'm not just talking about food," said Brandon. "You come out to LA, but you won't surf, you barely dance, and you wouldn't get on that high trapeze."

"Look who's talking! You haven't done any of those things either."

"I'm producing a channel and promoting the brand. What are you doing? You sit behind that sewing machine and wait for the guinea pigs. You let someone else test the waters before you go in."

"Chase would say you're mixing metaphors." Mia put down the sandwich, no longer hungry.

"What would *you* say?" Brandon picked up his sandwich and bit into it.

Mia leaned back in her seat and crossed her arms. "I'd say I'm not going to let you rile me." She side-eyed the camera as the boy filmed.

Brandon chewed, swallowed, and wiped his mouth with his napkin. "Is your uncanny sense of control nature or nurture? Did you have to keep it together for your mom because she was sick?"

Mia put her elbows on the table and leaned into Brandon. "Are you kidding me right now?" she said in a low growl.

Brandon leaned back, shrugging. "We all adapt to our family roles. Was yours the same in your family as it is in the house here? You're 'The Mom'?"

"You're clearly 'The Shit Disturber.' Is that how you get attention in your family?"

"That would be my older brother." Brandon's eyes narrowed at Mia. "I'm trying to decide if you're a reserved young woman or just a bitch."

Mia flung her napkin on the table and rose. "That's it. I'm out."

Brandon retrieved the camera from the kid with one hand while reaching up to catch Mia's hand. He pulled her back. "Thanks," he said to the kid, who nodded and went back to breakfast with his dad.

"Now we can talk." Brandon let go of Mia, who saw that the camera was now off. She took a deep breath. The restaurant was filled to capacity, with all the patrons engrossed in their own conversations. They had privacy.

Mia sat. "I thought we were producing the channel so that people could see what our life is really like. You just made up that whole scene!"

"No one gives a fuck what our life is really like," said Brandon. "That's why they give us challenges and try to steer us. They're escaping their lives into the life they *want*. If you keep doing it *knowing you're doing it*, you'll come out of this smelling like the roses you're embroidering on your T-shirts."

"They don't have a scent. No one wants to have my life." Mia sipped her water.

"Yes, they do. You're a fucking American Dream story to a lot of people."

Mia put the water glass down. "What's *your* story?"

Brandon poked his plate with a chopstick. "I am Maz's middle son."

"Your reputation precedes you."

"You mean my mugshot."

"You're not the first person to have a mugshot. I mean, look at Presley."

"Yeah, look at her. *She* probably posted her mugshot on social as a fuckin' public pity play. She's a white girl from Georgia.

Lyndon's sister? A white British woman. I'm surprised anyone remembers she's a killer."

"So you didn't beat the crap out of someone?"

Brandon dropped the chopstick. "I'm not going to talk about this right now."

Mia leaned forward. "Then why did you ask me here? You said you know what's happening. Tell me what you know."

"I know you feel responsible for everyone, like you're making up for some failure. I *get* that. I understand what that feels like." There was a sadness about Brandon that made Mia want to stroke his face. But he drew her in and pushed her away at the same time.

"Why didn't your dad clear up the story?" asked Mia. "Lyndon got behind Presley by hiring her as publicist."

"In my family, 'all press is good press.'" Brandon touched the camera.

Mia put her hand on the camera next to Brandon's. "Makes it hard to separate fact from fiction."

"No one is asking for that," said Brandon.

Mia played with the one thin gold bracelet around her wrist. "That's good, because Biker Extortion Night was not a prank."

Brandon leaned back in his chair, confused. "What?"

"The three bikers who came to the house are related to Ruby, the girl who worked for Otto Hahn at Wear National," said Mia.

"The one who almost went down for your buddy's murder?"

"Grace beat Ruby and framed her. It was all meant for Otto, but Grant showed up. He had no idea what was coming, and neither did Ruby."

"Man, wrong place, wrong time." Brandon shook his head. "But Ruby's okay now, right?"

"Her dad, brother, and new husband don't think so."

"That's not on you, Mia."

Mia looked into her tea, her face crumbling in despair. Brandon reached out and touched her wrist. "Hey . . ." he said gently.

"It's my fault Ruby went back to that house on July Fourth. If I'd made her stay with me at The Rabbit Hole, lives would've been saved. I tried to stop them both, because they were so wasted, but—"

"You tried. What more could you do? Physically restrain them?" Brandon's fingers moved to Mia's. "Besides, you didn't know what was going to happen at that house." He let the slightest beat pass. "Did you?"

"No!" Mia raised her voice, then looked around and lowered it. "But it's my mess. Her family is serious about restitution, and I'm going to pay them."

"That's insane." Brandon leaned forward. "It's Lyndon's mess. You should tell her."

Mia shook her head. "Absolutely not. I think those men are the reason Eve got hurt. If anyone else finds out, especially Lyndon, someone might end up dead."

Brandon took hold of Mia's hand. "Let me help you. We can go to my dad."

"No! Brandon, aren't you hearing me? Ruby's dad is a bad, bad guy."

"My dad's no angel."

Mia pulled her hand away, took a deep breath, and straightened. "I have the money. Just let me handle it. Please don't make me regret telling you." She locked eyes with Brandon to drive home her decision, but his gaze told her that he wouldn't let her go this alone.

"Come on." He held onto her hand as he stood.

Brandon drove Mia to the bank without asking any more questions. This time, Mia filled out the large cash withdrawal form. As Brandon watched, Max the Bank Teller eyed him suspiciously. Mia handed Max the form and put her arm around Brandon's waist. "I'm buying him a car, too."

Brandon pulled her in and kissed her cheek. "I'm a lucky guy."

Now that Mia had saddled him with her secret, she wasn't so sure this was true.

TWENTY-TWO

That Thursday afternoon, Mia took the envelope of cash from its hiding place inside a bin of zippers. After sliding it into her satchel, she punched the address for The Golden Strand salon into her phone's Google Maps. She told the other seasonaires that she had an appointment at Mood Fabrics to get a specific kind of jersey for some sample tops she was going to make. What she didn't say was that Lyndon hadn't yet approved the designs Mia had emailed over.

Brandon followed her to the car. "I've been around the business long enough to know that you don't need an appointment at Mood."

Mia stood at the driver's side. "I'm going to see Ruby," she whispered.

"I'm going with you." Brandon leapt around to the passenger's side.

Mia got in and locked the door. "No."

Brandon smacked the roof of the car, which Mia started. Mia rolled down the window. "I need to talk to her myself."

Chase passed them to get a surfboard in the other garage. "Lover's spat?" He grinned.

Brandon let Mia leave.

She followed her phone's nav to Corona. She wound up Kanan Dume Road, passing the spot where she had met with Teddy and Rocko. When she was over the hills, she merged onto the 101 South. Driving the tiny car on the freeway was nerve-wracking. Driving *any* size car on an LA freeway would have been nerve-wracking to her. She took the exit into Corona, a neighborhood of oatmeal-colored clone homes surrounded by the green of the Santa Ana Mountains.

The Golden Strand salon was ensconced in a stucco outdoor mall across from a Costco. She pulled into the large parking lot and slid into a space just far enough from the salon that she could quickly abort mission. She entered the salon and was met by the smell of ammonia and floral hair products. Blow-dryers whizzed. The stations were basic, with black vinyl salon chairs and veneer wood drawers. They were topped with glass jars filled with scissors and combs bathing in aqua-blue cleaning solution.

Across the salon, Ruby sat in one of the basin chairs. Her legs were crossed in vintage Lee overalls over a white tank, red Converse on her feet. She didn't see Mia because she was reading an *Us Weekly* and drinking an orange Fanta soda.

Mia stood at the reception desk. "Do you have an appointment?" asked the receptionist, who looked a decade older than Ruby, as did the other stylists and colorists.

"Yes." Mia almost said her real name but remembered: "Justine Timmons for Ruby."

"I'll go get her." The receptionist walked to Ruby, who looked up and saw Mia. Her face registered a split second of shock, which she quickly covered with a friendly smile as she approached Mia.

"Justine, hi! I'm Ruby. You're a new client?" Her smile remained plastered on, while Mia's heart raced.

"Yes." That was all Mia could get out of her mouth. She followed Ruby to a station. On either side, stylists worked with clients, snipping, coloring, and styling. Mia sat and noticed the cosmetology license on the wall. The date on it was three years earlier. Ruby must've gone to cosmetology school before she became a Wear National seasonaire. Ruby leaned over Mia's shoulders to shake out a slick black smock and whispered, "I would tell you to get the fuck out of here, but I'd lose my job." She stood back up and smiled again. Mia moved her hair to expose the nape of her neck so Ruby could snap the smock. "I love this job," Ruby said louder. Mia could tell that she meant it.

On the counter next to a hand mirror was a framed photo of Ruby and Caleb at their wedding. Ruby, in a loose, strappy white dress, was on her tiptoes kissing Caleb's cheek. In a robin's egg blue tux, Caleb had his mouth open wide, tongue out, and was making devil horns with a hand.

"You're married?" asked Mia.

"Newly. You, Justine?"

"Nope. Not me."

Ruby stroked her fingers through Mia's strands. "Marriage has gotten a bad rap. It's nice to commit to someone forever." As she caught a knot, Mia winced slightly. "I can barely commit to hair color, but I'm ready to go a little unicorn. Like yours." Mia eyed Ruby's pink hair—its long waves falling over her slim bare shoulders.

"Since you're a brunette, it would be a process that takes more than one time. I'd have to bleach it first. Do you live around here?"

Mia shook her head. Despite the fact that Presley had consistently called her hair "mousy" the summer before, Mia didn't have the patience to sit in a salon chair for hours on end. Today, with Ruby, she didn't have the fortitude to do it either.

"Then I'd suggest hair chalk," said Ruby. "With your hair and the fact that you seem kind of reserved, I'd do ocean blues." Mia was wearing white Lyndon Wyld chinos and a short-sleeve check- ered blouse with slip-on sneakers.

"I'm not as reserved as you think. But I trust you," said Mia.

Ruby gave Mia's shoulder a patronizing squeeze and walked off. Mia could see her tattoo sunflower's petals peeking out from the back of her tank. She stared at the wedding photo. After a few moments, Ruby returned with a box of hair chalk, which she set on the metal tray stand next to the chair.

"I can't see the whole thing, but is that a sunflower on your back?" asked Mia.

"Yes."

Mia's sunflower tattoo was covered by her pants. "Does it mean anything?"

"Nothing except it's behind me," said Ruby with a wry smile. She brushed Mia's hair, firmly but softly. Mia hadn't had her hair brushed since her mom used to do it when she was little. Then she'd become the one to do the hair brushing when her mom *had* hair between chemo treatments. She closed her eyes for a beat as the bristles stroked her scalp.

"You swim?" asked Ruby with a curious expression.

"I taught myself this year."

"Chlorine'll really do a number on this." Ruby ran a hand over Mia's hair.

"I've been swimming in a saltwater pool this summer."

Ruby raised her eyebrows. "How nice for you *and* your hair."

Mia shifted uncomfortably. Her phone buzzed with a text, so she lifted it out of her satchel, which she had hung on the chair's arm. It was from Presley:

You lil slut. Seamus AND Brandon? 🌿 🌿

Presley had obviously seen footage from the "breakfast date" and made assumptions, which was Brandon's goal with his fabricated scene. Mia dropped her phone back in her bag. "I have a friend who's dealing with *so much* drama."

"Your *friend* needs new friends." Ruby sprayed Mia's hair with water from a translucent plastic bottle, then clipped sections.

"She fucked up," said Mia. "And she's doing everything she can to make it right, but nothing seems like enough."

"Maybe instead of fixing it, she should leave it." Ruby ran a stick of chalk along a vertical chunk of Mia's hair, depositing the azure color.

"She can't leave it."

Ruby tilted her head to appraise her work with a focus that Mia had never seen before—Ruby had always been ethereal and flighty, mostly due to the drugs. But there was a somberness to her that came with the focus, like she needed to concentrate on something other than the life that was handed to her. Mia understood the need, because she had felt it for a long time.

After a few more artful strokes, Ruby offered Mia a hand mirror so she could see the results from all angles. The blue was subtly woven through Mia's brown locks. She caught Ruby's eyes in the mirror.

"You're finished," said Ruby, unsnapping Mia's smock. She strode off with it. Mia blinked at her own reflection, then rose.

At the front desk, Ruby wrote up the ticket, handed it to the receptionist, and, with a closed-mouth smile, said, "Thanks" to Mia—the one word Mia knew she hadn't meant. Ruby disappeared as Mia paid the receptionist.

"I'd like to give Ruby a cash tip," Mia said to the receptionist.

The receptionist looked around. "I think she went out for a break. I can give it to her."

"I'd rather give it to her myself."

"She's probably out back."

Mia exited the salon and walked around to the other side of the building. She found Ruby leaning against the wall, smoking a cigarette.

"I didn't want you to think I stiffed you on your tip," said Mia.
Ruby exhaled. "Shit happens."

Mia moved in closer. "I'm sorry about everything," she whispered.

"It wasn't your fault." Ruby couldn't cap her emotion, and neither could Mia. The tears rose, and they kissed. Mia had found a true soul connection with Ruby when they'd met in Nantucket, but she'd never felt Ruby's lips on hers. They were soft, like Ruby's heart, though she no longer wore it prominently on her sleeve.

"I need to tell you—" Mia's voice caught in her throat. "I called nine-one-one."

"I know—the night I overdosed." Ruby scoffed. "Do you want my thanks? You're still working for the sister of the hag who beat and tried to frame me." She stepped off to the side, away from Mia.

"Grace is in prison."

Ruby's eyes went wide with dismay. "You think that's enough?"

"It's not. That's why I have this for you." Mia pulled the envelope of cash from her satchel. The words rushed out. "I went after you that night, to see if you and Grant were okay."

Ruby squinted. "What?"

"When I got to the house, Grant was already dead." Mia glanced down at the ground, squeezing her right fist so that her nails dug into her palms. "*That* nine-one-one call." She looked up at Ruby, whose face twitched in confusion.

"You?"

Mia swallowed and nodded. Presley had already suffered the accusations and tumbled through the rumor mill, so Mia didn't want Ruby to know Presley had been at the house, too.

Angry red spread up Ruby's chest and neck. "Leave now, Mia. I told you to leave. *Leave now.*"

"I could never live with myself if Grace wasn't getting what she deserves," said Mia.

Ruby's arms wrapped tightly around her body. "*I* almost went to prison. *I* almost died. But I'm glad *you* can live with yourself."

Mia wanted to tell her that she had been the one to lead the police to Grace after Ruby, in her ever-wasted state weeks later, mentioned that the last person she'd seen before losing consciousness was "a blonde girl." But if Mia revealed this now, she'd risk exposing Cole, his job, and cause even more damage. All she could say—again and again—was "I'm sorry."

Ruby tossed the ashy stub down and snuffed it out with her sneaker.

"I don't have any right to ask you this," said Mia. "And I know your dad is just being protective, but can you please call him off."

Ruby offered a bitter smile. "He's not protective. Greedy, selfish, and controlling, maybe. But protective? No. He's the reason I *went* to Otto. Out of the two, Otto was a better choice."

Mia's brow knit. "I can't imagine that."

"Don't try."

"This is for *you*, not him." Mia closed Ruby's hand around the envelope and walked off. She wanted to take a deep breath but couldn't.

Her chest was tight and remained that way through her whole drive back to Malibu—a hazy dream with a classic rock soundtrack. Led Zeppelin's cover of "When the Levee Breaks" came on the stereo and Mia turned it up full blast. Her visit with Ruby didn't feel like closure; instead it felt like threads left hanging when a garment was stitched in a panic. A text buzzed in, but unlike the other drivers, she refrained from looking. After she pulled up to the house and into the garage, she saw it: from an unknown number with a 951 area code that was noted as Corona, CA.

Couldn't stay away from her, could u?

Mia sucked in a breath and deleted the text. *The threads were loose.*

As she entered the house, Eve and Alex crossed her in the foyer. "Are you making new clothes for the emperor?" asked Eve. Brandon was sitting in the living room, adjusting a camera.

Mia looked at Eve blankly, her mind still on the text. "What?"

"*The Emperor's New Clothes*. Where's the *fabric*?" Eve chuckled.

Mia held out her palms. "Oh. Guess I came out empty-handed."

Alex touched one of Mia's blue streaks. "But not empty-headed. I'm loving this look!"

"It's temporary," said Mia. Brandon gave her a curious look. Mia had the sinking feeling that Teddy would be back for more.

TWENTY-THREE

Lyndon finally emailed Mia her approval on *some* of the drawings, asking for samples of the nature-inspired pieces:

> Your charity T-shirt project is sweet and so are its
> roses, but sweet = bland. You're in California. Let me
> see some pieces that look like the wild West! And I
> don't mean bolo ties.

Mia was worried that if Lyndon didn't approve all the pieces, she would have to repay the loan. She tried calling but got voicemail. Hearing Grace again turned her stomach. She didn't leave a message.

That afternoon, she put on a Lyndon Wyld athleisure ensemble and running shoes. She found Brandon in his studio, editing footage from their breakfast date.

"You gave Presley a sneak peek?"

"She spins it on social. It's entertainment." Brandon glanced up at her. "What happened with Ruby?"

"I handled it," said Mia, tying a loose shoelace. "Chase, Oliver, and I are going for a hike, because I need some inspiration. I'm not sure whether Lyndon approved my designs. She was vague."

"That's a way to get you to do more work. If you want a straight answer from someone like Lyndon, you're going to have to ask a straight question."

"What I *want* is for her to be happy with the work. That's how I'm going to get to the finish line." Mia motioned to the door. "Want to come?"

"I don't hike." Brandon turned his focus to the monitors, which showed the two of them at Delicious Food Corner. Mia rolled her eyes. Brandon pressed a keyboard button to stop the frame where Mia got up and he grabbed her arm. "If Chase and Oli ask about our date, make sure you say I'm a motherfucker."

"I won't say that—not because you aren't one, but because I've never liked that term." Her small smile said she was only half-joking.

"The more drama we create, the less people are going to dig, because we're spoon feeding. That includes the people in this house and Presley."

Mia exited as Brandon continued editing. Chase had promised his mom he would visit after a shooting scare at his brother's school the previous day. "Since my parents' divorce, she needs my opinion on everything, and she wants to talk about putting him in private school." They would stop for lunch with his mom before hitting the trails, which were close to his house.

Chase maneuvered the Tesla around the curves of Sunset Boulevard through Pacific Palisades, a sleepy-looking, high-class hamlet where the majority of luxury strollers were pushed by nannies and pretty au pairs. A middle-aged woman in an electric

BMW inched out from a side street. She made a peace sign as Chase let her into the lane. A few streets later, when he tapped his horn to prompt her to look up from her phone at a green light, she flipped him off.

Oliver tipped his straw fedora to the woman, who ignored him and zipped ahead.

Chase chuckled. "Ah, my 'hood."

"I wouldn't call it a 'hood," said Mia as they passed beautiful home after beautiful home.

"There's an actual gang here. It's a fancy gang."

"Shut up." Mia snorted in disbelief.

"My mom will repeatedly tell you how much this little 'hamlet' has changed since she grew up. Pacific Palisades still has the Fourth of July Americanism Parade, but instead of sweet blue-haired old ladies from the Woman's Club sitting in folding chairs on street corners, paparazzi are hiding behind lampposts. This is where the stars with families live."

"Is your mom a star?" asked Oliver.

"In her own mind. That's everyone's mind-set here now. Even my rabbi has done TV series guest spots. He canvases for gigs after Rosh Hashanah services."

Mia thought about the church kiosk in Monterey Park and the protestors at Pride. "Maybe religion is just another way for people to spin a story to their advantage."

"'The mind is its own place, and in itself can make a heaven of hell, a hell of heaven,'" said Chase.

"*Paradise Lost*," said Oliver.

Chase grinned and steered the car right and down into Rustic Canyon, an enclave between Pacific Palisades and Santa Monica. The streets' canopy of trees sheltered the expansive craftsman and midcentury modern homes.

"My mom's a holistic nutritionist—at least that's what she calls herself. She does hot yoga seven times a week and we're forbidden to eat anything that's not from the farmer's market. She sources everything, because an organic egg could secretly be from a chicken that ate Twinkies."

Oliver licked his lips. "Sounds like a delicious egg."

"We'll have lunch and leave." Chase pulled the car into the wide driveway of a sprawling one-story woodsy home with mission-style lanterns and a stone chimney. Adirondack chairs sat next to a gurgling stone fountain. He lifted the Tesla's hatch and slung on his backpack, then motioned for Mia and Oliver to follow. "*Mi casa es su casa.*" He put the key in the lock of the wood-inlayed door and opened it.

A short, round-faced older woman in a #*MeToo* T-shirt, jeans, and a kitchen apron crossed the foyer with a laundry basket in her arms. She stopped and leaned in for a kiss on the cheek from Chase. "*Hola,* Rosa." Chase emptied his backpack of laundry into the basket.

"*Guapo,* your mom misses you." Rosa patted Chase's cheek and continued out of the room with the laundry.

Mia lifted her chin towards Chase. "So *this* is why you stopped at home. You wanted your mom to do your laundry."

Chase chuckled. "My mom doesn't do laundry."

A striking, slender woman in black yoga pants and a drapey sweatshirt that fell off one toned shoulder entered the warm, wood-paneled foyer. Her dainty rose-gold anklet matched the shade of her pedicured toes. She embraced Chase like she hadn't seen him in years. "Hi, baby!"

Chase introduced Mia and Oliver, who eyed the surroundings with awe. They turned and smiled. "Nice to meet you, Mrs. Edelstein."

"Oh, I'm not 'Mrs.' anymore. Call me Sharon."

Sharon hugged Oliver and Mia. Wrapped in the softness of the sweatshirt, the smell of lavender soap and mom-energy, Mia didn't want to let go. She forced herself to step away. "You have a beautiful home, Sharon."

"Thank you, Mia." Sharon smiled at Chase. "We like it, don't we, lovey?"

Chase jumped on the staircase banister and slid down. "It's ai-ght."

Sharon touched one of his sea-matted bleached-blonde locks. "This needs coconut oil." She ushered them through the house, with its stone fireplace, leather couches, and Native American woven wool blankets. They sat on the deck by the pool in the backyard—the green plants and vines popped with fuchsia bougainvillea flowers and fragrant night-blooming jasmine. Rosa brought out a tray of kombucha tea and a colorful Mexican pottery bowl of fresh fruit, which was conspicuously absent of berries.

Sharon scooped some fruit onto Chase's plate. She looked at Mia and Oliver. "California strawberries are tainted with fumigants! I mean, fumigants are how we lost our shepherd rescue, Stella. I was at my healer's house and I let Stella roam around the garden during my session. The next morning, our sweet girl was dead." She plunked the silver serving spoon back in the bowl. "My healer had no idea that his gardener was using pesticides."

"I'm sorry," said Oliver.

Chase tilted his glass and let a splash of his kombucha fall onto the deck. "Pour one out for Stella."

Sharon poured some of hers out onto the wood deck. Oliver and Mia awkwardly did the same. Mia sipped, then put her glass down when the fizzy vinegar beverage filled her mouth. She restrained herself from making a face.

"I had blood tests done afterwards to check my environmental toxin level and it was through the roof," said Sharon, raising a hand above her head. Her beaded bracelets jangled with charms. "I had the kids' blood tests done, too. Thank God they're okay!" She turned to Mia. "You should do it, Mia, since you have a family history of cancer." She squeezed Mia's hand. "I'm so sorry about your mother."

Chase tossed an apple slice on his plate. "Mom!"

Sharon looked at him, wide-eyed. "When you told me, you didn't say it was a secret."

"Keeping a secret is tough nowadays," said Oliver, tapping the arm of his chair three times.

Chase mouthed "Sorry" to Mia, who gave his hand a pat. Her mother's cancer was a tragedy, but not a secret like the one she was holding. Chase turned to his mom. "I thought you wanted to talk about the shooter scare at Josh's school," he said in a deliberate tone.

"I do. He's in his room processing it. He says he's fine, but I'm having him talk to his therapist and write in his journal. Maybe he can use some of this as grist for his bar mitzvah speech."

"We had an active shooter on my campus," said Oliver. "It was pretty terrifying."

Mia shivered at the memory of Oliver's naiveté regarding the bikers' visit and prayed he wouldn't bring it up.

Sharon placed her palms flat on the table. "I want all your opinions on the situation. You're millennials. You understand that this is the way of the world now: shooter scares and bomb threats. Do you think that public school is a safe place anymore?"

"Considering I went to private school and six kids in my class ended up in rehab for heroin, I think it's a mortality toss-up," said Chase.

Sharon shifted to Mia and Oliver. "Did you go to private school?"

They shook their heads.

"Did you get into a good college?"

"I didn't go to college." Mia cleared her throat. "Well, I'm probably starting in the fall."

"Better late than never!" Sharon lifted her glass to Mia.

Oliver folded and refolded his linen napkin. "I went to public school and got into a good college. But I'm not sure either have anything to do with how I turned out."

Sharon put her hand on his. "You're polite, which is more than I can say for Chase's friends."

Mia leaned into Chase as she grabbed a purple baby carrot from the crudité platter. "I can't argue with that."

Sharon forked a white hunk of jicama and waved it towards Chase. "Your father says it's this house or private school for Josh." She plunked it back on her plate. "I don't love this area anymore, but it's my home. It's gotten so hoity-toity since I was a kid." Chase, Mia, and Oliver shared an amused glance.

They picked at the kale and dried date salad, which adhered to Sharon's alkaline ash diet. She explained that it helped her overcome a host of maladies, from inflammatory arthritis to IBS. Mia privately marveled at her skating rink-smooth complexion, wondering how she could eschew toxins but inject Botox and fillers into her face.

While Chase disappeared to check on his little brother in his room and gather clean clothes, Sharon gave Mia a rose quartz crystal. "We're both empaths. I know what you're feeling. Keep this in your pocket." Mia slipped it inside her back pocket and hoped that Sharon didn't know *all* that she was feeling.

When she sat in the car and headed off with Chase and Oliver, the sharp edges of the crystal jabbed her butt cheek. "Ow," she muttered as she lifted herself up and pulled the crystal back out.

Chase grabbed it. "I love my mom, but—" Chase threw the crystal out the window. The three laughed, though once it was gone, Mia felt the pang of missing her own mother.

They backtracked on Sunset and found street parking near the mouth of Temescal Canyon. Chase had said finding parking in LA was like swiping right once and meeting your soulmate. They started the trek towards Skull Rock.

"You can always tell the real hikers. They're wearing hiking shoes instead of sneakers," said Chase.

Mia flashed on Teddy and Rocko's motorcycle boots on the side of Backbone Trail, and the smoking cigarette butt by her own shoes. "*We're* wearing sneakers."

She looked around and saw a variety of trailblazers—some in serious hiking gear and carrying walking sticks, the others in curated outfits for selfie sticks. "That's gonna sting if she falls," she said about one girl who adjusted her tiny shorts so they rode up just enough for some ass cleavage.

The three passed a grassy knoll with bright rainbow awnings, beverage coolers, tables topped with bottles of sunscreen, and banners that welcomed summer campers. A group of eight-year-olds raced each other, playing tag and chucking water balloons. A boy in swim trunks broke from the water balloon chuckers and loped to the perimeter where Mia, Chase, and Oliver walked. He spread his legs and peed without removing his trunks. "Dogs and cats do it," he said and loped back to the water balloons.

Chase shook his head and chuckled as they continued on. "Being a camp counselor is the best tube-tier. The last time I hiked up here was with surf camp. A kid picked up a used condom and put it on his hand like a puppet."

"No!" cried Mia as she and Oliver cringed.

Chase cackled. "He pulled out his hand and asked why it was sticky."

"How do you respond to that?" asked Mia.

"I said 'Ask your nanny,' then told him to wash his hands and eat his lunch."

Oliver wrinkled his nose. "That is so foul. But could you teach *me* how to surf?"

"Anytime, man. How about you, Mia?" Chase poked Mia's waist. Mia yelped once and jumped away from him.

"I hate being tickled almost as much as I hate swimming in anything where I can't see what's underneath me." She flashed back to searching for Ruby in the dark sea around Brant Lighthouse without knowing how to swim. Ruby had found *her*.

"When you surf, that's all going to change," said Chase.

Mia smirked. "*If* not when."

Chase filmed them with his phone as they trekked into the woods, past the quaint wood visitor center shack. People gathered, scanning maps and retying their shoes. Moms ready for their daily workout put hats on their babies, who they carried in matching front packs.

They walked the thin dirt path above the campgrounds, where campers were tie-dying T-shirts.

"At Y camp, tie-dye inspired me to become a fashion designer. I would grab any unwanted item of clothing at home and make it my own." Mia stood for a moment, watching. Her breathing had quickened with the uphill climb. "Maybe we can stop at an art store on the way back. I can buy some good, old-fashioned fabric dye and rubber bands."

"There's no art store close by, but there's a drugstore," said Chase.

"That'll do." She looked at Oliver's crisp white tee. "I'll tie-dye your shirt, Oliver."

Oliver swatted away a yellow jacket. "I don't do boho well. But I need to pick up a prescription . . . EpiPen."

They took longer strides up through the hills, surrounded by spiked cacti that bared bright flowers, and trees that looked like they belonged in a Dr. Seuss book. Oliver trailed. "My parents shipped me off to sleepaway camp every summer. I think it was so they could have the whole house to themselves and *really* kick the crap out of each other."

Chase shook his head. "Dude, that's gnarly. My parents went to a therapist who taught them how to speak to each other in this insanely ridiculous way. My mom'll try to do that with me, and I'll just fuck with her. Like I would say, 'I need to honor my subconscious,' and since water is a symbol for the subconscious, she would let me surf all day instead of go to school."

"At least they didn't blame their marriage problems on you."

"Divorce is never the kids' fault," said Mia.

"My parents are still married," said Oliver. "They stay together because of me, but I wish they wouldn't. I thought when I went away to college, they would use it as a chance to finally find their own separate happinesses. And then I'd get a chance to be happy."

Mia realized that she had rarely heard Oliver utter anything but pure optimism. It was also strange that he had been trailing behind them—he had the most energy of anyone in the house, even if he wasn't the most athletic. Now, he looked listless.

Chase motioned back to him. "Come on, Oli. Getting to the top of this mountain will make you feel like a king!"

Mia smiled at Oliver. "Should we try?"

Oliver nodded but didn't look convinced.

They crossed a small metal bridge over Temescal Falls. Chase explained how it had become a meager trickle during the recent drought. The trails twisted and turned, rising out of the canyon, then settling to a more gradual incline. They reached a ridge with an unobstructed view of the coastline.

Oliver sat on the ground, sweat dripping from his forehead. He took off his glasses and wiped his stinging eyes. "At the risk of sounding like a pussy, I don't know if I can climb all the way to Skull Rock."

"Are you okay?" asked Mia.

"Sorry. I have a splitting headache." Oliver's eyes were bloodshot. Mia had never seen him so lethargic.

Chase tossed his bottle of water to Oliver. It dropped in the dirt. Oliver brushed it off and drank. "Let's jog down. It's actually easier and more fun than walking," said Chase.

"Yeah. Let's do that. Sorry." Oliver passed the water bottle back to Chase.

"Don't apologize!" Mia put her hand out for Oliver and pulled him up.

They started to trot down. Chase was at the front, with Mia in the center. "It's meditative because you can't concentrate on anything but exactly what's in front of you." Mia found Chase's adage to be true. As they wound and skipped around rocks, crevices, and tree roots, Mia's mind was on putting one foot in front of the other.

"How's it going, Oli?" shouted Chase without turning back. There was no answer, and Mia realized that she hadn't heard the thump of downhill footsteps and rustling of leaves behind her for a while. She stopped and turned around but didn't see Oliver.

"Chase!"

Chase stopped and turned.

Mia lifted her arms. "Where's Oliver?"

Chase glanced around them. He shrugged.

Mia pulled her phone from her backpack and texted Oliver. No response. She called, but he didn't pick up. "Dammit!" She took quick strides back up the hill.

"Where are you going?" asked Chase.

"To find him!" Mia halted in her tracks at a chorus of buzzing, and turned to see a dry creek bed. In its center was a beach ball–sized slab of honeycomb with hundreds of bees blanketing the holes. "Oliver! Oliver!" she shouted.

Chase caught up to her. "What's with the freak-out? He's not a lost camper."

"I know." Mia was as breathless from nerves as she was from running.

Chase pointed to the hive. "That's cool!"

"He's allergic!"

Chase motioned to the trees, bushes, mountains, and vistas around them. "Maybe he needed some alone time. Being in a house with six people is a lot."

"Eight people," grumbled Mia.

"Wyatt and Nils are like puppies."

"Nine, including Boomer." Mia continued upward. She and Chase veered off one path onto another. Mia's gut feeling was that Oliver was in that direction. Chase followed, doing an Instagram Story: "The Mystery of the Missing O."

Mia didn't find it funny. She came around a bend to find Oliver by a sycamore.

"Hey," she said.

Oliver whipped around with his pocket knife open towards her. "Don't sneak up on me like that!"

"What are you doing?" Mia gestured to the tree.

"Eve would say he's defacing US Forest Service land and it's a misdemeanor," said Chase, his phone trained on Oliver.

Mia glared at Chase. "Then why are you filming it?"

Chase lowered his phone. "That's very artful." Mia stared at the trunk of the sycamore. In it was an incomplete carving of Munch's *The Scream*.

Oliver closed his pocket knife. "Sorry," he said to Mia and Chase. He patted the tree. "Sorry." His shoulders dropped. "I shouldn't be here."

"Because of the bees?" asked Chase.

"No. Because of *me*. I shouldn't be here in Malibu. I shouldn't be a seasonaire. I'm not like the rest of you."

Mia shook her head. "You're *you*, Oliver. That's better than the rest of us."

"I wouldn't go that far. I mean, Alex is so cool . . ." said Chase. Off Mia's look—"Kidding!"

Oliver motioned to them. "You're all good-looking . . ."

Mia smiled at him. "You're *very* handsome, Oliver."

Chase held up his phone and pointed to the screen. "Consensus online is that you're 'adorable.'"

"You're all talented," said Oliver.

"And *you're* talented, though indiscriminate." Chase gestured to the tree carving.

"I just don't feel right." Oliver put his hands to his head.

Mia reached out to him. "That's okay. We all have days when we feel like that."

"It's not the same."

"You belong with us because you're our friend." Mia stepped up to Oliver and kissed him on the cheek.

"Gimme some of that." Chase moved in and they all hugged.

"They're making out!" screamed a boy. A group of campers and their teen counselor—all wearing *Camp CaliSun* T-shirts—crossed an adjacent trail. The kids laughed loudly.

"Oooooh. Oooooh!" called the boy.

"That's why, kids, if you find a condom, keep it," said Chase. "Unless it's used."

"Don't be a tool," said the pretty counselor, who ushered off the kids.

Oliver shrugged at Mia and Chase. "I'm sorry. I'm being a p—"

Mia put her finger to his lips. "You're *fine*."

"I know the best way to get down this mountain." Chase motioned to Oliver to hop on his back. He carried Oliver back to the trail's mouth. Mia followed. She watched Oliver's face. His sweet grin was gone. He was a different person.

TWENTY-FOUR

Oliver locked himself in the bedroom. Chase used the obstruction as an opportunity to surf. Brandon used it as a chance to film him, since it was golden hour. Mia sat up the beach from Brandon and watched Chase ride the waves. His graceful, curving dance on the water seemed effortless, reminding Mia of the way Sean threw a ball. She pulled her phone from the kangaroo pocket of her hoodie and dialed.

"Hey," answered Sean.

"How are things?"

"Things are fine." There was a long silence. Mia thought the call had dropped.

"Sean, are you there?"

Brandon passed to follow Chase's movements with the camera.

"Sean?" repeated Mia.

"I'm here," said Sean.

"How'd it go with the Twins?"

"Fine." His voice sounded tight. "Listen, can I call you back? I'm just doing something."

"You have the apartment to yourself, so I don't want to know what that something is." Mia chuckled.

Sean didn't laugh. "Talk later?"

The corners of Mia's mouth descended. "Sure." Sean hung up.

———

Mia was glad that Oliver wasn't part of some nightmare she had made up about being taken by the bikers in the woods. But six days went by and he remained in bed, refusing to talk to a soul, even when Mia brought him food, which he barely touched. The shades to his room stayed down during the July Fourth fireworks that the others watched from the bluff. Barges along the coast launched the spectacular display. The brand didn't host a party, because Lyndon refused to compete with all the other high-profile celebrations in Malibu. Their big event would be a Labor Day fashion show.

Everyone knew better than to bring up Mia's Fourth of July in Nantucket, though the fatal event sat heavily in the air like the smoke over the ocean after a sparkling blast.

In the morning, the group stood around the kitchen island. Oliver was conspicuously absent. They all had to make their own lattes. Breakfast consisted of cold pizza from the night before instead of fresh pancakes.

Alex poked at a mushroom. "I should have known. One of my best friends struggles with bipolar disorder."

"How can you be so sure Oli is bipolar?" asked Mia.

"There are signs: the high energy and compulsion to entertain everyone."

"That sounds like you, Alex," said Chase, polishing off a slice.

"The compulsive cleaning and cooking—" Alex motioned around the kitchen.

Eve put her hand on Alex's arm. "That's definitely *not* you."

Despite the fact that Oliver had neglected the kitchen for the past few days, it still smelled like the rosemary mint–scented cleaner he always used.

"And now *this*," said Alex, motioning upstairs towards the bedrooms.

Mia tossed down her pizza crust. "I can't get him to come out."

Brandon filmed their conversation. Mia crossed to get a water from the fridge and put her hand over the lens. Brandon lowered the camera. "Don't ever do that," he snapped.

Mia glared at him. "Can you keep it out of here right now? And out of his room?"

"I'm not that much of an asshole."

Eve peered over her coffee mug at them. "Why don't you two just fuck already?"

Mia's phone buzzed with a call from Lyndon. She exited the kitchen and answered it when she reached the living room.

"Is he taking his meds?" asked Lyndon.

Mia's mouth screwed with curiosity. "How did you know he takes meds?"

"The same way I knew you had a fake ID last summer. Well, has he?"

"I haven't asked him. I didn't know." Mia remembered the hike: Oliver had wanted to stop at the drugstore for an EpiPen, yet she never saw him use the one he already had. He was probably going to refill a different prescription but was too ashamed to say anything. "Maybe this isn't the right environment for him," Mia said as she entered her workspace. The view from her floor-to-ceiling windows revealed a postcard-ready beach day.

"Or maybe we should use it as an opportunity to educate people and help remove the stigma. If you all support him

through it, others will see that they can get through it as well."
Lyndon's tone was officious, not empathetic. *Oliver was chosen for
a reason*, Mia thought. *We all were.*

Mia scratched her head. "We're not mental health experts."

Lyndon's voice softened. "I wasn't either, but maybe if I'd done
more for my sister, she wouldn't be in the position she's in now.
And Grant might still be alive."

Oliver trudged down the stairs and into the hall towards
Brandon's studio. He looked like a ghost—pale and wane from
days in the dark without food.

Mia looked up at him. "Oli?"

He didn't answer.

Mia cupped the phone with her hand. "Do you want to talk
to him?"

"I'm talking to you. You're talking to him. Same thing."

"I should go." Mia clicked off. Brandon stepped into the living
room. Mia motioned him to his studio, where they found Oliver
sitting on the stool in front of the backdrop.

Brandon spoke gently. "Hey, man, whatcha doin?"

"My confessional."

"You sure?"

Oliver nodded.

Mia motioned to the door. "Do you want me to leave?"

Oliver shook his head as Brandon started rolling camera. Mia
watched the monitor. Oliver's eyes looked like liquid blue saucers
as he stared into the lens and began to speak.

"Why do we do it? We put on the face we want everyone to see and
then we're upset when people don't try to dig deeper. But it's our own
fault. It's *my* own fault. I didn't want to be separate from anyone else.
That's why I did shit like take ecstasy at our beach party, which is not
smart for someone with bipolar disorder." Oliver gave Lyndon what
she wanted. Then he took it away. "I wanted to be what I *thought* was
normal, but the most normal thing I can do is go home."

He rose and crossed the studio without looking at Brandon or Mia. The door closed behind him.

That afternoon, the doorbell rang. Mia answered the door to find Presley.

"There's no *I* in quitter, I can tell you that much." Presley jangled her keys. The Volvo sat in the driveway. "Lyndon wants me to take him in case there's any media fallout. But he'll be a trivia question before he even boards the bus. No one cares."

"That's a huge part of the problem, so I'm coming, too." Mia slung her purse over her shoulder.

Presley crossed her arms. "Don't you trust I can get him to the station?"

"I don't trust what will happen *between* here and the station. He's really fragile, Presley."

"You're reinforcing a generation of snowflake baby-men."

"And you just proved my point. I'm going," said Mia.

Oliver descended the stairs with his suitcase and backpack. The other seasonaires joined. Presley handed him a paper pharmacy bag. "Your Risperidone, Oli." He looked mortified, but Mia stroked his arm while scowling at Presley.

Brandon filmed as Oliver said his good-byes.

"Love sandwich!" cried Eve as she and Alex embraced Oliver.

"Repeat after me," said Alex. "What you think of me is none of my business."

Oliver smiled between these two friends. "What you think of me is none of my business."

Chase manned the camera while Brandon pulled Oliver in for a hug. Only Mia could hear him as he said, low in Oliver's ear, "If you need anything—*ever*—I'm here for you." They parted.

Mia exited with Presley and Oliver, who rode shotgun. They headed to the Santa Monica Expo Line's western terminal station for the Metro Rail that Oliver would take to reach the Greyhound bus station downtown. Oliver stared out the window as the Volvo whipped along the sparkling coast. "I blew this one pretty good."

Mia leaned forward to rub his shoulder. "You didn't blow it."

"Ya, kinda did," mumbled Presley.

Mia glared at her, then looked at Oliver. "Were you afraid to come here? Because I was."

"Shaking in my loafers."

Presley tapped the steering wheel. "That's because you wear loafers and not MazzyLyn kicks. You're going to miss the store opening."

"I know."

"We'll send you some shoes. I promise," said Mia.

"Thanks."

Mia sat back. "You faced your fears, Oliver. You didn't need to get on a trapeze or climb to some skull-shaped rock to do it."

"No. I ignored my fears and they smacked me right in the face."

"You know you're loved, right? I mean, look at this." Mia handed Oliver her phone to show him a steady stream of comments coming in on the good-bye posts:

> Oli, you're our fave!
> Keep it real, O.
> Live your truth.

"They're strangers," said Oliver, returning the phone to Mia.

Mia clicked the screen black because she knew Oliver was right. "But *we're* not." Mia gazed at Oliver. She shifted to Presley, who instead of agreeing, honked at a weaving driver.

Presley yelled out the window. "Who the fuck taught you to drive?"

Oliver's phone dinged with a text. Oliver looked at it. "Lyndon says she's sorry to see me go." He put his phone down. "She can't be that sorry—she gets to keep ten grand."

Presley pulled up to the terminal's lot but didn't get out. Instead, she started scrolling on her phone. Oliver gathered his luggage, and Mia followed him to the platform. They stood facing each other. "*Don't* be a stranger, Oli."

Oliver reached over and pulled a quarter from her ear. He put it in her palm. "Don't spend it all in one place." They held hands for a beat. Mia's mouth turned up in a soft smile. Then, Oliver brought his fist around from Mia's other ear and opened his palm. In it was the pocket knife. "Whittle." He handed it to her and disappeared inside the station. Mia had the urge to go with him—not to make sure he would be taken care of but because he was taking care *of himself* by leaving. She'd thought that with this summer in Malibu she'd be taking care of herself, but it was like painting over a giant hole without spackling first. She sighed, dropped the pocket knife in her purse, and walked back to the car.

She climbed into the passenger's seat. Presley put her phone down and peeled out. She side-eyed Mia. "That dork was trying to get with you, huh? Lyndon thought he was nerdy-hot, but he was straight-up nerd."

"She's pissed he left. If she wasn't, she would've called him," said Mia.

"You should consider that Lyndon didn't trust *you* to drive Oliver off after your heart bled all over Ruby last summer."

"I never gave Ruby any information that had to do with Lyndon or the brand. We were just friends." Mia watched three high school girls on a corner by the Santa Monica Place shopping mall snap a selfie. "But that was enough for you to backstab me like some jealous high school girl."

"Jealous?" Presley scoffed. "That urchin is gluing extensions in bumfuck Corona while I'm traveling across the globe and living in penthouse suites. I'd bring you to see mine, but I don't want to deal with the traffic back from Brentwood." She steered left on Ocean Avenue and past the Santa Monica Pier and headed down the tiny street that split at two beautiful beachfront hotels. She pulled up in front of Hotel Casa Del Mar—a stunning blend of brick and Spanish architecture. "This'll have to do for a business meeting."

"What business meeting?"

"Oliver's replacement. We need one."

Presley exited the car and dropped the keys into the strapping young valet's hand. "We're here for the view. As they say, 'Take a picture, it'll last longer." She handed him her phone and ensured *his* view of her ass in a snug pencil skirt as she led Mia to the ornate lead glass doors. She turned and posed, while Mia tried to smile as the valet snapped shots. "Good eye," said Presley as she surveyed the photos while sashaying through the doors, Mia close behind. As she stepped across the mosaic-tiled foyer, Presley filtered, then tagged Mia and the hotel, and posted.

A stairway led up to the lounge, where well-heeled guests and patrons enjoyed drinks in living room–like nooks accented with palms and hanging ferns. Presley commandeered an empty corner, sitting in a Balinese chair. She caught a server by the sleeve and ordered two champagne cocktails.

Mia settled onto one side of a plush sofa. "So you *do* know where Ruby lives."

"As do you—from the look of those god-awful blue stripes." Presley leaned forward and swiped at one of Mia's azure-chalked locks. "No salon in this neck of the woods would dare put their name on those."

Mia tucked the lock behind her ear. "It's washing out, but I like it."

Presley waved a hand. "No, you don't—though we're not here to discuss your lapse in judgment, which won't happen again. Will it, sugar?" She locked eyes with Mia.

"Is that coming from you or Lyndon?"

"Same thing." Their cocktails arrived in their long-stemmed flutes. Presley sipped hers. She lifted her iPad from her white snakeskin tote and opened it. "Let's talk boy replacements. He needs to be from the East Coast, because Midwesterners like Oliver don't seem to be able to handle the heat. Let's have a look, shall we?" She propped the iPad next to a white ceramic bowl of artisanal potato chips. Clicking on a file named *Wannabes*, she scrolled through photos of twentysomething men who were good-looking and good-time-seeking. "Here's Jared from New York. He's a music major at Pace."

"Brandon will bury a musician," replied Mia.

Presley scrolled and pointed. "Charlie from Maine who lives on a salmon boat. The dad bod is cute, but he might not assimilate due to too much time alone at sea—plus a fishy stench that would rival Eve's. Garrett from Virginia, Michael from Rhode Island, Jackson from Jersey, which is a hard no for me.'" She closed the file and opened her photos library, finding a shot of Sean, shirtless on the beach. Staring out at Nantucket Harbor, he wasn't posing for the camera. He probably didn't even know it was there. "Your brother pretended he didn't like his visit last summer, but I can tell when a man is enjoying himself."

"No." Mia put down her glass. "Why don't you get Wyatt or Nils to take Oliver's place? As it is, they're basically living at the house."

"We already have Chase and his tar-sticky feet. But that reminds me—Lyndon wants you to boot the doofus twins once and for all."

"I tried."

"Trying is for losers. *Do it*. If people think they can live in our house for free, why would anyone apply to be a seasonaire? Those two soggy rats are sponging off us. Their social is getting bigger every day they fart on the rec room couch."

Mia picked up a chip, then dropped it back in the bowl. "I know."

"You don't want your brother stepping in their dog's shit."

"My brother isn't coming."

Presley sat taller, eyes on Mia. "Lyndon thought he was perfect back then, and her opinion hasn't changed."

Mia leaned towards her. "Didn't you hear him last summer? He thinks seasonaires are a bunch of assholes. And frankly, we are."

"Not Sean. He's the real deal."

"One seasonaire has already left. The drama has ramped up. Sean steers clear of drama like the plague. And since our mom died, that's the last thing he needs."

Presley pulled a Minnesota Twins roster up on the iPad screen. "He's not on it."

Mia's heart stopped. Sean hadn't called her back, and now she understood why. "How did you know that he was being scouted by the Twins?"

Presley gazed at her reflection in the mirrored wall next to the couch and brushed an impeccable brow with her forefinger. "You're aware there are cameras at the house, right?"

"*Inside* the house. I was outside on the beach when I talked to him. That was a private conversation."

Presley rolled her eyes. "Oh, honey, you have to let go of that 'privacy' shit." She put a hand on Mia's leg. "Where Sean is concerned, people are allowed to change their minds. Do you know for certain that at this particularly low point in your beloved brother's life he would pass up twenty grand and a cushy Malibu vacay?"

Mia looked out at the blue-on-blue view through the arched windows at the far end of the lounge.

"Don't you think he deserves it?" asked Presley.

"He likes cold weather. That's why he wanted the Twins," replied Mia.

"Take him to Universal Studios. Harry Potter World has snow year-round. This city has it all!" Presley pulled two tickets from her tote and waved them. "Including baseball." She clapped once.

"Wouldn't you know it? The Dodgers are playing the Red Sox! Dugout Club seats. He can schmooze."

"Sean doesn't schmooze."

Presley slapped the tickets on the table. "If you don't ask him, I will. Your brother and I have a good relationship." Presley recrossed her long legs.

Mia mimicked Presley's single clap. "You don't have a relationship."

"Well, I have his sweatshirt. I wear it to bed." Presley shifted on the couch cushion. Mia was never sure if Sean and Presley had hooked up during his brief Nantucket visit.

"Are you going to ask him, or should I?" Presley clicked off the iPad and slipped it back in her tote. Mia tapped her fingers on her thigh. Presley straightened. "I take it from your resistance that you'd like *me* to offer up the invitation." She removed her satin makeup bag and reapplied her red lipstick, rubbing her lips together for a perfect pout.

"It's going to look like nepotism. I already have enough problems with my backstory," said Mia.

"Maybe little sister is worried that big brother's gonna steal her thunder. I mean, you've been so humble about your nice payday. Why don't you let the world know what you're worth? Show off those peacock feathers!"

Mia crossed her arms. "Wow, you really have the inside scoop, don't you?"

"Always." Presley clicked her compact closed.

"Lyndon suggested that I keep my fee under wraps." Mia wondered how long Presley had been simmering over this information.

"I say a press release is in order. I'll have a chitchat with her. I'm persuasive, as your brother knows, so let's get him on the phone." Presley nodded to Mia's purse.

Mia stared at a potted palm, pondering for a long moment. "I'll pass on the press release, but you can persuade Lyndon to pay Sean more to pinch-hit here."

"Then *you* make it happen with him right now," countered Presley.

"Deal." Mia took her phone from her purse and started to dial.

"I want to see his face when we make the offer!" Presley reached over to press the FaceTime icon on Mia's phone. Sean answered, looking more disheveled than usual—dark circles under his eyes. "Sorry I didn't call you back," he said.

Presley moved next to Mia, into frame. "Surprise!"

Sean ran his hand over his face and groaned.

"Come seasonaire with your sister!" said Presley.

Sean snorted. "Now 'seasonaire' is a verb?"

"One of ours had to go home." Mia held up the baseball tickets. "There are Dugout Club seats in it for you. Oh, and thirty grand instead of the customary twenty."

Presley choked slightly and took a sip of her drink.

"That's about what the Twins would've paid you to start on an affiliate team, but you'll be making it in way less time," added Mia.

"With way less effort. So whaddya say, Sean?" asked Presley, scratching her nails back and forth on the sofa's woven fabric.

Sean answered without a beat. "Screw the Twins."

"Screw the Twins," replied Mia, offering an empathetic smile. She looked at Presley. "Presley will email you your plane tickets— first class, of course, because that's how the Daniels siblings *seasonaire*. See ya, turd."

"Whatever, turd." The siblings flipped each other off and FaceTime ended.

Presley glared at her. "First class? What the fuck, Mia?"

Mia rose. "I'll take a Lyft home. I wouldn't want you to get stuck." She strode out of the hotel.

At the curb, Mia took a deep breath of the sea air, then looked down at her phone to order the car. The sidewalk's steep incline made her feel a little off balance. Before she pressed the button to confirm her ride, a motorcycle's roar echoed on the thin street, causing her to drop her phone.

"Need a ride?" said a deep, gravelly voice.

As Mia retrieved her phone from the ground, she looked up and saw Teddy on his bike in front of her at the curb. He patted the space behind him on the seat. "Get on."

"No, thank you." *He knew where she was—had he been following her?*

"You think it's dangerous?"

Mia didn't answer.

"I can take you to the bank," said Teddy.

Mia's voice was small. "Why do I need to go to the bank?"

Teddy lifted his goggles onto his half-helmet so he could look Mia in the eyes. "I told you to stay away from Ruby."

Mia didn't avoid his stare. "The money is for her."

"I'm her father."

"She's an adult."

Teddy smiled, his teeth bared like a shark who ate anything in its path. "I make the rules. I'll always make the rules."

"I told her I was sorry." Mia wrapped her cotton cardigan around herself.

Teddy's smile turned into a scowl. "You told her more than that." He put a gloved finger on Mia's arm. "That'll be another twenty."

Mia's breath caught with panic. "I don't have that now."

"Then get it."

Mia stammered. "I can get it to you by the time we leave Los Angeles—when I get paid."

"When does your cunt boss pay you?"

"The day after Labor Day."

"If it's not in my hands by then, you *won't* be leaving." Teddy roared off on the bike. Mia shuddered—the engine's gnarl shook her to her core.

TWENTY-FIVE

The Tesla pulled up next to Sean, who blinked at the cacophony of car honks. The window lowered and Mia called out from it, "Ready to seasonaire?" She put on her most cheerful smile, even though she'd already vomited twice that morning. Alex and Eve attributed it to the unusual amount of tequila she'd been drinking since she'd run into Teddy a week earlier. The secret was making her sick. Lyndon wasn't returning her calls, instead sending emails demanding more samples. Mia hadn't been paid for any samples, though she had sewn, tailored, and embellished dresses, pants, skirts, tops, and jackets.

Sean looked tired and overwhelmed as the Tesla's back doors lifted to reveal all the seasonaires. Alex beamed from the third row. Eve, arm still in the sling, wiggled her fingers in a wave. Sean lifted his hand in a return wave. "Hey," he said as he slid in next to Mia. "Nice whip."

"How was your flight?" Mia tried to give him more room.

"They kept offering me hot towels."

"Worth the first-class ticket," said Brandon from the front passenger seat. He was filming the arrival.

Chapped, Eve pulled her hand back from her intended shake. "You flew first class?"

"That's Eve and Alex." Mia gestured back, then to the front. "Brandon and Chase."

"Hey," said Brandon from behind the camera.

Chase reached one hand off the steering wheel to give Sean a vape pen. "Welcome!"

"Thanks." Sean took the vape and smoked as Chase steered them up Fairfax. Mia watched him exhale, leaning his head against the headrest.

Mia tapped Brandon's seat as he filmed. "Can you ease him into this?"

"I don't care," said Sean, exhaling the weed smoke.

Mia sat back, unnerved by his indifference.

Brandon kept his camera on Sean. "You're not wearing any Lyndon Wyld."

"Nope."

Brandon stopped filming. "You will. Plus, you got here in time for next level."

"The opening of the MazzyLyn store," said Alex. "Is Lyndon going to be there?"

"No," said Mia. "She was at the Malibu opening, so she's leaving this to Maz."

Eve tilted her head. "Maybe it's also because she understands she's not representative of true streetwear. So many people wear it but don't have any understanding of the streets."

Brandon snickered. "*You* don't have any understanding of the streets. But you're the kind of people who've turned resale into a basement business. I'll bet your college boyfriend bought his books reselling Yeezys."

As they passed the gleaming red and silver metal waves of the Petersen Automotive Museum, Chase pointed to a trashcan filled with flaming paper. "Yo! A real dumpster fire!" Three firefighters emerged from their truck to wake a homeless man sleeping on the bus bench next to the smoking garbage, plastic grocery bags full of belongings and newspapers next to him. Tourists and summering teens walked around the strolling Orthodox Jewish men in their heavy, black suits and black wide-brimmed hats, some in fur *shtreimels*.

Alex watched them out the window. "It takes devotion to wear all that in ninety-degree weather."

"It's Shabbat. They're walking to synagogue. Their devotion kicks my devotion's ass," said Chase.

"Devotion means something different to everyone, and it means kicks, caps, and jackets to *these* people." Brandon nodded towards young shoppers streaming in and out of the stores: Supreme, Flight Club, and Diamond Supply Co. "Fairfax is being overrun by what I call 'trendhounds.'"

"What are 'trendhounds'?" asked Mia.

"Dickbags who chase what they think is cool. We gotta pretend we love them because they buy."

Mia ogled the lines around the stores. Some people waited in folding chairs. "I'll never understand what's so amazing about those sneakers." Mia pointed to one of the stores with a window display of kicks. "Do they make you fly?"

"They make you cum. They're *shoes*." Alex held his phone over the seat to show off a post of his walk-in closet, its color-coordinated shelves stacked with every kind of shoe from high-top kick to stiletto pump. "But I don't wait in line for anything."

Brandon grinned. "You won't have to. But if you did, that would be it." He nodded to the line that stretched around the block from the MazzyLyn store. It broke to allow hungry patrons to enter Canter's Deli.

They parked in one of the three reserved spots behind the MazzyLyn store. Brandon led them around front to enter so the cluster of paparazzi would snap them. Some waiting shoppers yelled, "What the fuck?" and "Get in line!" Others screamed Brandon's name, begging for selfies. A few recognized Mia and Alex—mostly the girlfriends of the impatient guys. They obliged with photos.

House music blared out of the open glass doors from a deejay who was spinning behind the window. The seasonaires entered past two enormous bouncers, who slapped palms with Brandon. Mia remembered them as Maz's bodyguards, Skullcrusher and Wrecking Ball. They had accompanied Maz when he dropped off Jade at the Nantucket house. The two giant men nodded to Mia. She managed a small, twitchy smile.

Inside, the bright lights bounced off the slick white floor. Sean squinted. "Now I understand sunglasses indoors." Brandon was still wearing his.

Chase scanned around, his eyes wide. "This is epic!"

"It is pretty cool," said Sean.

The two walls on either side were covered with shelves holding the coveted footwear. The back wall was a mosaic of caps and hats. T-shirts, jackets, tracksuits, and pants hung on white racks. The shapes were edgy, but the colors and patterns were pure Lyndon. She managed to keep her signature elegant style in a bold, noisy niche.

Maz, in a MazzyLyn leather vest/puffy jacket combo over diamond stitch carpenter jeans and jewel-embellished kicks, posed in front of a logo backdrop. Nearby, Presley courted the photographers and journalists. She sidled up to Maz and whispered something. He looked over to see Brandon and the group but continued his star turn in front of the cameras.

"King of the castle," mumbled Brandon.

Like court jester, Presley giggled and canoodled with celebrities, who also stood for photos in the clothes, shoes, and accessories.

She offered a pageant wave to the seasonaires, mouthed "Sean!" and blew him a kiss.

He glanced at his feet. "Yeah, no."

Eve winced. "She's single-handedly killing the progress of an entire gender."

"True, but those are giving *me* life!" Alex made a beeline to the platform sneakers with saw-tooth rubber soles, which took up an entire row of footwear. He pulled Eve with him.

Chase elbowed Sean. "We get free shit, so let's start with the libations." Sean shrugged at Mia. He followed Chase to the bar that was set up in the corner.

A photographer motioned Mia and Brandon together. "New couple alert." Snap-snap-snap and he was gone. Mia leaned into Brandon. "Do *not* tell your dad anything, please."

Brandon removed his sunglasses so he could look her in the eyes. "I promised you I wouldn't. Why would you think I would?"

"Because you told Presley about my brother and the Twins."

Brandon jeered at Presley, who ran her finger along the chest of a good-looking rap star. "I try to have as little contact with that girl as possible. I overheard you talking on the phone about it. My dad's a baseball fan. I thought he'd be impressed that Sean made the team."

Mia frowned. "Sean didn't make the team."

By the backdrop, Maz was shaking Sean's hand. Mia was happy to see a smile on her brother's face. She searched around. "Is Jade going to be here?"

"My sister is working my dad's other side of the world," said Brandon. "That's why he was forced to have *me* here." Brandon's whole demeanor seemed to shrink in the presence of his father. This humility softened Mia's anger at him.

"I need a drink. How 'bout you?" asked Mia. They turned and bumped into Marcus, who scowled and walked off to the register counter. He had gone from screenwriter to seasonaire caretaker to cashier.

Maz ambled up to Brandon and smacked him on the back. "Marcus is not happy with you, son. You fired him without asking me first."

"He was working for the seasonaires, so I made a decision," said Brandon. "You always tell me to be decisive." He shoved his hands in his pockets.

"You also have to suffer the consequences of those decisions. He was my second pair of eyes—some extra protection for you."

Mia noticed the black silk rope of Maz's medallion necklace disappearing inside his collar. Brandon didn't dare look at her. He kept his focus on his father. "I don't need protection. I'm not you."

"You might be if your older brother keeps fucking up."

"I appreciate the confidence, Pops. If you're that confident, then you know I made the right choice. Marcus is a bottom-feeder. I know he's a buddy of yours, but he's using you. And he was about to use *me*, because he was planning on writing a screenplay about me."

"It wasn't just about you," Maz responded and glanced at Mia. "It was about the seasonaires."

Brandon scoffed. "So you *knew*?"

"He pitched it to me. I told him it's all about the execution, and I highly doubt he'd be able to execute that. You worried for no reason."

"He made me uncomfortable," said Mia. "I didn't want him there, so Brandon did it for *me*. After last summer dealing with Otto, I wanted to keep our circle tighter." She flashed to Teddy on the motorcycle, baring his fangs at her. "But we should have consulted you before we made the decision."

Maz put his hand on Brandon's arm. "No. You're right, son. This seasonaires endeavor is yours. You take care of it." He leaned into Brandon. Mia heard him whisper, "You're on your own."

Presley stepped up to them. "I'm glad you're getting word out on the channel about MazzyLyn, Brandon. I wanted Wyld World to be a platform for cross-branding when I originally suggested it to Lyndon."

Brandon narrowed his eyes at her. "You what?"

"Wanted cross-promotion," replied Presley, adjusting her fitten denim MazzyLyn jacket.

"No, the second part. The only way I would've become a sea-sonaire was if I could produce a channel. Lyndon knew that." Brandon's amber eyes burned into her, but her bright smile never flinched.

Maz moved his hand to Brandon's shoulder. "As long as the channel is kicking ass, its inception is irrelevant." He turned to Mia. "Is it kicking ass?"

Mia's eyes shifted back and forth between Brandon and Presley, then landed on Maz, who smirked at her discomfort. "I think it's been fun for people to watch," she said.

"I hate the word *fun*. It's a non-description," said Brandon, who walked off to talk to some press at the backdrop.

Presley followed. "I'm going to make sure he has fun." Mia was left standing alone with Maz.

"You were diplomatic," said Maz.

"Self-preservation," replied Mia.

Maz stuck his hand out for her. "I'm Maz. We met last year when I dropped my girl Jade off at the house."

Mia shook his hand. She thought it was ingratiating that he saw fit to reintroduce himself, though she would've bet he didn't remember who she was. "Mia," she said.

Maz leaned back and crossed his arms. "You were wearing a classic skirt with polka dots. I wish Jade would go classic sometimes."

"My style and Jade's are very different. I could never pull off anything she wears." Mia smiled. "I miss her."

"She talks a lot about you. You were the only genuine friend she made in Nantucket besides that sheep J.P. She talked me into letting him design a couple hats for my M-Kat collection. Since they got kicked off the island last summer, Lyndon would eat dirt before she'd let him anywhere near this line."

"He must be really excited about M-Kat though."

"I think he shit his skinny jeans when I offered him the gig. He definitely needs more confidence. Jade's gonna eat him alive."

Mia chuckled.

Maz glanced at the deejay. "I like to nurture new talent—music, film, art, fashion." He shifted back to Mia. "Brandon says *your* upcoming collection for Lyndon is fire. Are you happy with your compensation?"

Mia shifted on her feet.

"I could do better," said Maz, touching the dime-size black diamond stud in his left ear.

"I'm flattered." Mia clasped her hands. "I don't mean any disrespect, but I'm not really comfortable having this conversation. I wouldn't be here if it weren't for Lyndon."

"That might be true, but the fact is—you're here now. Where you go is up to you."

Mia glanced down at the slick floor.

"Is she keeping you safe? After last year, I would hope so."

"Yes. Of course." Mia twisted the silver ring around her index finger.

"Self-preservation." Maz stood for a long moment, examining her face, then walked off. Mia watched him join Brandon for photos. Maz could be her ticket out of the mess with Teddy, but then she'd have a lawsuit with Lyndon on her hands and she was dealing with enough trouble. She scanned the store for Sean and caught Marcus glaring at her instead. She turned away and found Presley standing next to her.

Presley eyed Maz and leaned into Mia. "Having a little tête-à-tête with the man of the hour?"

"He was just being friendly."

"Maz isn't friendly unless he wants something."

"He wants us to promote this brand."

Presley snapped a photo of Alex strutting in a red pair of platform sneakers that made his Lyndon Wyld track pants and basic tee look runway-chic. She posted on the MazzyLyn feed. "Then do your job, Mia. Gather your minions and go say 'cheese.'" She pointed at the backdrop while snapping a photo of Sean. "Maybe I'll end up sleeping in that one, too."

Sean was trying on a sweatshirt. In Nantucket, Presley had made his Boston College sweatshirt hers. She grinned at Mia and walked off.

TWENTY-SIX

I n Mia's workspace, she and Alex started putting together looks for the Labor Day fashion show. They pulled from new pieces Lyndon had shipped over. Mia FaceTimed with Lyndon, who stood against the windows of her Manhattan penthouse office.

"MazzyLyn sales are rising exponentially since the launch, and my core brand's summer styles have flown off the shelves," said Lyndon, "but the goal of this show is to get people in stores and online for autumn."

Mia aimed her phone at Alex, who held up two long-sleeve jersey tops with lace inlays. She'd used the jersey that Lyndon had provided instead of trekking to Mood. "If you want to try to squeeze these in, they're quick to manufacture."

Lyndon pursed her lips. "Make them look like they're *not* quick to manufacture and I'll think about adding them towards winter."

"Can they be in the show?"

"I don't know, my darling, can they?" Lyndon batted her eyes once. "Alex, I want you in not just one but *two* white-on-white looks. You're the only one who can wear it without getting dirty."

Alex beamed. "I do my best."

Lyndon continued, "We're going to hold over some summer styles past Labor Day. Fuck the rules! Right, Mia? Fuck. The. Rules."

The only rule that Mia had broken that summer was giving money to Ruby instead of Ruby's father. She wasn't going to brag about that.

Alex found a white pencil skirt and men's blazer. He placed the skirt over his body as he admired his reflection in the mirrored wall. "Eve was telling me that some clothing companies burn their unsold inventory. You don't do that, do you?"

Lyndon's eyes opened wide. "Don't be daft!"

"I'd like to donate unsold items from the Malibu store to the SoCal LGBTQ Center. They distribute clothes to homeless LGBTQ youths."

"Brilliant, Alex! Why don't you go talk to the manager about the inventory?"

Alex replaced the skirt and blazer on their hangers. Grinning, he left, mouthing to Mia, "I love her." Mia wished she felt the same way, but getting Lyndon's sign-offs was like pulling tigress teeth.

"Mia, get resourceful, too," said Lyndon.

"I have been. What do you think of the samples?"

"I think you have more in you. You haven't really had to answer to anyone but yourself."

Mia knew this wasn't true, but she couldn't say anything.

"Now you're accountable. This is an invaluable lesson," said Lyndon.

"But I could really use the money."

"I already gave you money. Again, it's time to be responsible for *yourself.*"

"Lyndon—"

"You can do it, my darling!" Lyndon's eyes opened wide with a regal smile. "I'll see you at the show." And with that, Lyndon clicked off. Mia put her phone on the desk and looked around at the chaos of her workspace. She rubbed her brow, then made her way down to the rec room.

"Sean, I need to fit you for the fash—" Through a cloud of weed smoke, Mia could see Sean sitting cross-legged on the floor, bent over the glass table. She stopped in her tracks. Sean was snorting a line of coke with a rolled bill. Nils lounged nearby on the couch. The water from the bong he held gurgled as he pulled. He blew the plume into Boomer's face. The bulldog sneezed. Eve and Wyatt took a break from eating each other's faces in the faux-leather recliner. Wyatt laughed hysterically at the pooch.

Nils caught Mia's disapproving expression. "Cannabis is healthy for dogs!" Eve retrieved the bong from him, knocking over an open bottle of elderberry wine in the process. Already wasted, Eve let the burgundy liquid spill onto the sand-colored carpet.

Mia stared at her brother. "Sean?" Sean ignored her and whiffed up another line. Mia scanned the room. "Where's Chase?"

Eve stroked Wyatt's leg. "Waxing his board."

Mia's focus went from Wyatt to Nils. "I know I've asked you this about a million times before, but don't you two have homes?"

Nils opened his arms wide. "Yeah, but we've told you about a million times before, yours is so much nicer." He leaned his head back in his hands.

"That's because we're seasonaires and you're not," snapped Mia.

Wyatt snickered. "Are you fucking kidding me with that shit? Who made you queen?"

"In Lyndon's absence, I'm not asking—I'm *telling* you to leave." Mia grabbed an empty potato chip bag and an apple core, and dumped them in the wastebasket. "You're trashing our place and totally disrespecting us."

"If Chase wants us to go, then we'll go. But until then, you can suck a dick," said Wyatt with a shrug.

Mia threw out the toppled wine bottle. "Why don't *you* suck a dick?"

Sean released a laugh, wiping white powder from the rim of his nostrils. Mia eyed the camera in the upper corner of the room and tried to position herself to block its view of Sean. She pointed at Nils and Wyatt. "You're leeches, sponging off our work."

Wyatt unwrapped himself from Eve's good arm and walked to the coffee table. "Work?" He leaned over and did a line. "You're getting paid to do what we're doing. You're just wearing a price tag." He gestured to Mia's polo dress. "You couldn't pay me enough to wear that uptight bougie shit."

Mia crossed her arms. "All the more reason you should leave."

"You're being elitist, Mia," said Eve.

Wyatt crossed his arms. "I'll tell you what she's being: a whore."

Without thinking, Mia kicked Wyatt in the balls. He cupped his crotch, doubled over, and fell, groaning. Eve knelt down to him and looked up at Mia. "We're supposed to be the evolved sex! You use violence and go for his manhood?"

Mia plucked at her dress and glared at Eve. "*You're* promoting 'this bougie shit,' so he just called *you* a whore, too!"

Eve ignored her and caressed Wyatt's body while he writhed in pain. Mia grabbed Sean's shoulder as he did another line. "Get up, Sean."

Sean popped a Percocet from Eve's open vial on the table. "Baseball injury but look—" He jumped up and slapped his knee. "I don't even feel it." He tripped over the coffee table and gashed his shin on the glass corner. He cackled.

"That's because you're not feeling anything." Mia yanked him up the stairs by his sleeve. She opened the front door and pulled him outside, across the driveway and to the bluff.

Sean chuckled, stumbling over himself. "Wow, this Malibu air has made you strong."

Mia let go of his arm and got in his face. "It's making you stupid. You don't do coke!"

"I do now."

"That's how you're spending your seasonaire's fee?"

"Nope." Sean grinned. "It was a trade with Nils for the Dodgers tickets. I definitely got the better end of that stick, because baseball is boring as fuck. I mean I put my body through the hell of training. And for what?"

"Well, you won't have to worry about that again if someone sees you doing drugs. There are cameras!" Mia pointed towards the house.

Sean shrugged. "I don't care."

"That's crystal clear. But *I* care. You've been here a week and haven't been to my workspace to see *why* we're here—all the new looks."

"You mean all *your* new looks." Sean picked up a rock and chucked it over the cliff.

"*You* might want to throw away any chance at a sports career. But I'm proud to be your sister. Aren't you proud to be my brother?"

"Oh, spare me the guilt trip." Sean gestured at her. A ground squirrel popped out of a sage shrub and stared at them, then scampered off.

"You're making good money, Sean. And you can still go out for a team."

Sean scoffed.

"I want to make Mom proud," said Mia. "Don't you?"

Sean lunged and yelled into Mia's face, "Mom's gone, Mia! She doesn't care!"

Mia blinked back hot tears. "But *we're* here—together! Talk to me, Sean."

Sean glanced around. "Where's the camera now? I'll do a stupid confessional."

"There's no camera." Mia turned Sean to her. "Don't make me regret letting you come here."

Sean put his hands to his head. "*Letting me*? I thought that maybe when you asked, you needed me. But you don't seem to need anyone. After Mom was gone, so were you—like a bat outta hell. I think you were relieved!"

Mia clutched her gut. "How can you say that?"

"I get it. You took care of her most of the time." Sean pointed at her. "But *you* made that choice."

Mia wept. "Who was going to take care of her?"

"I made sacrifices, too." Sean paced, words tumbling out of his mouth. "Did you know I got into schools outside of Boston? But I didn't want to leave Mom! Maybe if I'd gone to one of those schools, I would've ended up on a team. I would've ended up with the Twins. My whole life would be different. You're living your dream with an actual contract. I've got nothing except a kinesiology degree and no desire to do anything with it."

Mia mirrored his pacing. "You could get into sports medicine . . . or become a team manager. You could coach!"

Sean stopped. "Those who can't do, teach, right, Mia? How would you feel if you ended up teaching—I don't know—*sewing*? Or working at that thrift shop forever?"

"Then that would be my destiny, because I'm doing my best."

"Maybe this is my destiny." Sean backed up towards the bluff's edge.

Mia reached out. "Sean, that's the drugs talking. It's not you."

"I hear my voice." Sean backed up again. "It's me. It's my life." The waves seemed to get louder.

Mia's hands shook. "Please, Sean!"

Out of nowhere, Chase tackled Sean. They grappled on the ground, stirring up dust. Chase pinned Sean. "Dude. Chill!" Sean surrendered with a frustrated sigh.

"Hate to break it up." Brandon stood nearby, holding a purple wetsuit. "Mia, your fans are challenging you to surf." Mia saw the camera. It wasn't on, but it was by Brandon's side.

Sean picked gravel out of his bloody shin. "So much for my confessional."

Chase helped him up. "Come on. Salt water is nature's miracle." He led Sean towards the Tesla. Two surfboards sat on the roof rack.

Mia touched Brandon's arm—the one with the camera. "Please tell me you didn't."

"Mia, if I keep editing shit out, we're going to be left with nothing." Brandon lowered his voice. "Our biggest story is a secret, so we have to give viewers *something*."

Mia grabbed the wetsuit. "How about if I drown out there? Will *that* be something?"

"You can't sell clothes that way," said Brandon, chuckling.

With an exasperated huff, Mia marched towards the house. Brandon followed, but stopped at the car where Chase and Sean stood. "Your sister put herself on the line to have you here, Sean. You're being an asshole."

"Isn't that a requirement for the job?" Sean got in the backseat of the car. Brandon took his place, shotgun.

Overhearing, Mia continued striding towards the house. She entered and took two stairs at a time. In her bedroom, she plucked a one-piece from a drawer, tore off her clothes, and yanked it on. She struggled into the wetsuit, which was thick and tight, and made her feel like she couldn't breathe. But she wasn't going to back down from this challenge even though drowning *was* a possibility.

She got in the car with the boys. Chase drove them off. "Surfrider Beach is the best spot for kooks like you, Mia."

Mia's eyes narrowed. "Excuse me?"

"A kook is a beginner surfer."

Sean, mouth twitchy, bounced his leg and tapped on the window. Brandon turned around. "Could you not?" Sean ignored him, though Mia looked equally annoyed with the coke-addled fidgeting.

After snagging a parking spot, they made their way down to the beach. Mia carried the heavy nine-foot, single fin board that Chase had spent the morning waxing.

"Need help?" asked Brandon.

"I got it," answered Mia.

Sean plunked in the sand. He pulled his knees to his chest and focused on the girls in bikinis bumping a volleyball back and forth while their boyfriends were out on the water. Chase tilted the bigger board towards him. "You wanna surf, Sean? You should do it before Malibu washes away."

"Nah. I'm good."

"You can trust me. I'm not nicknamed 'Chase' for nothin'."

Mia pulled her hair back into a ponytail. "Chase is a nickname?"

"Born Gregory Michael Edelstein. But when my mom took me to the beach as a kid, she couldn't keep me out of the water. All I wanted to do was chase waves. Thus, the nickname."

"You do *not* look like a Gregory," said Mia.

Sean shielded the sun's glare with his hand to look at Mia, who smoothed her wetsuit. "You do *not* look like a surfer chick."

"Not yet, but I adapt." Mia surveyed the water—past the breaking waves a quarter of a mile out, the ocean was calm. She waded into the tide with the board. Her arms and legs were exposed in the wetsuit, and the water's frigid temperature sent a shock wave through her body. "Holy shit, that's cold!"

"Invigorating, right?" Chase grinned and stayed close to her. The rocks jabbed at Mia's soles, forcing her to bellyflop onto her board and start paddling. Chase had Velcroed the leash around her right ankle, just below her sunflower tattoo. Maneuvering the longboard felt like driving a bus. The water that slapped against Mia's board jumped straight into her nose. The salty burn slid down her throat.

"Waves here break right, and First Point's are the mellowest." Chase nodded towards the Malibu Pier, which was simpler and less colorful than its Santa Monica counterpart. He helped Mia turn her board to face the shore.

Mia's heart raced as she scanned the dark blue liquid parking lot of surfers waiting for waves. "It's crowded out here."

"It's zooed for sure, but focus on yourself." Chase pointed to an incoming wave. "Take one after it turns to whitewash."

"I'll wait 'til everyone else goes."

"No, you won't." Chase gently pushed Mia into a small, foamy wave as it broke. Mia managed to get up, but she was too far forward, forcing the board's nose into the water. In a flash, she wiped out. Tumbling in a washing machine spin cycle, she couldn't tell which end was up. She remembered her time in the Y pool: she knew how to sink. She tried to exhale and let her body go limp. *If I surrender, maybe all my problems would disappear with me*, she thought. But the ocean wouldn't allow it and drove her to the surface. She coughed in fits and sprays and blinked the stinging sea from her eyes.

Chase was by her side with his ever-present beatific smile. "You bit it, but it's cool. You've got this, Mia!"

Mia tried again, managing to get up for what seemed like half a second longer before a baby wave knocked her off the back of the board. After toppling off no less than half a dozen times from waves that never grew above two feet, and getting snaked by other surfers, her frustration riled her. *I will stay on this damn board if it's the last thing that I do.* Then she caught one, and before she knew it, she was riding straight towards shore. She didn't let out a sound for fear she would knock herself off balance. Fast-moving rocks flashed in the water below her—except she realized the rocks weren't moving, *she* was.

Then she wiped out again. Exhausted, she paddled back out to Chase, who'd observed from his oblong throne like Poseidon. "Almost there!" he said. "Next time, lean forward to try to get an angle going. And don't drop in. That guy wants to kick my ass now." He offered a shaka sign to a surfer giving them the stink-eye. "You took that last wave and dude already grabbed it. But smile. Cute girls are forgiven."

Mia slicked back her wet hair and smiled. The corners of the pissed-off surfer's mouth lifted. The mandate to ingratiate herself stoked her fire. "I'm doing this." She saw the swell and gathered all her energy to furiously catch it. As the wave started to break, she centered herself, girded her core, and stood up with such an effort of control that she grunted. She followed Chase's directions to lean forward so she rode at the right angle.

The world became almost dead-quiet—the sound of the water faint, a whisper of wind through Mia's ears. That ten-second ride was effortless in a way that felt like bliss, because nothing for Mia had ever been effortless. She dismounted with a splash and turned back to Chase with the biggest shit-eating grin. She screamed with joy. Chase met up with her as she pumped one fist in the air, the other hand on the board she had conquered.

Chase chuckled. "Yo. Keep it cool."

Mia looked to the sand to see Brandon grinning from behind his camera. But Sean was gone. Her smile waned. "I'm fried." She and Chase tramped out of the water and onto the beach.

The three found Sean up at the car, leaning on the door, smoking weed from the vape pen. Mia decided she wasn't going to let anyone or anything ruin *her* high, including Sean. Chase drove them back to the house, doling out kudos for Mia. He moved to put the boards back in the garage.

As Mia, Brandon, and Sean entered, they heard Boomer barking. "He's usually the quietest out of the three," said Mia. They headed downstairs to find the rec room a bigger mess than when they left. "They're pigs."

Boomer barked at the closed bathroom door. They could hear Eve's muffled voice: "No. Stop."

Brandon tried the knob. It was locked. After more rustling inside and another "Stop," he kicked in the door. Mia could see Eve, bent over the sink—naked below the waist. Wyatt stood behind her, shorts down. Nils was against the wall, member in hand. Brandon yanked out Wyatt and started punching before Wyatt could pull up his shorts. Nils zipped up, leapt out, grabbed an ashtray filled with smoked joints, and thwacked Brandon on the head with a "She wanted it."

Brandon grabbed the ashtray and threw it on the ground, where it shattered. "Say that again."

Nils didn't back down. "She wanted it."

Brandon turned his rage on Nils and pummeled his face to a pulp, despite Sean's attempts at breaking it up. "Brandon! Stop!" yelled Mia, who helped Eve get dressed.

Brandon stood over both sprawled boys, fists still clenched. "Mia told you to leave. Now get the fuck out, or I will finish you."

Beaten, Wyatt and Nils left, with Boomer whining after them. Sean escorted them out. He looked back at Mia, his expression stone sober.

Eve buttoned her shirt. "I don't remember much after you left—" She wiped tears. "I woke up in the bathroom. What I do remember is that I sure as fuck didn't want The Devil's Triangle." She turned to Brandon. "Thank you for stopping them."

Mia stroked Eve's hair. "We should report this."

"You know what'll happen, right? Nothing. Wyatt and I have been together. And I was wasted."

"That doesn't matter! What they did to you was wrong!" replied Mia.

Shoulders hunched, Eve trudged towards the stairs.

"Do you want me to come up?" asked Mia.

"It's okay. I'm going to take a shower." Eve left.

Mia shook her head. She plucked a towel from the bathroom and moved to the bar's fridge. Wrapping the towel around ice, she walked to Brandon. Taking his hand, she led him to the couch and gently placed the pack on the back of his head, where blood clumped in his hair.

Brandon stared into space. "That's exactly what the fucker said about Jade."

"Who?"

"The reason for my mugshot." Brandon reached up and took the ice pack, putting it down on the side table. "I was working a party after Jade made the sexual assault allegations against Otto. When I walked by some scumbag, he said that she asked for what she got."

Mia shook her head. "That's horrendous." She remembered the video of Jade at the Summer Solstice party in Nantucket. Otto had crashed it. The two had been doing tequila shots—Jade had let him lick salt off her chest. She'd been trying to get her father's attention for a long time. That was her misguided way, and Otto—an old family friend—had been taking advantage of her need for attention for just as long.

Brandon's T-shirt was ripped. Mia lifted the Tibetan medallion and ran her finger along the eight symbols. "What do they mean?"

Calming down, Brandon pointed to each symbol. "The parasol is royal dignity and protection."

"Naturally."

"The two golden fish mean we shouldn't be afraid to drown in the ocean of suffering."

Mia shrugged. "I'm drowning in debt."

Brandon searched her eyes. "Why won't you let me help you?"

"You've helped enough." Mia lightly grazed his bloody knuckles with her forefinger. She brought it back up to the medallion. "What's this shell mean?"

"The right-coiled white conch is an awakening from ignorance." Brandon pointed to the next symbol. "The lotus is an opening to clarity; the victory banner means earned wisdom; the vase—long life and prosperity; the golden wheel has an eight-fold path, but I'm not sure what those paths are."

"Is anyone sure?" asked Mia.

Brandon stopped on the eighth symbol: an entwined pattern. "And this is the eternal knot, which is our connection to everything." Their fingers touched as they both held the medallion. Brandon stroked her cheek and she let go of the necklace, keeping her palm on his chest. They locked eyes and kissed. He felt and tasted good, so she let his mouth linger on hers. She gently pulled away. "This kiss means something."

Brandon lifted an eyebrow. "Oh, yeah?"

"It means that the footage of Sean doing blow ends up in the same place as the footage of your turn as the Incredible Hulk. No one needs to see either." Mia eyed the camera in the corner.

"Okay," whispered Brandon. They kissed again.

TWENTY-SEVEN

After the incident, Eve spent more time alone on the beach, though she wouldn't go for walks and film herself for her followers. Instead she'd sit on the steps and stare out at the sea. She wouldn't talk about it, even with Alex.

Mia joined her one afternoon, nodding to Crispy Tanned Rock Sculptor, who had returned to add rocks to his masterpiece. "What do you think his mandala symbolizes?"

"Maybe it doesn't symbolize anything. Maybe it's just a mound of rocks," said Eve, her voice flat.

The two sat in silence for a few minutes, watching the sandpipers with their long, thin beaks. They didn't bother Mia as much as the beach chickens.

"Are you okay?" she asked.

"No."

"How's your shoulder?"

"Fine." Eve touched the sling.

Mia reached to put her hand on Eve's leg. Eve's flinch made her think twice, and she touched the grainy wood between them instead. "Can I do anything?" she asked.

"Can you delete a memory like you can delete a post?"

"Believe me, I wish we could," said Mia, picking at a splinter. She didn't know what to do. The spark was gone from Eve's eyes. She hoped she would see it again by the season's end.

The incident had a more transformative effect on Sean, who took his partying down a notch. He still seemed sad and lost to Mia but settled into the groove of Malibu life. He ran on the beach with Alex. The group watched the channel's episode featuring Mia's surf adventure, which inspired him to try it. On the water, Chase found a new friend in Sean and seemed relieved that the old ones were gone. When Mia had told him what happened to Eve, he'd seemed disappointed but not surprised.

Sean even relaxed for selfies with customers at the Malibu store.

Presley stopped by the house to "personally" show him how popular he was becoming on the social media accounts she'd created for him. Mia found her scooting next to Sean on the living room couch.

"I knew you would be my 'get' for Lyndon!" she said, scrolling through posts. "And you wear both Lyndon Wyld and MazzyLyn so well!"

Sean's expression revealed relief at seeing Mia, who held up the T-shirt she'd hand-embroidered with roses. "How do you think this will look on Katie?" she asked.

Presley squinted, assessing the tee. "It's cute. I'm not sure how it'll sell in stores."

"Let's see what Katie thinks," replied Mia.

"Another hospital trip?" Presley fluffed a throw pillow. "You're on your own. The press isn't going to cover that twice."

"I'll go with you, Mia," said Sean, who stood. Presley looked disappointed, especially when he left the house wearing the MazzyLyn sweatshirt she'd bragged she'd snag.

Sean was tense walking in the hospital's sliding doors, but his whole demeanor softened when he saw Katie's giant smile as Mia handed her the T-shirt.

"I love it so much!" said Katie, running her delicate fingers along the tee's roses.

"Yes!" Mia clapped triumphantly.

The three hung out for a while. Sean and Katie played checkers, with Mia helping Katie strategize and win.

Returning to the Smart car, Sean took a deep breath. "I miss Mom, but I don't miss the hospital."

"I know, but now that I've been there in a different way, I don't mind it so much," said Mia as she got in and took the steering wheel.

Sean stared at the sights along Sunset as they headed back through Hollywood and Beverly Hills. "*Life* feels so different."

Mia glanced around them—at the mansions set back from the street. "It is different here."

Sean looked at her. "It feels different everywhere."

Mia nodded. "Yup," she said softly.

They listened to music as they wound their way back to Malibu. The classic rock station played Train's "Calling All Angels."

"Mom would've said Train isn't a classic rock band," said Sean with a sneer.

Mia flashed back to Presley tossing a pink daiquiri in the face of The Rabbit Hole's bartender, whom she'd been seeing. Presley had thought he was singing the song for Ruby. "Reminds me of last summer," said Mia. She changed the station to jazz.

Out of the corner of her eye, she saw Sean's raised eyebrow. "Since when do you listen to jazz?"

Mia shrugged. "It's grown on me." They let the easy, syncopated rhythm fill the small car, the notes connected yet not monotonous—unlike Seamus Galloway's pop-rock tunes.

Sean gazed out the window as they wound through Brentwood. The hills bore scorched spots from the fire. "Did you get a chance to see Ruby?"

"I did." Mia tapped the steering wheel nervously and then to the beat of the music.

Sean turned to her. "Is she okay?"

Mia nodded. She could never ask Sean to help her with the money she owed Teddy, because she could never tell Sean about her mounting mistakes.

"Are *you* okay?" Sean pressed.

Mia slapped on a grin. "How could I not be? Look where we are." The beach spread out before them as they zipped along PCH and she settled into the smile. That view never ceased to be beautiful.

After Sean spent the next afternoon throwing the ball around with Brandon on the beach, he told Mia that Maz had scored him a meeting with the Dodgers' coach. "The season will have already started when we're done here, but there's a chance I can play for the team next year."

Mia tilted her head. "You love winter. You know that doesn't exist here."

"Like you said before you conquered those waves, 'I'll adapt,'" said Sean.

⸺⸺

In a nudge to give the brand a more down-to-earth vibe, Lyndon sent the group to Leo Carrillo State Beach for an overnight "staycation." Presley had wanted them to do a photo shoot in the cactus-dotted landscape of Joshua Tree, but Brandon, during their conference Skype, labeled the rustic, artsy location "a wasteland for space blues and desert disco, which is synonymous with bullshit and more bullshit." Lyndon laughed, which caused Presley to bristle. Malibu Creek State Park, a popular camping site, was the location of some random shootings, so Lyndon put her foot down about Leo Carrillo.

"There are never shootings in Malibu," scoffed Chase after the Skype ended. He didn't see Mia shudder.

The group arrived at the seaside spot. "I don't camp," said Alex, propped inside the crook of a tree in the beach-adjacent woods while Chase and Sean set up the fully outfitted tents. Mia was pleased that neither did Presley, who claimed she had more important tasks to accomplish.

"The closest Mia and I have come to sleeping outside is almost getting evicted," said Sean, pulling the top of a tent over poles.

"This isn't camping. It's glamping," scoffed Eve as she unrolled the plush, sherpa-lined sleeping bags.

They wandered through the brushy paths dotted with yellow daisies and purple wildflowers, and down the wood plank path to the beach. Mia forewent venturing into the caves with the others.

Brandon perched with her on some rocks. "Check that out," he said as he pointed to three dolphins that curved their slick bodies up and down in the water. Mia had been so engrossed in thoughts about her impending Labor Day situation—*obsessed* was a better word—that she hadn't noticed. She gasped at the sight and smiled. Brandon snapped a photo of her. "There you go. Letting in a little magic."

"You're right. We have to capture it," said Mia. She turned Brandon around and took a selfie, pointing at the dolphins between them in the distance.

That night, the six sat around a fire in one of the designated fire rings near the tents, passing a flask of bourbon and making s'mores. Even Alex partook in the gooey treats. "All this nature is making me insane. Maybe an earworm crawling around here burrowed into my brain."

Eve blew out the flames that engulfed Alex's marshmallow. "Carcinogens."

Mia's anxiety had turned up when the sun had gone down, but the atmosphere remained as calm as the tide pools they'd combed that day. Chase rolled joints instead of smoking from a vape because "that's how you do it when you're in the '*Wyld*' World." Brandon laughed, victorious that he got this sound bite on film.

Alex and Eve played Fuck, Marry, Kill, which seemed to resuscitate Eve's humor but added to Mia's jitters. She knew it was a silly game, but the game that the bikers had started was too serious to forget, even under the sea of stars.

Sitting next to Mia, Brandon searched around for something on their blanket. "Dammit. I lost a lens." The others continued to drink, smoke, and eat the chocolate-gooey treats. "Don't all get up at once," he said, annoyed as he rose with his camera and trudged back up towards the lot where they had parked the car.

Sean leaned into Mia. "You shittin' where you eat again?" he said in a low voice.

"That saying is so gross," replied Mia, mid-bite of a s'more. "And give me a break, Sean, please."

Sean patted Mia's knee. "It's okay. I thought Brandon was a total asshole."

"The feeling was mutual." Mia chuckled as she swatted his hand away.

"But he's cool," said Sean. "Plus, I get that it's part of the whole thing." He held up his phone with Mia and Brandon's dolphin selfie.

Mia sneered. "It's not part of 'the whole thing.'"

Sean raised his eyebrows. "Oh, so you *are* hooking up."

Before Mia could answer, Brandon reappeared, looking pissed. "The car's gone."

Mia chucked her s'more in the fire. "What?"

They all ran up to the lot and saw that the space where the Tesla had been parked was empty.

Sean smacked his hand on his forehead. "You gotta be shitting me."

Mia whipped at Brandon. "Is this another prank for the channel, Brandon? Because it's not funny."

The other seasonaires glared at Brandon, who bristled. "Why would I leave us stranded in the middle of the night? No Uber or Lyft is going to drive all the way out here right now. Or ever."

"We gotta hoof it," said Chase, who, barefoot, was as undaunted as he was high.

Alex and Eve groaned. Sean shook his head as Brandon and Mia shared a look. This didn't sit well with Mia, but she wasn't going to say anything else in front of the others. They gathered as much of their stuff as they could and started their trek back to the house. Mia tried to call Presley—no answer.

She turned to Chase. "What about your mom, Chase?"

"She took my brother to a forest bathing retreat."

"A what?" asked Alex.

"It's some fancy tree spa," answered Chase.

"Exposure to nature has calming neuro-psychological effects," said Eve. "That's why we have to protect it."

Mia thought about Oliver on their hike. Being lost in nature had not inspired a sense of calm. And even this close to the beach in the moonlight, Mia was a bundle of nerves. She shoved her hands in her jacket pockets.

Chase walked backwards to face the group. "The retreat was against my brother's will, but she wanted him to 'get with himself before he becomes a man' at his bar mitzvah. Before mine, we went floating."

"In those isolation tanks?" asked Alex.

"That always seemed so unsanitary to me," said Eve with a sniff. "People trading places all day, lying in that salt water."

Alex crossed his arms. "You don't flush after you pee."

"It's conservation!" Eve gave her ringlets a strident toss.

"It's nasty."

The next seemingly endless hours of walking on a dark highway exhausted everyone and prompted quarrels about manscaping, attention whoring, and unwashed dishes. Sean put in his earbuds to listen to music. Mia tuned out the spats, because with every movement in the dark, her insides jumped. All she had was Oliver's pocket knife for protection.

Brandon filmed but soon grew weary of the bickering. He stepped in line with Mia. "I reported the car stolen. The cop told me to call towing lots."

Mia looked at him, her brow knit. "What if Ruby's family took the car?"

"Why would they do that?"

Mia showed Brandon her phone. "I checked the news. Lyndon was right. There *were* a series of murders in Malibu."

"Are you saying the bikers are serial killers?"

"No, but if something happened to us, people would assume we're like the other victims. The cops would follow *those* leads, away from Ruby's dad."

Brandon touched Mia's arm. "I can call my dad. He's back in New York, but he can send Marcus out to get us."

"No. We're almost home."

When they finally arrived at the house, spent, with blisters on their feet, they stared at a sight in the driveway. Sean pulled out his earbuds. "What. The. Fuck?" The Tesla was there, but no driver.

Safe and sound, they all fell into bed and slept most of the following day. Mia and Brandon were the only exceptions. Brandon edited in his studio while Mia worked on her pieces. Her eyes stung and her hands cramped from the embroidery, embellishments, and beadwork. She'd given Katie the original tee, so she sewed more roses onto another Katie tee sample. As she stitched, she thought of the roses Lyndon had sent. When the bloom wore off, they started to stink.

That night, Presley made a visit to the house while the group watched the botched glamping episode. In the footage Brandon had edited together, they seemed like one big happy family—until they trudged home along the dark side of the road and their petty differences got the best of them. The viewers took sides, but they all wondered what happened to the Tesla, because Brandon had left out the fact that it had been found in their own driveway.

Eve took a beat from a mutual foot massage with Alex to clap. "A cliffhanger! Genius!"

Presley lifted the Tesla key. "You can all thank *me*. *I'm* the fucking genius."

"Why would you do that?" said Alex, peeling off a Band-Aid from his heel and blowing on a blister.

Presley threw the key on the coffee table. "Because you're all lazier than cut dogs. You couldn't even drag your asses to Joshua Tree. Everyone loves Joshua Tree!"

"It *is* pretty cool," said Chase. "I took shrooms there once and watched a tortoise climb over a rock for like five hours—really drove home the moral of 'The Tortoise and the Hare,' because that tortoise got exactly where he wanted to go."

Mia squeezed her eyes closed.

Brandon's ire was focused on Presley. "Lazy?" He motioned to the widescreen. "This channel takes effort to produce."

"Effort doesn't equal excitement. I've been the one to add any spark to this game," said Presley. She pointed to a thumbnail of Wyatt and Nils on the side of the screen. "Now, *that's* a show. Shockingly, their new channel is getting interesting."

"I doubt it," said Chase, staring out the window at the beach. He hadn't said a word about his two former buddies since they got the boot.

Presley took the remote from Brandon. "Let's watch." She clicked on the thumbnail.

Wyatt and Nils's faces filled the screen—scabbed, black, and blue. They dove into their rant about the seasonaires. Nils leaned in towards the camera. "You can't tell one from the next, because they're all douche canoes. But let's try."

Brandon snorted with disdain.

Wyatt lifted up one finger. "You've got Mia, that uppity Mom jeans twat."

Nils held up a finger. "And Chase, who couldn't land a gig with a surf brand or as a *real* ski resort seasonaire like he's always wanted 'cause he sucks. So he's slumming it in bougie rags."

Chase continued to stare out the window.

On-screen, Wyatt leaned against the back of a ratty futon. "And then there's that mouthy bitch, Eve. She thinks she's pure sex, but she just lays there like a starfish while she spews her Antifa bullshit."

Eve stormed out while the two surfer scum insulted Alex on-screen. Nils pulled on the brim of his surf logo hat, which was propped at an angle. "I say end those six robots. They're not real people anyhow."

Mia grabbed the remote from Presley and clicked off the TV.

Presley pointed a thumb upward. "Their channel's subscriber numbers are rising while yours are falling." She flipped her thumb the opposite way. "If our little Labor Day shindig doesn't go off with a bang, there will be consequences. So here's *my* challenge—" She walked to Sean and caressed his shoulder. "Sean opens the show."

Sean shook his head. "I can run bases, but I have no idea how to walk a runway."

"That's why it'll be entertaining, sugar. Besides, if your sister can do it, anyone can. Lyndon will close the swan song show." As Presley sashayed towards the door, she pointed to a small box on the floor. "Mia, this is for you." She exited.

In the studio, Brandon and Mia sat with Chase while he did his confessional, talking about loyalty and the loss of friends. He ended it with Shakespeare's words: "Love all, trust a few, do wrong to none."

Back in her workspace, Mia opened the box. Inside were jersey long-sleeve tops with lace inlays. They looked like Mia's samples but were trimmed with contrasting satin instead of lace.

Alex, who was helping her prepare for the show, held one up. "These are gorg, Mia!"

Mia furrowed her brow—her name wasn't anywhere on them.

TWENTY-EIGHT

L abor Day came, and so did the event.

"This is the last hurrah!" said Alex, who helped Mia load the car with their fashion show ensembles. He was as excited about that as Mia was anxious. She didn't know how she would get through the night, let alone the following day, since she didn't have the bikers' money.

"Why don't we have the party at our house?" asked Sean, getting into the Tesla with the others.

"The beach party was here, so I'm wondering that myself," said Eve.

"It wasn't here," replied Alex. "It was on the beach."

"Exactly." Brandon slid into the passenger's seat next. "Lyndon would rather make a mess in someone else's place." That place was the Shoreline House, a beachfront members-only club that Lyndon rented out for the occasion. They arrived to fanfare, photographers, and a smattering of protestors.

A poorly dressed middle-aged man held a protest sign that had a slash through *Lyndon Wyld*. "Menswear is called menswear for a reason!" he yelled.

Alex, in evening makeup and a silk tunic over trousers, locked eyes with the man. "The *wrong* reason." The seasonaires entered the light-blue clapboard building.

Unlike the "summer of love" beach party, this event was gimmick-free so that the focus would be on the brand. The minimalist décor was accented with Lyndon Wyld table linens and monogrammed pillows. On the wraparound terrace that sat over the water, green and beige cashmere blankets were available for the guests, who hung onto the last bastion of summer in clothing that was also minimalist. The Hollywood wattage was high: reality TV celebrities, athletes, and music artists, as well as the action star with his artisan jewelry-crafting wife, drank and picked at the artfully displayed buffet of artisanal cheeses, chilled seafood towers, and gluten-free desserts.

Eve took it all in but frowned. "I wish Oliver were here." Alex gathered them for a selfie and posted with the caption:

> Miss you, @olivertwistsss #BuWyld
> #LaborDayWeekend

Mia leaned into Brandon. "Is Seamus Galloway coming?"

"He's on tour in his magic school bus." He moved off to spin as deejay Monarch. He had set up cameras all over the venue to live stream on their channel. In the upstairs sitting room, the seasonaires readied for the fashion show. Sean paced, drinking a local small-batch beer. "What the hell am I doing?"

Mia unzipped a suit bag for him. "You're putting on the clothes and walking like the rest of us."

Sean ran his hand through his hair and exhaled. "But I'm going *first*."

Alex, shirtless, pulled on the fitted white blazer. "If you're not going to eat this shit up, Sean, I will punch you in the neck. Some models won't even walk without being guaranteed first or last. Brandon's mother only walks first."

Presley entered and patted Sean on the ass. "Sean, strap on your nards and get dressed, or I will dress you myself." She stepped up close to him. "And we both know how that will go."

Sean glowered at her. "Why do you feel the need to put everyone in the most uncomfortable situation?"

"You put yourself in this position. And you're getting paid a shitload for it."

"You're exactly like I remember you from last summer. You think you're pulling the strings, but *you're* the real puppet," said Sean as he took the suit bag from Mia and shoved his empty beer bottle in Presley's hand. Presley blinked at him and dropped it in the wastebasket.

The fashion show began to a thumping house beat. In addition to her other work, Mia had spent the last month meticulously embellishing the autumn clothes with accents that represented each seasonaire. She didn't want any holes, loose threads, or dropped stitches.

The cool night air at the tail end of the summer would keep them from sweating—save for Sean, whose forehead glistened with anxiety.

"Don't blow this." Presley practically pushed him down the stairs to the terrace. Sean looked like a deer in the headlights as flashes burst, then he took slow steps across the lacquered wood floor in a brown herringbone flannel suit over a black diamond applique tee. The cheers—especially the whoops from the girls— put confidence in his step and a smile on his face. Mia peeked from the top of the staircase. She was proud and relieved.

Mia had embroidered Eve's jumpsuit with green vines and blue flowers. "Chakras. You have a huge heart and you should keep speaking up." During the show, Eve—her healing arm sans the sling—wore the jumpsuit with her head held high, but not as high as at the summer's start.

Alex inspired a standing O as he owned the runway in the white blazer, pencil skirt, and black-and-white MazzyLyn platform sneakers—Mia had sewn rhinestones on the blazer's lapels. His strut was "epic," as Chase put it, watching. After Alex took his last step, he hugged Mia. "We're shining so hard, the sun is jealous."

Chase loped out shirtless, in long olive canvas cargo shorts that featured the MazzyLyn logo in spray-paint graffiti and a beige Lyndon Wyld cashmere sweater tied loosely around his neck.

Mia was the last seasonaire to walk. She wore tan plaid culottes and the jersey lace top that Presley had delivered. The applause was loud, but it was loudest when Lyndon followed to close the show. Under a black denim duster coat, she wore the green Mia dress, with the fringe that had won Mia her contract. But the neck was higher and the hem longer for autumn. The duster coat was also Mia's design, though the jaunty epaulets had been replaced with large brass Lyndon Wyld monogram buttons. This whole fashion show was Mia's baby, but Lyndon basked in the adulation.

When the show was finished, the seasonaires gathered back in the sitting room. They embraced, so pumped about the show they didn't notice that Lyndon wasn't there. Mia texted her:

Can we talk?

They all changed back into their summer party attire and dispersed to celebrate. Mia searched around for Lyndon, to no avail. She retreated into the bathroom. Eve joined her, high on the experience and the champagne she was drinking. "I want to say I hated that, but it was a complete blast." She put her flute on the granite countertop and entered a stall to pee, leaving the door open.

Mia smiled. "It *was* fun." After washing her hands, she held them under the blower. They weren't fully dry when she noticed Brandon on the TV that was set into the mirror. Presley was standing close to him while he took a break behind his deejay equipment. "We should spice things up. We'd make a great team," she told him.

Eve's eyes went wide as she watched. "What the f—"

On the screen, Brandon adjusted the mixer. "You're not my type."

Presley inched closer. "I'm everyone's type. That's how I got here. Girls want to be me. Men want to fuck me."

"Is that why Lyndon stuck you in an office and not on a beach?"

Mia didn't know whether Presley was putting on this show for detractors who wanted to undermine Mia's relationship with Brandon, which was playing out on camera. Or was she doing it because Sean had dressed her down before the fashion show and she craved ego-soothing?

Eve stared at the TV screen, then glanced at Mia. "Are you jealous?"

Mia didn't answer.

Eve washed her hands. "I could've called it the minute I saw her two years ago on social when she was first a seasonaire. I knew so many girls like her in college. They were in sororities, with their secret handshakes and hazing rituals. I rushed just to see what the process was like. Two top houses invited me to pledge. I should've felt complimented, but instead I was disgusted."

Mia observed her own envy bubble up as she watched Presley and Brandon. "This is her way of being a seasonaire and the boss's right hand at the same time. She had to have her hands in every pot." Mia's phone buzzed from her clutch on the counter. She pulled it out and saw a text from Lyndon:

Crow's nest.

Eve went back to the party while Mia exited the bathroom and asked a passing server how to get to the crow's nest. The server pointed to the small elevator.

A security guard in a dark green suit with beige tie stood in front of the elevator door. "Who are you?" Mia showed him Lyndon's text message. He placed a key card over a flat black button. The door opened. Mia stepped inside. The security guard reached to press the third-floor button. Mia stepped inside the small compartment and the doors closed. Brandon's music played, and the TV in the wood-inlayed wall showed partiers dancing on the terrace: Eve joined Alex and Chase, who were letting loose. Sean was nowhere in the frame.

The door opened to reveal Lyndon sitting in a tall woven chair with a green cashmere wrap draped over her lithe legs. The small open deck had an unobstructed 360-degree view. It was chilly but cozy enough for the most private conversations.

Lyndon sipped a martini. "You did a nice job tonight, my darling. This summer was a success, don't you think?"

"I'm not sure."

"What do you mean?"

"You're wearing my dress and coat, I'm wearing my top, but no one knows they're mine."

"That's because they're mine. *You're* mine."

Mia put her hands in the pockets of the chevron-patterned shift dress she'd also made. She didn't want Lyndon to see them trembling. "I don't think Maz would agree with your sense of ownership. But I hope you trust my loyalty," she said.

Lyndon studied her for a beat. "Do you think that telling me Maz tried to poach you is going to make me want you more? I already *have* you."

"I thought I owed you the truth."

"People don't flirt unless you give them a sign."

"I think we both know that's untrue. There are plenty of men who push themselves on women who don't want the attention."

"Maz isn't Otto, whose balls were the size of these blue cheese–stuffed olives." Lyndon plucked the two green intrusions from her martini and dropped them in the potted fern next to her chair. "I asked for a twist."

Mia shivered and pulled her arms in closer to her body.

"I'm not talking about flirting in a sexual sense," said Lyndon, brushing the blanket with her hand. The diamonds from her watch glinted in the moonlight. "I'm talking about opportunists approaching you because you have an approachable disposition."

"Are you saying I'm a sucker?"

"I'm saying that you came here because you had an agenda."

"My mother died. I needed an income and I wanted the summer you promised."

Lyndon put her martini glass down hard, and a splash of clear liquid jumped out onto the side table, missing her suede purse. "Stop playing the victim, Mia. You'd better get over using Mommy as a crutch in your continued desire to fail."

"I've spent the whole summer here after what happened in Nantucket. I took your deal because I want to succeed."

"You signed the contract to ride on my coattails, not underneath my wings. I don't feel the obligation to protect anyone, especially someone who isn't completely on my side. Your alliance with Ruby last summer cost me, Mia."

Mia's heart raced. "What do you mean?"

"Ruby's family came to me demanding money for what my sister did. Of course they were too base to go through the right channels and attempt to sue me properly. But I was able to structure a deal, demanding they help pump up our channel's popularity with a little visit. Actually, that visit was Presley's idea, but I demanded she let you think it was yours. You see, ultimately, I give credit where credit's due." She straightened her jacket's lapels.

"Presley knew? I don't understand. Why would you . . . ?" Mia paced.

"It's like the small print in your contract that deems it's *my* right to choose which pieces have your name on them, if any. My approval is the last word." Lyndon rose. "If you think that would be different with Maz, you're mistaken." She picked up her purse.

Mia buzzed with a combination of fear and rage. "When I took the seasonaire's job this summer, I knew I was stepping into the lion's den. But I thought the lion's den meant *this*." She held up her phone. "I would be putting myself out there for everyone's entertainment again. Then I found out about the channel, and that felt even more dangerous. I realized this summer that *you're* the lion. People get hurt when they go into business with you."

Lyndon waved a hand and chortled. "Oh, Mia, don't be a drama queen. No one got hurt, except for some koi. I wasn't happy about the untimely death of those lovely fish, but Ruby's family got their money and I got my footage before those tattooed wankers broke the camera."

Mia stared at Lyndon, unable to tell if she knew about the bikers' further demands. She was torn—until the rest of the seasonaires left for home, they were in danger. She couldn't risk saying anything more. *She just needed the money.*

Lyndon shifted a hip. "Cat got your tongue?" When Mia failed to respond, Lyndon strode to the elevator and pressed the button. The door slid open and she stepped in. Mia rushed in before it closed.

The elevator descended. Before the knot hit the pit of Mia's stomach, she pulled the Emergency Stop button. The alarm sounded. Lyndon's expression registered irritation instead of fear. "What are you doing, Mia?"

"I understand the small print. But since you need designs to steal, I'm worth something to you."

"I never said you weren't."

Mia stood taller. "Then pay me. I gave you designs and samples. I want my fee for them."

A smile spread across Lyndon's face. "Don't ask. Demand. You're finally learning." She admired Mia for a beat. "I'll wire it to you."

Mia blinked, surprised by Lyndon's acquiescence.

"Tension equals excitement." Lyndon's smile disappeared. "Now let me down."

Mia pushed the Emergency Stop button back in. The alarm ceased bleating, and the elevator descended. Lyndon pulled six white envelopes from her purse. "Tomorrow, give the seasonaires these checks for the balance of their pay. In your envelope is also a one-way ticket to New York. You can choose to use it or go back to Boston. As long as you continue creating for me according to our contract, the choice where you do it is yours, though I'd advise you against the distraction of MassArt studies."

Mia felt her chest tighten with the decision she would have to make.

"Oh, and you won't have to worry about dealing with Presley in either location. She'll be in London taking over our European PR department."

The elevator doors opened.

Mia took the envelopes. "You won't be here to give them out?"

"I need to go see my sister in the prison hospital." Lyndon's eyes flashed sadness.

"What happened to her?" asked Mia.

"Grace tried to commit suicide. Like Ruby, she didn't succeed, but we're all paying for her mistakes nonetheless." Lyndon turned and strode out the exit.

Mia stood there, lost for a long moment. Presley strutted past, looking at her phone on her way to follow Lyndon. "Someone's looking for you."

Mia slid the envelopes in her handbag. "Who?"

Suddenly, hot pain shot through her left ear. She turned to find Seamus's girlfriend Spider Eyes clutching her teacup poodle in one hand and Mia's gold hoop earring in the other. "That's for putting a dick in your mouth that belongs to someone else!"

Guests turned and, seeing the two girls in a face-off, started snapping photos and filming on their phones. Presley had vanished.

Mia held her ear with one hand and gestured to Spider Eyes with the other. "Your boyfriend kissed me, but that's all that happened."

"You're a lying, trashy, slutty gash!" Spider Eyes chucked Mia's earring. It bounced off Mia and clinked on the wood floor. "I'm from Milton. I always wanted to fight a scrappy Southie slut. You think you're so tough over there."

Mia chuckled despite the pain. "You're not going to fight me. Who's going to hold your little dog? And I'll only wrestle if you have some Neosporin and a plastic pool full of Jell-O."

The crowd started chanting, "Jell-O! Jell-O! Jell-O!"

Brandon approached and ushered Mia off. He waved at the crowd. "Yeah, yeah, show's over."

Spider Eyes huffed and sashayed out of the club with her pup. "Watch your back, bitch."

"You just ruined her big media moment," said Brandon.

"Planned by Presley, I'm sure." Mia touched the blood that ran down her neck. "I need to get home, because *this* is not a good look." She scanned around. "Where's Sean?"

Brandon showed Mia his phone. "He saw this and said he needed to get some air." It was a post on Lyndon Wyld's Instagram of Sean walking the runway. The comment was from *hounddogdayz*.

No loss for the Twins.

"Shit," said Mia. *Could this night get more fucked up?*

Mia and Brandon exited and searched for Sean. Since the Shoreline House sat over the water, there weren't many places to hide if the goal was to stay dry.

Guests started streaming out of the club. Two girls wobbled down the highway's shoulder in their stilettos.

"Hey, why the mass exodus?" asked Brandon.

One girl took off her heels. "Some fuckstick called in a bomb threat."

"We had to evacuate—so lame," said the other. The two padded away.

"Could've been the protestors. Could've been those chode friends of Chase's." Brandon headed back into the club. "I'm going to get my gear. I'll meet you at the car."

Mia walked a bit farther and noticed a shiny black Harley with tall handlebars parked on PCH, wedged between two Priuses. She smelled cigarettes and looked down at a cluster of beachside rocks just out of high tide's reach. Sean sat next to Rocko, who smoked, while Sean drank from a bottle of Jack Daniel's.

Rocko retrieved the bottle. "You don't look like you belong around seasonaires any more than I do."

Sean saw Mia in the moonlight as she stepped down the rocks towards them. "I was talked into coming," he said.

"You're a sucker, man. Your boss don't pay enough for a job." Rocko stared at Mia as he finished off the Jack.

Sean turned to Rocko with a curious expression. "Were you going to be a seasonaire?" Mia knew that he would never have watched the channel before landing in LA, so he didn't recognize the biker.

Piss-drunk, Rocko started laughing hysterically. "Nah, I was never gonna be a seasonaire, but close enough."

Mia shivered, chilled to the bone. Rocko stood and lobbed the empty bottle into the ocean. He walked up to PCH and disappeared into the exiting crowd.

Sean furrowed his brow at Mia. "What was he talking about?"

"If he drank most of that whiskey, who knows?" Mia put her hand out for Sean. "C'mon, we've gotta go. Supposedly, there's a bomb inside the venue."

Standing, Sean saw the bloody mess on the side of Mia's head. "Did it blow off your ear?"

Mia didn't answer. They met the others at the Tesla as the police arrived to clear everyone else out. Brandon examined the wound. "I have something better than Neosporin and Jell-O."

"Do *not* offer me painkillers." Mia side-eyed Sean, who patted his pockets and turned over his empty palms.

"Wyatt stole mine," grumbled Eve.

Chase pulled a plastic-wrapped chunk of brownie from his shirt pocket. "I was gifted an edible. I ate most of it but—"

Mia waved it away.

"My remedy is tacos, and I don't mean drive-thru," said Brandon, pushing Chase from the driver's side door. He nodded to the passenger's side.

Chase, whose eyes were stoned slits, ran a hand down his belly. "I could eat."

"Always," chuckled Alex. They all got in the car.

Brandon drove through the city, stopping off at a drugstore for peroxide, cotton, and Neosporin. In the backseat, Alex cleaned Mia's split earlobe. Mia winced at the sting. Alex lifted the cotton ball. "Don't be a pussy. You have no idea what *I* do for glamour."

"I wouldn't call this glamorous," said Mia as she checked the wound in her phone's camera screen.

They drove east another half hour—the streets and freeway were fast and easy at the late hour. "Where are we going?" asked Chase, gazing out the open window as they crossed the LA River into Boyle Heights.

Brandon steered past colorful murals, Mariachi Plaza, and a historic synagogue. "Everyone watches shows and movies set in LA, so they think they know it: Beverly Hills, Hollywood, Malibu. But that's not the *real* LA. There is no *one* stereotype. It's many things." He smiled.

"Sounds like you love it more than I do," said Chase.

"I wish I could live here, man—in all of it, not just the part west of La Cienega," replied Brandon with a smirk.

Chase flicked him on the arm. "Why don't you? We could keep hanging out."

"My dad's corporate office is in New York. That's the hub," said Brandon. Mia knew that he meant *his dad* was the hub.

He cut the motor at the curb near a small park, and the seasonaires spilled out of the car to be met by the savory smell of grilled meats, onions, cumin, and other spices. Brandon led them to a corner stand, with its long-smoking, grilled, and juicy al pastor on a vertical spit. The cooks shaved off slices to heap onto freshly made tortillas.

Eve adorned hers with toppings from the salsa bar. "One-dollar tacos? I didn't think you could buy anything for a dollar anymore."

They brought their plates to the park and ate carnitas, barbocoa, and asada tacos on the grass. Brandon had challenged Sean to eat a tripas, and Sean was up to the task. Alex scrunched his face in disgust. "You're eating intestines."

Sean finished off his plate. "Yeah and they're pretty damn good."

"Wipe your hands, everyone," said Mia. She didn't see any reason to wait another day to pass out the envelopes. Everyone except Brandon peeked inside at their checks. "Lyndon says thank you. I say thank you. This summer has been real," said Mia, smiling. "Well, it hasn't been *real*, actually, but I've felt a real connection with all of you."

Chase lifted his Mexican Coke. "And Oli." The others lifted their bottles.

Mia held hers. "The one rule I forgot to mention is that we should look each other in the eyes when we toast. It wards off bad luck."

They each locked eyes and toasted. Brandon held his gaze on Mia as they touched bottles. Afterwards, while Alex pushed Eve on the swings, and Chase and Sean goofed around on the monkey bars, Mia hung back with Brandon, talking quietly.

"Lyndon's wiring me what I'm owed," said Mia.

Brandon caressed her knee. "I knew she would. She's cutthroat but not a thief."

Mia's tone became even more hushed. "Really? She hired the bikers."

"Why would she do that?"

"They came to her first for money over Ruby, but she'd only pay them if they tried to scare the shit out of us."

Brandon chuckled, plucking out blades of grass. "That's kind of ingenious. No wonder why you took the credit."

"I took *responsibility*, not credit, because I thought they came because of me."

"We *did* get a bump in our channel's subscribers when it aired." Brandon snapped photos of Alex and Eve zipping down the slide.

Mia put her hand on Brandon's jacket sleeve. Brandon lowered the camera. "It's not ingenious," she said. "It's fucked up, Brandon. What if she knows that it didn't stop there? What if she's taking back my pay that way?"

"Why would she do that? She doesn't need the money. I mean, the company slipped after the murder, but she's recovering. Plus now my dad's money is funneling into her business."

Lyndon always knew how to squeeze the most out of a situation. But Mia's payday *did* seem like a pittance in Lyndon's world. Mia plucked blades of grass, thinking about the other person who knew about her design contract fee. "Lyndon said the visit was actually Presley's idea. It would be just like Presley to work with the bikers behind Lyndon's back for a cut."

"Now *that* would be fucked up." Brandon took Mia's hand. "But honestly, I don't think Presley is remotely ingenious." He stroked Mia's cheek, trying to calm her. "It'll all be over tomorrow."

When they returned to the house, Mia tried reaching Presley but got her voice mail—her outgoing message sweet as sugar. "This is Presley Parker. Leave a message at the tone and you just might get my attention." *Beep.* Mia hung up.

TWENTY-NINE

Mia woke with a sharp inhale, jolting up in bed. She didn't remember having a nightmare or feeling of falling. Alex opened his eyes and stretched. "You okay? Did you have a bad dream? Because *I* did—Presley stole my entire collection of Manolos."

Mia managed a smile. "She would never admit to wearing the same size shoe as you." Mia understood her nightmarish feeling, even without the dream. More *what ifs*: *What if Lyndon didn't transfer the money?*

Eve rustled and pulled one earbud out of her ear. She searched around her bed. "I lose one every single night!"

Alex ran his hands over his light stubble. "Maybe it's up your ass."

"And every morning you say that. I'm so ready to leave this place," said Eve.

Alex pressed the button on the wall between his bed and Mia's. The shades rose, unveiling another perfect Malibu morning. "You mean *this* place?"

Eve turned from the blue sky view and shrugged. "It's not about the location. It's about the people."

Mia got out of bed, squinting at her. "Really?"

Eve fluffed her auburn ringlets. "Honestly, I've thought about it long and hard. I love you both, but this brand is not my people."

"Your people?" Alex raised an eyebrow.

"If you're referring to the fact that I'm white and hetero—" Eve fished around under the sheets but came up empty-handed. "Why are my contributions diminished?" She huffed, vexed.

Alex reached and caressed Eve's foot. "Is it that time of month, honey?"

"Even *you* don't get to say that!"

Mia's ear throbbed. "Hey, chill. Do you have any aspirin?"

Alex unzipped a satin cosmetic bag and searched. "It's in the kitchen."

Eve rose and rummaged through her packed suitcase. She slipped on a T-shirt that wasn't Lyndon Wyld. "I tied with Alex for the most followers this summer, but I won't be coming back as a returning seasonaire. I have offers from three other brands that are more reflective of my views."

Mia's brow knit. "Oh."

"Do you mean they pay more?" asked Alex.

"Combined, yes, but the opportunities also made me see that I don't need to be tied down by one brand."

Alex looked genuinely concerned. "Are you still pissed about the hate rant Wyatt and Nils posted?"

Eve's neck reddened. "None of you clapped back at them for me."

"I thought you didn't care about haters. That's what you told me on that first day when we met," said Mia.

"I do have *feelings*, but that's not the point."

Alex rose from his bed. "Feelings are never the point when you're in the public eye. But words can still sting like hot wax strips when you rip them off." He stroked Eve's arm. "The sting passes."

"I don't wax. And my philosophies are what counts. Honestly, I don't know how you both did it—how you had an effect on Lyndon. She's ignored all my suggestions. I sent her an email about hemp pieces—no response."

"Hemp's not really on brand." Mia zipped a Lyndon Wyld hoodie over a tank and slid on a pair of jeans.

"That's why I'll do better as a free agent, promoting not just one brand but different brands that reflect my philosophies— environmentally conscious and body positive. I can't continue to support a company that charges more for a bra in a bigger size." Eve held up a bra, which she folded and put in her suitcase.

Mia glanced at Eve's white envelope on the nightstand. "Well, everyone has been paid, so now you can move on." *Not everyone*, Mia thought, her mind on the bikers.

Alex poked Eve in the ass. "You're a greedy bitch like the rest of us." His throaty laugh made Eve loosen up and laugh. Mia left them to finish their packing.

She entered her workspace, opened her laptop, and logged in to her bank account. The money hadn't transferred, but Mia thought the lag might be because of Labor Day. She closed her laptop and went downstairs for a final group breakfast.

After finishing most of what was left in the fridge, the seasonaires took their farewell selfie on the bluff. Brandon posted, captioning:

This was everything. #BuWyld

But Mia knew it wasn't. She had one last crucial piece of business to handle. Brandon ordered a car to take Eve and Alex to the airport. At the passenger door, Mia breathed Alex in when he embraced her. "I will miss how good you smell."

Alex kissed her cheek. "I want to see *you* in peacock feathers."

Eve stepped up to Mia. "Handshakes are for introductions. Hugs are for good-byes." She and Mia wrapped their arms around each other.

The car drove off with the two seasonaires.

Chase strapped on his backpack filled with dirty clothes and walked down the steps towards the beach. He and Sean exchanged the shaka sign.

The two siblings remained on the bluff and watched Chase traverse the shore as the wind blew his bleached-blonde twists. Brandon filmed for the channel's closing episode.

Mia walked back into the house. The money still hadn't transferred.

She helped Sean pack. Maz was putting him up at a loft downtown so he could be closer to Dodger Stadium. While Brandon was editing the final episode before packing up his gear, Mia slipped into her workspace—still no transfer.

She went down to the living room bar and poured herself a tequila. She tossed it back, exhaled the burn, then poured another one. Stepping out onto the deck, she walked to the infinity pool. She placed her drink down, stripped, and dove in for a last swim. She let herself sink to the bottom, then floated back up. Swimming to the edge, she looked out—night was falling, and the Queen's Necklace had started to sparkle. She got out and dressed. After she finished her drink, she visited Brandon in his studio.

"We can run around naked now. I turned off all the cameras in the house," he said.

Mia touched the camera on the tripod in front of the logo backdrop. "Turn this one back on. It's time for my confessional."

Brandon lifted an eyebrow but didn't question her. He walked behind the camera while Mia sat on the stool in front of it. Mia spoke directly into the lens and never wavered:

"Here's my confession: I honestly don't give two shiny shits what you people want. I'm here because *I want* to make clothes. I'm not here for your entertainment. Most of what you're getting from me is fake. Who knew I was such a good actress? Now I want to ask *you*: Why do *you* care? What do you really get out of watching us? What do you get out of the likes, follows, and comments? Maybe you have a few new friends you would've never met before, but the rest—that's because you crave validation. We all crave validation. But are we getting it from the twenty-five photos we take to find that one 'perfect' shot, then the twenty-five minutes more doctoring it to be even *more* perfect? How long did you think about your caption? Your hashtags? How many should you use? What's the best time to post?" She stopped for a beat. "I say, fuck it—and you should, too." She got up from the stool. Brandon turned the camera off and stood, staring at her.

Mia grabbed him and kissed him. They tore off each other's clothes and made real what had been pretend for much of the summer. Afterwards, they breathed into each other, listening to the waves outside the open windows.

"If I don't get them the money by tonight . . ." said Mia.

"You will. And I'm with you."

Mia's eyes filled with tears. "You might not want to be with me . . ." She could barely get the words out. "I wouldn't blame you after . . . I . . ." She swallowed.

Confused, Brandon looked into her face. "What is it? You can tell me."

"I felt horrible about letting Grant and Ruby go back to the house," whispered Mia. "So I went to see if they were okay. And they weren't—" Mia took a deep breath. "They were not at all okay. I made sure help would come and then—" A tear fell. She sniffed.

"Shhh . . ." Brandon touched Mia's cheek. "You couldn't change what happened." He lifted his necklace over his head and slipped the black silk rope over Mia's. Mia touched the cool medallion against her bare chest. She would have protested and given it back to him, but she didn't. She couldn't. She was scared.

A text buzzed from her phone on Brandon's desk. She grabbed her tank top and held it to herself as she sat up to reach for the phone. She saw a text from Presley:

Help

Mia's heart stopped. She texted:

Where are you?

The return text:

Hotel

Mia put the phone on the ground and whipped on her clothes. Brandon could read the text exchange.

He scoffed. "You're not serious. This is one hundred percent theatrics."

Mia tied her sneakers and raced out down the hall, past Sean's bedroom. He was closing up his suitcase.

"Where you running?" he called out as Mia flew down the stairs.

"Presley's in trouble." She grabbed the keys from the bowl by the front door.

Sean followed her out and to the Smart car. "She calls and you jump?"

"She's demanding, but I've never heard her apologize *or* ask for help. She's never going to apologize, but she did ask for help." Mia got in the car. "Have Brandon take you to your new place. I'll come see you tomorrow before I leave."

"I'm not ready to leave Malibu yet."

"Sean, go!" Mia had been relieved that everyone was gone and out of danger, but she didn't want to be obvious. Now it was getting late in the game. She needed him to leave. Sean furrowed his brow, but she didn't have time to explain.

She drove off and stopped down the road to put Hotel Brentwood into Google Maps on her phone. Following the directions, she sped along PCH and up through Santa Monica Canyon, racing along San Vicente Boulevard. Even at night, joggers strode along the grassy meridian, with its parade of coral trees.

She pulled into the circular driveway of the Hotel Brentwood, a stately compound surrounded by palms and exotic flowers. She jumped from the car.

"Miss!" The valet held the ticket out for Mia, but she ran inside without it.

A tuxedoed clerk at the front desk hung up the phone and looked at Mia, who was breathless in front of him. "Can I help you?"

"I need to get to Presley Parker's room. She's in the penthouse."

The clerk scanned the computer screen. "She's not in the penthouse, but we can't give out her room number." It was just like Presley to exaggerate her accommodations, though Mia was sure that every room at this hotel was luxe. She showed the clerk the text message. He called over a security guard, who brought Mia up to the room. Mia knocked on the door. No answer.

The guard pounded. "Miss Parker, this is security. Are you alright?" At no response, the guard used the master key to open the door. Presley was lying on the floor, unconscious. Turned to the side, she had vomited.

"Oh my God!" Mia knelt down.

This time, Mia waited until the paramedics arrived. They told her that Presley had ingested some kind of poison, though they were not sure what kind.

"Thankfully, you got here in time," said one of the paramedics. "She should be fine, but we're going to take her to UCLA Medical Center."

Mia nodded. She knew that if she didn't get Ruby's family the money, the fate of Sean or Brandon—or both—could be worse. She excused herself to get some air and left. Out front, she found her car still sitting near the perturbed valet. She handed him the last twenty from her wallet and drove off—back to Malibu.

THIRTY

M ia snuck back in the house. Thankfully, Brandon and Sean were out of sight. She wasn't ready to tell them what had happened or admit that she had left Presley, whom she'd gone to help. In her workspace, she quickly logged into her bank and was relieved to find the money wired into her account. She texted the Corona phone number:

I have your money. When to meet?

A phone dinged and Mia's heart stopped. She turned to find Teddy and Rocko in the doorway. "Now," said Teddy. Mia hadn't seen their motorcycles when she drove in.

Mia pointed to her laptop screen. "I have the money, I swear."

The nose of Rocko's .45 was pointed at her head. "All I see is that stupid fucking logo." Mia's laptop screen saver was the Lyndon Wyld logo.

"Get up," growled Teddy.

Mia reached to close her laptop. Behind it, among paper clips, pens, and errant stick pins, was Oliver's pocket knife. She slipped it in a zipper pocket of her sweatshirt as Teddy yanked her up by the hood. He ripped the black bandana off Rocko's head. Rocko held Mia's arms behind her back while Teddy tied the bandana around her eyes and wrapped rough rope around her wrists.

Mia's heart pounded. "Wait, wait, wait!" Her voice was a breathy squeak. She was picked up and slung over a shoulder. Her whole sense of balance was thrown off as she was carried through the house and outside. Her endorphins kicked in—flight over fright—and she flailed her legs. "Let me down!"

She heard the front door of the house open and slam shut behind her. The night air was cool, but it didn't temper her sweat. She was dropped and stretched horizontally—her arms pulled over her head. Rope wrapped around her ankles. She wrestled against the four hands that held her like vices.

She tried to open her eyes, but the black bandana was pressed taut against her lids. *This is a joke. This is a joke.*

As she wrenched her body, her phone fell from her back pocket, and she heard it smack on the driveway's concrete. A trunk door creaked open.

"What the fuck are you doing?" she yelled, trying to stay angry instead of letting her terror take over.

She was shoved inside a space that felt not much bigger than her body. The man mitts maneuvered her like a bag of groceries and the trunk door slammed over her. The cool air was gone.

She woke up when the trunk creaked back open, then she was pulled out the same way she was pushed in. She had no idea how long she'd been inside. Placed on the ground, she could feel rough gravel underneath her sneaker soles instead of the smooth concrete of the driveway or the asphalt of the street. The bandana was removed. As Rocko untied her feet, Mia saw Sean—hands rope-tied behind his back—kneeling by the back door of the black '80s Camaro that had held her in its trunk. He was puking. Brandon stood on the car's opposite side. His hands were also tied. Caleb had a revolver trained on him.

"You okay?" Brandon mouthed to Mia.

Mia nodded at him, though her body trembled and ached. She looked around. She could still see Malibu's twinkling Shangri-la lights, but they were farther away and below.

The car's headlights shone on an abandoned tower a few yards ahead—a looming structure of concrete slabs covered in graffiti. Rocko shoved Mia, Sean, and Brandon forward with the nose of Rocko and Caleb's guns at their backs. There were no homes on this high, isolated Malibu mountaintop. Mia noticed a black matte Harley with two helmets hanging from the handlebars—a half helmet and a full face with violet flames across the top.

Mia noticed the "No Trespassing" sign and a small, empty security booth. They each slid through a jagged opening of the metal fence that made the space feel like a lion's den once inside. A *lion's den*, Mia thought.

At the foot of the decaying structure, Teddy stood with Ruby. He opened his arms wide. "I call this Resurrection Tower. Some people say it's not what it once was."

"Part of a missile defense program," said Rocko.

Caleb spoke over him. "Radio tower."

"But it's still standing." Teddy planted his boots apart on the dirt under him. "Our family's been through a lot, but we're still standing, too." Small and thin, Ruby looked like a little girl next to her imposing father. He lumbered over to Brandon. "You think your family stands taller than the rest of us, don't you?"

Brandon stared straight ahead.

Teddy got in closer. "I don't give two fucks about your big daddy or your pretty sister, though apparently Otto Hahn gave more than two fucks about her."

Brandon spit in Teddy's face. Mia held her breath.

Teddy capped his cool. "Protective. Commendable."

Brandon locked eyes with him. "Fuck you."

Teddy took the black bandana from Rocko's hand, wiped his face, and handed it back. He lumbered back to Ruby's side so he could be in the glowing spot of the headlights again.

"Unlike Otto Hahn, I'm here to admit I've seen the error of my ways. I love my daughter—too much for my own good." He turned to Ruby. "But I learned the hard way that you need to give those you love what they are owed."

He gestured to Mia. "Don't you agree, Mia?"

Trembling, Mia nodded.

"Yet you haven't done that." Teddy put his arm around Ruby's tiny waist and yanked her in close. "I promised Ruby I would help take care of her and my new son-in-law, and now you've made me break my promise."

Caleb gazed at his boot, digging his thick heel into the ground.

Mia leaned forward in desperation. "I'm going to pay you! I swear!"

"Yes, you will," said Teddy. "Because you also broke my rules by telling people other than your seasonaire coworkers." Teddy took his arm from around Ruby to point at Sean.

Rocko rushed Sean while Caleb held Brandon.

"He doesn't know anything!" cried Mia.

Rocko punched Sean in the stomach. Brandon struggled to get free. "He's one of us!"

Mia ran to Sean and dropped down to him. "Sean!" She tried to get his attention. He stared at the ground, wheezing.

Rocko stepped on Mia's hand. "So you didn't tell your own brother you bailed on my sister at that house last Fourth of July?"

Mia wept. "It looked like she might have killed Grant. I didn't know what to do!" She sobbed. "This is *my* fault! I deserve your punishment, but no one else. I was only thinking about myself. I left my mother last summer, I left Ruby in that pool house, and now, I've left my brother to the dogs."

Rocko pressed the toe of his boot down harder. "Are you calling us dogs?"

"You *are* a damn dog," growled Teddy. "Let her up."

Mia stood, opening her hand with a pained wince. She walked towards Ruby, ignoring the guns trained on her. "I want to make what happened to you right. I don't know what else to do." As she got closer, she could see Ruby's arms in the shine of the car's headlights—the scars that were raised diagonal slashes on the inside of her bare forearms.

Ruby refused to look at Mia. "This isn't my decision."

"It's *your* life, Ruby," said Mia.

Ruby's eyes finally shifted to her. "No. When you left me for dead with that gun near my hand, you *took* my life."

"Then reach in my pocket and take mine." Mia nodded to the left pocket of her sweatshirt.

Ruby unzipped it and pulled out Oliver's pocket knife.

"Do to me what you did to yourself, but finish the job," said Mia, looking at the horizontal scars on the inside of Ruby's wrists.

"Putting my baby in a nasty position once again," Teddy scoffed. "Like I said, you're not a friend."

The sound of his voice made Mia's stomach turn and her blood boil. "You're not a father," she said, her stare burning into him.

Teddy grabbed the medallion necklace Brandon had given Mia. With his other hand, he spun her so her back was against his chest, then he yanked the black silk rope. He pulled it tight around her throat. "You told Ruby what you want, but she's my good girl. She won't do it, but *I* will." Mia choked and rasped as he twisted.

Brandon tried to run towards Mia, but Caleb restrained him. Rocko kicked Sean in the stomach.

The rope strangled tighter and tighter until Mia's body weakened. Teddy suddenly let go of the rope, howling in pain.

Free, Mia gasped for air and stumbled away. Ruby had stabbed Teddy in the neck with the pocket knife but missed the carotid artery—blood trickled instead of spewed. Teddy glared at Mia. "*You* are a bad influence." He nodded to Rocko's gun. "Son, I'm done with her."

A shot rang out, echoing off the tower, the mountain range, and the canyons. Teddy fell to the ground—dead—a bullet hole in his chest. Mia and the others turned to see Marcus holding a gun. Skullcrusher and Wrecking Ball stood behind him with rifles trained on Rocko and Caleb, who put their smaller guns down.

Mia moved towards Ruby, who was in shock.

"Let's go!" yelled Marcus.

Brandon grabbed Mia and pulled her away, then helped up Sean. Marcus ushered the three to a black Escalade, leaving Maz's two bodyguards behind. As he drove them away, Mia caught Ruby's eyes. Ruby's face was a mixture of pain and relief. Mia knew that feeling all too well.

The police would never arrive.

THIRTY-ONE

Marcus drove Mia, Brandon, and Sean down the canyon and onto PCH. In the car, Brandon explained to Mia and Sean that his dad had a way of handling "these types of situations," though he didn't realize that Marcus was worth his weight in MazzyLyn streetwear.

Marcus looked at Brandon in the rearview mirror. "Your father would've been here himself, but he's back in New York."

Brandon snorted. "No, he wouldn't have."

"You're right. That's why he has me." Marcus chuckled. "Here's his mandate: you don't tell Lyndon what happened. News of Teddy's untimely death will come out, and then she'll know. He had a lot of enemies. No one will question it. The other three will be spared, unless they get out of hand again."

Brandon looked at Mia. "Are you cool with this?"

Mia nodded and turned to Sean. "Sean?"

Sean stared straight ahead. "I don't ever want to think about this again."

Marcus dropped them off at the house. He leaned out of the driver's side window. "FYI, I love koi fish."

Sean went straight up the stairs, passing Mia without looking at her.

"I'm sorry, Sean." They heard the bedroom door slam. Brandon poured Mia a tequila from the bottle she'd left on the bar earlier that evening. She tossed back the drink. Brandon was pouring one for himself when his phone buzzed with a call. He pulled it out of his jeans pocket and saw a FaceTime coming in from Maz. He glanced at Mia, then answered it.

"You don't have to thank me," said Maz.

"Then I won't," replied Brandon.

Mia stepped into frame. "*I* will."

Maz nodded to her. "You're welcome. I sensed things weren't right when we talked at the store. As the daddy of six kids and even more companies, I've grown antennae." He winked. "A tracking app doesn't hurt."

"Are you going to say I told you so about Marcus?" asked Brandon. His jaw clenched as if he was bracing himself for words he'd been hearing his whole life.

"No. He's had to prove himself like you do."

Brandon looked at the ground, because these words weren't any better.

"I've paid Ruby," said Maz.

Brandon shook his head. "Why does that trash family get any money at all?"

"Just like I don't want you to tell anyone how that fucker died, I want them to keep their mouths shut, too."

"I understand," said Mia.

Maz pointed at Brandon. "You understand?"

"Yup."

"I knew you would, son. I'll see you soon. Your mama wants you back home." Maz clicked off. Brandon put his phone back in his pocket.

"How did your dad know where we were?"

"Since I was a little kid, he's had two parental sayings." Brandon lifted his forefinger. "Number One: 'Remember your name.'" His second finger lifted. "Number Two: 'I know where you are every second.' Sometimes he's bluffing, but rarely."

"Maybe you can look at it as a gift? Speaking of . . ." Mia started to lift the medallion necklace over her head. "Here—"

Brandon touched her arm. "It wouldn't be a gift if you gave it back to me. It's yours now." Mia brought her arm back down. She had felt that silk rope wrap around her throat, but she'd ended up safe.

"I lost the sea glass necklace your sister gave me last year. I don't know if I can be trusted with this," said Mia, studying the medallion.

"You can." Brandon kissed her forehead.

Superstitions be damned—Mia wanted to keep Brandon's necklace.

Mia was supposed to close and lock up the house the following morning, so she headed upstairs to her room to pack. She stopped at Sean's closed bedroom door. She took a deep breath and knocked. "Sean?" No answer. "Sean, please let me in. I promise to stand in the doorway behind the invisible shield." Still no answer. "You remember the invisible shield?"

"Fine," said Sean. Mia winced and opened the door. Sean was lying on his bed, tossing Brandon's signed Dodger baseball up and catching it. He couldn't look at her.

Mia stood stiffly, as if she'd been against a real invisible shield. "Sean, I'm so sorry about what happened."

"Why didn't you tell me what you saw in Nantucket?"

"Would you have told *me*? I didn't know you were dating your last girlfriend until after you broke up."

Sean held the ball for a beat, keeping his eyes on it. "Did you really just make that comparison?"

"I could keep apologizing forever—"

"Don't," snapped Sean.

Mia could see that she wasn't going to get anywhere with him, so she left. She packed, sitting on her suitcase by herself to close it—not an easy task. She didn't want to sleep alone, so she led Brandon to her room. They showered together—she didn't take off his medallion necklace. In bed, Brandon wrapped himself around her and they stayed in that entwined position until morning. When Mia woke after the deepest sleep she'd had since she'd arrived, she slipped out of his arms and into her workspace.

She called Presley, who didn't answer, then dialed UCLA Medical Center. She knew that information wouldn't be readily released, so she attempted her best Georgia peach lilt. "This is her sister, Gemma Parker." She found out that Presley had ingested antifreeze, and she flashed back to Presley's favorite drink—a strawberry daiquiri in its wide, round glass, melted and sweating—on the hotel nightstand. When Mia learned that Presley was in stable condition, she said "Thank you" and hung up. As Presley had assured her, "I'm not going anywhere"—except London. Mia could've bet on it. She told Brandon what had happened.

"Antifreeze. One of Teddy's crew obviously got to her," said Brandon as he loaded Mia's luggage into the back of the Tesla. When Sean exited the house with his suitcase, Mia gave Brandon a look that told him the conversation was over.

Brandon and Mia drove Sean to his new downtown digs. Heading into the physical center of LA, they saw the cluster of skyscrapers jutting out from a crisscross of freeways. They wove around gleaming buildings into the Arts District and its blocks of warehouses that had been converted to apartments and lofts.

Mia got out of the car and walked towards the entrance of a block-long brick building. The words *Shoe Factory Lofts* were painted on the side. Brandon touched Sean's arm before he disembarked. "We have to be there for our sisters."

Sean offered a small nod.

"She's doing the best she can," said Brandon.

"She always has."

"You understand that's not what she thinks."

Sean took this in for a beat, then exited the car and met his sister next to the building's front door. Mia shuffled, hands behind her back. "Hey, at least there weren't any earthquakes. And it wasn't a total loss—you get to meet with the Dodgers."

"It wasn't a total loss because we got to hang out. We never really hung out at home."

Mia gazed upward, pondering this, then looked back at Sean. "You're right. We didn't."

Sean lightly kicked Mia's shoe. "You're a good person, turd."

Mia smiled. "So are you." They embraced. Mia headed to the car. She turned back to Sean. "I'd say 'Break a leg,' but I won't." They flipped each other off and Sean entered the building. Mia climbed into the passenger's seat.

Brandon noticed her wipe tears from her eyes. "How about a challenge?" he asked.

Mia shook her head, sniffing. "Oh, no. Our channel is done for this summer."

Brandon tapped the steering wheel. "It's not for the channel. It's for me."

"What's the challenge?"

"Skeeball."

"I don't even know what that is," said Mia.

Brandon grinned and drove them to the Santa Monica Pier. He parked in a spot on Ocean Avenue, against a grassy stretch that overlooked the beach. A homeless man talked to pigeons that surrounded him, while a group of elderly women went through their slow Tai Chi moves. Mia and Brandon walked under the Santa Monica Pier arch and down the steep, narrow sidewalk that led to the rides, arcades, and a sea of people.

Mia took in all the sights and sounds. "I've never been to a pier or an amusement park."

Brandon held her hand. "I've been to all the good amusement parks, but only when they were closed. That's the way my dad had to do it."

"I actually like the word *fun*, and that sounds fun to me."

"It wasn't. Part of going to places like this is watching people— you know—that 'sense of wonderment about who they are.'"

Mia bumped his shoulder with hers. "Are you teasing me?"

"No." Brandon bumped her shoulder in return. "I think I forgot how to just watch and wonder."

They reached the bottom and stepped onto the pier's wood planks, strolling past a few old fishermen in floppy hats. Brandon leaned into Mia. "I hope that's catch-and-release, because Eve would tell you that no one should eat fish from this water."

They walked under the curving Pacific Park sign and past the Seaside Swing and the Shark Frenzy, where riders were whirled around while sitting between sharp white teeth. Brandon stopped at a row of mini bowling machines. "Skeeball."

"Ah." Mia nodded.

Reaching into his back pocket, Brandon pulled out some quarters. He stuck a couple in the slot of adjacent machines and the red wood balls slid down a column, clacking against each other when they hit the bottom. He lifted one out, aimed, and rolled. The ball jumped up and landed in the highest circle, marked *50*.

"Oh, that *is* a challenge!" Mia smiled and picked up a ball. She rolled it and it veered off to the right, sliding down into the bottom curve that offered no points.

"Keep your eye on where you want it to land and let go of the effort." Brandon rolled another ball. It popped into the *50* again.

"No effort, huh?" Mia picked up another ball and breathed. She thought about surfing the wave and how effortless the ride had felt. She drew her arm back, stared at the *50*, swung slightly, and released the ball. It landed where she wanted it to go. She threw her arms in the air. "Yes!"

They rolled side by side. Brandon won, but Mia was close. In the second game, they tied. They ate cotton candy and watched people ride the roller coaster that zipped around the park.

Mia turned to Brandon. "Let's do it." They rode, reaching their arms in the air and laughing as they were whipped along the red track.

The Ferris wheel was their final ride. They climbed into a bright yellow gondola and sat on the same side. The wheel slowly started to turn. As they came around the top, Mia could see even farther out across the ocean than she could at the house. The ride went around one more time and stopped at the top.

Mia furrowed her brow. "Is it stuck?"

Brandon looked below. "Sometimes a kid doesn't want to get off. It'll start again."

The wind was strong. Brandon noticed the goose bumps covering Mia's arms, so he gave her his jacket.

Mia pulled it around her shoulders. "I didn't peg you for a gentleman when we first met."

"My brother doesn't care much for being polite, but manners are important to my mom. Open a door for a lady, out before in in an elevator."

"Out before in—that's an unspoken law for everyone. My dad used to say that, too, in our building . . . before he left us. But he wasn't a gentleman. Gentlemen are thoughtful. And they don't care if it's not cool to be a gentleman anymore."

"It will always be cool to be a gentleman." Brandon put his arm around Mia.

"I wish my mom would've had the chance to come to a place like this. She never went to amusement parks either."

"You two were close, huh?"

Mia nodded and entwined her first two fingers.

Brandon looked at her. "Do you think you look at Lyndon as some type of mother figure? My dad's been doing business with her since I was a kid, so I know Jade did. And I'm pretty sure Presley does. She even dresses like her."

"That style is new for Presley. But her attempt to talk like Lyndon is terrible," said Mia.

"Lyndon looks out for number one, and so does Presley." The wind howled. "Do you think Lyndon knew what Grace was going to do in Nantucket?"

Mia slid away from him. "What do you mean?" *When will this Ferris wheel start up again?*

Brandon sat back. "Lyndon has her stamp on everything. I think she either encouraged Grace or didn't try to stop her."

Mia didn't say anything, because Brandon was saying what she had always thought. He inched closer. "She needs full control. I don't know what'll happen with her and my dad, because they're playing a game of chicken. He needs full control, too. Like he's going to hold this summer over me for the rest of my life."

Mia shook her head. "That's an excuse, Brandon. No one controls you. It's like letting followers and fans direct our whole life. Your father shouldn't be able to do that either."

Brandon gazed out over the water as the Ferris wheel started to turn again. "I don't know who I am if I'm not my father's son."

Mia put her hand on his leg. "I don't know who I am if I'm not my mother's daughter."

Brandon turned to her and caressed her cheek. "Then we're meant for each other."

"No, it means we're not meant for *anyone* right now." Mia held Brandon's hand as the Ferris wheel brought them to the bottom. They got out of the gondola and began walking back towards the arch.

"After last night, I know what it's like to want to give up," said Mia. "I felt like I'd failed everyone. But I've really been failing myself. Growing up with a sick mom is always like that. You have your first kiss, but your mom's dying. You score the winning home run for your team, but your mom's dying. You sign a contract for your own clothing line, but your mom's dying. Making my life matter felt selfish."

"It's not selfish." Brandon gave her hand a squeeze. "*You* matter." He stopped Mia, turning her to him. "*You* matter." They kissed. A clown skipped by and made a balloon flower, then stood there until the two stopped kissing. Brandon handed him five dollars. "Man, you're freaking me out." The clown kicked out one of his giant red shoes and scooted off. Brandon gave the balloon flower to Mia. They continued to stroll back up towards the pier's exit.

As they walked past Pier Burger's red-and-white awning, Mia saw the Santa Monica Route 66 sign she had missed on the way down. It read:

END OF THE TRAIL.

They stared at the sign. "It's not," said Mia.

Mia showed the airline's gate agent her one-way ticket to New York. MassArt could wait. She walked through the tunnel, into the plane, and found her seat in first class—this time next to the window. The seat next to hers remained empty. After a friendly flight attendant handed her a flute of prosecco, the crew was directed to get ready for takeoff. Buckling up, Mia took a deep breath. She was ready for the turbulence. She looked out as the plane rose above the City of Angels. The veil had lifted.

ACKNOWLEDGMENTS

I want to express my immense gratitude to everyone who helped me get to this novel's finish line. To Jessica Case, my editor for her guidance and astute notes. My appreciation goes out to the entire Pegasus team. To my literary agent, Adam Chromy, who has an uncanny way of curbing my "nervousing," and whose compassion motivated me to keep putting words on the page. To my publicist Kathleen Carter for her strategic thinking and for answering my green author questions. And to Abrams Artists Agency—especially Manal Hammad for her pragmatism and persistence.

My thanks to talented authors Charles Blackstone and Erica Wright for their support of *The Seasonaires*. And I so appreciate all the readers, reviewers, bloggers, and bookstagrammers who embraced that debut novel.

ACKNOWLEDGMENTS

I couldn't have made it through this intensely challenging year without my amazing family and wonderful friends. Gratitude forever from the bottom of my heart.

A special note to my sister: I love you and wish you were here to read this. May you rest in peace.